REEVE

USA TODAY & WSJ BESTSELLING AUTHOR

SIOBHAN DAVIS

Paperback edition © December 2023

ISBN-13: 978-1-916651-12-8

Edited by Kelly Hartigan (XterraWeb) editing.xterraweb.com

Proofread by Lunar Rose Editing Services

Cover design by Shannon Passmore of Shanoff Designs

Cover imagery © depositphotos.com and © bigstockphoto.com

Formatting by Ciara Turley

Note from the Author

This is not a stand-alone book. It is a companion novel to *Say I'm the One* and *Let Me Love You* and you must have read those books before reading *Reeve*. While it is preferable you have also read *Hold Me Close*, it is not essential to read the optional epilogue novella.

This was so emotional to write, but I am glad I did it. It offers us additional insights into Reeve's character, and their earlier years as friends and then a couple. I hope you come away understanding his motivations more clearly. He isn't a bad person, but a good person who made some bad choices that had far-reaching consequences. And boy, did he love Vivien so much! It has given me some closure and I hope it does that for you too.

Thank you for reading. Make sure you have some tissues close by!

Siobhán.

DEDICATION

I dedicate this book to all the readers of the *All of Me Duet* spoiler group on Facebook. Thank you for your enthusiasm, excitement, commitment, and crazy love for these characters and this world. This book exists because of you.

REEVE

Chapter One
THEN – age 6

"Stay right here." Beth points at Viv and me, trying to look scary, but it doesn't work. My best friend smiles sweetly, waving as her nanny leaves the room with her cell phone pressed to her ear. Her boyfriend is always calling her when Viv's parents go out. Lauren would be mad if she knew. But Viv doesn't want to snitch because we get away with lots of stuff when Beth isn't looking.

"Come on." Viv grins as she tugs on my arm. "The workers are gone. Let's check out the treehouse."

I shake my head and hold her wrist. "Your dad said we weren't to go out in the garden." Jonathon left to drive Lauren to the airport. She's going to Ireland for her movie premiere. Vivien begged her to let us go with her, but she said we couldn't miss school.

"Reeve." Viv puts her hands on her hips and gives me that look. The one that says she's the boss and I'm to do what she wants or else. "Daddy will be gone for ages. We'll be back inside before Beth even knows."

"It's dangerous," I say, looking out the window at the area at the top of the garden where the men are building our new tree-house. Last year, they built an obstacle course, and before that, they built the playground Viv and I play in every day. I know it's going to be mega, and I can't wait. But I don't want to get in trouble. Mr. Mills said we weren't to go near it, and he'll be angry if we do. I don't want him to tell me I can't come over anymore because I hate my house.

I hate my daddy.

Well, not really. He's my daddy. I love him even if he's always shouting at me. "And my dad will be mad if he finds out."

Vivien scowls. "Your daddy is mean! Who cares what he thinks."

I do. "He'll shout at me."

"Then I'll kick his ass!" Vivien balls her hands into fists, looking like she's ready to go into battle with my daddy.

A weird fluttery feeling spreads across my chest. "We'll just wait until your daddy comes back, and then we'll ask him to take us out to see it."

Vivien's long dark hair falls around her shoulders as she shakes her head. "It will be too dark then." She looks over her shoulder out the window. "It's already starting to get dark now." Reaching out, she grabs my hand. "Let's go."

I sigh. I might as well just give up. If I don't go, she will only go by herself. "We're only going to look at it." I try to wear the same face my daddy does when he's warning me about something.

"You shouldn't worry so much." Viv links her fingers in mine as she leads me toward the door. Her palm is warm against my skin, and it makes me happy. "We're kids. We're supposed to be naughty." Her eyes twinkle, and I'm smiling as we run quietly down the hallway, past the door where Beth is giggling on the phone to her boyfriend, and around the corner toward the side door that leads outside.

My nose twitches as I smell the roses while we run across the grass. Lauren planted this huge garden with different colored roses a while ago. Viv and I helped her with some of it until Viv got bored and wanted to play on the swings and slide. I wanted to stay.

I love Vivien's mommy. She's so nice. She always gives me hugs and kisses and sneaks me chocolate and candy on the weekends. She is always telling my daddy it's not good enough. I don't know what she means. Viv and I eavesdrop on their conversations sometimes, and my name comes up a lot. I feel sad if my daddy is telling Lauren I'm not a good boy. I try really hard, but Daddy always gets mad at me. I think that's why he works so much, and I don't see him during the week, and why he never wants to play with me when he's home on the weekends. I spend most of my time at Viv's house.

I wish I lived here all the time.

I wish Lauren and Jonathon were my mommy and daddy.

"Reeve!" Vivien tugs on my hand, and I blink as I stare up at the large oak trees. I don't even remember getting here. "Look how big it is!" Viv lets go of my hand, squealing and jumping up and down as we both look up. The treehouse is being built between two of the biggest trees in the garden and it looks ginormous. Lots of metal poles are pushed against the trees. There are planks of wood between the poles the men stand on when they are working. Earlier, when Viv and I were watching from her bedroom window, we saw the men climbing up and down with tools strapped to their belts. The roof is on and all but one side of the house is built.

"It looks awesome." Excitement bubbles up my throat. "It's going to be so cool."

"I'm going up." Viv races toward the poles at the side of the first tree.

"No." I run after her. "You can't go up there. You might fall."

"Don't be silly." She bats my hand away and lifts her foot onto the first pole. "I'll climb it like the men do."

"Please, Viv. Don't go up there. I don't want you to get hurt."

"Reeve." She turns around and flings her arms around me. "I won't get hurt. It will just be like rock climbing, and I never fall when I'm on the wall." Every Saturday, Viv's daddy, Jonathon, takes us to the rock climbing wall at the local indoor climbing gym. It's fun, and we always race one another to the top. Viv hates it when I win, so I sometimes slow down on purpose. I don't mind losing to my best friend. I never want her to be sad or mad.

"You don't have a harness," I say into her hair as I hug her close.

"I don't need one." She gives me one last hug before starting to climb.

Another fluttery feeling starts in my chest, but it feels different than the last time. I wrap my arms around myself as Viv moves higher. "Be careful," I call out.

"I always am!" she shouts back. But that's not really the truth. If Viv wants to do something, she just does it. Sometimes, she does stupid things and gets into trouble.

I bite down on my lip and tip my head back as I watch her climb higher and higher. There's a weird taste in my mouth, and my stomach is all jumpy. I feel like I did that time I had a stomach bug and I puked everywhere.

Viv screams, and I watch in horror as she loses her footing and lets go of the metal poles. She is freefalling in the air. Her arms and legs are moving around, and I don't realize I'm screaming and shouting at first because I'm so scared I kinda zone out. Then I snap out of it and move. I have a sharp pain in my chest as I hold out my arms to catch her.

Viv lands heavily on top of me, and I lose my balance, falling to the ground at an awkward angle. But my arms are around her, tightening automatically so I won't let go. My ankle hurts, but I barely feel it because Vivien is screaming and holding her arm, and I'm more afraid than I've ever been.

"Viv." I sit up and keep my arms around her, ignoring the pain in my ankle. "What's wrong?" I ask, wiping the tears running down her face.

"My arm," she sobs. "It really hurts, Reeve." Her crying gets louder as she buries her face in my neck and leans into me.

"I told you it was dangerous." I wince as I attempt to stand and my ankle wobbles and shakes. I drop back to my butt, hugging my best friend.

"Make it stop, Reeve. It hurts real bad." Vivien's tears soak through my T-shirt, but I don't care. I only care that she's hurt. I should have made her stop; then none of this would have happened.

I rest my chin on her head. "Beth is coming," I say, spotting the nanny racing toward us with big eyes and pale skin. "She'll fix it."

"I'm scared." Viv cries. "Daddy is going to be so mad at me. Do you think I'll have to go to the hospital?"

I shrug. "Maybe."

"I need you." She holds me tight. "Don't leave me." Viv stares at me through big, watery hazel eyes as she clings to me with her good arm.

"I won't ever leave you, Viv. You're my best friend, and I'm staying until you're all better."

Chapter Two
NOW – age 17

"Good luck, babe." Viv presses her lips to mine, and I reel her into my arms, deepening our kiss and holding her flush against my body. My girlfriend's touch has always had the power to soothe me at times of stress.

If home is a person, Vivien Mills is my home. She is the other half of my soul, and I'm only truly content when I'm with her.

There will never be another girl for me.

Viv is the one.

I've known that truth before I could even put words to the things I was feeling. She is all I see. All I need and want. Vivien has been there from the very start. She knows me inside and out like I know her. She is my past, my present, and my future.

It's as simple as that.

Right now, I need her to ground me because I'm nervous. I'm always the same before auditions. The fact I have already secured the part of Camden Marshall in *Cruel Intentions* hasn't taken the edge off my anxiety. The part of my leading lady hasn't been cast yet. I've tested with eight actresses to date, and none of them were right, so today is a big deal. I'm worried if I don't connect with someone, the studio will change their mind about me and cancel my contract. My new agent, Bianca, says that won't happen, but I can't stop worrying. It's part of my DNA.

The studio headhunted someone they believe is the perfect fit for the role of Abigail Hearst-Manning. I don't even know who the actress is because they want to keep it under wraps. Buzz is already building for this movie, and if the predictions are correct, this film will be the one to put me on the map. To launch the career of my dreams.

Building the kind of career I've dreamed of means having the financial independence and freedom to start creating the life Viv and I have always desired. A lot is riding on this movie, and I'm going to do everything in my power to ensure it's a success. To ensure more movies are made in the series and that my future with Viv is secure.

For years, I have been counting down to the day I can break out on my own and prove to my father I'm not the failure he believes me to be. I want to make something of myself so my mother's sacrifice isn't in vain. She died giving birth to me, and my father has never forgiven me for it.

Vivien breaks our lip-lock. "Hey." She clasps my cheeks in her soft palms, examining my face with concern. "You were a million miles away."

"Sorry." I plant my hands on her slender hips. "I'm a nervous wreck."

"Breathe, babe." She kisses the tip of my nose. "You've already got this in the bag. Today is a formality, most likely, so there's no need to be nervous."

"There's still a lot riding on this audition. It all hinges on us having chemistry."

"Trust the process, Reeve." Viv's hands lower to my shoulders. "And if it doesn't work out with this actress, they will find the perfect Abby. I've seen my mom go through so many auditions over the years, and they always find the best leading man to work with her. These people are pros. They know what they're doing, and it's a good thing they are taking their time to find the right leading lady. It means they are completely invested in this adaptation." She kisses me softly. "Do you want me to come with? I can ditch school. Mom won't mind."

Warmth floods my chest as I shake my head. I pull her in closer. "The auditions are closed. They wouldn't let you in even if I was selfish enough to let you skip school to come with me." I pepper kisses across her gorgeous face. "Thank you for offering, and thanks for everything, Viv. I wouldn't have this part if it wasn't for you."

"Don't talk shit, Reeve. You have this part because you are mega talented, and you worked your butt off for it." Her fingers move over the new definition in my arms. "Not many actors transform their bodies and their look so completely for auditions." Her fingers trek up my arms toward my hair. I have it cut and dyed so it matches the description of my character from the book. Camden Marshall is ripped in a way I wasn't, which is why I hit the gym and hired a personal trainer four months ago when I first heard of the part.

"Your encouragement and support made all the difference."

"I love you. Your dreams are my dreams. Helping you to fulfil those is not a chore."

I slam my lips on hers and kiss her with all the love coursing through my veins. "I love you so much, Viv," I say when we break apart. "Nothing means more to me than you."

"Right back at ya, sexy." She waggles her brows and grins as she pinches my ass. "Now, get your delectable butt in the car before you're late."

"I'll call you the minute I'm done," I promise, pecking her lips one more time.

"Try to relax. You've got this." She blows me a kiss as I walk off, and some of the tension has eased from my shoulders as I get into my car and drive away.

"You made it by the skin of your teeth," Bianca says when I arrive at the studio with minutes to spare.

"Traffic was hell." Not a lie, because traffic is always hell in L.A., but it's not the full truth either.

"Let's talk in here for a sec." Opening the door to a small office, she quickly ushers me inside. We don't bother sitting. "The actress you're auditioning with is Saffron Roberts," she confirms.

My eyes pop wide.

"I see you've heard of her."

I nod. "It would be hard not to. She was plastered all over social media last year." Saffron is notorious for having an affair with a top movie director and his wife. After that news leaked, an ex of hers sold naked pics of her, and she was trending for weeks. Offers were flooding in, and she's been in a few big-budget Netflix films and shows, and there is talk of other productions in the works. "Isn't she supposed to be working with Scorsese on his new project?" At least that's the gossip doing the rounds.

"She was too young for the part, which is lucky for us because it means her schedule has opened up." Bianca opens the door. "I think you and Saffron will look good together, and she'll help to build hype for the movie."

I follow her out of the room, trying to steady my nerves. "She doesn't exactly fit the description of Abby in the books," I admit as we walk down successive hallways toward the set where the audition is taking place.

"Films adapted from books are never identical. They can't be. It's a different medium. The studio will retain key elements to keep the existing readership happy, but this film opens the series to a whole new audience, and the film must engage and hook that audience for it to be a success. Abby's physical characteristics from the book are not sexy enough to appeal to a wider, older audience, so they're adjusting it. Saffron *is* small and dark-haired like the description in the book."

"But she doesn't have a ballerina's body," I remind her as we push through double doors.

"They are rewriting those parts, so Abby is a contemporary dance student, not a ballet dancer, and Saffron's curvier figure will work in that context."

"That makes sense."

"Right." Bianca slams to a halt just outside the door to the set, and I almost career into her back. She grips my shoulders. "Ready?"

"As I'll ever be." I shove my nerves aside and remind myself I have the part and I know this material inside and out. We are shooting three different scenes today, challenging various aspects of our characters' personalities and different elements of the relationship between Cam and Abby. I have been rehearsing for weeks with Vivien, and I could recite the scenes in my sleep at this stage.

"You were born for this, Reeve." Bianca gives my shoulders a squeeze before releasing me. "There is no doubt in my mind you are going to be the shining star of this movie. Own it. Go in there and show everyone who is the king."

Her words help, and I'm projecting confidence as we enter the room. Saffron is standing with her agent, the casting director, and the director in front of the camera that faces the large room. It's been split into three different sections, each one set up for the scene we're about to perform. My eyes scan the large bed propped against the wall, and I wipe my clammy hands down the front of my jeans as nerves fire at me again.

Sex scenes are awkward, or so it's said. I have never done one. I have kissed my costars in plays and on the small screen, but this will be a first. Having to act intimate with someone I have just met only adds to the awkwardness, but this is the life of an actor, and I need to get over myself.

Saffron's head lifts as we approach, and a wide smile ghosts over her mouth. She cuts off her conversation to walk toward us. A formfitting black and gold dress molds to her body, and the matching stilettos give her added height. The dress manages to be both demure and sexy, and it's exactly what Abby was wearing when she was accosted by Camden in the parking garage after her ballet show before they drove to Lauder's party. I guess we're starting with that scene.

Rea, the set costumer, stands to one side, patiently waiting for me, and I tip my head in acknowledgment, silently conveying I won't be long.

"Reeve." Saffron's big blue eyes are welcoming as she leans toward me. "It's so lovely to meet you."

I bend down, and she kisses my cheeks. "The honor is all mine," I say as I straighten up.

"I was just running through a few things with Nick and Jeremy. I haven't had much time to prepare, so I hope you'll forgive me for any slipups."

"I know the material well, so I'll help."

"That would be great, thanks!" She leans in closer so only I can hear. "I'm so excited for this movie, and I really hope I get the part. I think this could be massive for both of our careers."

"I agree, and I'm rooting for you."

"Aw, thank you." A faint blush stains her cheeks. "I have a

feeling you and I are going to get on famously. Fingers crossed I get the part because I would love to work with you. I'm relatively new to acting, and Bianca was telling me all about you. She said you've been taking drama and acting classes since you were eight, which is so inspirational. I want to enhance my skills and continue pushing myself to deliver the best possible performance. Working alongside good actors is crucial, and I think I could learn a lot from you."

"I'm not sure I'm worthy of such praise, but I will do my best to live up to it."

She flashes me a pretty smile. "I have faith in you. I have no doubt you will live up to my every expectation and more."

Chapter Three
Now

"Hey, Reeve." A familiar-looking blonde cheerleader sidles up to me as I wait alongside the bleachers for Alex to finish practice. I snagged a ride with him today because my car is at the garage for a routine service. I could have gone with Viv, but she had shopping plans after school with Audrey, and I don't like asking Charles—the full-time driver my father employs—because he's dealing with medical stuff, and he really should retire.

"Uh, hi." I offer her a polite but strained smile. Since the news broke about my high-profile role, girls have been regularly hitting on me, and it's starting to grate on my nerves. Random girls accosting me in the street don't know I'm in a committed relationship, but the girls at school know I've been dating Vivien since we were fourteen. They know better, and yet they continuously ignore the truth.

I was so freaking happy when I got this part. After successive rejections chipped away at my self-esteem, I was losing faith in my ability to make it as an actor. Missing out on the

Riverdale part at the last minute gutted me so much I even considered quitting acting.

But it's in my blood.

It's my other passion, and I can't walk away when it gets tough. I am sure there are plenty of tough times ahead. I try to remind myself of this when the less-than-appealing elements of winning the part are drilled home. Like enhanced attention from the press and on social media and when girls repeatedly hit on me.

"It's so exciting about your new role," a brunette cheerleader says, coming up on my other side. I don't know her name either.

"Thanks." I fold my arms over my chest and stare out at the players on the field, willing Coach to end the session so I can get out of here.

"There's a party at the Jennings' place on Friday," the blonde says, pressing her body up against me.

"We were hoping you'd meet us there." The brunette pushes up against my other side, licking her lips and grinning salaciously as she eye fucks me with zero shame.

"I have plans with my girlfriend every Friday, and this week is no different." Every Friday night, Viv and I order takeout and watch a movie at my place. She stays over, and I get to worship her beautiful body with my mouth, my fingers, and my cock all night long.

Nothing beats Friday nights with my girl.

"We'll make it worth your while," the blonde says as both girls lay hands on my arms and blatantly ignore my comment.

"We're down for a three-way if you are." The brunette makes a grab for my crotch, and I circle my fingers around her wrist, halting her.

"Don't fucking touch me," I snap, dropping her wrist and moving out of their reach. "I love my girlfriend, and I'm faithful to her. I have no interest in either of you or a threesome, so you're wasting your time."

"Your loss, asshole," the brunette says in a sneering tone.

"And there's no need to be rude," the blonde adds, drilling me with a venomous look.

"The fame is already going to his head," the brunette scoffs as she loops her arm through her friend's, and they cast nasty looks over their shoulders at me as they walk off.

"Good fucking riddance," I mutter under my breath as Coach ends the session and Alex jogs toward me.

"Hey, man." Alex clamps a hand on my shoulder. "I see your fan base is expanding." He smirks as he bends down to grab his duffel bag.

"It's no joking matter. It's pissing me off. Most of these girls know Viv, and they don't give a fuck about disrespecting her. It makes me mad on her behalf."

"What did you expect?" Alex slings the bag over his shoulder, and we walk toward the exit in the direction of the parking lot. He's showering at home tonight because we're under pressure to pick the girls up on time for our double date—dinner at The Shack and then the movies is something we do every Wednesday. "It's only going to get worse."

I groan. "Don't say that."

"Dude, it's the truth. You better prepare yourself and Viv for the oncoming storm."

***

"Knock, knock," I say ninety minutes later as I rap my knuckles on the half-open door to Lauren's home office. I purposely arrived at Viv's house ten minutes early in the hope I'd catch her mom for a quick chat. "Do you have time to talk?"

"For you? Always." Lauren smiles as she gets up from

behind her desk and walks toward me. "Come in and close the door."

After shutting the door, I turn around and I'm instantly enveloped in the familiar woodsy floral scent of Chanel No. 5. "How are you?" Lauren asks as she bundles me in a loving hug.

"I'm good." I hug her back, closing my eyes and offering silent thanks for this woman. My childhood would have been a lot worse without Vivien's parents. Lauren went to bat for me a lot when I was growing up, and I can never repay her for her loyalty and kindness.

"What did you want to talk about?" she asks, gesturing for me to take a seat on the velvet couch in front of the fireplace.

"I was looking for your advice." I wet my suddenly dry lips as I sit down beside Viv's mom. My knee taps on the ground. "It's a bit awkward." Heat creeps up my neck.

"You can ask me anything, Reeve, and this conversation can remain between us if that's what you prefer."

She knows me so well. I slowly nod. "Normally, I ask Viv for advice, but I didn't want to go to her with this because it might upset her, and I never want to do that."

Her features soften. "I know, honey. You love my girl good."

"She's the love of my life. My everything."

"I love the way you two love one another. It truly warms my heart. Jon and I have always known it was inevitable. I wish you could have seen yourselves when you were little. The bond was there right from the very start. It's been magical watching it happen."

"You don't think we're too young?" I've had that shit thrown at me at school.

"You *are* very young, but who am I to tell you what is right and what is wrong? Love knows no age limits. Let your heart guide you. It will never steer you wrong."

My heart swells behind my rib cage, and it's pure emotion

that has me speaking these next words. "I hope you know how much I love you. Jon too." I rub the back of my neck. "I'm so grateful for everything you have done for me."

"You're our son in every way that counts, Reeve, and we love you very much."

A lump forms in my throat.

She takes my hands and squeezes. "I'm so proud of you. Proud of the man you're becoming. I know life hasn't always been smooth sailing, and it would be easy for you to feel bitter, but you don't, and that is a true testament to your inner strength and your purity of heart. Your mother would be so damn proud, Reeve." Tears fill her eyes. "I still miss Felicia every day."

"I wish I'd had the chance to know her."

"Me too, honey." She squeezes my hands. "Me too." Lauren lets go to dab at her eyes. "What's troubling you?"

"Sex scenes," I blurt because there's no way of easing into his conversation.

"Ah, yes, I see." Compassion floods her expression.

"How do you handle them? I had one scene at the audition with Saffron, and I froze. I couldn't relax. It felt like I was betraying Viv, and I couldn't get out of my head. The only lips I want to kiss are Viv's. The only person I want to touch is her. I felt ill kissing and touching Saffron, and I don't know how I'm going to do it. I don't want to fuck up before we've even begun filming." The studio publicly confirmed Saffron for the part the day after the audition, and the paperwork is all signed now. It's a done deal.

"Sex scenes are never easy, and that is the least of it. It's hard being intimate with someone you don't really know, especially when you're in a room full of other people and you're told exactly what pose to hold, how you should kiss, how you should fake making love, and what sounds and expressions you should make. Even closed sets are challenging. Fewer people, but it's more intense. And you must make it look real even if you loathe your costar." Her face pulls into a grimace. "I've filmed a few projects where I intensely disliked my male lead, but I still had to fake sex. It's probably the most challenging aspect of acting and as stressful as any emotional scene to pull off. It's where our skills are stretched to the max."

"So how do you do it?"

"You have to approach it the same way you approach any scene—as your character. It's not you and Saffron in that bed; it's Cam and Abby. Each day when you step on set, shed your skin, Reeve. You are Camden Marshall the moment you show up, and you don't unsheathe his persona until you finish for the day. Keep your professional and personal lives strictly separate. You are there to do a job, and you're not cheating on Vivien by fulfilling your contractual commitments."

"You make it sound simple, but it's not."

"It absolutely isn't." Lauren turns a little on the couch so she's facing me. "It takes practice and time. If you trust and respect your costar, it is easier. I've had some costars who went out of their way to ensure I was comfortable, and it helps. But I struggled with a lot of the same concerns when I was starting out. They are still not my favorite scenes to film, but I separate who I am from my role, and that's the only way I've been able to do it. Maybe you'll find a different way that works for you, but don't beat yourself up over it, Reeve. Vivien will understand. Like you, she's grown up in this industry, so she knows what's involved. I'm not saying it will be easy for her to see, because I already know she won't like it, but she'll get used to it. As long as it's her you're coming back to each night, you will both find a way to deal with it."

Chapter Four
Now

"What is with you tonight?" I ask Alex as we finally drive through the entrance gates at the front of North Beverly Park after security has cleared us. "You're acting so weird."

My best buddy accosted me after school and manhandled me downtown, where we grabbed food and then shopped for my upcoming trip to Big Bear. It's a surprise for Vivien. It's my eighteenth birthday tomorrow, and I already know my father will be a no-show.

It took years for me to figure out why he was never around for my birthdays despite the promises he made—he won't celebrate the day his beloved wife died. I have zero desire to hang around my house, being reminded of how little I matter, so I booked a luxury cabin at Big Bear for the weekend. I'm looking forward to celebrating my birthday with my girl.

The impromptu shopping trip was not necessary, but I indulged Alex. He also insisted on heading to his place on the way back, forcing me into showering and changing there.

Like I said, the dude is acting weird.

We are forgoing our usual Friday plans for a double date with our best friends. Audrey and Alex wanted to toast the birthday boy tonight before we disappeared for the weekend, and neither of us could say no.

"What the fuck?" I blurt, sitting forward in my seat as Alex drives his Jeep through the open gates toward my house. Tons of vehicles are parked on either side of the long driveway, and the area in front of the house is crammed with cars as we draw closer.

Alex shoots me a wide grin as he swings his car around the water feature, stopping at the bottom of the steps leading to the double front doors. Viv and Audrey are waiting for us, wearing matching smiles and pretty party dresses. The dots start connecting in my brain as my heart jumps through hoops and adrenaline punches through my veins. "What did you do?" I ask my best friend when he kills the engine.

"Ask your girlfriend," he says with a wink before climbing out.

Viv opens my door and pulls me out of the Jeep. Music filters through the open door as our fellow students wander in and out of my house. "Surprise, baby." She flings her arms around my neck, and a familiar perfume cloud surrounds me. "Happy birthday, Reeve. I love you so much."

My arms band around her slim waist as I lean down and press a lingering kiss to her lips. "You threw me a party?" I say when we end our kiss. My heart is doing cartwheels as I hold her close, the organ swollen with so much emotion it feels like I might burst.

"Yes." She chews on the corner of her lips as she scrutinizes my face. "Are you mad?"

"Not even a bit." Tears prick the backs of my eyes. "At least now I know why Alex was acting so strange."

"I needed to get you out of the house so I could set up," Viv explains. "Audrey helped, and Mrs. Thompson was in on it too." Mrs. Thompson has been our housekeeper since I was a baby, but she took a more active role in my life after my nanny, Eleanor, left when I was ten. Between her and Lauren, they tried to ensure I didn't miss out on anything.

"Very sneaky, but I approve." I peck her lips before standing back to admire my gorgeous girlfriend. Blood rushes south as my eyes track over every glorious inch of her body. Viv's dress is a pretty pastel-pink color. It's strapless and rests mid-thigh, hugging her curves like a glove. A light-pink mesh layer covers her from chest to neck, along both arms and at the cutout panels at each side of the dress. Silver closed-toe stilettos complete the outfit, and she looks so fucking gorgeous I feel an urge to pinch myself because this is one of those moments where I can't believe she is mine.

"Sexy but so sweet," I purr as my hands glide over her sides. "How did I get so lucky?" Vivien is my every wet dream come to life with her stunning thick wavy hair, soulful hazel eyes, plump lush lips, high cheekbones, flawless skin, tempting long, long legs, and luscious curves in all the right places. "You take my breath away, babe. Every time."

Viv beams up at me, and it's like being bathed in the most wonderous sunshine. My heart kicks off, and things are getting interesting behind the crotch of my jeans. "You're so romantic." She swoons in my arms. "And it's me who's the lucky one because you are so freaking hot and so freaking awesome. My heart still goes crazy, and I get mad butterflies whenever I see you." She wraps her arms around my neck again. "I hope it's always like this for us, Reeve." Trusting greenish-brown eyes lock on mine. "I never want to stop feeling the things you make me feel."

Subtly, I nudge my semi against her stomach. "Feel that, babe," I tease, and I'm rewarded with another dazzling smile.

"As much as I'd love to hide away with you in your bedroom and let you do all manner of naughty things to me, it'll have to wait."

"Now she tells me," I joke, poking her stomach with my now rock-hard length.

"You're only eighteen once, and you deserve to party! Come on."

I sling my arm around her shoulders, and we walk over to where Alex and Audrey are making out by the stone pillar.

"Rey, get your tongue out of his mouth!" Viv hollers from two feet away, causing both our friends to almost jump out of their skin. "It's time to par-taay!"

It takes time to make my way through the house because everyone stops to wish me happy birthday. I'm sure I've got the cheesiest grin on my face. I think Viv must have invited everyone from our grade. Well, not everyone, I mentally correct, thinking of Marnie Gibson. That bitch has tried her best to make Viv's life a living hell since we started high school. I'm confident Gibson and her boyfriend Jennings are not here.

"Holy shit, babe," I exclaim when we reach the ballroom. "I can't believe you did all of this!"

The large room has been completely transformed. Dad's generations-old furniture has been temporarily replaced with glossy high tables and matching stools dotted around the perimeter of the space. A stage has been erected at the top of the room, and a DJ is spinning tunes as a lively crowd throws shapes on the dance floor. At the other end of the room, our friends and fellow students are swarming the free bar like booze is going out of fashion. To one side is a self-service buffet. On the other side is a table hosting a large three-tier cake. Mountains of presents rest underneath. A candy cart is tucked into one of the two alcoves behind the bar, and a photo booth with props is in the other. Birthday banners cling to the walls, and black, gold, and white balloon centerpieces adorn every table.

"I wanted to do more, but time was an issue," Viv says.

I haul her back into my arms. "It's perfect, babe. *You're* perfect." Emotion clogs my throat. "Thank you so much. I thought I didn't want a party, but I was wrong. This is the best surprise of my life, and I can't wait to show you how grateful I am later." I waggle my brows and thrust my hips against her. Thankfully, my semi has gone down, but one touch from Viv is usually all it takes to get my juices flowing.

The party is a roaring success and I'm enjoying it. I spend time with the guys, drinking, laughing, and eating, and then my girlfriend drags me out onto the dance floor, and we work up a sweat, grinding on one another and making out.

I'm struggling to hold my emotions in check when Vivien takes to the stage, asking everyone to join her in singing "Happy Birthday" to me. My girl has the most beautiful voice. She could pursue a career in the music industry if she wasn't allergic to the spotlight. Viv's chosen passions are costume design and writing, and she prefers to be behind the scenes. Shame to hide such natural talent, but I would never push her to do something she didn't want to do.

After she serenades me, I cut the cake, and we take turns mashing chocolate-fudge goodness into our mouths in between kisses. I can't remember the last time I had so much fun, and I never want the night to end.

It's after four before the house is cleared out and we stumble upstairs to bed.

Wasting no time, I carefully strip my love out of her clothes before tearing my own off, and then we're tumbling into bed, kissing, and groping like our lives depend on it. I slide easily into my girl, hovering over her as I go rigidly still, peering at her flushed face, vibrant eyes, and swollen lips as I savor the moment. "Tonight was the best night of my life, Viv."

"The night's not over, stud," she says with a cheesy wink and a skillful thrust of her hips. "You promised to thank me with your body, and I'm calling it in." Stretching up, she nips at my chin with her teeth. "Fuck me, Reeve. I want it hard and fast. Don't hold back. Give it all to me."

And I do.

"Just smell that," Viv says, tipping her head up as she stands in front of the luxury cabin I rented for the weekend at Big Bear. We left a little later than initially planned, thanks to our late night, but we've still got about three hours of daylight and all day tomorrow. "I love the crisp, clean, minty air," she says, swirling around in her snow boots. "The snow always smells so … pure and fresh. Like a baptism."

I chuckle, loving how unique her mind is. "I know what you mean," I say, closing the trunk after I lift the last of our bags. "It's like another world up here."

"I think we should buy a place here when we're married." Viv takes one of the grocery bags from my arms.

"That's a good idea." We've been coming to Big Bear every year with Viv's parents, and it's always something I look forward to. I like the idea of continuing that tradition with our own family. "I'll add it to our life plan."

Viv tucks her arm into mine. "Everything is going to happen fast now." She smiles adoringly at me, but I spot something else hidden at the backs of her eyes. "I know these next few years will be busy, but it's exciting getting closer to realizing all of our dreams."

"Exciting and a little scary." I place my hand on her lower back as we climb the three steps to the cabin.

"The best things in life are always a little scary." Viv sets the grocery bag on the hall table as I close the door. Sitting on the bench, underneath the coat rack, she works her snow boots off while I do the same beside her. "It would be boring if we got everything we wanted with little effort. It's good to work for things."

"You're very wise and philosophical today, my love." I bundle her in my arms and touch my nose against hers.

"I find myself getting more introspective the closer we get to your leaving." A wave of sadness washes over her face before she quickly disguises it. She's upset I'll be gone for three months. I am too. But it needs to happen for everything we've planned to slot into place.

"We've still got six weeks," I remind her, pressing a kiss to the top of her head.

"It will go too fast, and I bet the time you're gone will pass at a snail's pace." She sighs, and I pull her onto my lap.

"We knew this would be our reality when things started happening for me." I brush messy strands of hair off her face so I can see her eyes. "It won't be easy, but these are stepping-stones. When I'm more established in my career, I can be choosier about the projects I take on and limit them to a few a year so the separations aren't as bad."

"I'll just miss you." She buries her head in my neck, and we silently hold one another for a few beats. Viv lifts her head and runs her fingers through the light stubble on my cheeks. Tingles spread over my face from her touch, like always. "I'm being selfish. I don't want to ruin this weekend after you've gone to so much trouble."

"It's not selfish. I understand you have concerns. I do too, but it's an adjustment, that's all. We'll figure it out." I dust a feather-soft kiss over her lips.

She moves to straddle me through our thick jackets and jeans. "I know we will, because you and me are written in the stars, Reeve. We have always been meant to be together."

"Amen to that, my love." I clasp her face in my hands as she settles on top of me, examining her makeup-free face, noting the delicate smattering of freckles dotted across her red-tipped nose, the rosy glow to her cheeks, and her wide, vibrant eyes. Viv is shielding nothing from me, and I see her love as clearly as I see her fear. I wish I could carry it for her to lighten the load. "It will be scary, but like you said, nothing worthwhile in this life comes easy. I love you and you love me, and that's all that matters. That won't ever change."

Chapter Five
Then - Age 9

Fighting tears, I hang my head and rest my hands on top of the table in the kitchen, trying not to look at the clock again.

He's not coming.

He promised, but he always breaks his promises.

"Let me try your dad again." Eleanor gets up from the seat across from me with her cell phone in her hand. "I'm sure he's on his way." Her smile is barely a smile as she walks out of the room to make the call we both know will go unanswered.

"I made you some hot chocolate," Mrs. Thompson says, placing a mug in front of me.

"I shouldn't be drinking that before breakfast," I mumble.

"It's your birthday. The rules don't count when you're the birthday boy."

I wish that were true, but today is no different than any other day. My daddy is not here, like always. He promised he was just going to the office for one early-morning meeting and that he'd be home to have breakfast with me before we'd go out for the day.

But he's still not here, and he's almost two hours late now.

He won't come.

It's the same every birthday.

I don't know what I did to make him hate me, but I must have done something wrong. Nothing I do is right. Nothing pleases him. And sometimes, when I catch him looking at me, it's like he wishes I would disappear.

"Reeve," Mrs. Thompson says in a soft voice, causing me to lift my head. My eyes sting, and I'm trying not to cry in front of her. She looks sad as she brushes her fingers across my cheek. "I got you a gift. Go ahead and open it." She slides a package wrapped in blue and green paper toward me, and I snatch it up, ripping the paper open and gasping when I see what is inside.

My lips curl into a smile as I run my fingers across the shiny cover. "You got me the new Harry Potter book!" Tears are building in my eyes again, but this time, they are happy tears. "Thank you." I fling myself at her, clutching the book in one hand as I hug her. "This is the best gift ever."

"You're welcome, sweetheart." Her body shakes against me for some reason.

The doorbell chiming echoes in the kitchen, and I hop up off the chair, holding the book to my chest as I race toward the hallway and the front door.

He's here! He didn't break his promise this time!

"Reeve!" Vivien screams, running toward me as my steps slow down.

It's not my dad.

Viv throws herself at me, and my arms go around her on autopilot as I look over her head at her parents. They are talking in hushed tones with Eleanor at the door.

"Happy birthday," she gushes, squeezing me tight.

"Thanks." I try to force my sadness away because I'm happy she's here. If my daddy isn't coming, then I want to be with my best friend and her family. It's usually what happens every time it's my birthday.

"I made you chocolate chip pancakes." Viv wiggles a plastic box in my face. "Well, Mom made them, but I helped. I stirred the batter and put the chips in, and I helped pour it too." She loops her arm in mine. "C'mon. I'm hungry."

"Vivien, wait." Lauren strides down the hallway and crouches in front of me. She pulls me into a warm hug. "Happy birthday, Reeve."

"Thank you," I choke out, clinging to her as she hugs and kisses me. Vivien's mommy gives the best hugs. I always feel all warm inside when her arms are around me.

Lauren straightens up and takes my hand while Vivien takes the other. We walk back to the kitchen, where Mrs. Thompson is already putting plates and silverware on the table. The two women look at one another a bit funny as Viv drags me over to the table.

Lauren takes the box and removes the pancakes, stacking them on a large plate in the center of the table while Mrs. Thompson ferries maple syrup, chocolate syrup, sliced straw-berries, and chopped bananas from the counter.

"We're going to have the best day ever," Vivien says, practically jumping in her seat. Her pretty eyes go wide as she looks over at her mom. "Can I tell him now, Mom? Puh-lease?"

Lauren smiles, ruffling her daughter's hair before she presses a kiss to the top of my head. "Go on," she tells Viv.

"We're going to Universal Studios, and we're going to go on that new *Revenge of the Mummy* ride! Daddy already talked to the man, and we don't have to wait or anything. He said we can go on it as many times as we like!"

I have been there before with Viv and her family, but we're really excited for this new ride. We didn't get to watch the movie because Lauren said it's too violent, but we're both tall enough to go on the rollercoaster, and Jonathon said they would take us one day. "This is so cool," I say as my sadness gives way to happiness. Hope swells in my chest when I look up at Lauren as she puts some pancakes, fruit, and chocolate syrup on my plate. "Is my daddy coming too?"

She pulls a weird face for a second before she turns to me with a smile. "Not today, but we were hoping you'd be okay to go with us, and we have another surprise for you later."

I rub at the tight pain in my chest as my lower lip wobbles.

"Your daddy's an asshole," Vivien blurts before shoving a pancake in her mouth.

"Vivien Grace Mills!" Lauren stares at my best friend with an angry face, and I hope she won't get into trouble. "I never want to hear that word come out of your mouth again, do you hear me?"

"That's not fair," Viv says over a mouthful of pancake, glaring at her mom. "I heard you saying it to Daddy! Why can you say it and I can't?"

Lauren mutters something under her breath, but I can't hear it.

"Princesses don't curse," Jonathon Mills says, entering the room carrying a massive box covered in red and blue wrapping paper. My eyes almost bug out of my head as I watch him drop it on the end of the table.

His eyes are kind as he bends over me. "Happy birthday, son," he says, messing my hair. "Eat your pancakes, and then you can open your gifts."

I shovel pancakes into my mouth superfast as the adults chuckle.

"Go slow, Reeve," Mrs. Thompson says as she pours me a glass of orange juice. "You don't want to choke."

Viv and I finish our breakfast in record time, and we sit on the floor with the box in between us as my best friend helps me to open my present. Inside are several boxes, and warmth spreads across my chest as I look at them one at a time.

"I picked this one," Viv says, handing me a large set with Justice League action figures. She shoves a big box of Legos at me. "That's from my daddy." Another box gets thrust at me. "Mom picked the Power Rangers tank set." She doesn't explain who picked the art materials, books, games, or the movie and McDonalds vouchers, but I don't care. This is the best birthday ever.

"Do you like it?" Vivien asks, and it looks like she's holding her breath.

"I love them." I lean forward and hug my best friend.

"Yay!" Vivien kisses my cheeks. "You're my bestest friend in the whole world, Reeve, and this is the bestest day because it's your birthday."

I hug her again. "You'll always be my best friend, and I want to spend every birthday with you." I climb to my feet and hug Lauren, Jonathon, and Mrs. Thompson. I don't know where Eleanor disappeared to. "Thank you for my gifts. I love them all."

"You're welcome, honey." Lauren's eyes look glassy when she smiles down at me.

"Open your card," Viv says, handing it to me. Two pink spots bloom on her cheeks. "I made it for you."

I open the envelope and smile at the picture Viv drew on the front.

"That's us," she says, pointing at the boy and girl holding hands in front of a large tree.

"That's our treehouse," she adds.

"I guessed." I hug her again. "I love it."

When we pull apart, the grown-ups all have this strange look on their faces.

Jonathon rubs his hands together and smiles. "Who's ready

for some rollercoasters?" he asks, and Viv and I scream yes and jump up and down.

Lauren laughs. "Go to the bathroom and freshen up, and we'll go then."

I grab Viv's hand, and as I'm leading her out of the kitchen, I hear Mrs. Thompson say, "Thank you for this."

"I want to throttle him with my bare hands," Lauren replies, but I don't hear anything else as Viv drags me to the bathroom.

I have the best day at the theme park. We go on so many rides, eat burgers and hot dogs, take photos, and drink milkshakes, and then we go back to Vivien's house where Jonathon orders pizza delivery. After, Lauren comes out with a big chocolate cake with "Happy 9th Birthday Reeve" on top, and I get to blow out the candles. Viv says I have to make a wish, and I wish that every birthday is as good as this one and that Vivien, Lauren, and Jonathon are always there.

When Lauren says I can sleep over if I want, I want to cry with happiness. I'm still mad at my daddy, and I didn't want to go home, so this is perfect.

"Can I show him now, Mom, pretty please?" Vivien's eyes are all lit up as she wraps her arms around her mom's waist and peers up at her. "I can't keep the secret any longer."

"I'm surprised you kept the secret at all, princess." Jonathon smiles at Vivien.

"It was hard," she says. "But I did it for Reeve because I wanted to see his face when he sees it."

"See what?" I ask because I have no clue what they are talking about.

"Come on." Lauren removes Vivien's arms from her waist. "Let's show Reeve his surprise."

I'm kind of in a daze as I hold Vivien's hand and walk upstairs with her parents. After everything, they have another surprise for me? "Pinch me. I need to know this isn't a dream," I whisper in her ear when we reach the landing. "Ow." I rub the sore spot on my arm she just pinched.

"You asked." She giggles. "And it's not a dream, silly. It's real." She kisses my cheek, and my skin feels really hot. "Did you feel that too?"

"Yeah," I whisper, suddenly feeling shy.

"Princess, no kissing boys until you're at least thirty," her daddy says.

Lauren laughs, swatting his chest. "Jon, you're ridiculous."

"Vivien won't be kissing other boys even when she's thirty," I say, holding her hand tighter. "The only boy she'll be kissing is me." I don't know where the words come from, but they feel true.

"All boys are gross except for Reeve." Vivien smiles at me, and I smile back at her, and I've forgotten all about the surprise. "So, you don't need to worry, Daddy," she says, keeping her eyes on my face, "because I know you love Reeve as much as I do."

Lauren looks like she's going to cry.

Jonathon bends down in front of us, his eyes moving to our joined hands. "I do, princess." He kisses Vivien's cheek and then mine. "We love both of you so much," he adds, "but there will be no talk of kissing until you're much, much older." I might be imagining it, but he stares straight at me when he says it.

I bob my head, and he seems happy again.

Grown-ups are freaking weird sometimes.

"Come on, cuties." Lauren ushers us toward the guest bedroom I stay in when I sleep over. "Time for your surprise."

"You're going to love it." Vivien squeals, tugging me forward.

The grown-ups stand outside the room as Vivien pulls me

inside. My mouth hangs open, and that fluttery feeling is back in my chest, swooping into my belly as I swallow and turn around, marveling at the bedroom that has been transformed into a Harry Potter bedroom.

The walls are painted orange, and there are wood panels on some of them. A map of Hogwarts is hanging on the wall behind the large bed with Hogwarts Express printed on the top and bottom. The comforter has pictures of the book covers on it. The side table is round with an owl holding it up, and all the Harry Potter books are on top. A giant Professor Dumbledore cutout is standing in one corner alongside a thick wooden box and a chalkboard. On the other side is an alcove with a wooden desk and shelves of books behind it. String lights that look like floating candles hang from the ceiling. The small navy couch in front of the TV holds cushions shaped like stars, the moon, and dragons. A quidditch stick and a quaffle ball are hanging on the wall alongside framed book covers. When I look closer, I see the pictures have been signed by the author, which is *wow*. New blue curtains and a spongey blue carpet finish the room.

"Reeve," Vivien whispers as she yanks on my arm. "Why are you crying? Are you sad?"

I didn't even realize I was crying. I shake my head, but I can't make any words. It's like I have forgotten how to speak.

"Honey." Lauren bends down to me. "Are you okay?"

I smile through my tears as I nod. "I love it," I whisper, forcing words out of my mouth. "You did this for me?"

"It was my idea," Vivien says, puffing out her chest. "Mom said she wanted to make a special bedroom for you, and I told her it had to be Harry Potter because it's your favorite."

I squeeze Viv's hand. "It is my favorite. This is awesome."

Lauren wipes my tears with her fingers. "We want you to have your own room here, Reeve, and to know that you are always welcome."

"You are a part of our family," Jonathon says. "Our house is your house too."

"I wish you were my mommy and daddy," I blurt, not understanding all the things I'm feeling.

Lauren starts crying, but she tries to hide it. Jonathon pulls her into a hug, and then he pulls me and Vivien into a hug with them. It feels nice. Safe. And I'm really happy. "We are here for you whenever you need us, Reeve," Jonathon says. "To us, you are already our son."

Chapter Six
Now

After a brisk walk in the forest, we return to our cabin and I light a fire in the open fireplace while Viv throws a couple of frozen pizzas in the oven and sets about making salad and garlic bread. We take turns grabbing quick solo showers, and then we congregate in the living room, sitting on cushions on the floor in front of the fire, while we eat our food and sip chilled champagne.

"I should probably learn how to cook before we get married," my girlfriend says in between bites of pepperoni pizza.

I shrug. "We know the basics. Between us, we'll cope."

"I want to be a good wife," she says, adding her last slice of pizza to my plate. "You can have it. I'm stuffed." Rubbing her flat stomach, she lies back against the couch.

"You will be a good wife. That's not up for debate. Whether you can cook cordon bleu meals or not doesn't matter. In all the ways that count, you excel."

"You'll give me a big head." She grins.

"I'd like you to give *me* a big head," I joke, waggling my brows as I grab my dick through my sweatpants.

She rolls her eyes. "Cheese city."

I throw a cushion at her. "Come here. You're too far away over there."

She crawls over to me, snuggling under my arm and resting her head on my shoulder as I finish my food.

"I dream about it all the time, you know," she says in a soft voice. "Our wedding. Getting to call you my husband, building our dream house, waking up beside you every day, and going to sleep beside you every night."

"Your belly swollen with our babies." I easily continue the vision because it's occupied my headspace every night for years. "Your gorgeous face glowing as you cradle our newborn in your arms. Me pushing our kids on the swings in our garden."

"A garden with a treehouse, an obstacle course, and a playground."

"Don't forget the roses." I grab both empty plates and twist around to place them on the side table before lifting our flutes. I hand one to Viv. "Is it crazy to crave the day I get to call you my wife?" I peer into her beautiful eyes. Eyes that are the gateway to her soul and my forever. "Because I daydream about that constantly." My lips kick up at the corners. "I may have doodled it on every school notebook at one time."

Viv snorts out a laugh. "I've been writing Mrs. Reeve Lancaster on my notebooks since I was ten."

"I feel sorry for those who haven't found their soul mates," I say in between sips of champagne. "Imagine having to go out there and find your other half?" I shudder at the thought. "It makes me feel physically ill."

"We're lucky, Reeve." Viv straightens up and turns to face

me. "So fucking lucky that we found one another so early and we shared the same feelings."

I press a kiss to her brow. "I remember how terrified I was to move us from the friend zone to more. I was so scared you didn't feel the same and afraid I would ruin our friendship."

"Is that why you kept me waiting for years before you properly kissed me?"

"That and your dad."

She arches a brow.

"Remember that birthday when I got the Harry Potter-themed bedroom? You kissed my cheek out in the hallway and your dad made it clear there was to be no kissing for a long time."

Viv shakes her head, smiling as she finishes her champagne. "You're too noble for your own good, Reeve. It's a miracle I'm still talking to my parents." Her eyes sparkle, and she dazzles me with a blinding smile. "First, they scare you into not kissing me, and then they cockblock me until I'm legal."

Now it's my turn to arch a brow. "Ahem. Neither of us was legal when we lost our V-cards to one another."

"You still held back until you were almost seventeen. I was ready to jump your bones at fourteen."

I almost choke on the last of my champagne. "Neither of us was ready at fourteen. I'm not sorry we waited. The anticipation was next level, and it's not like we weren't having fun finding other ways to explore and get one another off."

Viv plucks the flute from my hand, placing both glasses on the table beside the plates. Crawling into my lap, she straddles me, moaning softly when she feels me hardening underneath her. She rocks her pelvis against me as her hands gravitate to my hair. "You do have very talented hands and a very talented mouth." Leaning down, she kisses me slowly and passionately, and my hands press into her back, pushing her chest flush with mine.

"Want me to show you how talented my cock is too?" I whisper in her ear before nibbling on her lobe as I thrust my erection up against the softest part of her. Only sweatpants and long-sleeved shirts separate our bodies, and I can feel her heat through our clothes.

"Yes, please," she purrs, yanking on my hair and pulling my head back. "I'd like that very much."

Unlike last night, when it was almost a race to shed our clothes and fuck, tonight we take our time.

Viv remains on my lap as I slowly pull her top off. She's not wearing a bra, and I'm as hard as steel now. My fingers sweep across her silky-smooth skin, dancing a light path down her body. Groans pepper the air as I circle her nipples and softly squeeze her magnificent tits before cupping them in my hands. "These are mine." I push them together and lower my mouth over one nipple and then the other, sucking gently on the taut peaks. "I'm the first and last to touch them, to see you like this."

"Yes," she rasps, gyrating on my lap with her head thrown back, her hair hanging in soft waves over her shoulders, and her eyes partly closed. "You're the only one who gets to kiss me, touch me, fuck me."

My dick jerks at her words, fueling the possessive beast inside me. "Lie back," I command, lifting her off me by the hips and placing her down on the soft blanket I laid on the floor before we started eating. "Touch yourself, baby." My fingers curl in the waistband of her sweatpants as her hands roam her smooth skin. Precum leaks from my cock as she fondles her tits and tweaks her nipples. "Fuck, that's hot."

"Reeve, I *need*."

"I know what you need, Viv, and I'll give it to you."

I roll her sweatpants and flimsy lace panties down her legs

and toss them aside. Flames crackle and dance in the hearth as I lay my love out like the goddess she is. "Spread your legs," I instruct as I yank my shirt off and stand to kick my sweatpants away. I didn't bother putting underwear on after my shower. The heating is cranked to the max, and with the fire, the cabin is nice and toasty. Clothing really is optional.

Kneeling between her legs, I take a moment to enjoy the view. "You're exquisite, Vivien, and I love you so fucking much."

Her eyes bore into mine. "I love you too. More than words can describe."

Pressing my naked body down over hers, I kiss her tenderly before slipping my tongue into her mouth. A whimper escapes her lips as she parts her legs wider, and I nestle my throbbing cock between her soft thighs. My palms hold her face steady as I kiss her deeply, not rushing on purpose because I want to enjoy every second of this weekend and commit every moment to my memory bank so I have it to draw upon when I'm feeling lonely and missing her.

"Reeve," she pants in between kisses. "I need you inside me. I ache for you."

"I ache for you too, baby, but I don't want to rush this. I want to worship every inch of your beautiful body and remind you of all the ways you are mine and I am yours."

I kiss my way down her warm flesh, licking the valley between her tits, before swirling my tongue around her nipples as I massage her soft mounds. My lips blaze a trail as I move lower, over her ribs and down to her stomach. I tickle her belly button with my tongue, and her flesh quivers as she moans while I move my lips across her pelvis, bypassing her pulsing core to suck on the tender skin at the tops of her thighs.

Pressing my nose to her pussy, I close my eyes and inhale her intoxicating scent before my tongue darts out and I lick a line up and down her slit. Viv arches, moaning and whimpering and thrusting her cunt in my face. Placing one hand on her lower belly, I hold her in place as I devour her with my lips and tongue. She's crying, whimpering, and squirming under me and I love it. "Hmm," I murmur before plunging my tongue in and out of her slick channel. "You have no idea how much I'm addicted to how you taste, Viv."

"Stop talking," she pants. "More licking and tongue fucking."

I chuckle against her lower lips. I love how open and honest we are with one another about our needs. Pushing two fingers inside her, I watch as she writhes on the floor, her neck and face flushed, her nipples hard and standing at attention. With her eyes half closed, she parts her lips to pant as I pump my fingers in and out of her pussy, cursing under my breath when I feel her clamping down around my digits. She's close, so I move my mouth to her clit and flatten my tongue against it as I curl my fingers inside her and stroke her inner walls in a consistent fast motion.

"Reeve!" she shouts as I graze her clit and drive another finger inside her cunt. "I'm going to ... agh!" Her pussy strangles my fingers as she comes, and I suck her swollen bundle of nerves as I continue stroking her through her orgasm. "Holy fucking hell, Reeve." Her lust-coated eyes pin mine in place. "You are so unbelievably good at that." She reaches down, grabbing hold of my shoulders. "Now, get up here and fuck me."

I kneel, staring at her glistening pussy as I suck my fingers dry. "Delicious."

Viv sits up abruptly and grabs my cock, wrapping her slim fingers around it and giving it a few tugs. Leaning in, she licks the crown, and I see stars. "You're not the only one who's addicted." She peers up at me as she sucks on the tip. "I love how you taste too," she says before swallowing me.

I rest one hand on the couch to steady myself as she sucks me off, hollowing her cheeks so she can take more of me in. A familiar tingling at the base of my spine warns me I could come like this. But I want to come inside her, so I pull out of her mouth with a pop and reel her into my arms, hugging her for a few seconds. Tipping her head back, I stare at her gorgeous, gorgeous face. "I'm going to make love to you now, Viv."

"Halle-fucking-lujah," she says over a grin.

"Do you know how beautiful you are?" I whisper, my fingers caressing her delicate facial features. "How sexy you are?" I add, moving my hands lower and fondling her tits. "How much I crave you? Need you? Adore you?"

"Reeve." Moisture pools in her eyes. "I'd say about as much as I crave, need, and adore you too."

With tenderness, I lay her back down on the blanket and settle myself between her thighs. "Life hasn't always dealt me a good hand, but I hit the jackpot with you." I kiss her swollen lips as I position my cock at her entrance. "No day will pass where I won't be in love with you," I promise as I slowly inch inside her. Ripples of pleasure wash over me as I enter my love. It feels as magical as it did the first time we had sex. "I will love you for eternity, Viv."

"Reeve," she whispers as I slide all the way home. "I won't ever stop loving you. You're my reason for existing." Her legs wind around my back as I move carefully and precisely inside her, feeling every drag of my cock against her velvety-soft walls as I dust kisses along her neck and across her collarbone. Desperate hands clutch at my back as I thrust in and out, rotating my hips, lifting her ass up, and angling my cock so it hits the perfect spot inside her.

"Oh fuck," she says in a breathy tone, squeezing my ass as I pick up my pace and rut into her with more urgency. "You feel so good." Her back arches off the floor, and a shiver works its way through me as her pointed nipples brush against my chest. My hands hold her hips in place as I work my dick in deeper and push her legs up higher on my waist.

"Every time is incredible," I tell her, plunging inside her with greater need as the tingling returns to my spine and my balls pull up. "I will never get enough of you, Vivien. Never."

"Reeve!" she cries out as her pussy clamps down hard on my cock, and I almost detonate on the spot. Throwing her legs over my shoulders, I adjust our position so I have easy access to her clit, and I rub two fingers against her swollen bud as I ram into her hard.

"Yes! Right there, oh fuck, yes, Reeve."

I roar as my release thunders through me, shooting jets of cum into her body while her pussy pulses and shakes around my dick and she moans and writhes through her own orgasm.

I collapse on the floor alongside her, pulling her onto her side with my dick still jerking in her pussy. Circling my arms around her, I press my sticky flesh against hers and close my eyes, relishing the feel of her in my arms and the warmth of her cunt as it nestles my cock. I dot kisses all over her face and into her hair as we cling to one another, basking in the strength of our love. I often lack confidence, but the one thing I never doubt is Viv and me. I'm more than confident in the connection forged since we were little kids with an arrogance that is born of true belief and commitment.

A lot of things about the future are uncertain, but never us.

Never Viv.

Nothing will come between us because we were always destined to be together, and nothing will ever tear us apart.

Chapter Seven
Now - Age 18

"Come on," Alex says, looking like a man on a mission as he charges out of the locker room after practice. "Let's get out of here."

I fall into step alongside him, not questioning it.

"Don't worry, Reeve," Guy Fenwick shouts after me. "We'll take *real* good care of Vivien while you're gone."

Alex grips my elbow as I slam to a halt. "Don't, man."

"She'll be so busy on her knees she won't have time to miss you," his sidekick, Keith York, adds.

My fists ball tight at my sides as I grind my teeth to the molars. Fuck this. I can't let it go. Turning around, I stride toward the pack of assholes loitering outside the locker room.

"Don't be a dick, dude," Nate says, pushing his way through Guy and his crew of jerks, with Zeke in tow.

"I'm not the one who was mouthing off about pounding Lancaster's pretty princess until she can't walk straight." Guy's lips kick up at the corners as he arches a brow in Nate's direction.

Alex narrows his eyes on Nate, and I full-on glare at him.

Nate swings his gaze to mine. "I was drunk and talking through my ass. I didn't mean it."

Yeah, sure. Everyone and his mother know Nate has a hard-on for my girl. We have come to blows a couple times in the past over Viv.

"Don't worry, dude." Guy slaps Nate on the back. "We'll make sure you get a turn."

Guy levels me with a salacious grin, and I instantly see red. Reacting on autopilot, I dump my book bag on the floor and lunge at the dick. His crew surrounds him, straightening their backs and clenching their fists, practically frothing at the mouth. Before I can land the first punch, Alex yanks me back. "You can't show up on set bloody and bruised," he says low into my ear.

Right now, I don't fucking care. I want to pummel these jerks into the ground for daring to disrespect Vivien. Guy has been taunting me about her for years, and I'm mostly able to let it slide. Mainly 'cause I have always been here to protect my girlfriend. This time is different. I'm leaving tomorrow for three months, and I won't be here to keep her safe. How do I know they are only trying to bait me? How do I know they won't try to hurt her? Guy has a bad rep with girls for a reason. I want that douche nowhere near the love of my life.

"Don't give him what he wants," Alex whispers as he drags me back. A bunch of other guys from the team stand with us as we face off against Guy and his supporters. "Viv won't give those jerks the time of day."

"I know," I hiss. My girl is loyal. "I'm not worried about that."

"I won't let them harass or hurt her," he promises. "I'll watch her back."

I offer him a tight nod. "I'm good now," I say, shucking out of his hold. I'm not, but I won't start a fight and leave under a cloud. I need to take control of the situation and ensure he keeps his grabby hands off my girl.

A smirk rolls over my lips as I step up to him. "Speaking of women on their knees. How is your mother doing these days?"

The smug grin slides off his face, and my grin grows wider.

"I was going to say my dad misses her cunt, but that would be a lie. Since she hit on me, when I was *fifteen*," I add, playing to the mushrooming audience, "he hasn't been so keen on taking her to his bed. But I hear she's not short of lovers."

Guy's nostrils flare, and he looks like he's seconds away from punching my lights out. "Shut your fucking mouth, Lancaster." He shoves my chest, and I laugh.

"The truth hurts, huh, bruh?"

"At least I have a mother," he retorts.

"Your mother is a wannabe pedo," I say in a cutting tone, ignoring the stabby pain in my chest. "Or maybe a full-fledged one." I shrug. "Who's to say I was the only underage boy she hit on? Maybe others weren't so quick to push her away."

A flash of something passes over his face, gone too fast for me to decipher it, but it's clear I've hit the right button. Smiling, I push my face all up in his, talking in a low tone so only he can hear. "It wouldn't take much for me to start that rumor. I've got a massive following on social media. One word from me, and your mother's reputation—and her marriage—would be ruined. You wouldn't be able to show your face around town." I drill him with a caustic look. "Stay away from Vivien. If you or anyone from your crew so much as breathes in her direction, I will unleash hell on your family." I grab a fistful of his shirt. "Do we have an understanding?"

A muscle pops in his jaw as he reluctantly nods.

"Good." I shove him away as I release my hold on his shirt. I point my finger in his face. "I will keep my word as long as you do. Don't even think of double-crossing me." Turning around, I take my bag from Alex's outstretched hand and stalk off.

"I see you pulled the ace out of your sleeve," Alex says as we walk toward the exit. The hallways are virtually empty at this time on a Friday, and the girls left straight after their last class to get ready for our dinner date tonight. I hung around as I had some paperwork to complete. Today was officially my last day at Blackrock Prep. My last day of high school. I won't be back for graduation, so I'm handling everything today.

"Knew that would come in handy someday." A shiver works its way through me as I recall the time Maritsa Fenwick tried to seduce me. Only my dad and Alex know what went down, and it's not something I like to think about. It still makes me want to puke. I feel a little bit sorry for Guy. His mother is too busy spreading her legs to have time for him and his sisters. Growing up in his household wasn't fun either I'm guessing. He's still an ass, though. At least he won't torment Viv while I'm gone. That fleeting expression on his face confirms it.

"Lancaster!" Nate yells as the sound of running footsteps tickles my eardrums. "Hold up."

"I'm not in the mood for dealing with his ass," I warn Alex. I don't get how he tolerates him. Both sets of parents are long-time friends, but foisting their kids on one another isn't right. Alex has said that's not it. He says there is more to Nate than meets the eye, and his persona is a front. I don't care. I have little patience for the guy. If he wasn't so blatantly obvious about wanting my girl, it might be easier to be around him.

I only turn around for Alex. He hates playing referee. "What do you want?" I work hard to keep my tone neutral.

"I'm sorry, man." Nate runs a hand through his hair as Zeke leans against a locker, chewing on a toothpick as he watches this go down. Nate's best buddy is an all right guy. Don't know how he tolerates Nate either.

"If you said that shit, that's not cool," Alex says, grabbing on to the straps of his bag.

"I know, I know." Nate drags his fingers through his hair again. "I was trashed when I said it, but I know better."

"I tolerate you because of Alex," I say, eyeballing him. "And he's the only reason I'm not shoving your head through the wall." I step up closer. "I have told you over and over to quit saying shit about my girl. To stop looking at her like you're picturing her naked. It's disrespectful."

"I don't mean to disrespect you, I jus—"

I prod his chest with my finger. "It's disrespectful *to Viv*, Nate! She's not into you. She's with me. We're forever." I jab my finger in harder. "When are you going to get that through your thick skull?"

"I know you two are for life. I'm trying not to crush on her, but it's hard because she's gorgeous and hella cool."

"Try." Jab. "Fucking." Jab. "Harder." Jab.

"You and I will have problems, bro, if you don't quit this bullshit," Alex adds.

"I'll stop. I promise." Nate pierces me with a sober look. "I swear I won't pull any shit while you're gone. I don't mean to." His eyes lower to the floor as he combs his hand through his hair again. I step back, ready to be done with this. He lifts his head. "Sometimes shit comes out of my mouth before I have time to consider it, let alone stop it. I never mean to disrespect Viv. She's always been nice to me and ... yeah, I'm quitting while I'm ahead," he adds, seeing the warning look in my eyes.

"Don't pull shit with Viv while I'm gone, Nate." I level him with a lethal look. "I won't be gone for long, and you don't want to see what I'll do if you mess with my girl."

The next morning, I sneak into Viv's empty room trying to ignore the heart-wrenching pain in my chest. It's been there since last night as I held her in my arms in my bedroom while she slept. I didn't sleep a wink. Didn't want to waste a second of our last hours together. Watching her sleep has always comforted me, and I needed to memorize every soft curve, every tiny freckle, every little sigh. I need a mental stamp of every minute detail so it keeps me going over the long nights ahead.

I have never been apart from Vivien for any length of time, so this is going to be hard on both of us.

Lifting her pillow, I slip the small mesh bag containing the silver locket, chocolates, and card underneath. My gaze rakes over the familiar room as tears prick my eyes. I drop onto the bed and bury my face in the soft pillow, inhaling the floral scent that reminds me of my girlfriend.

I'm excited to begin filming the movie, but I'm traumatized at doing this without my rock. Viv has been with me for every pivotal moment in my life, and I'm not sure I can do this without her by my side. But I've got to get a grip.

Placing the pillow down carefully over the surprise gift, I exhale heavily before climbing to my feet. I'm eighteen. I'm a man now, and it's time to prove it—to Vivien, to my father, to Lauren and Jon.

But most of all, to *me*.

This is my time to shine. I'm capable of being responsible and independent, and I'm *not* going to fuck it up.

Chapter Eight
Now

"**C**ome here, baby," I plead, feeling something dying inside me as I watch the silent tears coursing down Viv's face. She has been fighting tears the entire ride to the airport, and she can't hold them at bay any longer. I bundle her in my arms in the back seat of the car, attempting to comfort her. The rents already got out, giving us some privacy. "Please don't cry. It's killing me."

"I'm sorry," she says in between sobs as she climbs into my lap. "I swore I wouldn't cry, but my tear ducts obviously didn't get the memo."

Mine didn't either. A few nights ago, the reality of our separation hit me full force, and I had a mini breakdown in my room, crying myself to sleep. I know this might seem excessive, but no one gets it. No one understands how much we are a part of one another. Leaving her is akin to leaving half my heart behind in Cali. It's like chopping off crucial limbs and hobbling my way through life without them.

That's how important this girl is to me.

She is everything.

Everything.

Saying I will miss her doesn't come close to describing how it will feel.

But I can't be selfish. I can't let her see how devastated I am because it'll be worse for Viv. She'll be stuck here without me, surrounded by our memories and our love. I'm the one getting to experience new adventures, and I'll have plenty to distract me. It's going to be harder for my girlfriend, and I need to do what I can to make it easier for her. "It's only three months, not forever. I'll be home for prom before you know it." I kiss the tip of her nose.

She grips my face in her hands. "I'm so damn proud of you, Reeve, and really excited for you."

I press my forehead to hers and indulge my vulnerability for a moment. "I needed to hear that, because I'm scared shitless. What if I fuck this up?"

It's not just thoughts of leaving Viv that have given me sleepless nights lately. This is my first big role. I'm working with actors who are more experienced than me. The director is highly sought after, and the studio is one of the best in the business. The budget is massive. The projected outcome is beyond my wildest dreams. There is a lot resting on my shoulders, and there are a lot of people depending on me. When I let those thoughts linger, I am petrified I'm going to mess it all up.

Her eyes pop wide. "Are you kidding me? There is no way you can fuck this up. We've been running lines religiously from the moment you got the part, and even I could recite Cam's lines in my sleep. You've got this, babe. You are going to kill it."

I swoop in, claiming her lips in a deep kiss that conveys everything I'm feeling. Viv moans into my mouth as I slip my tongue between her lips, and she grinds on top of me. We've indulged in a fucking frenzy this week, both of us desperate to get our fill of one another, but it's not enough. It would never be enough with this girl. Blood flows to my cock, and I'm already sporting a semi.

"I love you," I remind her as I circle my arms around her back and hold her close. "I love you so damn much. Don't forget that." My eyes shutter as I hug her tight, never wanting to let go.

"I won't." She rests her head on top of mine, and I commit the feel of her to my memory bank.

"I mean it, Viv." Reluctantly, I lift her up and settle her on the seat beside me. My arm glides around her shoulders. "Things are going to get crazy, but nothing matters to me as much as you do. You are my entire world, and that will never change."

Nothing will be the same after this, and my desire to protect what we have is stronger than ever. This is going to be the first real test of our love, and while I'm confident we'll weather the storm, I'm not going to lie and say I don't have concerns. Neither of us has gone this long without one another, and it won't be without challenges or pressures.

"Stop it." She playfully pushes my chest while her eyes turn glassy again. "Stop being so damn romantic. So damn perfect, because it just makes our separation even harder."

Dad opens the door and pops his head in. "It's time." He shoots an almost soft look in Viv's direction, which surprises me. Simon Lancaster takes less than minimal interest in my life, and he's never said much about Viv or us as a couple.

"Just give us one more minute," she says, picking up the silver-wrapped package from the floor as Dad nods and closes the door.

Anxious butterflies swoop into my belly at our impending separation, and bile swims up my throat.

How am I going to do this?

How am I going to live without her?

I'm used to talking to her constantly, even when I'm not with her. I'm used to loving kisses and touches and her tempting body curled around mine in bed.

How will I survive without her encouraging commentary, her playful laughter, her sexy smiles, and her loving eyes?

"Open it on the plane." I snap out of it when Viv hands the gift to me.

I wish *she* was packaged in silver foil and I was taking Vivien with me.

It's those kinds of thoughts that confirm I need to do this alone. It's not right to rely on her to the extent I do. I know that. Maybe this time apart will be good for our relationship and help both of us to be a little more independent. This will be a good thing for us. We'll emerge stronger than before.

I cling to those sentiments as I prepare to say goodbye.

"I left a gift for you on your bed," I say.

Her eyes fill up again, and we move as one, pressing our lips together in a tender kiss. Then I help her out of the car and hold her hand as I watch the last of my luggage being secured on the Studio 27 private jet. The studio has arranged for a car to pick me up from Logan International and take me to the hotel I'll be calling home for the first few weeks. Thereafter, we'll be on location in different parts of Massachusetts.

"Good luck, son," Jonathon Mills says, pulling me into a bear hug. My heart skips a beat like it always does when Jon calls me son. He's been doing it since I was little, for as long as I can remember.

I feel more like his son than Simon Lancaster's.

I can't wait until the day when it's official. When I marry Viv and Lauren and Jon are my legit parents.

They are the only parents I have known growing up, and I love them so much for everything they have done for me. Just thinking about them draws tears to my eyes.

"We're rooting for you," Jon adds, squeezing my back.

"Enjoy the experience, honey." Lauren pulls me into an embrace next. She takes my hands in hers while kissing both my cheeks. Warmth floods my chest at her tender touch. Lauren Mills is the best woman I know and the most amazing mother. I'm lucky to have had her influence in my life. I shudder to think how much worse my childhood would have been without her in it. "And I'm only a phone call away if you need me. I know from personal experience how daunting it can be, so call any time, day or night."

I know I can count on her to help, but I need to do this on my own. I need to prove to everyone that I can stand on my own two feet. That I don't need to rely on them anymore. That I'm an adult and capable of handling my own affairs. How else will I prove to Lauren and Jon that I'm worthy of their only daughter?

"Just focus on the work," Dad says, yanking me out of my head. "Don't let anything distract you."

Without conscious thought, I reach for him.

I don't know why.

I can't ever remember him hugging me.

My arms are around him, and his are hanging loose at his sides, like he's forgotten how to hug. Pain spears me from all angles and I'm just about to break our embrace when he lifts his arms and hugs me back. Tears stab my eyes, and I'm struggling not to cry. My dad's arms feel good around me even though it sends me back in time and I feel like a lost little boy again. Squeezing my eyes closed, I pray that this will be enough. That I'll do him proud, and he'll forget that I killed my mother and love me the way I want to love him. It's not entirely his fault. Something broke in him the day he lost my mother. Imagining what it would be like if I lost Viv in such a soul-destroying way helps me to empathize. I know I would never be the same. So, I can relate in some way.

What I don't understand is how he could all but abandon me.

I'm his last link to my mom. The woman he loved more than life itself. Shouldn't he cherish me for that? If I was in his shoes, I would cling to my little boy and shower him with love because he was a parting gift from the love of my life and all that remains of her on this earth.

I will never understand how my presence in his life seems to have had the opposite effect.

Sometimes, I think he's a lost cause. That there's no point trying to win his affection. I've made vows to myself to stop trying in the past. But I always break them. I hate to admit what he thinks matters to me, but it does.

I want him to love me.

I think I need it to feel whole.

I wish I didn't, but there's always this hollow ache inside me without my father's love and respect.

"You've done well, Reeve," he says, ending our hug. "Your mother would be so proud of you."

Wow. I stare at him in a bit of a daze. He has never said that to me before. My heart swells behind my rib cage, and emotion clogs the back of my throat. Viv wraps her arms around me as a full-body shudder whittles through me.

"We're *all* proud of you." Lauren squeezes my shoulder, and I'm dangerously close to losing it completely. I knew today would be hard, but never this emotional.

"You need to board the plane, or it will have to leave without you," Dad says, glancing at Viv with the same soft expression I saw on his face a few minutes ago.

Viv shakes in my arms. "I love you," I say, holding her tight to my body.

"I love you too," she says through her tears.

Holding her gorgeous face, I kiss her beautiful lips. "Stay strong, babe."

She bobs her head and sniffles.

I kiss her one final time, and it's killing me to let her go, but I have to. I walk toward the plane with Viv's gift tucked under my arm, fighting the tsunami of emotions swirling inside my chest.

"Be epic, babe," Viv hollers. "And know I'm cheering for you every step of the way."

Spinning around, I blow her a kiss, smiling when she jumps up and catches it.

Vivien loves me so good, and I'm incredibly lucky to have her in my life. She wants me to succeed and she's proud of me. Those sentiments are what will keep me going in the weeks and months ahead.

Tears fall as the plane takes off, leaving the love of my life behind on the runway. It feels like my heart is ripped in two, and the pain is so intense it's a miracle I can still breathe. After somewhat composing myself, I open her gift, inspecting every carefully chosen item, knowing how lucky I am to be loved like this.

Then I wipe my tears and promise myself there will be no more. I'm going to give this movie my all and build the kind of career I have dreamed of because it's how I'll ensure Viv's dreams come true too. And getting to share my life with her in the way we have planned is all I have ever wanted.

Chapter Nine
Then - Age 10

I hold my hand over my hot ear as I stumble down the hallway toward Dad's bedroom, sobbing as the pain gets worse. I'm crying too hard to notice the weird sounds coming from his room before I open the door and run inside. "Dad," I sob. "My ear..." My words fade, and my tears stop as my mouth falls open. I watch in silence, trying to make sense of what I'm seeing. There's a strange lady on the bed, and she's got no clothes on! Dad is leaning over her, and he's naked too! His butt flexes as he thrusts against her, and the woman's big titties wobble and shake as the back of Dad's bed slams against the wall. She cries out, and my daddy grabs her hips and curses.

"Dad! You're hurting her!" I shout, forgetting about my sore ear for a second.

The woman screams, and both my ears hurt now. She shoves Dad away and pulls the sheets up under her chin. At the same time, another naked woman walks out of the bathroom, and her eyes pop wide in horror when she sees me.

"Reeve!" Eleanor whispers my name as Dad roars at me.

"Get the fuck out of here, you little shit!" Dad yells,

climbing off the bed and coming toward me wearing his angry face. I've never seen his penis before, but it's so much bigger than mine. It's hard, like mine gets sometimes, and it's standing straight out. "Go back to your room!" Dad shakes my shoulders, dragging my gaze to his angry face, as Eleanor approaches from behind. She's got my daddy's shirt on now.

"I'll take him," my nanny says.

"No." Dad grabs her elbow, keeping her at his side. "He made his own way here. He can make his way back." He waves his finger in my face. "What have I told you about knocking, boy? How dare you barge in here! It's the middle of the night. Go back to sleep."

"But, Dad—" I'm about to tell him I'm sick when he shoves me.

"Go, Reeve! Get out of my face before I do something I'll regret."

Eleanor pushes past Dad and wraps her arm around my shoulders as I start crying again. "Don't speak to him like that, Simon." She glares at him. "He's only a little boy."

"He's old enough to know better." An icy look fills his eyes. "And old enough to not need a nanny any longer."

Eleanor stiffens. "Don't do this. He needs me."

Dad snarls. "Neither of us needs you." He stalks to the other side of the bed, scoops up some clothes and comes back, throwing them at her. "You're fired. Clear out the rest of your room, and be gone by the time I get home from work tomorrow."

"Baby," the woman in the bed says, batting her eyelashes at my dad. "Come back here and finish what you started."

"You're an asshole," Eleanor says, hugging her clothes to her chest as she keeps me tucked against her side.

"Never pretended I wasn't," Dad says, pushing us out into

the hallway and slamming the door in our faces, like we're trash.

Eleanor sniffles, and she's shaking all over. "Are you okay?" I ask as I pull at my sore ear.

Her face softens as she crouches down to my level. "I'm fine, sweetheart." She looks at my hand pressed against my ear. "What's wrong, Reeve?"

A sob bursts from my lips. "My ear hurts."

A sudden loud *thump, thump* frightens me, and I cling to my nanny. Eleanor scowls at the closed door and straightens up, taking my hand and leading me back to my bedroom. She makes me get under the covers while she goes to fetch the first aid kit. When she returns, she's wearing jeans and a blouse and carrying a tray with a glass of juice and the box. My nanny takes my temperature and gives me some medicine.

"That should ease the pain, and I'll get the doctor to come over first thing in the morning. You might need an antibiotic."

"What's wrong with me?" I ask, scooting down in my bed.

"You have an ear infection." She presses a soft kiss to my brow. "But you'll be right as rain in a few days."

"Nor?" I whisper, grabbing her hand. "You're not leaving, right?"

"I will talk to your daddy in the morning when he's less angry." She tilts her head to one side and softly combs my hair with her fingers. "I'm sorry you had to see and hear that, Reeve. I'm sorry I ever crossed a line. More sorry than you'll ever know," she adds in a soft voice.

"Why was my daddy hurting that lady, and why were you wearing no clothes?"

She tucks her hair behind her ears and licks her lips. "He wasn't hurting her. Remember when we talked about sex?" My face feels like it's on fire. Eleanor walked in on me touching my dick last month. I was embarrassed, but she told me it was

normal to feel these urges, and she told me about sex. I'd heard stuff in school, and next year, when Viv and I start middle school, we'll have sex education class, but I didn't realize that was what my daddy was doing, and now I feel stupid.

"Did you have sex with my daddy too? Is that why you were naked?"

She rubs her hands down her face and sighs. "I don't think your daddy would like us talking about this, and you should put it out of your mind. Just know your daddy wasn't doing anything wrong. It's what grown-ups do." She leans in and kisses my cheek. "Go back to sleep, Reeve, and the doctor will be here when you wake."

The doctor examines me in the morning and confirms I have an ear infection. He gives me more medicine and tells me I need to stay in bed and rest for two to three days. Normally, I would be happy to miss school, but I don't like that Viv has to go to school alone. I got in a fight with Guy Fenwick two weeks ago because he said he was going to kiss her. I got really angry and punched him. He punched me back, but then a teacher broke it up. Dad had to come to school, and he was really angry. Not that I got detention for a week, but because I got caught. He told me next time to be more discreet and to never punch first.

Now Viv will be alone in school, and I won't be there to protect her. I try telling the doctor I feel much better today and I am able to go to school, but he just chuckles.

And then things go from bad to worse when Eleanor comes to say goodbye. Her eyes are red, and she cries when she hugs me. I am crying too. I want to call Dad and beg him to let her stay, but she says it wouldn't make any difference. I know that too. He's the biggest asshole, and I hate him.

Vivien drops by after school, and it's the only thing to bring a smile to my face all day. "Hey, bestie." She jumps on my bed and it bounces. "Are you still sick?" Her face is scrunched up with worry.

"I'm okay. The doctor gave me medicine, and it doesn't hurt as much now. I tried to go to school, but he wouldn't let me."

Viv rummages in her book bag as she talks. "I missed you today. School sucked." She pulls out a bunch of candy bars, dumping them on the bed. "I stopped by the store on my way home." Her eyes light up, and when she smiles at me, I feel that urge in my dick again. It's not the first time it's happened when I'm with my best friend. Thankfully, she's never noticed, and my comforter hides me now. My eyes drop to her lips, and butterflies swoop into my chest. I wonder what it would be like to kiss her.

"Look what I found?" Her grin widens as she pulls the latest Harry Potter book from her bag.

"No way!" All thought of kissing her vanishes as I greedily take the book from her hands. "I was planning on going to the bookstore this weekend." It released Monday, and I've been on a countdown.

"Now you'll have something to read while you're getting better."

"You're the best." I pull her into a hug, and the familiar smell of peaches and vanilla has my dick jumping again. What is with that?

"I'm the MVP of besties," she says, giggling as she puffs out her chest.

"You totally are," I agree before blurting, "The asshole fired Eleanor."

"No way!" She turns on her side, tucking her hands under her face. "I thought he was going to keep her until we started middle school?"

"I walked in on him having sex," I admit, and her eyes pop wide. Lauren talked to Vivien about sex around the same time Eleanor talked to me. "He had a naked lady in his bed, and Eleanor was naked too."

Vivien blinks rapidly, and then her nose scrunches up. "Ugh. Gross."

"I don't think sex is very nice. The lady was screaming and crying when Dad was poking her with his dick."

"Stop, Reeve." Viv places her hand on my bare chest, and fiery tingles shoot across my skin. "I think I'm gonna puke."

We both laugh, and I press a kiss to her hair as I lie on my side so we're facing one another. The smile slides off my face. "I think it's my fault Eleanor got fired. I should have knocked."

"It's not your fault," she rushes to reassure me, like always. "Your dad is the biggest asshole. He's the king asshole of assholes. It's his fault, not yours." She holds my hand. "At least you still have Mrs. Thompson, and you have me. You don't really need Eleanor anymore."

"I guess not." I shrug, but it still hurts. Eleanor became my nanny after Mildred, my original nanny, left. She's been with me since I was four and I loved her. She promised she would call me, but I won't hold my breath. Dad has a habit of promising me things and letting me down, and I think she might be the same.

"What happened at school?" I ask, wanting to forget about Eleanor and my dad and what I saw last night.

She bites on her lip. "I might have gotten in a teeny tiny bit of trouble."

I'm instantly on alert. "What happened?" I sit up, resting my back against the headboard, and Vivien does the same.

"Promise you won't get mad." Her eyes hold mine in place.

"I'm not promising anything. If somebody hurt you, I'm kicking their ass."

She fights a smile. "You're not to do anything. I handled it. Okay?"

"Handled what?" I chew on the inside of my mouth.

"Guy tried to kiss me, but I told him to fuck off, and I kneed him in the balls."

"I'm going to kill him," I hiss, grinding my teeth as I get angry.

"Reeve." Viv holds my face in her hands. "He didn't touch me, and I made him pay. He was crying and holding his penis for ages after." Her proud smile eases some of my anger.

"I told him to leave you alone."

"He's an idiot." She rests her head on my shoulder, and warmth fills me. "I got detention though."

"Detention sucks."

"I thought Mom would be angry, but she told me to never let any person touch me without my permission. She said she doesn't condone violence and next time I'm to go and tell a teacher, but she didn't even ground me, so I think she just said that cause she had to."

"I hate Guy Fenwick," I snarl, clenching my fists. "I'm still going to kick his ass."

"Don't. You'll only get detention again."

I smile as a plan comes together. "Then we'll be in detention together."

Vivien grins.

It seems I'm not done teaching Guy a lesson.

Chapter Ten
Now

I knew it would be hard, but I didn't think it would be this hard. It's only two weeks into filming, and I already feel like I'm drowning. "Hey, man." Rudy—my costar who was cast as Jackson Lauder—slaps me on the back as I leave my dressing room, ready to head back to the hotel. "A few of us are going to the sports bar. You should come." We finished early today because of some tech glitch, which paused filming. Not that I'm complaining. I'm exhausted and planning to take advantage of the extra few hours of downtime. I haven't been sleeping well, and it's starting to show.

"Thanks, but I'll pass. I want to call my girlfriend and then crash."

"Ride with me." He lifts one shoulder as he heads toward the line of drivers waiting outside. They shuttle cast and crew to and from the hotel to the studio every day.

We grab the first available town car and hop in the back. As soon as the privacy screen is in place, Rudy turns to face me. "Talk to me. I can tell you're struggling, and I want you to know I'm here for you." Rudy is five years older than me, and he's been acting in big-budget shows and movies since he turned eighteen. "I've been in your shoes," he adds. "And it's not easy."

"I'm a little out of my depth," I admit, dragging a hand through my hair. "I'm finding it hard to switch off at night and not getting much sleep."

"What's troubling you specifically?"

"I'm feeling the pressure to perform, and I'm really missing my girl. She's my rock, and I'm not sure I can do this without her." I feel like a pussy for admitting it, but from what I've gleaned about Rudy so far, I think he's trustworthy. He's already known as the prankster on set, but there's depth to the guy.

"We're so alike in many ways." He leans back in the seat and stretches his legs. "I got my big break at the same age, and I had a childhood sweetheart as well."

That's news to me. "You do?"

"I *did*." He drills me with a look rimmed with pain. "We broke up a few years ago." He stares out the window for a few minutes as if lost in thought. His features are composed when he turns to face me again. "Maybe my story can help you to avoid making the same mistakes."

Rudy grabs a couple waters from the ice bucket in the back, handing one to me. "I met Poppy freshman year when she transferred to my school from out of state. It was love at first sight, man." He smiles as he takes a swig from his bottle. "We had this instant connection, and we were joined at the hip from the moment we met. I got the gig that changed my life just after we graduated high school. She went to college while I moved to South Carolina to begin filming." His knee bounces. "I remember feeling out of my depth too even though the other actors were all newbies like me. We were all scared together."

"I feel like an imposter most days," I say before chucking back water. "You guys are way more experienced than me."

"Dude, you're more talented than all of us combined." He eyeballs me solemnly, and I see no lie in his expression. "You also know the material better than any of us." He taps a finger to his head. "Whatever lack of confidence you're feeling is all in here. It's not showing on set. You're nailing it."

Air whooshes out of my mouth. "Thanks, man. I needed to hear that."

"It's good to be humble, but don't let it go too far. Believe in yourself, Reeve. We all do." His tongue darts out, wetting his lips. "Don't take this the wrong way, but you need to let loose a little. Hang out with us off set. Don't shut yourself away in your hotel room. The rest of us are bonding, and you're missing out."

"I'm not big into partying."

"You don't have to be. You can still show up and then take off. It's all about balance."

"How can I achieve balance when we have such grueling long days and daily early-morning workouts? I'm exhausted when I fall into bed each night, but my brain is wired and won't shut off. It feels like I'm running on empty most days." Frankly, I'm shocked I'm turning in good performances because I feel dead on my feet a lot of the time. "I sound like an ungrateful bastard, but I'm really not. It's my first time away from Vivien, and I'm not coping well. She's usually the one talking me off a ledge, but I don't want to tell her I'm struggling because she'll only worry."

My cell phone pings.

"I sent you a link to a meditation app I use when I'm having trouble sleeping. It's a bit weird at first, but I swear it works if you persevere. It helps calm your mind and lull you into sleep."

"Thanks. I'll try it."

"As for your girl, I think you're right. You need to do this without her holding your hand. I speak from experience. Poppy was my rock too."

"Where did it go wrong?"

Rudy moves around on the seat, the leather squelching with the motion. "I shut her out without explaining it, and we gradually drifted apart. Losing her is my biggest regret. I still miss her."

"I'm sorry. That sucks."

"Yep." He drains the rest of his water and tosses the empty bottle into his bag. "My parents are creative. Mom's a writer, and Dad's an artist. I asked Dad for his advice when I was in your position, and he said I had to be selfish. All artists have to be selfish if they want to succeed. Making sacrifices comes with the territory. He said I couldn't perform my role if I was too distracted by Poppy. That I needed to separate my personal and professional lives to succeed."

It's similar to what Lauren told me.

"The mistake I made was not explaining that to my girl. I was a totally selfish prick, and I got angry with her when she didn't understand. I was the creator of my own demise." He pins me with a serious look. "Don't do what I did. Talk to Vivien. Explain you need to be selfish and what it means in practical terms. Like you might not always be able to call her and hanging out with the cast off set is important and has to be your priority. Tell her it doesn't alter who she is to you, but you have to be selfish to pull this off, and you need her support and understanding. If she loves you, she'll agree."

***

"This is a nice surprise," Viv says, beaming at me through the cell phone screen.

"Filming finished early today," I explain before adding, "Fuck, I miss your beautiful face." I reach out to brush the screen with my fingers, wishing my fingers were touching her soft skin. "I think you get more gorgeous with every passing day." She's wearing yoga pants and a crop top with her hair pulled back in a ponytail and no makeup, and she's still the most stunning woman I've ever seen. Viv's beauty is effortless.

"I wish I was there so I could jump your bones."

I groan, adjusting myself behind my sweats as my dick instantly swells. "Don't fucking tease me. My blue balls don't thank you." I'm jerking off daily, but nothing eases the ache for my girl. I'm used to regular sex, and abstinence is hard. Pun intended.

"Don't *you* fucking tease *me*." She waggles her finger up and down. "At least dry yourself properly after your shower and put a shirt on. I'm ridiculously jealous of those water beads rolling down your chest, and that's plain pathetic."

I burst out laughing, instantly feeling lighter. "I'm jealous of those clothes you're wearing and that bed you're sitting on because they're touching you and I can't."

Now she's giggling. "I'm glad we can be pathetic together."

"I miss you so fucking much, baby."

"I miss you too." She blows me a kiss. "It feels like you've been gone longer than two weeks."

"Same, but we'll get through it. Before we know it, it'll be prom, and I'll be holding you in my arms on the dance floor." I'm purposely downplaying my feelings because Viv will feel responsible if I tell her how badly I'm missing her and how much I'm not sleeping. Thank fuck for makeup artists. Gina, the woman who does my makeup on set every day, gave me this tube of concealer to hide the dark shadows under my eyes, and it's been effective. Viv hasn't noticed anything off.

"I was talking with Rudy earlier, and he gave me some advice." I proceed to tell her about our conversation.

"I get that," she instantly says. "That's what it's like for my parents when they're on set. It's why they try not to book projects at the same time, so one of them is home with me. Though they both try to call me daily when away, it's not always possible. I don't want you to put yourself under additional pressure to call me every day if it's not doable, babe." Sadness lingers behind her smile until she tilts her head to the side, and it disappears. She angles the phone so the large vase of flowers is visible. "You show you care in many ways." Warmth floods my chest at the adoring expression on her face. "Thank you for the flowers. It's so thoughtful and sweet."

I arranged weekly deliveries for every Monday so I could wish her a good week. I just want her to know I may be across the country but she is never far from my thoughts. "I love you. Even if I can't call, you are always on my mind and in my heart."

"We knew this would be challenging, Reeve." Her expression turns more somber. "I never want to make it more difficult. If you can't call, just shoot me a quick text so I know you're okay, but it's fine to be selfish. There is no point half-assing this. Go big or go home, right?"

"Fuck, I didn't think I could love you any more, but every day, my love grows because you love me so fucking good, baby. I would be nothing without you. I'm not worthy, Vivien, but I'm trying to be."

"You're already worthy, Reeve. Don't be so hard on yourself. I love you for eternity. That's never changing."

"This means a lot to me. Thanks, babe."

"Whatever you need, it's yours. I know you'd do the same for me."

A knock sounds on my door. "I've got to go. I said I'd hang out with the cast tonight. I've been turning them down, but I need to bond with them more. I think it'll help."

"Go do your thing." She blows me a kiss. "Love you to the moon and back."

The knocking grows more insistent at my door. "I love you too. Have a good night and sweet dreams. I'll text you later when I'm going to bed."

Viv waves and blows me one final kiss before the screen turns black. I hop up and swing my door open.

"Hey, movie star." Saffron grins as her eyes dart quickly over my bare chest. "Thought you were hanging out with us?" A few of the guys are lounging against the wall in the hallway behind her.

"I am. I just lost track of time. Give me five, and I'll meet you guys in the lobby," I say as Rudy emerges from the room next to mine. He gives me a thumbs-up before I shut my door.

An hour later, I'm nicely relaxed in a booth in a private section of the sports bar close to our hotel, sipping a beer and laughing as the gang tells funny stories of times spent on other film sets in between watching college basketball that's showing on several screens around the room. Most of the main cast are here—Saffron, Rudy, Jacob, who plays Sawyer, Jolina who plays Jane, Conrad who plays Drew, and Ed who plays Tristan. Darren and Rob, who are cast as Charlie and Xavier, are the only ones missing.

"Did you talk to your girlfriend?" Rudy asks as the conversation splits between different groups at the table.

"Yeah. She was cool with it." The tension that has been cording my shoulder muscles into knots already feels lessened after my call with Viv. "It helps her parents are in the industry. She understands."

"Whose parents are in the industry?" Saffron asks, leaning forward and staring at me as she sucks her cocktail through a straw.

"My girlfriend's," I confirm, taking another sip of my beer and shaking my head as the waitress offers me a fresh one. I'm not a big drinker, and I don't intend to start now. I still have to get up at five, and I'm planning on leaving shortly.

"This is the girl in the pic beside your bed?" she inquires.

I nod.

"She's beautiful."

I smile. "She is. Inside and out."

"Aw, that's so sweet."

"It's the truth."

"So, who are her parents, or is it some big secret?"

"It's not a secret. Her parents are Lauren and Jonathon Mills."

"Get the fuck out!" she splutters, almost choking on her drink.

"Vivien is Hollywood royalty," Rudy says, chinking his bottle against mine. "And Reeve is definitely off the market."

A frown briefly appears on Saffron's face. "I don't think I like your insinuation, *Rudester*, and in case it needs to be said, I'm fucking Jeremy."

I had suspected something was going on between the assistant director and my leading lady because they are constantly flirting on set, much to the director's chagrin.

Rudy holds up his hands. "I wasn't implying anything, Saff. It was just a statement of fact."

"I'm a professional." Saffron pouts, fixing Rudy with a pointed stare. "I resent any implication otherwise."

"I wasn't implying you weren't, and everyone is always fucking everyone else on set. I'm a judgment-free zone."

She smooths a hand over her long, dark hair. "Sorry, I'm a little sensitive sometimes. You know, after what went down." Her eyes bounce between me and Rudy. I assume she means the details of that affair she had with a director and his wife.

"It's cool, Saffron. No one is judging you for that. At least, we're not." I can't really speak for the rest of the cast and crew but the vibe is good on set and I haven't seen anyone giving her shit. I don't think the director would stand for it.

"Thanks, Reeve. That means a lot, and please call me Saff. All my friends do."

"I'm out," I say fifty minutes later, finishing my beer and standing.

"Peace, dude." Rudy pulls me into a man hug, and I say goodbye to the others.

"Hold up, movie star," Saff says, hurrying to finish her third cocktail. "I'll come with. I'm tired and want an early night."

I put my jacket on and wait for Saffron to say her goodbyes, and then we leave the bar together. "I'm glad you came out with us tonight," she says, and I slow my stride when I see her practically running to keep up with me.

"Me too. I had fun."

"I love the cast and crew for this movie. Everyone gels and gets along. It makes life so much easier on set."

"Yeah, they're a good bunch."

"I hope we can be friends," she adds as we turn the corner, heading toward our hotel. "And if you ever want to run lines in advance or talk through a scene, I'm open to that."

"That's a good idea, especially for some of the more emotional scenes."

I hold the door to the hotel open for her because the porter is MIA. "Thanks, Reeve." She smiles up at me. "I'm a good listener too, so if you ever need to talk or get anything off your chest, I'm your man." She giggles as we walk past the reception desk, her high heels clicking on the tiled lobby floor as we make our way to the elevator.

"I appreciate it." I step back to let her inside the elevator first. Our rooms are on the same floor, like all of the cast. It makes it easier to take group pics each day for social media. Cassidy, the PR person hired by the studio to promote the movie, has issued us with a list of dos and don'ts. Top of the list is ensuring someone posts a group pic on socials every day.

"I hope I'm not overstepping, but I've noticed the dark circles under your eyes. Are you getting enough sleep?"

I cross my arms over my chest as the elevator ascends. "It's been challenging, but I'm sure it'll settle down."

"It's commonplace on movie sets because of the long hours and the pressure."

The doors open on our floor, and I step aside to let her exit first.

"You're such a gentleman, Reeve." Her smile expands. "I hope Vivien knows how lucky she is."

"We're both lucky."

"And there you go again." She squeezes my arm briefly. "You're one of the good guys, Reeve, and I hope you never change."

We reach her door first. "Goodnight, Saffron."

"Saff," she reminds me as she swipes her keycard. "And hold on for a sec. I have something for you."

I stand in the doorway, keeping the door open with my foot as Saffron, *Saff*, kicks off her shoes and enters the en suite bathroom. She returns a few seconds later holding a pill bottle in her hand. "Here, you can have these. Take one when you're ready to go to bed, and they'll help."

My brow furrows as I examine the label. "I don't like taking pills."

"It's only Xanax. My doctor prescribes them to help with anxiety and insomnia." She curls my hand around the bottle. "I got a large prescription filled before I left home, so I have plenty. I won't miss these." She shrugs. "Take them or don't, but it's good to have some support, right?" Her eyes probe mine. "They won't hurt."

"What if I oversleep?" All the guys on set have to attend a rigorous workout with the studio-hired personal trainer every morning at five a.m. to ensure we're in top shape during filming. The male characters are all ripped, and it's important we look the part.

"Get your assistant to call you, or use the hotel wake-up call service."

I pocket the pills, still not convinced I'll take them, but I don't want to offend her when she's only trying to help. "Thanks, Saff."

She stretches up and kisses my cheek. "Thanks for walking me home, Reeve. I hope you sleep well."

Chapter Eleven
Now

I roll over in bed and grab my cell, groaning when I see the time. I have to get up in two hours, and I still haven't slept a wink. It's beyond a joke at this stage. My eyes home in on the bottle of Xanax Saffron gave me last week. I haven't taken them. I'm not into drugs and I don't want to fall down that slippery slope. But it's tempting in the early hours of the morning when I've been tossing and turning nonstop.

My brain won't switch off. Not helped by the fact we're acting the sex scene from the audition later today. It's one of the steamier scenes, and I'm on edge. Sleep deprivation is the last thing I need. Instead of trying to blank my mind, maybe a distraction will help instead.

Clamping my eyes shut, I run through memories of my birthday weekend in Big Bear, smiling to myself as I remember every precious moment. I miss Viv so much. I know if she was here, curled around me like a koala, whispering reassurances, I would have no problem sleeping.

"Jesus, dude," Rudy says, slapping me on the shoulder as we amble from the hotel gym. "You look dead on your feet."

"I'm not far from it," I admit, lifting the hem of my damp training top to wipe my sweaty brow.

"Still not sleeping?"

I shake my head. I got one hour of sleep before my alarm went off.

"You should talk to the set doctor. He'll prescribe you some sleeping pills."

Yeah, no. The last thing I need is it being official I'm a basket case. I'll have the director and Bianca on my back. I'd much rather handle this alone, under the radar, and not cause any fuss. I only ever want to be known for my acting prowess on set. I have zero desire to be known as a broken mess.

"Here." Saffron thrusts a coffee cup into my hand. "I made it extra strong. It should help."

Great. Can everyone see I'm a hot mess today? Nick barked at me earlier when I fluffed my lines. It's the first time it's happened, and I was mortified. I know this material inside and out, so there's no excuse. But I am literally dragging my body around the set. It doesn't bode well for the closed-set sex scene we're due to film shortly.

"Thanks." I try not to grimace as the hot, bitter black coffee slides down my throat. I take my coffee with cream and sugar, but my costar obviously has me pegged as the classic type because she's fixing me black coffee every day. Saffron is only trying to help, and I don't want to seem ungrateful, so I accept the black poison and force it down my throat every day. On this occasion, maybe it will help. Mortification will be the least of my worries if I actually fall asleep when we get into that bed.

"You're not taking the pills, are you?"

"Don't take it personally. I'm just not into it." I've seen most of the cast snorting coke or popping uppers at some point by now, and I've been around the industry long enough to know it's nothing unusual among actors. But I always said I wouldn't go there and don't want to compromise my principles. I'm not that desperate.

Yet.

"Take this." She slips a small pill into my hand. "It will help reenergize you."

"No thanks." I pass it back to her. "I don't do drugs."

"It's honorable, Reeve, but everyone can see you're not coping. You fluffed your lines, and that's not you." Concern bleeds from her eyes as she stares up at me. "You don't want Nick breathing down your neck. You're the star, Reeve. Everyone is looking to you. If you start floundering, it'll impact more than just you."

"You think I don't know that?" I hiss, rubbing at my sore temples. "I know I need to get my shit together, but drugs are not the answer."

"It's not that big of a deal, Reeve. Everyone does it. The odd pill here and there will help. It'll only become a problem if you let it. Why do you think most actors use? We're not machines. Our bodies aren't built for these long-ass days. It's necessary to get through it."

"I won't compromise myself, Saff. That's not who I am."

She loops her arm in mine and smiles. "Like I said, you're honorable. I just hope it won't be your downfall."

"Cut!" Nick hollers as tension rolls through the closed set. "Reeve. A word, please," he snaps, jerking his head to the side.

Saffron shoots me an apologetic look, but it's not her fault I'm fucking the scene up. I can't get out of my head. I'm trying to channel my character, like Lauren advised, but it's not working. All I'm thinking as I'm touching and kissing Saffron is how much of a betrayal this is to Viv, and my movements are jerky and wooden. Not the actions of a guy head over heels in love and lust with his girl.

I climb off the bed wearing tiny flesh-colored boxer briefs as I walk to the side where the scowling director is waiting to tear strips off me.

"What the fuck is going on with you today?" Nick whisper-hisses when I reach him. "I've seen more life in a corpse."

"I'm sorry." I drag a hand through my hair. "I'm all up in my head."

His features relax a little as he sighs. "Is this about your girl?"

I nod.

"Look, kid. I know it's not easy. Especially if you're in a relationship, but you can't let that hold you back. You are not you in that bed. You are *him*. She's not your girl; she's Cam's."

"I know. I'm trying, but I just keep seeing Viv's face when I look at Saffron, and it feels like I'm cheating."

"So, flip it on its head."

I frown. "How?"

"Imagine she's Viv. If you're already visualizing her face, it shouldn't be an issue. Get into that bed and fuck your girlfriend."

"That feels like an even bigger betrayal."

"It's not a betrayal, Reeve. This is your job." He fixes me with a look that says it all. We are only three weeks into shooting. It doesn't happen often, but there have been occasions where leading actors have been replaced during production. That is not going to be me.

"Okay." I hold my head up and my shoulders back. "I've got this."

He eyeballs me for a few tense moments before clapping me on the back. "Okay, kid." He squeezes my shoulders. "Let's do this."

"Are you okay?" Saffron asks when I climb back over her.

"Yeah. Sorry."

"You don't need to apologize. I know this is hard for you. If I can do anything to make it easier, you know you only have to ask."

"It's not you, Saff. This is all on me."

The director calls for quiet, and I get into position between her legs, hovering over her semi-naked body. Like me, Saff is wearing flesh-colored underwear, and she's bare-chested. I'm trying to remember she's vulnerable too and me messing this up is only making it more difficult for her. I just need to chill and do what the director says.

"Action," Nick calls, and I lean down, picturing Vivien as I smash my lips down on Saffron's and thrust my cock against her pussy. I zone out, remembering the time I fucked Viv the night of my party, when we were both wild with lust and desperate for one another. My hands roam her soft flesh as I pick up my pace, pounding against her as I devour her mouth and pepper kisses over her neck. She writhes underneath me, grabbing handfuls of my hair and scraping her nails down my back, before squeezing my ass and urging me to thrust harder.

I'm vaguely aware of voices in my peripheral, but I'm too lost to focus on anything but my girl. My skin is on fire, and I'm lost in Viv, starved for her touch, greedy and demanding. My cock is hard as steel, and it won't take much to—

"Cut!" Nick yells, and I'm ripped from my memory as the crew claps.

"Hot damn, movie star." Saffron stares at me with flushed

skin and swollen lips. "Who knew you had that in you?" Her eyes drift to my cock, straining against the flimsy material of my briefs, and I can barely swallow over the lump clogging my throat.

"Well done, Reeve." Nick slaps me on the back as I climb off the bed in a daze, grabbing the robe one of the set assistants hands me and quickly putting it on. Not that it hides anything. I'm pretty sure every person in the room saw my monster erection. "You went off script, but improvisation is good." He squeezes my shoulder, grinning. "We can work with what we have." I think he's just pleased I could pull it off, even if I didn't stick to the choreographed scene.

Bile swims up my throat as I force a smile and thank the crew before hightailing it out of there. Saffron calls after me, but I don't stop, flinging myself into the bathroom and barely making it to the toilet in time. Crouching over the bowl, I throw up repeatedly as silent tears roll down my face.

What the fuck was I thinking pretending she was Viv?

I slump on the ground with my back against the toilet as horror washes over me. It feels like the worst betrayal to use one of our precious memories like that, and I have never been more ashamed of myself.

"Reeve." My assistant, Wen, thumps on the door. "Nick says filming has ended for the day and you can head home."

"Okay. Thanks." I haul my tired body to my feet and splash water on my face. Gripping the edges of the sink, I stare at my haunted reflection in the mirror. Even with makeup disguising the evidence of my sleepless nights, I still look like shit. I can scarcely look at myself because I'm thoroughly disgusted.

I was hard.

On set.

With a woman who isn't my girlfriend.

I don't care what anyone tells me. It's wrong, and I want to rewind the clock and do it all differently.

I don't know how I'm going to get through future sex scenes, but I make a vow not to use Viv again, and I promise myself that is the last time I'm sporting an erection during filming.

I am still beating myself up fifteen minutes later when I exit my room. As I pass by Saffron's dressing room, the distinct sound of moaning filters out through a gap in the slightly open door.

"Fuck, yes," Saffron pants in a breathy tone, grabbing the back of Jeremy's head as he fucks her against the wall. Her legs are wrapped around his waist, and his head is buried in her big tits as he thrusts in and out. Her eyes pop wide, locking on mine through the door, and she smirks as the assistant director grunts and pounds her into the wall. Dropping my gaze, I pick up my pace and sprint along the hallway, more than eager to put this nightmare of a day behind me.

Chapter Twelve
Now

"You look like shit," Bianca says after storming into my dressing room the following afternoon.

"Hello to you too," I joke, wondering why she has made an appearance.

"Let's grab a coffee from the van outside. Some fresh air will do you good." She clearly checked the schedule and knows I'm on a break.

I pull a hoodie on over my jeans and grab my jacket before joining my agent as we make our way off the set. She chats casually with me until we're outside. My California bones protest the cold, and I yank my hood up as a blast of wind whips around us.

"I don't know how anyone lives on the East Coast." Bianca pulls the zipper up entirely on her fur-lined coat. "I swear it's fucking freezing every time I visit."

"It's been one extreme or the other. I hope it stabilizes and it's somewhat warmer by the time we finish on set." Shooting finishes here in four and a half weeks, and then we'll be on location, filming outdoors in various places across Massachusetts. I hope the heating in my trailer is top-notch, as I already know I'm going to need it.

"Nick called me." Bianca glances at me as we walk toward the silver van in the near distance. "He's worried about you."

Great. This is all I need.

"What's going on?" She blows on her hands.

"I'm not sleeping," I truthfully admit, "and I feel like I'm dragging myself around."

"Hmm." She narrows her eyes before we step up to the van. We order coffee and remain silent while the guy fixes our drinks. Bianca hands me my flat white before drinking her large latte.

"Why can't you sleep? You should be exhausted falling into bed at night."

"I am, but I can't switch my brain off."

"Why? What is keeping you awake?"

"Worries about fucking things up on set, going over lines in my head for the next day, and I'm missing Vivien."

She exhales heavily. "This is why I advise my younger clients to remain detached. You already have so much pressure on your shoulders, Reeve, without worrying about any girl back home."

I round on her instantly. "Vivien is not just *any girl*, Bianca. She's my everything. The woman I plan to marry."

Her lips purse, and she takes a few seconds before replying. I gulp back my coffee, ready to defend my relationship. When I signed my contract with Bianca, she suggested it would be better if I was single, and I made it perfectly clear how important Vivien is to me. She can't fucking turn around now and try to blame her for this. Missing Viv is only part of my issue, and it's not her fault—it's all on me.

"I know you're serious about her, and I'm not disregarding your relationship, but even you must admit it makes things harder for you. If Vivien is the one, she'll wait for you until the timing is right."

"I'm not breaking up with her, and I'm insulted you would even go there. You know where I stand on this, Bianca, and I'm not changing my mind."

"It would be easier if you didn't have external distractions, Reeve. And think about Vivien. Things are going to be insane when this movie releases. Buzz is already ramping up. She's going to be targeted. I've seen it happen before. Have you thought about what's best for her?"

"*I'm* what's best for her," I snap, draining my coffee and tossing the empty cup in the large trash can just outside the set entrance. "And now you're just pissing me off."

"That's not my intent." She holds my arm, stalling me. "You're my client, my responsibility, Reeve. A lot is riding on this production. They are all counting on you, and you're already struggling."

"Yes, I am," I shout, yanking my arm out of her grip. "But asking me to dump my girlfriend would only exacerbate the situation. Trust me, you don't want to see how badly I'd fall apart without her. She's my rock. Vivien keeps me grounded."

"Okay, okay." She holds up her palms in defeat. "I hear you." She clasps my hands in her bony ones. "But you need to do something, Reeve, before you jeopardize your role and ruin everything. Whatever you have to do to fix this, do it and do it quick."

That night, I pop a Xanax and sleep like a baby.

"You look good, babe," Viv says when we are on a video call a few nights later.

"I feel good. I think things are starting to settle down for me." I hadn't divulged how bad my sleep issues were, so I haven't mentioned anything about the Xanax I take every night. She won't approve. Hell, a big part of me still doesn't. But desperate times call for desperate measures. I was on the verge of fucking up all our dreams, and I'm not falling at the first hurdle.

"Hey, Reeve." Lauren pops her head over Vivien, smiling at me. "How are things?"

"It's all good here. I'm finally in a proper routine, and the cast and crew are awesome."

"I'm delighted to hear that. We miss you."

"I miss you all too. Tell Jon I said hi."

"Will do." She presses a kiss to the top of her daughter's head and waggles her fingers at the screen. "Remember, I'm only a call away if you need anything."

"Thanks, Lauren," I call out as she exits the room and closes the door behind her.

"Four weeks down now, babe," Viv says, sitting cross-legged on her bed. "A third of the way through."

"We've got this."

"We do." She blows me a kiss and then entertains me with stories of the big fight that blew up between Guy Fenwick and Keith York in the hallway at school that day and how the married janitor was caught in a compromising position with the much older single principal by a couple of students. "Oh, and Marnie Gibson tripped and fell in the cafeteria. Serves her right for wearing skyscraper heels and a tight-fitting dress. She had meatball sauce all over her hair and in her eyes. It was the best thing to happen in years."

"Karma is finally calling," I muse. "Wish I'd been there to see it." My phone pings.

"Just sent you the link to the video. It's all over school. Couldn't happen to a nicer person." Her eyes light up in a way they used to as a kid when she was up to mischief. "The bitch actually had the nerve to blame me. She said I deliberately tripped her because it happened just after she passed our table. If I'd thought to do it, I would have and happily claimed responsibility, but I'm not going down for her clumsiness."

"You'd think she'd get over it by now." I lean back on my bed with one hand behind my head. Can't say I'm sorry to have left all that petty high-school crap behind.

Viv lies down on her bed, and her top lifts with the motion, exposing a sliver of smooth, tan skin. My dick jerks behind my sweats. "She can't believe anyone would reject her for me. Bitch will be fat and gray and still trying to pull shit purely because you chose me."

"I will always choose you, Vivien Grace Mills. You are the other half of my heart."

"Aw." She places her hand on her chest, and my eyes linger on her tits. Viv is wearing a soft-pink tank, and it's obvious she's braless. Her nipples are poking through the thin material, and I'm rock hard now.

"Babe." I slide a hand down my bare chest, toying with the band of my sweats. "Are you up for trying something?" I can't believe I haven't thought of phone sex before now. Jacking off just isn't cutting it for me.

Viv's gaze follows my hand as I slip it under my sweats and grip my swollen flesh.

"I'm liking where this is going," she purrs, palming her tit over her top.

"Take your top off. I want to see my tits."

Viv props her phone up against her lamp and angles her body so I have a front-row view as she quickly disposes of her tank.

"Damn, baby. You are a sight for sore eyes," I admit as I

push my sweats and boxers down my legs and kick them off the bed.

Viv yanks the hair tie out of her hair, and waves of glossy dark hair tumble over her shoulders. Leaning in closer, she cups her tits and pushes them together, licking her lips and looking suggestively at me. "I'm imagining you are here and you're sucking my nipples and tugging on them with your teeth." Her eyes zero in on my hand wrapped around my cock as I give it a few quick pumps. "I miss your cock. I miss how it feels moving inside me."

"How wet are you right now?" I inquire, spreading my thighs and repositioning my phone so she has a better view as I stroke my erection.

"So fucking wet, Reeve."

"Show me."

Viv shimmies her shorts and panties down her legs as I watch.

"Let me see your panties," I demand, forcing my hand to move slowly on my dick. I don't want this to be over too soon.

Viv shows me the bottom of her panties, and precum leaks from my cock at the obvious damp spot on the material. But it's not enough. I'm greedy, and I want more. "Spread your legs and show me your cunt. I want to see if it's dripping for me."

Viv moves her phone, resting it against a mountain of cushions as she lies down on the bed stark naked and obeys me. My hand works my dick harder as I stare at her glistening pink flesh. "Ride your fingers, baby. Two to start."

"Oh, fuck, Reeve." Viv pants as she drives two digits in and out of her pussy, arching her hips with the movement. "I wish these were your fingers so bad."

"I know, baby. I know." I quicken my pace, jerking my cock with firm, fast strokes. "Rub your clit and add another finger in your pussy."

The sound of flesh slapping and moans fills the air as we both masturbate while watching the other. "Watching you jack off is so sexy," she pants, fixing me with dilated pupils and a lusty expression.

"Watching you fuck yourself is turning me on so bad, baby."

"I'm close," she rasps before throwing her head back and rotating her hips.

"Eyes on me, babe," I command as a familiar tingle forms at the base of my spine and my balls tighten. "We come together, watching one another."

"Agh, Reeve." Viv's gaze is locked on mine, alternating from my hand to my face, and I'm doing the same as we work ourselves into a frenzy. "Reeve!"

"I'm there, babe. Let go," I say, roaring out a grunt as my dick jerks and my orgasm races through me. Cum spurts from my crown, splaying over my thighs and my stomach. Pleasure lights up my limbs as my climax rolls over me while I watch my love writhing and whimpering with her fingers buried in her cunt and toying with her clit.

When we're both sated, we clean up and get dressed before lying down on our respective beds and staring at one another with stupid, goofy grins on our faces.

"I love you," I say, reaching out to touch the screen, like I often do, wishing it was my fingers caressing her beautiful face.

"I love you too." Leaning in, she kisses the screen before easing back. She pins me with a blinding smile. "That was so hot, and we're definitely doing it again."

I laugh, awash with sheer happiness, feeling like a ten-ton weight has just lifted from my shoulders. "Fact, beautiful. Now I know how awesome phone sex is, try stopping me."

Chapter Thirteen
Then - Age 11

"Race you to the treehouse," Viv says after she finishes the last mouthful of her pasta. She hops up from the kitchen table. "Bet I'll win again!" Her greenish-brown eyes sparkle as she sets the challenge, and I can't help grinning. Viv's shorter legs are no match for my much longer ones, which is why I let her beat me sometimes. Not enough that she has worked it out 'cause she'd kick my ass if she knew I was letting her win.

"No leaving until everyone is finished eating, princess," Jonathon says, eyeballing his daughter across the table. "You know the rules."

"Rules, shmules." Viv pouts as I shovel chicken and pasta into my mouth.

"Vivien Grace." Lauren stares at her daughter with her serious face, the one that warns her to behave.

Vivien peers innocently at her mom, like a pretty little angel. Lauren shakes her head, but she's smiling. She never stays angry with Viv for long.

"Hurry up," Vivien tells me, pointing at my plate, and I load more food into my mouth.

"Take your time, Reeve, or you'll choke," Lauren warns.

"You should listen to Lauren," my dad says from behind, startling me. "Unless you want to miss out on all the fun." I glance over my shoulder with a frown on my face as I chew. Dad is never home this early. He always works really late. Most nights, I don't even see him before I go to bed. It's why I eat dinner with Viv and her family almost every day.

"What are those?" Viv asks, leaning her elbows on the table and squinting at the tickets my dad is holding.

Dad waves them in the air as he approaches with a smug smile. Now, I'm really suspicious. I can count on one hand the times I've seen my father smile. Leaving work early and smiling is not the norm. Something is up. Is he sick or having an out-of-body experience?

"Who would like to go to the premiere of the latest Harry Potter movie?" he asks, staring at me as his smile lingers.

My mouth hangs open as Viv blurts, "What?" in a squeaky voice.

"Well, Reeve?" Dad stands beside my chair. "What do you say?"

I have to force my tongue to unglue from the top of my mouth so I can speak. "You got tickets? You said you couldn't." I begged him for tickets, but he said they were a hot commodity and as his studio wasn't producing the movie he didn't think it would be possible.

"I didn't think I could pull it off, but a contact came through for me today."

"At least that explains the limited notice." Lauren fixes my dad with a sharp look as she gets up to clear the table.

"We have two hours before we need to be there. It's enough time to get ready."

"Can Viv come?" I ask, pushing my almost empty plate away. There is no way I could eat now. He's holding several tickets, so I presume my best friend is coming too, but I want to make sure. If he doesn't have a ticket for her, I'm not going. It's both of us or neither of us.

"Of course. I have tickets for everyone." Dad smiles again, and it's like looking at an alien. I don't know what's come over him, but I'm not sure I trust it.

"Oh my freaking God!" Viv jumps up, screams, and starts dancing. "This is the best day of my life!" she yells. My grin is so wide it feels like my face might split in two. Viv races around the table and yanks me off my chair. We hug, jump around, and dance as the oldies look on with goofy grins on their face.

I am so excited I could pee my pants.

"Oh my God!" Viv shrieks again. "We can wear our Harry Potter T-shirts!" Lauren got one of the designers she knows to make shirts for us, and we haven't had much opportunity to wear them yet.

"Yes!" I holler, jumping up and down with her. "This is perfect!" I love she is as excited as me. Things are always so much better when I get to share them with my bestest friend in the whole entire world.

I notice the oldies covering their ears as they smile. Simon isn't even angry that we're making lots of noise.

"Come on." Viv takes my hand and moves toward the door. "We need to get ready."

"Go up to your rooms, and I'll be there in a few minutes to help," Lauren says.

I pull my hand from Viv's and run to my dad, wrapping my arms around his waist as I beam up at him. "Thanks, Dad. This is the best day ever."

He pats me awkwardly on the head. "I'm glad you're

happy. Go get ready, and I'll come over with the car when we need to leave."

Viv and I run out of the room and up the stairs, talking nonstop about the scenes we hope to see in the movie. She stops in front of her bedroom door, turns, and spins around. "I'm going to get my clothes, and I'll come to your room then so we can get ready together."

My eyes pop wide as an idea comes to me. "I'll put the last movie on while we're getting dressed!"

"Yes, yes!" She claps her hands. "This is going to be awesome."

"I'm so excited!"

"Me too," she says before she leans in and kisses me on the lips! It's quick. Only a second, but my lips are all tingly, and my dick is jumping around a little.

We stare at one another for a few moments, and two red spots appear on Viv's cheeks. Tossing her long dark hair over her shoulder, she says, "Go on, silly. I'll be there in a minute."

I guess we're pretending it didn't happen. "Okay." I walk off in a bit of a daze with my lips curling up at the corners.

Vivien kissed me! Maybe she's been daydreaming about kissing me like I've been daydreaming about kissing her! But Jonathon told me once Vivien couldn't kiss anyone until she was much older, so I have been trying to forget about it and be good.

Lauren comes in to help us get ready, and we sit on my couch to watch the movie while she goes to get dressed.

"You look really pretty," I tell Viv as we sit side by side, holding hands, while watching the TV. She's wearing some kind of tutu skirt with her T-shirt and sparkly sandals. Her mom pinned her hair up, and there's a big braid running around her head. Lauren even let her wear some lip gloss and perfume. I haven't been able to stop looking at her. Her eyes look really big, and her lips are really shiny.

"Thank you." She turns to smile at me, and I notice the blush on her cheeks again. She squeezes my hand, and tingles shoot up my arm. I love holding Vivien's hand. I always feel all warm and fuzzy inside when her skin is touching mine. "You look hot. I like your hair like that."

Lauren put some gel in my hair and smoothed it back off my brow. She said I looked classically handsome, whatever that means. I'm wearing jeans and sneakers with my T-shirt even though I'm a little worried Dad won't approve. On the rare occasions when we go out for dinner, he always makes me wear proper shoes and pants with these stupid stiff shirts. I'm glad it doesn't happen often because I hate going out looking like a pussy.

I shrug, like it's no biggie, but I'm secretly pleased at Viv's compliment.

Simon shows up a little while later with a limo! I've only been in a limousine one other time, so this is a big treat. "You look pretty," I tell Lauren as she takes my hand and leads me outside. She's wearing a long blue dress with sparkles on it, and she has lots of makeup on her face.

"Thank you, Reeve." She bends down to kiss my cheek. "You're such a good boy." She kisses my other cheek. "I hope you have the best time," she adds.

"Quick, Reeve," Viv calls out from inside the limo, patting her hand on the seat beside her. Her daddy helped her inside, and he's sitting across from her beside my dad. Both of them are wearing tuxes, and they're drinking champagne. I slide in beside Viv and instantly take her hand. We grin at one another like goofballs. I can't remember when I was this excited before. We have been to a few movie premieres with her parents over the years, but this is the best one yet.

Lauren sits beside me, and the driver shuts her door, and then we are on our way.

Dad looks at Vivien and me, smiling as he notices our matching T-shirts and our joined hands. "Are you excited?" he asks.

"Are we ever!" Vivien replies before I've had the chance to.

Dad chuckles, and I stare at him.

"You are lucky to have such a good friend," he tells me.

"I'm the lucky one," Vivien says, leaning her head on my shoulder. "Reeve is my world."

Dad's eyes pop wide as Jonathon chuckles. "The kids over-heard me and Lauren talking," he says, and my dad nods.

"Did you know your mom and I grew up together?" Dad says and I shake my head. He rarely talks about my mother to me. Sometimes, I find him crying when he looks at old photo albums, but any time I ask him to tell me about her, he shouts at me and storms out of the room. What little I know is from Lauren. She met my mom, Felicia, in high school, and they became instant best friends. My mom was my dad's girlfriend then, and later when they all went to college, Lauren met Jonathon through my dad.

Lauren has a weird look on her face as she stares at my dad. Simon looks out the window as he talks. "We were neighbors, just like you and Vivien. You remind me of us."

"What was she like?" I whisper, not wanting to waste this opportunity to find out more.

When he turns to look at me, his eyes are all watery. "She was the most beautiful girl I'd ever seen, and she had the biggest heart. She loved animals and nature and painting and singing, and she was the kindest person I ever knew."

A sob rips from Lauren's lips as she rummages in her purse, pulling out a tissue. "Your mother was the best friend I ever had." She clutches my hand as she dabs at her eyes with the tissue. "She had the purest heart. I see so much of her in you. She would be very proud of you, Reeve. So, so proud."

A muscle twitches in Dad's jaw as he stares at me. But it's like he's not seeing me. Like he's not even here.

No one speaks, and it's strange. Until Viv breaks it. "I love you," she tells me, peering directly into my eyes. "You're the best friend I've ever had, and it's forever and ever."

"I love you too." It's not unusual for us to say it to one another. Lauren and Jonathon always tell me they love me whenever we say goodbye, and Viv and I do it too. But this time, it feels different. I can't tear my eyes away from my best friend, and it's like she's the same.

"You two are so cute," Lauren says, ending the spell. She leans over and hugs us both. "We love you so much."

Simon squirms on his seat, remaining silent for the rest of the ride.

It's mayhem when we get to the theater. I hold Viv's hand tight in mine as we're surrounded by our parents and a couple of bodyguards. There are crowds of people lining up behind barriers outside the theater, waving banners, crying, and screaming, as different actors and actresses walk the red carpet. Lots of people shout for Lauren. We pose for group photos, and my eyes are blinking way too fast from all the flashes. Vivien clings to me, trembling a little, and I wrap my arm around her, keeping her close as we make our way inside.

Jonathon goes to get us popcorn and drinks while Dad talks to a group of men, and Lauren, Viv, and I get photos with some of the cast. They sign our T-shirts, and we have the biggest grins on our faces. Our seats are near the front and Viv and I take turns pinching one another because this is too awesome to be real.

It's officially one of the best nights of my life. One of the happiest times I spent with my dad because those were rare.

Chapter Fourteen
Now

"Oh my God! Some of these people are crazy," Saff says, giggling as I try to concentrate and zone her out. "Listen to this one."

"Saff-*ron*," Rudy says, drawing out her name on purpose, and my eyes fly open. My best friend on set is glaring at my leading lady. "We are trying to meditate. If you're not going to participate, at least keep your mouth shut. We're supposed to be helping Reeve."

The three of us are in my hotel room, sitting cross-legged on the floor as Zen music plays softly in the background. I tried the meditation app Rudy suggested, but it didn't work for me, so this is his Plan B. Alex would piss himself laughing if he could see me now.

Guilt churns in my gut as I think of my best friend back home. I only managed to call him one time, but I try to message him at least every couple of days. I have limited downtime, and it's usually late when we get back to the hotel from filming. I reserve those valuable minutes for my girlfriend, and I'm not purposely neglecting my closest male friend. I silently vow to find time in the next few days to call him.

Rudy changes the background music as he shoots Saffron the evil eye. He's hella serious about meditation and keen for me to discover the benefits. He says it's best to meditate without music, but opinions are contradictory. As I generally struggle to quiet my mind, he thought we should try a session with music first. We've been concentrating on breathing and emptying our minds and I was feeling relaxed until Saffron got bored and started reading comments on social media out loud.

"I *am* helping him," she protests. "Right, movie star?" She tucks her hair behind her ears, and I shoot her a warning look. I don't want anyone to know I accepted those pills from her. I don't care if others are taking stuff on set, I don't want it getting out that I do.

"You are helpful, but maybe it's best we do this alone."

"I'll be quiet." She makes a zipping motion with her lips as she climbs to her feet and flops down on my bed. "You won't even know I'm here."

"One more outburst and you're out." Rudy levels her with a firm look.

"I prefer your jokester other side." She scoots back on my bed, sitting up against the headboard as she scrolls through the feed on her phone. "That Rudester is a lot of fun. This one is boring with a capital B."

Rudy is a pretty complex character. He is constantly pulling pranks on set. The jerk replaced my shampoo with toothpaste, and it was a fucking nightmare to get out. I got him back though. I put itching powder in his boxers, and he chased me all over the set shouting threats while vigorously scratching his balls. It was funny as fuck, but I'm watching my back now as I know he'll retaliate.

When we go out, he's the life and soul of the party, but he's got a mellow, deep side too. He plays guitar, meditates, consumes self-help, historical, and philosophical books like they're water, and he follows a strict nutritional diet most of the time. He's my closest friend on set, and I have a feeling we'll become firm friends from this experience.

"One-dimensional personalities are not my thing." He shoves his middle finger up at her. "And I'm a man of my word, so zip it, Saff, or you're out."

It takes me a few minutes to get back into the zone, but then I relax. Saffron keeps quiet, and Rudy deems the session a success when he calls time on it.

"I bet you'll sleep better tonight."

"Thanks, man. I appreciate it."

"And if not, we can always try yoga next."

Saffron mutters under her breath and rolls her eyes. "Reeve is already sleeping better. He doesn't need all this new age hippy shit."

"Your ignorance is showing, darling," Rudy calls out as he pulls two waters from the mini refrigerator in my room. "Mindfulness is not just for hippies. It's for those who are self-enlightened and intelligent, so I can see why it's not your thing."

I bark out a laugh as she flips him off. "I take it back. You're not funny. Like at all."

"You two crack me up." They are constantly bantering on set, and it's entertaining as fuck. I pop the cap on my water and guzzle it.

"Glad we amuse you, movie star." Saffron pats the space beside her. "Get your ass up here and look at some of these comments. I'm cracking up reading them."

Rudy and I join her as she scrolls through the feed.

"What's a Saffhard?" Rudy asks.

"Loyal fans of mine." Saffron puffs out her chest, shooting

us with an extremely smug look. "Some instagrammers came up with the moniker last year, and it's stuck."

"They sure seem keen on shipping you with Reeve," Rudy murmurs, jabbing at the screen. "I'm guessing they didn't get the memo he's off the market."

"Don't be a dumbass. You know he can't declare that."

"Why the hell not?" I arch a brow in her direction.

"It's all about perception, honey. You have to look like you're single. I do too. The more fans ship us together, the better. Look at what Rob Pattinson and Kirsten Stewart's relationship did for the *Twilight* franchise and their careers? And there are countless other examples. Fans love this shit, and we need to feed the beast."

"I'm not comfortable doing that," I truthfully admit before finishing my water and throwing the empty bottle across the room and into the trash can.

"It's all part of the game. Hasn't your agent spoken to you about this? I wouldn't be sitting here if I hadn't made a deal with Bryan and his wife to leak details of our three-way relationship to the press. It was a win-win for all involved."

"That is entirely different," I say, rubbing a hand across my chest. What is with everyone trying to make me hide or dispose of Vivien? I don't fucking like it, and it's never gonna happen.

"It's two sides of the same coin," she continues. "All I'm saying is it would be best for the movie and your career if you kept your girlfriend under the radar and we played up the notion of us having an off-screen relationship. It's not like I'm suggesting we actually go there. No offense, Reeve, but you're like a little brother to me."

"None taken." I'm truthfully relieved. For a second there, I thought she was suggesting we purposely start something to leak it to the press and build buzz. "I don't have romantic feelings for you either."

"Honestly, it would be in Vivien's best interests too," Rudy says as he scrambles off the bed. "Some of these people online can be really nasty. If people don't know she's your girlfriend, they can't throw shade at her."

"Like I said, win-win." Saffron shrugs before pocketing her cell. She slips off the bed and slides her feet into her shoes.

"I'm out." Rudy heads toward the door.

"Thanks for the session, and I'll see you in the morning."

"I'll leave you to your beauty sleep," Saff says, leaning in to kiss my cheek.

"I need to finish ordering Viv's birthday gifts, but then I'm definitely crashing."

"Oh." Saffron's eyes sparkle. "Do you want some help with the gifts?"

I shake my head at first. "No, I'm ... actually, I wanted to order her some makeup, but I'm totally clueless. Could you help me pick something out?"

Her eyes light up, and she rubs her hands. "Now you're talking my language, movie star. Of course, I'll help!"

I lead her over to the desk and open my laptop. The lingerie store I was perusing earlier pops up on the screen, and I scramble to shut it down. "Ugh, hang on a sec."

"No! Wait!" Saffron puts her hand over mine on the keypad, halting my motion. "Is this another part of her gift?"

"Yeah. I was in the process of buying it when you guys showed up. It's fine. I'll just order it after."

"You're not seriously getting her that, are you?" Her brows climb to her hairline as she points at the pretty pink lace bra and panties set in my cart.

"What's wrong with it?" I ask over a frown.

"There's nothing wrong with it, per se, but do you seriously think any woman wants boring blush-pink underwear from her man?"

"Viv is a real girly-girl, and pink is her favorite color. I know the kind of lingerie she wears, so I was picking similar things I think she'll like."

She chuckles when she sees the confusion on my face. "Oh, man. You are so stinking cute." Her eyes pop wide. "You guys are childhood sweethearts so that means you've only been with her. Amirite?" She plants her hands on her hips, fighting a smile.

She's starting to grate on my nerves. "Fuck off, Saff. That's none of your business, and you know nothing about my relationship."

The smile slips off her face. "I apologize, Reeve. I didn't mean to embarrass you. I think it's so fucking adorable. Any girl would be lucky to have a guy like you as her boyfriend, and Viv sounds like a total sweetheart from everything you've told me. I didn't mean to insult you."

I drag a hand through my wayward hair. "It's fine. I overreacted." I move my finger over the pad. "What site is the best for makeup?"

"Can I just say one final thing? Please?" Her eyes plead with me. "I'm only trying to help."

I rub the back of my neck. "Okay, what?"

"Have you ever bought lingerie for Vivien before?"

I don't like divulging details of my relationship to anyone, but I can't lie either because I'm sure it's written all over my face. I shake my head.

Her genuine smile disarms me, and I relax. "I thought as much. Look, let me show you what girls are into now so you have some other ideas, and then you can decide what you want to order later. Lingerie is as much for the guy as the girl. I order off this store all the time, and they have some tasteful sexy pieces. Wouldn't Vivien want to look sexy for you when you return home after filming ends?"

"I'm actually seeing her in a few weeks for prom, but yeah, she would want that."

"Oh, I didn't know that. Cool."

"Nick worked the filming schedule around it so I have a full twenty-four hours off. I've got a private jet booked, and I reserved the best suite at Chateau Marmont for the night as a surprise. I'm already on a countdown." I cannot wait to see my girl. I'm going to shower her with love and affection and give her the best prom night any girl has ever had.

A dreamy smile ghosts over her mouth. "Like I said, so freaking cute."

Maybe Saff is right, and I should get some sexy stuff that Viv can wear under her dress. Blood rushes south at the thought of my girl wearing some of the stuff I've seen in the store. A mix of stuff I think she'll like with a few racier pieces can't be wrong, right?

I watch and listen as Saff scrolls through the store, pointing out items she thinks Viv would like, and I add a few to my cart before we move to the makeup store, and she helps me to pick a palette.

"I hope she likes her gifts," she says when I finish my purchases. I'm sending them all to Lauren's assistant, Moira, and she's going to package them up together and ensure they are hand-delivered to Vivien on the day of her birthday, which is fast approaching.

"Me too. Thanks for your help."

"Anything for you, movie star." She nudges my side. "I'm always happy to help, and I can't wait to hear her reaction."

Chapter Fifteen
Now

Sitting on my bed, fresh from my post-workout shower, I clear my throat and press record on my phone. "Hey, guys. Today is a very special day, because on this day eighteen years ago, the most important person in my life was born."

I fight a smirk as I hold up the cutest baby picture of Vivien. Lauren sent me a few after I told her I wanted to record a birthday video. My girl is probably gonna string me up by the balls for sharing this publicly, but I want the world to know I love her and how much she means to me. I can't think of a more perfect way to do that.

Plus, I'm missing her big-time today. This is the first time I have missed her birthday, and I'm all up in my feels. If I can't be with her, I still want her to know how much I adore her. I want her to feel surrounded by my love even if I'm thousands of miles away. I already got confirmation the lavender roses I sent her were delivered, and Moira confirmed she dropped my gift off at the house last night and her parents will give it to her today.

"I wouldn't be the man I am today if it wasn't for this gorgeous, smart, funny, compassionate, loving woman," I add, holding up a different photo. This pic is one we took while in Big Bear in January. We are wrapped up in one other, both sporting matching wide smiles for the camera. "Have you ever loved someone so much it physically pains you to be apart from them?" A tight pain spreads across my chest, confirming my words. I rub at the pain, but it does nothing to alleviate the perpetual ache for my girl. "As much as I am loving bringing Camden Marshall to life, I am missing my baby so much."

Emotion swirls inside me as I lean in closer to the screen, speaking these next words directly to my love. "I love you, Viv. You are the best thing to ever happen to me, and I don't even care that the guys are going to give me shit for this." I blow her a kiss. "You are my world, and I wish I could be there to hug you and kiss you. Only twenty-seven days until I see you again. I can't wait. Till then, have the happiest of birthdays, my love." I blow her one final kiss before ending the recording and pressing publish. I like the thought she will wake up and see my message first thing.

Predictably, when I show up on set, the guys give me a ton of shit for my "sappy" birthday message.

"Look what I dug up online." Rudy smirks as he holds out his cell phone while we are assembled around one long table in the cafeteria eating breakfast.

"Where the hell did you get that?" I swipe the phone from his hands so I can look at the picture up close. It was taken the night we attended our first Harry Potter premiere together, and I remember it as if it was yesterday.

"It's amazing what you can find when you google shit. There are tons of pics of you and Viv from when you were kids. I see what you mean now. There's no way you can hide your relationship from fans, and I don't think you should. You two are the ultimate Hollywood love story. I think fans will eat that shit up." A fake swoony expression coasts over his face as he places one hand over his heart. "Even my cynical ass believes in the dream."

Pity my agent and the studio publicist don't share that sentiment. I have tried making the same argument, but they are not listening to me.

"Aw, so cute." Saffron leans against my side as she peers at the phone. "Look how she's clinging to you! Viv was riding your coattails even back then!" She giggles.

"What the fuck, Saff?" I don't like her insinuation.

"Chill, movie star. I'm just teasing." She rolls her eyes and grips my arm. "It's obvious you two were already so close."

Air expels from my mouth as I relax. "We've always been close. No one knows me better than Vivien."

"Lemme see." Jolina snatches the phone from my hand. "This is so freaking adorable. You're wearing matching Harry Potter shirts! And look at you two holding hands. Aw, Reeve." Her eyes are suspiciously glassy. "This is the sweetest thing I've ever seen. You should have shared that online."

"He can't," Saff says. "Not unless he can obtain the original photo and request permission from the copyright holders to share it. Remember what Cassidy said. We need to be careful we don't breach copyright law with anything we post online."

"I can send you the link if you want to try and get a copy of the pic," Rudy suggests.

I would love to have a copy of that picture for us. "Send it. Thanks."

The day is busy, and I'm in back-to-back scenes, so I don't have any free time to call Viv. Despite my nostalgia for not being with my girl on her birthday, I'm in good spirits. I caved today and popped an addy Saff gave me. While the Xanax has been helping me to sleep, I'm a little sluggish on set every day, and I don't want to mess up again. I've seen some of the others popping pills each morning, and I figure there isn't too much harm as long as I don't become reliant on them. I'm continuing to try meditation, and our trainer said he'd do a weekly yoga session with us too, so as long as I'm only taking the pills when it's absolutely necessary, I won't get addicted. I'm in control and feeling better than I have in weeks. I'm bouncing around the set, full of energy, and smashing every one of my scenes. The vibe on set is more chill now I've got my act together, and Nick tells me every day I'm nailing it. Everything is how it should be.

I even performed a sex scene yesterday, and there was no repeat of the horrendous first scene. This time, I channeled Camden with ease. No hard-on, thank fuck. I approached it clinically, like any other aspect of this job, and crushed it in two takes.

I'm still besieged with guilt every time I think about that first sex scene. I never want to sport an erection on set ever again. And I never want to tarnish or use my girl or my memories to do my job. I have got to keep them separate, and I now have the coping tools I need to ensure that happens going forward.

"Goddamn it!" I drag my hands through my hair as I search every inch of my dressing room, and my phone charger is still nowhere to be found. Filming has finished for the day, and I'm in my dressing room attempting to phone Viv, but my cell is completely dead, my charger has disappeared, and my inept assistant is MIA. I'm sure Viv has tried calling me, and I desperately want to call her back. Her birthday party will be kicking off shortly, and I really want to speak to her before then.

I grab the quickest shower in history and get dressed in record time, planning to return to the hotel before heading to the club with the gang. I can talk to Viv from the privacy of my room before meeting up with the others. I'm just grabbing my wallet and keys when there's a knock on my door. I open it to find a scowling Cassidy. She manages PR for the movie.

"We need to talk." She barges past me without invitation, and I count to ten in my head. Cassidy is not my favorite person, and I doubt I'm hers either. She always seems to be busting my balls about something.

"About what?" I ask, closing my door and leaning back against it. I fold my arms across my chest and eyeball her.

Cassidy perches against the side of the dressing table and glares at me. "What did I tell you about keeping your relationship on the down-low?"

"Not this again." A frustrated sigh cleaves from my lips.

"You are not taking this seriously, Reeve!" Her eyes bore a hole in my head. "You are the main star of this production, and fans are already going gaga over you. In the online polls, you score way higher than all the other male actors. Women are fantasizing about you, and having a girlfriend will shatter that illusion. If you won't dump Vivien, you need to at least keep the relationship secret and pretend you are single. I shouldn't have to keep repeating myself."

"Fuck off, Cassidy." I push off the door and snarl at her. "I'm not dumping Vivien or hiding her. Fans will just have to deal with it. They'll come around in time. Especially if you take the story and run with it." I wish I had that pic now to show her. "We can spin this in our favor."

"Reeve." She loses the angry face as she stands. "I empathize. I do. I know you love her, but you are naïve if you truly believe that. You are too green to know your head from your elbow, and that is why you have Bianca and why the studio hired me. We have experience you don't. We have been in this position with other actors countless times. It never ends well for the girlfriends. You need to trust we know what we are doing and we have your best interests at heart."

"But do you?" I snipe, because it doesn't always feel like that.

"I won't even dignify that with a reply. Everyone is invested in this movie performing well. If it does, we all get more work. That's what drives us. There is no personal vendetta against you or Vivien, Reeve. Call Bianca if you don't believe me. She is not happy about this birthday video either."

"Well, it's out there now, and I'm not taking it back."

"It's no longer in your hands. I deleted it," she coolly replies, flicking her long black hair over her shoulders.

"You did what?" I roar, beyond incensed. "You have no fucking right to do that!"

"Actually, I do. Check your contract. The studio PR team has access to all the main actors' social media profiles, and you already gave permission for us to manage it how we see fit. I don't like interfering, and mostly, we just supervise and review the content you all post, but on this occasion, action was warranted."

I read over the contract thoroughly before I signed it, and Carson Park, my dad's attorney, reviewed it too. They have the legal authority to do this, but I honestly didn't think they would ever step in and do something like this. More fool me, because there is nothing I can do to refute it. Viv will be as upset as I am. The last thing I want to do on her birthday is make her cry or disappoint her.

"I should at least have been consulted before you did that."

"We're not obligated to give you prior notice, but I might

have shown you that courtesy if you hadn't been filming all day." She walks toward me. "Frankly, you should be thanking me." She pokes her finger in my chest. "You've been on set, and you didn't see how it was unfolding. Some of the comments were extremely nasty, and some very harsh things were said about Vivien. I did you both a favor removing it, and I sent you a copy of it so you can forward it to her privately." Cold, ice-blue eyes penetrate mine. "Which is what you should have done in the first place. There was no need to make it public."

"It's an important birthday and the first time I'm not there. I wanted her to know how much she means to me. I wanted everyone to know."

She shakes her head and purses her lips. "No one can know, Reeve. I feel like a broken record saying this all the time. Do you want to fuck everything up? Do you want the movie to flop and for it to impact negatively on all of our careers?"

"Of course not," I snap, shoving my hands in the pockets of my jeans. It's either that or I might just hit the bitch.

"Then you need to grow the fuck up and start acting like a professional. Your actions affect all of us."

I grind my teeth to the molars as I simmer with unbridled rage.

"Respect the rules, Reeve, and there won't be any reason for me to take corrective action. It's really that simple." Her shoulder brushes mine as she walks past me. "I trust we don't have to talk about this again."

I glance over my shoulder, seething and shaking.

She turns around with her hand curled around the door handle. "As far as the public is concerned, Vivien does not exist. You are young, free, and single, and theirs for the taking." She drills me with a stern look. "Ensure it stays that way."

Chapter Sixteen
Now

"Where is Wen?" I ask through gritted teeth, scanning the club for any sign of my wayward assistant. Saff tracked him down when we left the set, and he said he'd go to my hotel room and grab my spare charger. That was over an hour ago, and the fucker is still not here. I knew I should have gone back to the hotel myself, but I was in meltdown mode after my dressing-down from Cassidy, and Rudy and Jacob convinced me to come straight to the club to chill out. I wish I could say it has helped, but the two beers I've drunk haven't even made a dent in the anger coursing through my veins.

"He couldn't find your charger, so he's gone to buy you one." Saff's gaze skims over the screen of her cell phone as she reads the message he sent her. "He'll be here shortly." She snatches a cold beer from the bucket on the table and hands it to me.

Wen is a fucking moron. Fuck it. I'm going to complain about him because he's more of a hindrance than a help. I've been holding back because he's related to Nick. His second

121

cousin or some shit. It's clearly the only way he got the position because the idiot is more interested in screwing pussy on set than doing his job.

"You're still way too tense." Saffron's hands land on my shoulders, and she begins kneading my tight muscles. "You need to relax."

I shove her hands away, not wanting her to touch me. "I'll relax when I speak to Vivien."

"Call her from my phone." Rudy pulls his cell from his pocket and hands it to me.

"She won't answer a strange number." Jon and Lauren drilled plenty of things into our heads from a young age, and not answering calls from unknown numbers was one of them. It's far too easy for paparazzi and reporters to get celebrity phone numbers, and they often try to go through family members. Lauren also had a scary stalker a few years ago, and he managed to get Viv's number. He was calling and texting nonstop until the cops got involved.

If that idiot doesn't show up soon, I'll just go back to my hotel and call her from there.

Forty minutes later and I've reached my breaking point. "I'm out," I say, finishing the last of my beer and standing.

"Aw, Reeve." Saffron tugs on the leg of my jeans. "Don't go. I'll call Wen and rip him a new one if he doesn't get here stat."

"I'm not waiting any longer. I need to speak to my girl." It's just after midnight here, and with the three-hour time difference, it means Viv's eighteenth birthday will officially be over in a few hours. I won't let the day pass without speaking to her. I shouldn't have bowed to peer pressure and come out to the club. It hasn't done anything to alter my shitty mood. I should have gone straight to the hotel, charged my phone, and called my girlfriend.

I say a hasty goodbye to the others, ignoring Saffron's pout, and just as I turn around, Wen appears in my line of sight, fighting the crowd to get to me.

"Hey, man. Sorry I'm late, but I had to go to three places before I found one open." He thrusts a package into my hand. I don't bother tearing into him, rushing over to the socket at the wall behind our table and plugging my cell in to charge. I order a bottle of water and settle back for a few minutes to wait.

"I've been thinking," Rudy says, sidling up beside me. "You should speak to Bianca and propose an alternate plan. Like we discussed earlier. Sell her on the notion of you and Viv as Hollywood's new golden couple, and let her convince the studio and Cassidy of the merits of going public. Then it'll be a win-win."

I thank the server as she hands me a bottle of water. "Bianca wants me to be unattached. I doubt I can convince her of anything."

"It's worth a try though, right?"

I shrug, tipping my head back as I sip from my water, on a countdown until my cell is charged enough to go outside, where it's quiet, and make my call. I glance at it once it's powered on, noticing several missed calls and two messages from my girl, and one from the publicist with the video attachment. I forward the video privately to Viv, still seething over Cassidy's actions and words. Fuck that bitch. I genuinely loathe her.

Blood rushes south when I open the pic Viv sent me of her in the sexy black lingerie. Shielding the screen with my hand, I examine every inch of her gorgeous body as she strikes a sultry pose against the wall, leaning slightly forward so I get an eyeful of tempting cleavage. Lustful eyes and pouty full lips ensnare me as I ogle the photo like I'm a horny kid who's just discovered his dick for the first time. I'm already sporting a semi and wishing we had time for phone sex because *hot damn*. My woman is a sexy siren, and I'm dying to touch every curve.

The second pic is of Viv in her party dress, looking hot as hell. She made it herself, and she's so incredibly talented. It's a short, tight black dress with gold and green edgings. Her long legs are magnificent encased in high-heeled sandals, and she's wearing her hair down in soft waves, just how I like it. A pang of longing spears me through the heart. I should be there, holding her in my arms as we sway on the dance floor and share a lingering, passionate kiss. Worshiping her body all night long and ensuring she knows she is adored, desired, and so fucking loved.

I hate I am not there with her.

I fucking hate it.

Ten minutes later, I'm done waiting, and I head outside to call my love.

"Hang on a sec," Viv yells into the phone. I can scarcely hear her over the thumping music and the sound of chatter in the background. "It's loud as fuck, and I can't even hear myself think."

I chuckle, trying to remain upbeat so I don't rain on her parade. No sense in both of us being Debbie Downers.

"That's better," she says as the background noise dies down. "Hey, baby. I miss you."

Her soft, seductive tone wraps around me like a comfort blanket. "I miss you too, and I wish I was there."

"Thank you so much for my flowers and gifts, and that video message was beautiful. I tear up every time I look at it."

I'm glad she liked my gifts, but I'm dreading telling her the truth about the video. It's going to upset her. "I sent it to you privately since I was forced to take it down from social media." I inwardly cringe as I dance around the truth, but I'm trying to soften the blow. Viv will freak out if she discovers the PR people have control over my socials and the power to remove stuff without my permission. I'm feeling foolish for not challenging that clause. "I hope you don't mind."

"What do you mean you were *forced* to take it down? By who? Did Bianca make you do it?" Viv is immediately on the defensive, and I don't blame her. That one time she met Bianca she didn't warm to her at all.

I draw a long breath before explaining. "It wasn't Bianca. It was Cassidy. She's been hired to handle PR for the movie, and she threw a massive hissy fit."

"Why?"

The truth will hurt, but I can't keep it from her. Viv understands the way Hollywood works, so it shouldn't come as a complete surprise. "I guess it doesn't look good I have a girlfriend."

Her quiet "Oh" almost kills me.

"It's probably for the best. Some of the comments were nasty. The last thing I want is you becoming a target for crazy bitches." I am as unhappy as she is that the video was removed, but this is no lie. I don't want anyone targeting Vivien and making her life hell. Even if I got Bianca and Cassidy on board with the Hollywood golden couple suggestion, it would not mean every fan would fall in love with us. Vivien will still have haters. It's always the women who endure the hatred in these situations, which is so fucking unfair.

A subtle breeze blows at my back as loud music trickles outside the club.

"What was that?" Viv asks.

"Someone just opened the door."

"Opened the door where? Aren't you at your hotel?"

"We're at a club. We worked late tonight, and a few of us decided to go out for drinks," I explain.

"Dude," Conrad says, materializing at my side. "We're going to head back to the hotel bar."

"Okay." I'll probably join them for a nightcap.

"Wait. Is that your girlfriend?" Rudy asks, and I nod. He reaches for the phone and I pull it back, covering it with my hand and arching my brows.

"Let me say hello."

"Why?" I ask as the rest of our crew piles out through the door.

"Jesus, suspicious much?" Rudy chuckles. "I just want to wish her a happy birthday. I have no nefarious agenda."

I suppose it can't hurt, so I hand my cell over.

"Happy birthday, Vivien," he says, waggling his brows at me. I shove my middle finger up as he chuckles at whatever Viv says.

"I'm Rudy. Hasn't Reeve told you anything about me? I'm offended, man." Cocking his head to one side, he shoots me a mischievous grin. "And here I thought we had the bromance of the century."

I roll my eyes as he listens to whatever Viv is saying.

"Did he tell you about the lube in his sneakers?" Rudy asks, fighting a laugh.

"I still owe you for that," I remind him. It was his retaliation for the itching powder prank. I reach for my phone because he's hogged my girl for long enough. "Give me that."

"My turn," Saff says, snagging the phone from Rudy before I can grab it. I scrub a hand across the back of my neck, uneasy and on edge. Saffron is only a friend, but Viv is still a little iffy about her. Which is understandable on the one hand but a bit irrational on the other. Saffron is like a big sister to me, and she's no threat to Vivien. There is no woman on the planet who could ever replace my love in my affections. And it's not as if Viv has even met her. You shouldn't judge someone you haven't met.

"Hey, Vivien. It's Saffron. Happy birthday! Did you like the lingerie I helped Reeve pick?"

Oh, holy fuck. I tip my head back, staring up at the stars, wishing Saff had not brought that up. It's completely innocent, and I haven't done anything wrong, but I don't think Viv will like it.

"Viv?" she inquires, and I lower my head and lock eyes on my costar. She shrugs, waving her hands in the air in a quizzical manner. "We did it online one night after work. That photo he has by his bed is so sweet. You make a cute couple."

Jesus fucking Christ. Is Saffron trying to kill me here? There is no ill intent, but it's like she's got a foot-in-mouth disease. Possibly, the copious beers she's consumed have addled her brain. "Give me that," I command, reaching out for the phone. I need to do damage control before Saff says something else and digs me a bigger hole to fall in.

"I've got to go, but I'm so looking forward to meeting you. Buh-bye," she adds, thrusting the phone into my hand. "Sorry," she mouths, looking apologetic.

"Hey, it's me," I quietly say.

"Why was she in your hotel room, and were you in hers?" she barks, and it's clear she's totally worked up. I assume she's been drinking, and that won't help me to reason with her.

"Babe, calm down." I glance anxiously at my costars, not wanting to have an argument in front of them. I have been gushing about Vivien and our relationship, and I don't want to fight with her and make it look like it's all been lies. I also don't want to fight with my girlfriend on her birthday.

"You let her choose lingerie for me?"

Ah, fuck. Now she sounds hurt. If she realized how innocent it was, she would be fine with it. But I'm not sure it's a good idea to get into this when we've both been drinking. It's better we wait until tomorrow when we're calm to discuss it and put it to bed. "It's not as bad as it sounds," I say, hoping to defuse the situation.

"I'm glad you realize how bad it sounds," she barks, raising my hackles.

"Don't overreact, Viv," I say, eyeballing Rudy and communicating a silent message. He nods and starts ushering the others to the far end of the building to wait for the town cars.

"Don't tell me not to overreact! You know how I feel about her, yet you spend time with her in a hotel room and let her pick an intimate gift for my birthday. How the fuck do you expect me to react?" she roars, and it's clear there is no reasoning with her tonight.

"I can't talk to you when you're like this." I purposely lower my tone so no one overhears me. "How much have you had to drink?"

"How much have you?" she snaps as three town cars round the corner and pull up out front.

Rudy jerks his head in my direction, and I nod. "Our car is here. I have to go. We'll talk again tomorrow when you've calmed down."

"Reeve. Don't you dare hang up on me."

I don't want to, but there is no way in hell I'm continuing this fight in the car with everyone listening and forming the wrong opinion. "I love you, Viv. We'll talk soon. Go back to your party," I say before ending the call and jogging toward my ride back to the hotel.

Chapter Seventeen

Now

I'm roused by my alarm the following morning, and I groan as I roll over in bed. I feel like shit. I couldn't fall asleep after my phone argument with Viv as I replayed everything in my mind, so I popped a Xanax to mellow out and eventually fell asleep sometime after two. I'm in no mood for my early-morning workout, but I can't bail, so I force my heavy limbs out of bed. I'm yawning as I pull on my training top and shorts and rub my eyes while I unmute my cell. Panic is instantaneous when my phone continuously pings with repeated notifications.

What the fuck?

I open up Insta, and my feed is nuts. I've been tagged thousands of times, and it can't be anything good. I don't really have time to look, but I won't be able to focus on my workout if I don't identify what's going down. As I flip quickly through my feed, it doesn't take long to find the post that started all this madness.

All the blood drains from my face as I watch the short video of Nate and Vivien kissing. It's in slow motion, and their eyes are closed as they lock lips. Nausea swims up my throat, and pain eviscerates me on the inside. Tossing my cell on the bed, I bury my head in my hands. Tears prick the backs of my eyes. How could she do this to me? I shouldn't have hung up on her, but that is no excuse for cheating! And with Nate of all people. Pain slices through my heart, and I can scarcely breathe over the messy ball of emotion lodged in my throat.

No.

No!

Viv wouldn't do this. I don't care how drunk or angry she was. She wouldn't betray me.

I inhale and exhale as I attempt to calm down. I'm not going to overreact. I understand how things can get distorted online, and I'm betting this isn't as bad as it seems. There must be a logical explanation. I know my girlfriend, and she wouldn't do this. I stare at the frozen image of that prick Nate with my girl, and it feels like I'm suffocating. An errant tear leaks from my eye, and I hastily swipe at it. I bet this is his fault. I suspected he would make a move on her when I was gone despite Alex's assurance he would keep him in line.

Nate did this. He pounced on her when she was drunk and upset, and I'm going to fucking murder the bastard in cold blood when I get my hands on him.

I shut down the feed and set my phone on silent. Scrubbing my hands down my face, I try to erase the image of my love kissing another man from my brain, but I fear it's permanently imprinted in my subconscious. Even though I know deep down that Viv didn't do this willingly, it doesn't diminish the throbbing ache in my chest or the pain slithering through my veins.

Fuck, it hurts.

It hurts so bad.

Sniffling, I scrub at my eyes, telling myself to get a grip. I can't show up at the gym or on set with red eyes looking like a pathetic prick. It's just a big misunderstanding, and I'm going to treat it as such until I talk to my girl and get the truth.

It's only three a.m. in Cali, and I'm sure Viv's in bed, but on the off chance she isn't, I call her. It connects immediately to her voice message, meaning her cell is out of charge or she has it switched off. Fleeting doubt simmers in my chest, but I push it back down. It doesn't mean anything her phone is off. It most likely means she is just sleeping. "Call me when you get this," I say, keeping my message short and sweet.

I try to hold my shit together as I push myself to extremes in the gym. None of the guys have said anything, so they must not have checked social media yet.

Back in my room, I call Viv again, even though I know it's futile. I have to keep trying. My schedule is hectic today, and I won't have much time in between scenes to call her.

I need to speak to her.

I need to know what happened.

I need to tell her I'm sorry for last night.

If I'd gone straight back to the hotel and called her, maybe she wouldn't have been so drunk, we wouldn't have had any argument, and Nate would not have had any opportunity to pounce.

Bile explodes in my gut, and a red haze coats over my eyes. That fucker is going to wish he'd never been born by the time I'm through with him. Where my words appear to have failed, I'll ensure my fists drive the message home next time.

I leave another message and hop in the shower. After showering and dressing, I leave another message and one final one as I'm leaving my room.

In the town car, en route to the set, I send her a couple of texts, imploring her to contact me the minute she wakes. I also message Wen, telling him I need him close to me on set today and asking him to meet me there ASAP. That dickhead is going to help me today, or I'll threaten to report him to human resources.

"How are you holding up?" Saff asks, placing her hand on my thigh and shooting me a pitying look.

Great. She clearly knows something. It's not that I planned to keep it hidden from my friends on set, but I didn't want to discuss it until after I'd spoken to Viv and had all the facts. I know how this will look to them, and I don't want anyone hating on my girl. I deliberately didn't breathe a word when I met them in the lobby, and I've been trying to act normal, like nothing is wrong. Guess we're doing this now. "I'm fine." I work hard to keep my tone easy-breezy despite how every muscle in my body locks up tight.

"What's going on?" Rudy asks, lifting his head from the book he's reading. He's sitting across from Saff and me and beside a conked-out Ed.

Saff squeezes my thigh in a comforting gesture as she explains. "Reeve was tagged overnight in a video from Vivien's birthday party, showing Reeve's girl kissing another guy."

"What the hell, man?" Rudy's eyes pop wide as he slips a bookmark into his book and closes it.

"It's not how it looks." My voice holds more confidence than I feel. "That guy Nate has been chasing Viv for years. I wouldn't be surprised to learn he set the whole thing up to try to separate us. He's just that desperate."

"I hate to say it," Saff says, visibly wincing, "but it looks pretty passionate."

"Well, looks are deceiving, and it didn't look that passionate to me." I slant her a pointed look, daring her to challenge me. "It's been edited in slow motion to make it look like it's more than it is." I clear my throat as my gaze bounces between them. "Vivien would not cheat on me," I say in a firm tone.

"You need to talk to her," Rudy says.

"No shirt, Sherlock." Air whistles out of my mouth as I drag a hand through my hair. "It's still the middle of the night in Cali, and I haven't been able to speak to her yet."

Rudy and Saffron share a look I don't like.

"Don't do that," I snap, jabbing my finger in the air between them. "Neither of you know her like I do. She didn't betray me."

"Things seemed pretty heated on your call last night," Saffron reminds me. A grimace spreads over her face. "I want to apologize. I lose control of my mouth when I drink alcohol. I didn't mean anything by what I said, but I can see how she might have construed it. I'm really sorry if I caused issues in your relationship, Reeve."

"You didn't." I lift her hand off my thigh, because it's not appropriate. "Everything will be fine when I talk to Viv. I trust her, and it's not how it looks."

I stare out the window, with a muscle clenching in my jaw, as Rudy and Saff exchange another look. I want to rip through them for their obvious thoughts, but I'm not an idiot. I know how it looks to people who don't know us.

Things aren't much better when I get to the studio and find Cassidy waiting for me. She starts with her shit, and I'm not in the mood for this. I'm running on fumes at this point and tense as fuck. The last thing I need today is this bitch heaping more shit on my pile. "What the hell do you want me to say, Cassidy?" I yell as we walk down the hallway toward the dressing rooms. "I told you I'll deal with it."

"Do you have any idea how bad this makes you look?"

"What?!" I throw my hands in the air as I slam to a halt in the corridor. "What the fuck has that got to do with anything?"

I couldn't give two shits about my reputation right now. All I care about is ensuring Viv knows I love her and that whatever happened last night was only a blip. A blip we will get past.

She doesn't want Nate. She barely tolerates him most days. This isn't going to derail my relationship.

"You put out a sappy video declaring how much you love her yesterday, and a few hours later, a video shows up where she's got her tongue down another guy's throat! If you can't see the issue with that, then you're clearly lacking basic intelligence!" she shouts, folding her arms and glaring at me. "You look like a goddamn fool, Reeve!"

"Gee, tell me what you really think," I say, leveling her with a glare. "And she did not have her tongue in his mouth!" Shoving past her, I inwardly groan when I notice the line of cast and crew members congregating behind us in the hallway. I didn't realize we were blocking the hall and gathering an audience. I rub at my sore temples, embarrassed to have this playing out in front of others. Now, everyone will think I'm a gullible fool. Anger comingles with frustration as I storm toward my dressing room. Did Vivien even think of me before she let Nate put his lips on hers?

Maybe she did it on purpose to get back at you.

I punt that devilish voice from my mind because Viv wouldn't be that petty. Would she? She was pretty angry, but no, she wouldn't do that to me. It's not how we roll.

A few hours later and I'm starting to reconsider my beliefs. Wen is playing ball after my threat, and he rushes up to me after every scene with an update and hands me my cell phone. Still no return calls or messages. It's eleven here, which means it's eight a.m. her time.

It's early, but I thought someone would have seen what's going on and woken her by now. The video has been up for hours at this stage, and the longer it's live, the more harm it's doing. Wen told me my supporters are up in arms, posting vile comments and making threats toward Vivien. It's fast getting out of hand. Cassidy is trying to get it taken down, and she's in full damage-control mode.

"It's still up," Wen says, confirming what I already know and failing to hide his gleeful smile behind a fake compassionate expression. He's loving this, and I'm growing more irate by the second.

Where the fuck are you, Vivien?

Maybe she's with him. In his bed. That's why her phone is off. That's why she hasn't called you back.

No! Hell no!

Fuck that inner voice.

It's not true.

It can't be.

It isn't.

"I need privacy," I tell Wen as he moves to follow me into the small, empty office just off the main set. I slam the door in his face and call Viv again as the last shred of my patience flitters away.

Even if she hasn't seen the video, she knows what she did. She should have woken early to call me first thing. It's not acceptable she hasn't reached out yet, especially when I've left several messages and calls by now. If something like this happened to me, she'd be busting my balls for not calling her already.

"For fuck's sake, Vivien, answer your damn phone!" I yell into my cell. "I can't believe you did this. You didn't even give me a chance to explain before you sought comfort from Nate, of all fucking people! Do you know how stupid you made me look?! I look like a fucking idiot pining for you, posting how much I love you, and a few hours later, everyone sees you kissing that asshole. You have made me look like a damn fool!" I shout. "I'm so fucking disappointed in you."

It's the truth. Even if she didn't cheat, she put herself into this situation. She knows better than this. She knows how tenuous my situation is with the studio publicist and how important image is for the success of the movie. How could she have let this happen? And all because she's pissed I asked Saff for her help when choosing some of her gifts? It's a gross overreaction, and now she's really made a mess of things. I never thought Vivien would ever let something like this happen. She should have been more careful, and I'll be having words with my buddy Alex too. He was supposed to have her back. Where the fuck was he when this was going down?

I'm breathing heavily as I rub at the tightness in my chest. It's been a constant since I watched that damn video. "Do I even know you at all?" My voice cracks as the stress gets to me. I don't need this shit when I've already got so much on my shoulders. Vivien is supposed to be helping make things better, not making it worse. "I've got to get back, and I don't have another break. Call me tonight." My sigh is loud. "Or don't. I... I...I can't deal with this right now."

Chapter Eighteen
Now

An hour later and I'm all out of patience with Vivien. She is still not picking up her phone, and I'm on edge. I seek Saffron out before I call my buddy. I rap on her dressing room door, and she hollers to come in. The makeup people are getting her ready for the next scene, but she gets up and comes over to me, pulling me into a hug.

"What's that for?" I mumble, briefly hugging her back.

"You looked like you could use a hug." She rubs my back before breaking our embrace.

"It wasn't a hug I had in mind."

Her eyes widen.

"No! Not that either. Shit." I grab handfuls of my hair as air whooshes from my mouth. I lean down and whisper in her ear, "I need a pill."

Her eyes light up in acknowledgment. Taking my hand, she grabs her purse and pulls me into the bathroom, shutting the door behind us. It's a little cramped, and I press my back to the wall so we're not touching. "I know you don't want anyone to know," she says, rooting through her purse. "Even though no one would bat an eye. The makeup and costume people see mostly everything. It's par for the course." She hands me a bag of pills. "You can have those. I have more stashed back at the hotel."

"Thanks." I remove one and swallow it dry before pocketing the bag in my jeans.

"I've got your back, movie star." She stretches up and kisses my cheek. "Have you spoken with Viv yet?"

I shake my head. "I still haven't been able to reach her."

"It doesn't mean she's guilty or that she spent the night with the guy or anything."

"Thanks for that visual."

"Reeve." Concern splays across her face. "You should probably prepare yourself. I know you think she hasn't cheated, but this is your first time away from one another, and it's not impossible. Remember how badly you were struggling? What if she's been struggling too and hasn't said anything because she didn't want to worry you?"

Fuck. It would be just like Vivien to mask her pain so she didn't add to mine. Haven't I done the same with her? Hiding how hard it's been so she wouldn't worry? It's not inconceivable to think she's doing the same.

"Maybe she's not coping either, and she must have been upset last night after your argument, and you weren't there for her birthday, and maybe she drank too much. Good sense goes out the window with booze. Just..." Her features soften, and her eyes plead with me. "If she made a mistake, go easy on her. It's got to be very tough for her at home alone without you. She loves you, and you love her, and that's what matters, right?"

"Yeah." I bob my head. "Thanks, Saff." I give her a brief hug. "I needed to hear that."

I exit her dressing room and head to mine to hide the addy in my bag and to call my buddy in private. Alex stayed at Viv's last night. He might know what's happening. I only have a short break, so I'm silently praying he picks up. I'm calmer after talking with Saff and trying to control my emotions to avoid losing it with Alex.

"Reeve," he pants, sounding breathless, and I cringe.

"Shit, are you with Audrey?" My finger hovers over the end button, ready to press it if I hear even the slightest hint of a moan.

"I wish," he grumbles. "I just got back from a run."

"Where is Viv?"

"She's still sleeping, I think. I only woke an hour ago. I checked on the girls before I went on my run, but they were both passed out in Viv's bed. We're all pretty wrecked after last night."

"Were you there? Did you see it?"

"What do you mean? See what?"

"Come on, Alex. Don't pretend like you don't know. It's fucking all over social media."

"Reeve, I have no clue what you're talking about. I haven't checked social media today. My phone was dead when I woke. Vivien's housekeeper gave me a charger and I plugged it in before I left."

"Open Insta," I say through gritted teeth, pacing my room as I wait for my buddy to watch the video.

"Holy fucking shit!" he exclaims a few minutes later as alarm burns through his tone. "I didn't fucking see this. I swear! Audrey was helping Vivien stand when I found them outside the marquee. Viv was totally wasted. She puked every-where, and she was rambling and slurring her words and not making much sense. Rey and I helped her up to her room, and my girl insisted on sleeping in Viv's room 'cause she was scared she'd vomit in her sleep. Audrey said nothing about this."

"Of course, she didn't. They were probably hoping to keep it quiet."

"Or Rey wasn't there, and she doesn't know."

"Come on, man. Of course, she knows. Those two are thick as thieves. They tell each other everything."

"I'm going to kick his fucking ass," Alex hisses.

"That's my job, and I'm going to make him pay. Big time."

"I'm sorry, Reeve. I should have been there."

Despite my recent less than charitable thoughts, I can't hold this against Alex. "You're not her babysitter, Alex. I can't expect you to shadow her every move. This isn't on you. It's on that prick, Nate. I told you he's an ass. I knew he'd try something as soon as I was out of sight."

"If he did this deliberately, I'm done with him. I promise you that."

"Can you go wake Viv? I need to speak to her."

"Sure. Stay on the line."

A loud rap bounces off my door and Wen pokes his head into my room. "Nick has called you back to set."

"Fuck." I rest my head back against the wall.

"Alex, I've got to go, but get Viv to call me. I'll pick up when I can."

"Will do, and Reeve?"

"Yeah?"

"She didn't do this. I hope you know that. Vivien would never cheat on you. I'd stake my life on it. She was upset and very drunk last night. Whatever happened, this is all on Nate."

"I hope so." I can't even contemplate if it's not. I know we won't break up. Nothing or no one will tear me away from the love of my life, but shit will be rough if she willingly kissed a guy who isn't me.

"I'll get her to call you, and call me back later if you have time."

"Will do, buddy. Out."

I don't get another break for three hours. When I walk off set, Wen hands me my cell. "The video is gone, and the studio is pulling out all the stops to deflect attention."

I nod, feeling slightly relieved as I walk toward the bathroom. My heart pounds behind my rib cage when I spot the new flashing message. It's from Viv, and she left it twenty minutes ago. I wait until I'm in the bathroom alone before I hit play.

"Reeve, I'm so sorry," she says in a teary tone. "I didn't kiss Nate. That fucking prick kissed me! I don't even remember it. I was trashed and ..." Her anguished sobs tear strips off my heart, and I rub at my sore chest. "Look, I didn't cheat. I love you, and I'm so sorry. Please call me when you can so we can talk about it, and I'll tell you exactly how it went down. I would never betray you, Reeve. Please believe me." She dissolves into tears, and my heart is a mushy lump in my chest. "Sorry," she whispers before the message cuts off.

I want to call her right now, but I don't have enough time. This isn't a conversation that can be rushed, so it will have to wait until later. Her words have soothed my frayed edges. I knew this was all on that jerk, but hearing her confirm it has made it better and removed some of the immediate urgency.

I take a piss and wash my hands before leaving the bathroom. I check my other messages as I head back, spotting a recent one from Alex. I press play.

"Lauren's IT guy got the video removed, and lawyers have issued warnings to the media. You're not going to believe it, but this was Marnie Gibson's doing. Randy was at the party, and he filmed it and posted it online using a fictitious account. A few of us put the beat on him, and he admitted Marnie was furious not to be invited, so she wanted him to find something to use against Vivien in retaliation. Nate wasn't involved in the setup.

The idiot was drunk and thought Viv looked sad, so he kissed her. It doesn't excuse it, and if you want payback, I won't stop you. But he genuinely feels bad."

I roll my eyes as I listen. Alex is too soft on that guy. I don't care how drunk he was. No one puts moves on my girl without consequences. I thought I dealt with Marnie previously, but it's clear she needs to be taught a more permanent lesson. She's going to regret not letting go of her vendetta. It's been years, and it's fucking pathetic. And how useless is Randy Jennings that he's letting his girlfriend call the shots? I'll be dealing with that pussy too.

"Vivien is devastated, Reeve. She's a basket case. If you want to take it out on anyone, take it out on Nate. Don't take it out on her."

I exhale heavily as I step up to Wen, tapping out a message to Cassidy to tell her everything is handled before I hand him my phone. I physically feel the stress leaving my shoulders as I walk over to the director.

I knew Vivien wouldn't cheat on me.

Everything is going to be okay.

When I jump out of the shower after a long, tiring, stressful day, I notice I just missed a call from Viv. Toweling off quickly, I pull on some sweats, climb onto my bed, and grab my cell to FaceTime her.

"I'm sorry," we both say at the same time when the call connects, and it helps to defuse the situation. Seeing her beautiful face equally soothes and hurts. The thought of ever losing her feels like a knife driven straight through my heart. Emotion swells in my chest as I wish I was there so I can bundle her in my arms and keep her safe from predators.

"Viv," I whisper as tears stab the back of my eyes. Her eyes are swollen and red, and I hate how all this drama happened around a birthday that should have been special. Now, the memory will permanently be tarnished.

"I didn't kiss him!" She bolts upright on her bed, panic transparent on her face. "I would never do that, not even when we've been fighting. I was drunk. Audrey had gone to get me some water, and Nate was the only one at the table. He was drunk too, and he thought I looked sad, so he kissed me."

So I've heard. I hate that fucking asshole. He's lucky he's not in proximity because I would not be responsible for my actions. "I am going to punch that slimy bastard in the face until he no longer resembles himself." A muscle pulses in my jaw as I fight to remain calm.

"I think Alex already beat you to it."

"Remind me to thank him." My buddy didn't mention any beatdown on Nate, but I'm grateful.

"Nate is an idiot. You know I have zero interest in him, and he'd kiss any female with a pulse."

"Don't try to lighten this," I hiss, rubbing at my thumping temples. "Nate has the hots for you, babe. Everyone can see it but you."

"Whether he does or not doesn't matter. I don't have the hots for him, so you don't need to worry."

"And that's exactly what I've been trying to tell *you*." Viv has expressed concerns about my costar several times, and nothing I have said seems to reassure her. I don't know what more to say to convey how Saffron has no interest in me like that. The only woman I see is my girlfriend. No one can replace Vivien Mills in my life.

No one ever will.

Lying down on my side, I work hard to leash my anger. I'm not angry at Viv, and I won't take it out on her. "You have nothing to worry about with Saffron. *Nothing.* Even if she did have feelings for me, which she doesn't, I have zero interest in her."

A grimace crosses over her face before her features smooth out. "I think you're wrong. I think she has set her sights on you, and let's not forget she has a history of stealing other women's men."

Jesus Christ. Not this again. Saffron was in a consensual relationship with Bryan and his wife, and it ended amicably. For fuck's sake, the three of them banded together to maximize the opportunity, which helped all of their careers. She didn't steal anyone's man because the couple is still happily married. But Vivien seems determined to cast Saffron as the villain.

"Baby, please, believe me when I say you couldn't be more wrong." I sit up against the headboard and bring the phone closer. I need her to see my face when I tell her this again, hoping this time the message will get through. "I have told her point-blank how much I love you. She knows you're *the one*, and she's happy for me because she's my friend, in the same way all of my costars are my friends. Honestly, I couldn't have asked for a better crew. We all get along famously, and there are no airs or graces, especially with Saffron. If we weren't in this situation, I think you would really like her and you two would be good friends."

Bitter laughter greets my words, and I'm getting angry now. "I can safely say that will never happen," Viv says. Her tone and her expression are resolutely determined.

I close my eyes for a second, counting to ten, as I try to remain calm. "Viv, I need you to listen to me and listen good. She's twenty-one, and I'm eighteen. I'm like her little brother." I don't want my costar and my girlfriend at loggerheads. They don't have to be besties, but I would love it if they respected one another, at least. "She's not interested in me like that because she's told me," I continue, "and she's fucking the thirty-year-old assistant director."

"It hurt knowing she picked my gifts," she admits, lying down on the bed and bringing her knees to her chest. "It really hurt, Reeve. How could you do that?"

Ah, hell. The look on her face is killing me. All anger fades, quickly replaced with regret. "I didn't stop to think about it. I wanted to buy you lingerie, but I was bombarded by all the choices, and I was struggling to pick things you would like. She offered to help, and I accepted without thinking it through." I didn't think it would be an issue, but at least I'll know better in the future. I will not be asking Saffron or any other girl for gift advice going forward.

"You know me better than anyone, Reeve. Whatever you would've chosen for me would've been perfect. And girls know that helping someone's boyfriend with a gift is a no-no. Especially something so intimate. Unless it's the girl's bestie and there's an established friendship between friend and boyfriend like with you and Audrey." She chews on the corner of her lip as pain shimmers in her eyes.

I really fucked up, and I'm frustrated with myself. I wanted to do something nice for her, and the whole thing's been a shit show of epic proportions. "It wasn't intentional, babe, and the last thing I ever want to do is hurt you. I swear."

"I believe you. It's her motives I don't trust."

And here we go again. If Vivien was here, she would see Saffron is no threat to her or our relationship. I've seen my girl jealous over the years, as I've been when other guys have looked at her with noticeable want. I figure a small amount of jealousy is healthy, only this isn't. Viv's intense dislike of Saffron is coming from bullshit she's read online, and it's really not fair. I don't know what else I can do or say to make her see she has nothing to worry about.

"I was going to burn the underwear," she says after a few tense, silent beats. "But I couldn't bear to destroy such beautiful garments. However, I can't wear them either. I'm going to return the unworn items to you so you can get a refund."

"Babe, please, don't, I—"

"I can't wear things some other woman picked out for me, Reeve," she snaps, rubbing at her brow. "How would you feel if I got Nate to help me choose gifts for you? Would you ever be able to look at them without seeing his face?"

Tension bleeds into the air again, and the almost suffocating pain in my chest is back. But she's made her point well. I would be murderous if Nate helped Vivien pick any gifts for me.

But I would have just cause. Nate has been lusting over her for years.

It's not a like-for-like situation.

Vivien does not have the same reasons for hating Saffron. Not that I can make that argument. I just want to put this to bed and move on. "That was low, Viv, but I get the point. Send it back to me, and I'll return it." I drag my lower lip between my teeth, hating to have to admit this too, but it needs to be said. "You had better send the makeup back too."

"Not the purse or the bracelet?" she asks, sounding hopeful.

I shake my head. "She wasn't involved at all in those purchases."

Extreme sadness shrouds her face before she tucks it into her chin, looking anywhere but at me. I hate I put that look on her face, and I wish I could rewind time and not ask Saffron for her help. "Vivien. Look at me, babe."

Slowly, she lifts her head and her glassy eyes lock on mine. My heart physically hurts. I hate this separation. As much as things have settled down for me at the studio, I will never get used to the long distance keeping me from my love. "I'm sorry, Viv. I just wanted to make your birthday special, and instead I ruined it. If I hadn't upset you, you wouldn't have gotten drunk and that degenerate wouldn't have put his toxic lips on you."

"Why were you like that on the phone last night?" she asks. "If you had just talked to me, this could've been avoided. And how could you hang up on me knowing I was upset?"

"I didn't have the privacy to talk to you properly about it, and the guys were leaving and calling for me. The few beers I had probably didn't help either. I don't know what else to say except I'm sorry and it won't happen again."

"We have both made mistakes," she says, reaching out to touch the screen. "But this won't define us. Let's agree to put it behind us and not let anything like this happen again."

That is music to my ears. "I love you, baby. So, so much, and it's killing me being away from you. Especially now. If I was there, I would hold you in my arms all night, kissing you and making love to you until I'd banished every single doubt and every molecule of pain I have caused."

Tears flow down her face. "I miss you like crazy, Reeve. It's so much harder than I thought it'd be."

"I know, babe. I know. But we are nearly at the halfway point, and I'm going to see you in less than a month for prom."

"I can't wait." She smiles, and my heart melts. God, she is so beautiful, and she has my heart in the palm of her hand. "Just promise me one thing, Reeve."

"Anything, my love."

"I don't want her in your room with you alone or you in hers. The thought of it makes me ill."

I rest my hand over my heart. "I promise she won't be in here unless the guys are with her. Same goes for her room. If that's what you need to feel reassured, I can give you that." It's a small concession to make, and it's not like Saff is in my room alone that much. If Vivien needs this, I can give it to her.

"Thank you."

"I love you, Vivien Grace Mills. You are my heart. My soul. My world." I blow her a kiss. "Please never doubt my love. It will always only be you."

Her legs unfold, and she relaxes into the bed, beaming at me as her fingers brush the screen again. "I love you too, Reeve, in all the same ways. Let's never fight like this again."

"Amen to that."

Chapter Nineteen
Then - Age 12

"You are mega talented," I say, running my fingers across the soft material of the black top. "I can't believe you made these."

"Mom helped." She pushes her chair back and stands, moving away from the sewing machine.

"I did very little," Lauren says, walking into the room. "Vivien has worked really hard on these costumes. She didn't want to let you down."

"That's an impossibility. Vivien could never let me down." I lean in to kiss her on the cheek.

I'm very competitive when it comes to our annual middle-school Halloween event. They throw a party in the big hall at school every year, and there are prizes for the best-dressed students. We came in runner-up last year, and I'm determined to win this time. We only have one more party after this one before we graduate and head to high school, and Viv and I are going to dominate!

"Do you really like it?" she asks, chewing on the corner of her lip.

"I love it. It's perfect."

We decided to go as Zorro and Elena, drawing inspiration from *The Mask of Zorro*, which Lauren let us watch over the summer. Vivien has created a long-sleeved, loose-fitting black top with crisscross ties on the top. There is a matching black cummerbund with a gold pattern in the center, which I'll wear over plain black pants and boots. She has even made me a cape and a wraparound black eye mask.

"Where'd you find these?" I ask, picking up a hat and leather gloves just like the ones Antonio Banderas wore in the movie and a fake sword that is so well made it could pass as the real thing.

"Mom took me to The Costume House, and they made our swords especially for us!" She swipes her sword and steps back, brandishing it dramatically. "En garde!" Vivien dances from foot to foot, waving the sword in front of me, and I pick mine up, and we parry and thrust as we joke around.

Lauren snaps pics of us wearing a wide smile. "Are you sure you don't want to be an actress, sweetie, because you've definitely inherited a dramatic streak."

"I'm leaving the acting to Reeve." Viv grins as she sets the sword back down and lifts the dress she made for herself. It's a replica of a pretty dress Catherine Zeta-Jones wore in the movie. The long white dress could pass for a wedding dress except it has a red silk sash around the middle. "I think I'd like to make costumes," she says, hugging the dress to her body.

"I thought you wanted to be a writer," I say because Vivien is always entertaining me with stories that just pop into her head. She has tons of notebooks filled with stories and ideas.

"I want to be both," she confidently proclaims.

"You can do whatever you want, sweetie," Lauren says. "As long as you're happy."

"Thanks, Mom." Viv leans in and hugs Lauren. "I couldn't have pulled this off without your help. Maureen's too."

Last year, Viv started personal dressmaking classes with a friend of Lauren's. Maureen works with several studios, and she has her own custom design business. She doesn't normally teach classes, but she made an exception for Vivien.

"You're welcome, Vivien. You know your father and I will always support your passions." She ruffles her hair before doing the same to me. "You two better get a move on, or you'll be late!"

"Come on. Let's get dressed," Viv says. "First prize has our names on it!"

Heads turn when I walk into the transformed school hall with Vivien holding on to my arm. I'm instantly transported to the future, and I imagine I'm walking her up the aisle as my bride. Pride swirls through my veins as I escort the most beautiful girl into the room. Hushed whispers and finger pointing follow us as we stride to the dance floor. "Everyone is looking," Viv murmurs, keeping her head up high even though she detests being the center of attention.

"Because they know winners when they see it," Alex says, appearing in front of us with Viv's friend Audrey by his side.

"Oh my God, Viv." Audrey squeals before hugging her best friend. "You look like a princess."

"*Princess Bride*," Alex quips, and a blush heats Vivien's cheeks.

"I see you went all out this year," I tease, raking my gaze over his familiar costume. Alex came as Fred from *The Flintstones* last year as well.

"I'm only here to party," he jokes while Audrey rolls her eyes.

"Who are you supposed to be?" I ask her.

She punches me in the arm. "I'm Natasha Romanov from The Avengers." She shakes her head. "Philistine."

Alex and I burst out laughing. Since we learned that word in English, Audrey has been slotting it into conversations whenever she can. It's funny as fuck.

"Come on, my beautiful Elena." I sweep forward in an elaborate bow. "It's time to show these losers how it's done."

Viv doesn't like the spotlight, but she readily helps me learn lines for school plays and walk-on parts on TV shows, and she instantly agreed when I suggested we learn the Spanish tango so we could recreate the dance scene from the movie. Lauren coached us, and we've practiced hundreds of times, so we execute the routine flawlessly as our friends and fellow students form a circle around us, whooping and hollering as we dance. At the end, we withdraw our fake swords and mock fight as the cheering accelerates, and I know we've nailed it.

No one can rival our costumes or the show we've put on, and when we are announced as the first-prize winners, I feel on top of the world.

Together, Vivien and I are invincible, and it only confirms what I've been thinking lately.

Vivien Mills is not just my best friend; she's my soul mate. The girl I'm destined to marry and spend my life with.

As we grin at one another, it takes massive self-control not to grab her into my arms and kiss her. It's all I can think about lately, and when I touch myself at night, it's always to images of Vivien's smiling pretty face.

I want to kiss her so badly. To make her my girlfriend, but I'm afraid.

What if she doesn't feel the same?

What if I kiss her and she tells me to stop being gross?

What if I ruin our friendship and she never talks to me again?

What if Jonathon finds out and he bans me from their house?

These worries stop me from doing anything. I'll just have to wait and hope that Vivien makes the move to kiss me. Then I'll know she wants it too and we can be together in the way I want. For now, I need to be patient.

If I have to wait forever for her, I will because that's what soul mates do.

"I'm proud of you," Lauren says as she drives us home later after the party has ended. "You both worked so hard, and you deserve first prize."

"It was so fun." Vivien snuggles into my side as she looks at her mom through the mirror. "Everyone formed a circle around us, and they were clapping and cheering."

Well, not everyone. There are always a few jealous idiots who resent us. Guy Fenwick hates my guts, and the feeling is mutual. He says rude things about Vivien to piss me off, and we've had our fair share of fights over the years. I spotted him and his crew throwing scathing looks at us all night, but Vivien was oblivious, which is just the way I like it. She doesn't need to know the shitty things he says about her, and I have success-fully managed to keep her away from him. I swear, if he ever touches her, I will ruin him. Dad said he'd help. I think he's just annoyed he has to come to school at least a couple times a year to deal with the fallout.

When we get back to Viv's house, we change in our respective rooms and then sneak outside in our pajamas and robes with our sneakers on. Vivien has some secret plan I know nothing about. As usual, I tried talking her out of it, but she is stubborn when she gets an idea in her head, and there is no swaying her. I'm just here to try to keep her out of trouble.

"Here, hold this." Vivien slaps a large flashlight in my hand as we approach our treehouse. It's propped between the two biggest oak trees on the grounds.

"Can you tell me now what we're doing?"

"We're carving our initials into the tree. For posterity." Audrey isn't the only one throwing big words around these days. Viv is determined to know every word in the dictionary. She says it's important to be a writer, so she learns and memorizes a new word each day, choosing randomly and adding a tick beside them to keep track.

"What does that even mean?" Maybe I should be doing the same. An actor should have an extensive vocabulary too.

"For future generations." She removes a pen knife from her robe pocket. "We'll put our initials here, and our children will see and their children and so on."

Warmth floods my chest at her words. If she still thinks we'll have children, that must mean she sees me as her future boyfriend and husband. Right? The compulsion to kiss her returns, and I stare at her lips as she sets to work. Her tongue peeks out of her mouth as she concentrates, and it's so stinking cute.

I am so in love with her.

I don't care that I'm twelve—soon to be thirteen—and the oldies would say I'm too young to know what love is. I know what I feel in my heart. I know what I feel deep down in my soul. I know it's true love, and I will never love another girl for as long as I shall live.

"Reeve." Vivien wiggles her fingers in my face. "You're a million miles away."

"Sorry," I murmur, lowering my eyes to her lips. *Do it,* the devil on my shoulder whispers. *Kiss her!* I lean in, and Vivien puts her hands on my chest and frowns.

"Reeve, did you hear what I said?" Her brow creases further. "You're acting weird."

The moment is gone, and I step back, trying to ignore the tingling in my boxers.

"It's your turn." She hands over the pen knife and snatches the flashlight from me. "Carve your initials there." She points at a particular spot on the tree. She has already carved VM and a love heart underneath, and I work carefully to add RL in the space below. When I'm done, I pocket the knife, and we both stand back and admire it.

Her hand slides into mine, and I squeeze it tight. "It's perfect," she whispers, sounding a little choked. I look down at her, spotting the glassy sheen in her eyes that mirrors the emotion swirling in my chest.

"I love you," I tell her, and even though I have told her a million times, this time feels different.

Her eyes peer deep into mine as she says, "I love you too, Reeve. Forever and ever."

This is it. There will never be a more perfect moment. This time, when I lean down toward her, she doesn't pull a face or tell me I'm acting weird. Her eyes pop wide, and her chest heaves up and down as I move my face closer to hers, my gaze fixated on her mouth, watching as she licks her lips and little puffs of air escape. My heart is beating so fast, and my hands are clammy as I close the distance between us. I am just about to press my lips to hers when the garden floods with light, and we jump apart at the same time.

"Vivien Grace Mills!" A stern-looking Lauren strides toward us, bundled up in a coat.

Busted!

"Shit," I mutter.

"Let me handle it." Vivien tosses her hair over her shoulders and lifts her chin.

"What are you two doing out here, and what have I told you about sneaking outside after it's dark?" Lauren crosses her arms as her gaze bounces between us.

"You need to take a chill pill, Mom. We're almost thirteen, and it's not even that late."

"Don't you give me sass, young lady."

"This was important."

"What was so important it couldn't wait until tomorrow?"

"This." Vivien points proudly at the tree.

Lauren's features soften instantly. "Oh my."

"Exactly." Vivien grips my hand harder. "It's for posterity, and I want everyone to know we love each other."

"I still don't understand why this could not have waited until tomorrow. You could have cut yourself."

"Mom, we're not little kids anymore."

"I'm well aware." Lauren holds out her hand. "Hand the knife over."

I remove it from my pocket and give it to her.

"This is still dangerous, and it should have been supervised." Lauren drills us both with a serious look. "Don't do something like this again without checking with your father or me."

"You treat me like I'm five," Vivien grumbles as we make our way back inside.

"I'm your parent, and it's my job to ensure you are safe at all times. I know you're growing up, Vivien, but you are still a child, and you are still subject to house rules." She glances at me. "That goes for you too, Reeve."

"I'm sorry," I say. "It was my idea. Don't blame Vivien."

"Don't lie." Viv glares at me. "It was my idea, and you're not going to cover for me. Reeve didn't know what we were doing until we were outside. It's not his fault. If you're going to ground me, do it, but he shouldn't be punished."

"No one is getting punished," Lauren says, opening the door and gesturing for us to go inside first. "As long as you promise you won't do anything dangerous alone again."

"We promise," Viv says, smirking as she looks at me.

If Lauren thinks that will stop her daughter in the future, she's very much mistaken. Viv has a wild streak that can't be tamed. But Viv's parents shouldn't worry because I'll never let anything bad happen to her. As long as I'm there to protect her, she'll be safe.

"You don't need to worry, Lauren. I will always protect Viv. She's safe with me."

She pulls me into a side hug. "I already know that, honey."

"Let me guess?" Jon says as we enter the living room. "My little princess was up to mischief again?" The smile on his face shows he isn't angry, but Simon's expression is harder to read. I wasn't expecting our dads home yet. They were at some charity golf event earlier followed by dinner and drinks. I thought they'd be out until at least midnight.

"They carved their initials in the tree," Lauren explains, and the three adults share a look.

"How was the party?" Jonathon asks.

"Awesome," Vivien says as I say, "We won first prize."

"You should get dressed," my father says, eyeballing me. "Let's go home."

"But we're having a sleepover," I protest.

"You're always here, Reeve." Dad glides his fingers through his beard. "You can sleep at home tonight."

"Simon, it's fine." Lauren interjects like I knew she would. "Reeve is welcome here anytime."

"I know, Lauren, and I'm grateful. I truly am, but I'd like my son to come home with me tonight."

He has never been so insistent. It's weird. I would rather sleep here, but I don't want Lauren getting into a fight with Simon on my behalf. He can be really cruel at times, and she shouldn't have to hear that shit.

"It's okay. I'll get dressed," I say before exiting the room.

"Come with me," Dad says when we get home, and I head for the stairs and my bedroom. "I want to show you something."

I'm intrigued, and I don't argue because it's rare he wants to do anything with me.

I follow him into his study and take a seat on the hard-backed leather couch as he fixes himself a whiskey. Mrs. Thompson must have lit the fire, and I lift my hands, warming them in front of the dancing flames.

"You get your love of Halloween from your mother," he says, and I nearly fall off the couch. Dad never voluntarily speaks about my mom. Except for that time in the limo on the way to the Harry Potter premiere. Any other time I ask questions, he shuts me down on the spot.

"I do?"

He nods, plopping down beside me with a couple of thick leather-bound albums. "Felicia made me dress up every year, and we always attended a party. She always went overboard with our costumes." He drinks his whiskey while flipping through the photo albums. I soak it all up, afraid to say a word in case I break whatever spell he is under. He turns page after page, and I try to memorize the pictures because I don't know if he'll ever show me again.

"She was really pretty," I blurt when we are halfway through the second photo album. It's true. Lauren has shown me some photos before. Mom had gorgeous, long, wavy brown hair, and the shade is the same as my own except for the sun-kissed streaks I have acquired thanks to the California sun. But that is all I see of myself in her, and it saddens me. I wish I didn't look so much like my father. That I could see my mother when I look in the mirror and feel a connection with her. Felicia Lancaster is a stranger to me, and I hate I have no memories and minimal knowledge of my mother. Sadness clings to my skin as I stare at her photos.

"Your mom was a beautiful woman."

"I miss her," I whisper, not looking at him.

"You can't miss something you never had, boy," he clips out, instantly dismissing my feelings.

"Did she..." I look up at him, afraid to ask this, but I need to know at the same time. "Did she even hold me after I was born?" She died shortly after giving birth to me, so it's possible she had touched me before she was taken from us.

His Adam's apple bobs in his throat, and he drains his drink before pouring another large measure. A muscle clenches in his jaw, and his fingers dig into the glass as he knocks it back in one go. His hand shakes as he flips to the end of the album and removes a photo. "There," he thrusts it at me.

Tears prick my eyes as I stare at the picture of my mother holding a baby, *me*, in her arms. She's crying, but she looks happy. "Can I keep it?" I ask as tears roll down my face. I want to put it in a frame beside my bed.

"Keep it," he barks, pouring more whiskey into his glass.

I press it to my chest, over my heart as it pounds and pounds behind my rib cage. "Why didn't you show me this before?" My voice wobbles.

"*Why?*" he snaps, turning his head to glare at me.

I shrink away from him and the angry look on his face.

"Use your fucking brain, boy." With a roar, he throws his glass at the wall, raining whiskey across the papered wall and the hardwood floor. "It's hard enough to look at you sometimes, let alone think about that day."

I'm horrified when tears well in his eyes. My father has never cried. Simon Lancaster prides himself on being a cold, heartless monster.

"You think it's my fault?" I whisper, clutching her picture closer to my heart.

"Well, it's hardly fucking mine, now is it, boy?"

Pain hacks chunks out of my heart, and the pressure sitting on my chest makes it difficult to breathe.

"Go to bed," he snaps, getting up to grab another glass. "And don't put that photo where I can see it. Not unless you want to give me more reasons to avoid you."

Every cell and nerve ending in my body is in excruciating pain as I quietly get up and leave his study. Tears flow silently down my face as I walk on autopilot to bed. I have always suspected Simon hates me for being born because his wife sacrificed her life for mine. I don't need to wonder anymore. The brutal truth is staring me in the face. My father can't stand to be around me because I represent everything he lost.

I crawl into bed in my clothes, shivering and silently crying. Kissing the photo, I open the drawer of my bedside table and carefully place it inside. I'll ask Lauren to help me buy a picture frame, and I'll keep it in my bedroom in her house. If this is the only picture I have of me with my mother, I won't leave it anywhere near that monster downstairs.

If he got rid of it, I might just be up on a murder charge.

As I cry myself to sleep, I ask myself why it matters so much that I make my father proud. If he blames me for my mother's death, I don't know if there is anything I can ever do to make him love me.

I wish I could stop caring, but I can't.

Chapter Twenty
Now

"Are you sure it's done?" I ask Simon as I make my way to the hotel after a long day on set in one of the town cars.

"Her place at UCLA has been rescinded. Doug Simmonds is a good friend, and he personally handled it. She has already been made aware. You don't need to worry about Marnie Gibson. She won't be anywhere near Vivien to torment her."

Vivien hasn't said a word about what's going on at school, but Alex is keeping me updated. The bullshit online about Saffron and me is getting to her even though I beg her not to look at it and to ignore it. So-called insiders are spouting crap about how explosive my chemistry is with my costar, and other idiots online are saying I kicked Viv to the curb after she cheated on me. She's getting shit at school for that and the video, and that cunt Marnie is going to town on her. I was never going to let what Marnie did pass, but I'm determined to destroy her now for continuing to hound Viv. Enough is enough.

"Thanks, Dad."

Bianca called me a few days ago to say it looks like the studio is going to commission two more movies in the series. Nothing is set in stone. It's still being discussed and negotiated, so I'm not saying anything to Vivien yet. But, if it goes ahead, it means I won't be attending UCLA with her after all even though we have already accepted our offers. Like Marnie had, but she's just lost her place. There is no way I'm having that bitch around Viv on campus when I might not be there to protect her.

"What about the video and the pics we found?" Simon asks. "Do you want me to release those now?"

"Release the video of Jennings, but hold the pics back for now."

Dad has a lot of shady contacts, but they came in handy when I asked him for a favor. He had Randy's and Marnie's cells and computers hacked, and we hit the jackpot. It seems Randy is bi, and he's been fucking a few guys behind his girlfriend's back. The idiot even had someone film him. I'll enjoy ruining his rep and their relationship. Let him see what it's like to have a personal video blasted everywhere. Unlike us, he doesn't have the contacts to get it taken down, and it will haunt him for the rest of his days.

As for Marnie, I'm thinking I'll hold those nude pics of her in reserve for now. Maybe I'll release them just before graduation. I doubt she'll walk or show her face around town once they surface.

"Consider it done."

"Thanks, Dad."

Saff is waiting outside my hotel room, as prearranged, and we huddle in the shadowy corner, away from the camera, to make the exchange. I pass her a roll of cash, and she hands me two bags of pills that I promptly stash in my bag.

"Thanks."

"Anytime, movie star." Her lips purse. "Though I really don't enjoy shady meetings in hallways. I don't see why I can't go into your room or you can't come into mine? It's not like I'm going to jump you." She laughs, but there's a slight edge to her tone. "Why is Viv so insecure? Everyone who's met you knows you'd walk over hot coals for her. There is no boyfriend more devoted or loyal anywhere on this planet. Why is she punishing you when you've done nothing wrong? That seems grossly unfair to me."

She doesn't understand why Viv is making such a big deal of this, and I won't entertain her attempts to drag me into a discussion about it. My girlfriend asked this of me so she can feel reassured, and I'm not going back on my word.

"Babe." Jeremy calls out as he rounds the corner, rescuing me from answering. "Are you coming or what?" He leans against the wall with a towel wrapped around his waist. His room is in the adjoining hallway, and I'm guessing Saff is sleeping over tonight. Those two go at it nonstop. It's a running joke on set, and most everyone has seen her O face or heard him coming because they seem fond of leaving doors open. They were extra loud this evening just after we finished filming for the day. Nick isn't a fan, and I overheard him tearing into Jeremy earlier.

"Gotta go." She leans in and hugs me. "See ya tomorrow."

"I won't be here." I can't contain my grin. "I'll be at prom, remember?" I don't have to be on set again until four p.m. the day after next, so I'll get to spend almost twenty-four hours with my love. I am dying to see Viv, and I've been on a countdown these past few weeks.

"Oh, yeah. Have a good one, movie star," she says, waggling her fingers as she skips off down the hallway to her boyfriend.

———

"I don't understand," I say, scowling at Nick the following morning. I was in the car, ready to head to the airport, when the driver was instructed to drive me to the set. I had no clue what was going on when I called the pilot telling him to be on standby. "How could this even happen?"

"I'd like to know the answer to that question too," he says, full-on glaring at Jeremy. The assistant director is sweating bullets, and I wouldn't be surprised if he was fired. Though Nick probably won't do it. We only have three more days on set, and then we're on location for four weeks. I doubt he can let go of Jeremy this late in the production. I wouldn't be surprised if he's canned for the next two movies—if they get the green light.

"I don't know what to tell you." Jeremy frowns. "I backed them up. It must be a glitch."

"It doesn't add up," Nick snaps.

"The tech guys might be able to recover them," Jeremy suggests.

"We don't have time for that. We are going on location in a few days. The only free window we have to reshoot the missing scenes is now."

"You promised," I growl. "I have a private jet waiting for me at Logan, and I'm not letting my girl down."

"I'm sorry, Reeve. I hate to do this, but there's no other choice."

"Oh my God." Saff sidles up beside me. "This sucks. I'm so sorry, Reeve." She leans in to hug me as my mind churns possible options. "Have you told Viv yet?"

Ignoring her, I turn to face the director. "What about adding them to the reshooting list for August? Why can't we do that?"

"It doesn't make sense when we have a window today to reshoot. It would cost too much money to push those scenes to August."

"I'll pay."

"Reeve, it's not an insignificant sum of money."

"I don't care. Whatever it is, I'm good for it." I got access to half of my trust fund when I turned eighteen, and I get the rest when I'm twenty-one. I can afford it, and I want to do this because I can't disappoint Vivien. She'll be devastated if I don't show up.

He scrubs his hands down his face as he considers it.

"The extras are all here, and the props are set up," Jeremy says. "We should just do it now. We can't call everything to a halt because our leading man wants to go to prom. It's ludicrous."

"Maybe you shouldn't have lost the footage and the backup in the first place," I yell, clenching my fists. I'm ready to punch his fucking lights out. I get he's keen to rectify his mistake ASAP, but why should I have to pay the price for his fuckup?

"How about this?" Nick says, reclaiming my attention. "We'll shoot half the scenes now and the other half tomorrow."

"What time does that mean I'll get out of here at, and when would I have to be back tomorrow?" I was supposed to be off the rest of today and only due back on set at four p.m. tomorrow.

"We should be done by six, and I'll need you here by midday tomorrow."

"That means I won't get to prom until nine or ten, and I'll have to leave again by two to make it back on time." The time difference will cost hours, and I'll have to contend with rush hour traffic en route to the airport, and that's assuming we can get a new flight time. The suite I booked at Chateau Marmont will go to waste too, along with all the plans I had for worshiping my girlfriend all night long. Fuck this shit. It's so fucking unfair. He's got to give me more than this. "I'll need to leave at four, and I can be back by two tomorrow."

"Reeve, this is the best compromise I can offer. I'm going out on a limb to ensure you get to attend prom in some capacity. Take it or leave it."

I am so fucking pissed, and Vivien is going to be upset. But getting to show up for prom is better than missing it entirely. "I'll take it," I say through gritted teeth.

I have decided not to tell Vivien I will be showing up later because I won't let her down a second time should anything happen and the director reneges on his word. At least it will be a surprise if things work out. I already left a message for Alex so he knows to ensure Vivien stays at prom until I arrive. I plan to text him updates when I'm en route. My nerves are hanging by a thread as I make the call I've been dreading.

"Are you on the plane?" she asks in a gleeful tone, and nausea swims up my throat.

"Viv. About that."

"No, Reeve. Please don't say what I think you're going to say."

Pain crashes into my chest. "I'm so sorry, baby, but I'm not going to be able to make it after all."

"Why?" she chokes out and I feel like the biggest piece of shit.

"Something weird happened overnight. The last few shots we filmed yesterday were corrupted, so the director called us in this morning to reshoot them. I tried to get out of it, but it wasn't possible. We're on a really tight schedule, and there are no other gaps to reshoot them. I'm so sorry, baby. I'm as devastated by this as you are."

"I hate this. It's so unfair," she quietly says, and my heart is shredded matter in my chest. I can hear how upset she is, but she's trying to put on a brave face for me.

"I know. The guys were giving me crap because I was on the verge of tears, but I'm really upset. I don't want to miss tonight, and I would happily trade a limb if it meant I could be there. For years, I have dreamed of holding you in my arms all night at prom. I had booked a suite at Chateau Marmont as a surprise, and I was looking forward to ravishing your body all night long. I'm so sorry, Vivien, more than I can even say."

"I don't want to go without you, and I hate that prom is ruined for us, but this isn't your fault, Reeve. There isn't anything you can do, so don't feel guilty. It is what it is."

Her voice sounds devoid of all emotion, and this is hurting her bad. She's downplaying it because she doesn't want to worry me. But this is the worst news ever. She's been working on her dress for months, and we've both been clinging to this reunion. Things are strained between us, and we desperately need time together. I'm tempted to tell her I'll be there, but it will only hurt her more if something else happens and I don't show at all. Who knows what shit is going down on set. If footage can go missing last night, it's not inconceivable to imagine we might run into issues today. I am praying it doesn't come to that. I'm praying I get to spend some time with her at prom, but it's pretty much out of my hands.

As much as this is killing me and hurting her, it's better than having to make a second apologetic call.

"Viv. Baby, are you still there?" I ask, realizing she's been silent while I've been ruminating in my head.

"Yes. Sorry. I'm here."

"I want you to go to prom. Please don't stay at home alone. You know you can go with Alex and Audrey, and they'll ensure you have a good time. And I need to see photos. I've been imagining seeing you in, and out of, that dress for months." I'm expecting to have to force her into going, so I'm pleasantly surprised when she agrees without argument.

"I'll send you pictures, and I'll try my best to enjoy prom even if I'll be missing you every second of every minute of the night."

Chapter Twenty-One
Now

My phone pings with a text from Alex as I climb out of the car at the hotel and hand my keys to the valet.

I stride confidently through the lobby and down the hallway, heading toward the section of bathrooms just outside the ballroom where the prom is taking place. I'm almost gagging at the Hollywood theme. It's so cliché and unoriginal. I nod and say a quick hi to people I know as I pass by, but I don't stop, purposely avoiding being dragged into a conversation.

I'm here for one reason and one reason only—my Vivien—and I'm not wasting a second of our precious time on anyone else.

Reaching the restrooms, I plaster my back to the wall beside the door, hiding as best I can because I want to surprise her. Luckily, she's the next person to exit the bathroom, wearing her prom queen crown on her head, the corsage I sent her on her wrist, and looking more gorgeous than seems humanly possible.

I cover her eyes from behind and press up against her, feeling the bare skin at her back brush against the front of my tux. A hint of side boob has lust instantly stirring down south, and the beast in my pants roars to life. A little shriek rips from her lips, and it's time to show her I'm here. "Don't scream. It's only me." Lowering my hands, I drink her in as she whips around to face me.

She is a vision in a gorgeous red gown that takes my breath away. It molds to her full breasts, slim waist, and slender hips before falling to the floor. A sequined strip hems the dress at the collar, the sides of her tits, and in a line from the curve of her hip to the bottom of the gown.

Our eyes meet, and I instantly feel at home. Emotion stabs the backs of my eyes as hers fill up. Vivien throws her arms around my neck, suctioning her tempting body to mine, and my arms automatically band around her as we hold one another close. Warmth from the skin on her back seeps into my flesh, heating every part of me. Closing my eyes, I inhale the delicate floral scent of my girl and savor the feel of her in my arms.

I have missed her more than is normal.

Brushing her hair aside, I bury my face in her neck. "I've missed you so much, baby." The words aren't enough to properly convey how lost I have felt without her and how much I have craved her company. I dot kisses all over her neck, smiling when she shivers as I kiss that spot she loves just under her ear.

"Reeve." Her tone carries need and longing that match my own. I'm primed to explode. I need my woman in every conceivable way. Arching her neck, she presents herself to me, and I dive in, dragging my lips up and down the elegant column of her neck as she explores my back over my jacket. "I have missed you so damn much. It's been the worst pain."

Pain adequately describes the steel rod in my pants, pressing against my zipper. I need to be inside her. I need to connect with her in the most intimate way. I want to look into her eyes as I drive deep inside her, reminding her that I am hers and she is mine. Cementing all the ways we are perfect for one another and eliminating the stress of the past couple months. "I need to taste you," I say, lifting my head.

I can't wait a second longer to kiss her. I cup her beautiful face and bring my lips to hers. Viv holds on to my jacket, desperate to pull me even closer, and my heart is beating in tandem with hers and rejoicing. The kiss starts off tender but quickly transforms as every emotion I've been battling during our separation surges to the forefront. I devour her mouth, sweeping my tongue inside, demanding everything, and she gives it to me. Thrusting my hips, I poke her with my erection, grabbing on to her with even greater need when she moans into my mouth.

We move as one, pressed against the wall, touching and grinding against one another as our mouths drink greedily in a heady bid to consume one another. It's everything. She's everything. Everything I have been missing. Everything I need and want. As close as we are, it's not enough. I want to feel her clenching around me as I pound my cock into her pussy, but time is limited, and I don't want her to think I only came here for sex. For years, we have dreamed of dancing at prom, and I won't deny Vivien it. "I don't have much time," I pant against her lips.

"How long?" she asks, tearing her mouth from mine.

"My car will return in ninety minutes."

"Then let's make every second count."

I'm silently fist pumping the air when she grabs my hand and yanks me into the wheelchair-accessible bathroom. I lock the door, and when I turn around, Vivien is on her knees, looking up at me with dilated pupils and so much lust and love on her face that my legs almost go out from under me. She reaches for my zipper, and my cock is leaking precum like I'm a horny thirteen-year-old again, jerking off twice daily to thoughts of my best friend with her mouth on me. "Jesus, Viv."

This is even better than any fantasy I've ever had.

"I need to taste you too." She pulls my pants and boxers down while licking her lips, and I'm a goner.

"Fuck. You look beautiful, Viv," I say, my eyes rolling when she licks the tip. I spread my thighs wider. "I'm dying for you, baby. You have no idea how much."

She goes to town on my dick, and I gently thread my fingers through her hair as she sucks me off, already feeling a tingle in my balls. "Viv. I'm not going to last long, and I need to be inside you."

I pull her to her feet, stripping my pants and boxers fully away as I watch her lean back against the sink with her dress yanked up to her waist. She's wearing red lace panties, and I almost come on the spot. Tugging on my dick, I stalk toward her with purpose. "I love you," I say, wrapping her leg around my waist as I line my cock up at her entrance. "And I wish I had all night to show you how much." I thought we'd have hours tonight, and I had plans for ravishing her in so many positions. A quick fuck in the hotel bathroom was not on the agenda, and she deserves so much more, but neither of us can deny our mutual need.

I need to be inside my baby. NOW.

"You're here, Reeve." She drags her fingers through the stubble on my cheeks. "That's all the proof I need."

I drive into her in one fast thrust, and she cries out before my lips descend in a claiming kiss. I plunge into her heat like a man possessed as we kiss like it's going out of fashion. I cannot get enough of her, and she seems to feel the same. We're clawing at one another with lips, teeth, and hands as I fuck into her with savage need.

There's an intensity to our fucking that is hinged in desperation. I can't get deep enough. I want to bury myself so far inside her she never doubts what we mean to one another. I want to imprint her with my cock and write my name on her heart, but I can't get deep enough like this.

Proving how in sync we are, Vivien moves to pull herself up onto the counter so I can bury myself deeper. I pull out for a few seconds while I help her to get settled, and then I plunge back in. Her legs fasten around my waist, and she pivots her hips as I thrust deep, deep, deeper. "Oh God, Reeve," she rasps in between kisses, "you feel so freaking good."

"Fuck, Viv. I want to stay buried inside you forever. This feels incredible." Keeping a firm hold on her hips, I shove my dick really deep, and stars burst behind my eyes as her cunt hugs my cock so tight.

Sex with Viv is always phenomenal, but this is on a whole other level. I continue driving into her like a madman, knowing I won't be able to hold off any longer. Viv grips me hard as her back arches, pressing her tits into my chest and screaming as she gives into the orgasm tearing through her like lightning.

It's all I need to follow her over the edge, and I'm grunting and roaring her name as I fill her with my cum. I rest my head on her shoulder as I slowly come down from the best sex of my life. Holy fucking shit. Maybe long separations won't be so bad if this is the kind of reunion we have to look forward to.

"Wow," she whispers. "I think we needed that."

She's grinning as I say, "I love you," and then I kiss her, pouring all my affection into the soft, lingering kiss. I love her so fucking much. I don't have the words to adequately describe it. With her touch, Vivien has soothed all the frayed parts of my soul and made them whole again.

If it was an option, I'd get down on bended knee right now and beg her to marry me.

I stay inside her as we tenderly kiss, and it's almost impossible to pull away from her, but I manage it because I want to give her as much of the prom experience as I can before I have to go. "I would love nothing more than to spend my time balls deep inside you, but it's prom, and I promised you some dancing."

"You did." She is smiling as we both clean up and get dressed. "You look gorgeous," she adds, and warmth floods my chest.

"Stop stealing my lines." I encircle her waist from behind, and we look at one another in the mirror. "You are stunning, Vivien Grace. More beautiful than any mere mortal. You are a goddess among women."

"Thank you." Her gaze shines with emotion when she twists around in my arms to look at me. "Thank you for being here. I can't express how happy I am to see you."

"I'm sorry our plans were ruined." I kiss the back of her hand. "And I wish I could stay all night, but I had to beg the director to give me a few hours off."

"I don't care." Her hand lands on my chest. "I'll take whatever time I can get with you."

I pepper her stunning face with kisses before brushing my lips against hers in a fleeting kiss. "I hate being separated from you." I pull her closer. "It's the worst form of torture."

"I know. It's been killing me too."

I rub my nose against hers. "You're my home, Viv," I softly admit.

"I know what you mean." She palms my face. "Everything feels right when you're with me."

I take her hand in mine. "Then let's make the most of our time, because it's got to last us another month before I'm back home." I let my gaze rake over her again. "Damn, Viv. You're breathtaking, and that dress is exquisite." She is such a talented designer, and I'm in awe of her skill.

I keep hold of her hand as we make our way into the hall, ignoring classmates who reach for me and making a beeline for the dance floor. Alex approaches with a wide smile, slapping me on the back before he places my prom king crown on my head. I kiss Audrey on the cheek, and then my woman is in my arms as we sway to the music, grinning at one another like the lovesick fools we are.

My eyes latch on to Vivien's as we dance, and I have never felt closer to her. This right here is what makes it all worth it. I don't care that it took me hours to get here for precious minutes of time. I would do it all again to get to spend it in her presence. There is something so intimate about gazing into her eyes for long moments in time as I feel her body heat wrapped around me like a security blanket and know her heart is beating as fast as mine.

I twirl her around, basking in the glow on her face and the happiness that flows from her tinkling laughter. Even the sight of that idiot Nate doesn't detract from the joy I'm feeling tonight. I'm not wasting treasured minutes with Vivien to handle that prick. I'll deal with him when I'm home for the summer. He is right to cower in fear because he's not getting away with that little stunt he pulled.

Tossing the jerk from my head, I focus all my attention on Vivien, raining kisses on her as we dance and grind and work up a sweat.

All too fast, the night is drawing to a close, and my chariot awaits. It pains me to pull myself away, but I have no choice.

Viv insists on coming with me, and I don't protest. I'd have kidnapped her if she hadn't suggested it. The instant the driver deploys the privacy screen in the car, we're all over one another, kissing and groping like it's our first time making out.

The private jet is waiting for me when we hit the runway, and tears are pouring down Vivien's face. My heart hurts too, but I'm trying to be strong for her. "I love you." I wipe her tears away with my thumbs and my lips. "I love you so much, Vivien. Even when we are not together, you are my world."

"I love you too," she croaks, swiping at more tears as they leak from her eyes. "I'm on a countdown until you come home."

"We're at the final hurdle, and I'll be home before you know it."

"I'll be waiting."

I kiss her passionately, hugging her close. "Be brave, my love," I whisper in her ear before pressing my lips to hers one final time. My eyes shutter as I commit it all to memory. I'll need it to keep me going these next few weeks because tearing myself away from her again is as painful as the first time. "I love you forever, Vivien Grace. Never forget."

Then I climb out of the car and don't look back. I'm afraid if I do, I'll never get on the plane.

Chapter Twenty-Two
Now

"Hey, man, open up." Rudy raps on my trailer door as I lie sideways on the couch, tossing a stress ball into the air as I absently watch TV. I sigh as I swing my legs around and stand. Yawning loudly, I run a hand through my hair before walking to the door and opening it. I step aside to let my friend in.

"Have we been called back early?" I inquire, closing the door after him. The girls are filming back-to-back scenes today, and we were only needed on set once this morning, and we have another scene later where all the main characters are together.

Rudy dumps a large paper bag on the small table before bending down to the refrigerator. "Nope." He grabs two sodas and joins me on the couch with the drinks and the bags. "Snatched a couple of burritos from the food truck," he says, driving his hand into the bag and handing me a foil-wrapped package.

"Thanks." I pop the top on my soda and reluctantly

unwrap my burrito. I haven't had much of an appetite recently. Heartbreak can do that to a man.

"You're coming to the bar with us tonight," he says in between mouthfuls of spicy goodness.

I shake my head. "I'm not in the mood." I've been melancholy since prom. It's not as bad as it was at the start of filming, but only because I have a handy stash of pills to help me sleep at night and more to perk me up during the day. It's not a problem. I don't take them all the time, and I'm not addicted.

"Come on, dude." He nudges my shoulder. "We only have three weeks left, and we need to make the most of it." We stay in various hotels while on location, but it's always late when we get back there. The cast and crew usually take over the hotel bar for a nightcap, but it's not my scene. I pop a Xanax after my nightly call with Viv and then crash.

"I'm focusing on work."

"You're throwing a pity party for one, and I'm staging an intervention."

"Why do you care?" I ask before taking a reluctant bite of my burrito.

"We're buddies. And buddies don't let one another drown. I know you miss her, but you're gonna see her soon. She wouldn't want you moping around and isolating yourself from everyone." He nudges my shoulder again. "Come on, movie star. Live a little."

"I'll think about it." I won't. I have zero interest in going out drinking tonight.

Rudy scarfs the rest of his burrito before greedily eyeing mine.

"Have at it." I thrust it into his hand, chuckling as he devours it in record time.

He flashes me his signature grin before standing. "Saff wants you to drop by her trailer. Something about a script change for the pool scene tomorrow? She's on a break but due back in twenty."

Don't know why she couldn't have stopped by, but whatever. It's not like I have far to walk. "Okay." I shove my feet into sneakers and exit my trailer with Rudy. He heads toward the mobile gym trailer, most likely to heckle the guys while they train. It's actually a container attached to a semitruck. It comes with us to every location, and we meet the trainer there early every morning to get our workouts in. There is a lot of downtime on location, so we often head to the gym during the day for some quick cardio or to lift weights.

I raise my hand to knock on Saffron's trailer door when it swings open, and a disheveled-looking Wen looms over me. I narrow my eyes at my errant assistant. He's still an ass, and I can never find him when I need him.

"Reeve." He grins as he attempts to tame his hair. "I was just dropping off the updated scripts."

Yeah, buddy. I'm sure you were, I think as he wanders off. It's not like I care if he's banging my costar. I have no clue what is going on with her and Jeremy. It's unsurprising they're not exclusive, and it's none of my business. I have zero interest in Saff's sex life, so I never ask her.

"Hey, movie star." Saff appears before me, wearing a vibrant red silk robe that hits just below her knee. Although her hair isn't wet, beads of water cling to her bare legs and the slip of skin exposed at her collarbone, confirming she just took a shower. "Come in." She smiles as she steps back to let me in.

"I'll wait here," I supply, earning a fleeting scowl. "I just came for the new script."

She turns to grab some papers from the table. "That wasn't what it looks like," she says, walking toward me.

"It's none of my business who you fuck," I say, leaning against the doorway.

"It wasn't me." She thrusts the script at me. "He's bumping uglies with Nadine and just came from the makeup truck." Nadine is one of the younger hairstylists and far too sweet for a jerk like Wen if you ask me.

"What's changed?" I ask, ignoring her attempts to drag me into a gossipy conversation. I flip through the pages.

"Some of the dialogue has been updated, and they want you to remove my bikini top now." She shrugs, and I know it's no biggie.

Unlike lots of actresses, Saff didn't insist on any nudity clauses in her contract. She has no issue flashing flesh on the screen. I won't lie and say sex scenes are something I look forward to filming, but I've gotten out of my head, and I'm able to act professional on set. Except for that first disastrous scene, I have never gotten hard when acting out intimate scenes with my costar. Pretending to fuck her tomorrow in the pool, with her bare chest pressed against mine, won't turn me on either because she's not the girl I lust after. Saffron is like the supportive yet sometimes annoying older sister I never had.

"Okay." I roll the script up. "Thanks for this." Again, not sure why she summoned me to her trailer when Wen should have delivered my copy to me. But whatever.

I resist peer pressure and avoid hanging out at the hotel bar that night, but the following night, all the main cast and some of the younger crew members are staying at the mansion where we're filming for a few days, and there is no avoiding the party in full swing at midnight.

"Movie star!" Saff hollers from the pool. "Get your sexy ass in here." She stretches her arms back against the edge of the pool, displaying her bare tits for everyone to see. It's too hard to tell, even with the outdoor lighting, but I'm guessing pretty much every guy in the pool is sporting a semi or a full-blown boner if the looks they're shooting her way are any indication.

Jolina and Nadine are the only other girls here and both are wearing bikini tops. Wen has Nadine pushed into the corner and his hands are all over her. Jolina and Rudy are fucking around while the other guys are sipping beers and ogling Saffron. I've been hanging back on a lounger, slowly sipping a beer and reading, trying not to look like a party pooper. I only got off the phone with Viv an hour ago, and I'm missing her like crazy tonight.

"Dude, come on," Jacob calls, swimming up to the ledge nearest me. "The water is heated, and it's a great de-stressor."

They're all going to gang up on me, so I might as well just give in now. Setting down my phone and book, I pull my shirt over my head and toss it on the lounger.

"Take 'em off, movie star," Saff teases before whistling. Her eyes roam me from head to toe, and I roll my eyes.

She's incorrigible sometimes.

"The shorts stay on." I pin her with a look before I dive into the pool, spraying water everywhere. When I surface, they're all shouting at me, and I grin.

"Come talk to me," Saffron drawls, eyeballing me as she hits a blunt.

I swim over and rest my back against the wall, keeping a reasonable distance between us, before I kick my legs out in front of me.

"You need to relax," she says, passing the blunt to me. "I'm worried about you."

I hate everyone babying me. "I'm fine." I accept the blunt and take a drag.

"Don't lie." Saff peers at me with a puckered brow. "You've been all mopey since prom."

"It was hard seeing Viv and then having to leave so quickly. It reminded me of everything I'm missing one-hundred-fold."

We pass the blunt back and forth, and I feel the stress lift from my tense limbs.

"I told you it wasn't a good idea to do that. You pulled yourself out of the zone, and now you're paying for it."

"My acting is not suffering." I'm nailing it on set, and Nick hasn't said anything to me.

"You're miserable as sin, Reeve, and don't think it isn't showing. You could perform any scene in your sleep, but the passion you bring to everything is lacking. You know you're capable of more."

"Fuck off, Saff." She's starting to irritate me. I'm more than pulling my weight on set and this is just bullshit. "If I wasn't cutting it, Nick would be all over my balls."

She turns to the side and grips my chin so I'm forced to look at her. I'm trying not to look at her tits, but they're right there in my face, bobbing above the water. Her tits are fucking huge with big nipples and wide areolas, and while plenty of guys would get off on them, they're actually a big turn-off for me.

Vivien is a C-cup, and her tits are perfection. Pert little nipples, small pink areolas, and breasts that are more than a handful but not so big they're like two flopping mountains perched on her chest.

Saff looks like she's about to topple over some days because she's so small with this massive rack that looks disproportionate. Most of the guys on set are going gaga over her tits and loving how freely she flashes the goods, but I'm not most guys.

They do nothing for me.

My dick didn't so much as nod in her direction today during the filming of our last sex scene and she had her chest pushed up against my bare one and her legs were wrapped around my waist as we made out for the camera.

Sometimes, I wonder if it pisses her off I don't get hard for her during scenes. If there's one thing I've learned about

Saffron Roberts, it's that she loves being the center of attention. She loves watching men fall over themselves to worship at her altar. While our relationship is more akin to siblings, I think she's arrogant enough to be annoyed that I don't seem to be attracted to her like every other male on this set.

It's hard to ignore her when she's semi-naked right in front of me, and I wish she'd put her fucking top back on.

"Earth to movie star." She snaps her fingers in my face. "You were on another planet." She smirks, and my cheeks heat when I realize she thinks I was looking at her. It's possible when I zoned out my gaze was trained on her tits, and now I'm mad at myself. Viv would chop my balls off if she knew. Guilt is instant, and I pull back, placing more distance between us.

"I'm exhausted," I say, and it's no lie. "And I could do without you busting my balls. I'm missing my girl, and as long as it's not interfering with my role, I don't see how it's any of your business or Rudy's or anyone else's."

"We care about you," she says, closing the distance I just created and placing her hand on my arm. "Maybe because you're the youngest on set, and as the leading man, you have so much pressure on your shoulders. Or it's just we all know you're a good guy. You're well-liked, Reeve. Is it so bad people care about you?" Her big eyes shine with concern, and I feel like a bit of a prick for being so testy with her.

"No, it's not." I run a hand over my wet hair. "Sorry if I'm off right now. I'll snap out of it. I swear."

"I'm here for you. We're all here for you. If you need help with anything, you only have to ask."

Chapter Twenty-Three
Now

"You did what?" I yell, glaring at Cassidy as we FaceTime with Bianca, who is also in attendance. "You have no right to hack into my girlfriend's account and remove her post! That's fucking illegal, and I'll sue your ass," I bark, spewing the thoughts as they pop into my mind. Viv is going to throw a shit fit when I tell her about this. I'm betting the loving message I texted her first thing this morning and the flower delivery will be forgotten when she discovers what this bitch has done now. Just like prom, graduation has been tarnished, and I'm sick to my stomach.

"You should be fucking thanking me," Cassidy hurls back, her face contorting into an ugly grimace. "That little bitch is doing everything to ruin your reputation and sabotage this movie before it's even released! I'm saving your ungrateful ass!"

"Don't you fucking dare call her that!" Cassidy is lucky she isn't here because I might've thrown a punch for that remark. "And how the hell is my girl doing that? She only tagged me in a post, for fuck's sake." Vivien has been really good about not posting any pics of me or making any reference to me. She's also not reacting to the trolls who are spouting trash about her online, and she's not retaliated any time a Reeveron supporter has tried to bait her into responding. What more do they want of her?

I pace the floor of my trailer, growing more agitated by the second. "How dare you do this." I jab my finger at the screen. "This is not okay, and I'll be making a formal complaint. You can't do this."

"I think you'll find I can." She sits back in her chair and pins me with a smug smile that does nothing to dampen my ire.

"Reeve, you need to calm down," Bianca says, joining the conversation for the first time. I'm guessing that's why Cassidy brought her in on this call. "Cassidy may have gone about this the wrong way"—Cassidy levels her glare on my agent, and Bianca drills her with a warning look—"but she isn't wrong in her assessment." Bianca cocks her head to the side as her features soften. "I know you love Vivien, Reeve, but she isn't helping you. I thought you spoke to her about the importance of you appearing single? Keep your relationship clandestine, and no one has any issue with it. But Vivien tagging you in a post is anything but a secret. She needs to understand how damaging this could be for you. She didn't leave Cassidy much choice."

I narrow my eyes at the studio publicist. "That is fucking ridiculous! Celebrities get tagged nonstop on social media, and other friends have been tagging me in graduation posts all day!"

"This isn't about anyone else. It's about you and Vivien. You two have a public history we are trying to separate you from. She's not just some random person tagging you!" Cassidy retorts, spittle flying from her mouth.

"So what!? That doesn't necessarily blow my single-person cover! We've been friends our whole lives. We're practically family!"

Cassidy bolts upright and pokes her finger at the screen.

"That damn birthday fiasco was only a few weeks ago. In case you've forgotten, you professed your love, and thousands saw it before it was taken down. People are not idiots. Her tagging you so soon after that proves there is still a connection between you. A connection that cannot exist. A connection we're trying to confirm is in the past."

I still think they are completely overreacting, but I'm tired of going around in circles. It's really stressing me out. "You should've called me, and I would've asked Viv to remove it without the need to invade her privacy," I say through gritted teeth, working hard to restrain my anger. Every time I think of what she did, I'm beyond enraged.

"Be reasonable, Reeve," Bianca says. "You were on set all day."

"The longer it was live, the more damaging it was," Cassidy says.

"I don't agree, and why did you remove her post entirely? All you had to do was remove the tag and remove it from my profile."

"She could've re-added the tag, and I wasn't taking any chances. I had to make a judgment call, and I stand by it. I'd do it again if I had to."

"Do it again, and I *will* sue your ass. I'll also tell her parents and let them bring the full weight of their power and influence down upon you. Don't fucking think I'm joking, Cassidy. You leave my girlfriend alone!" I don't want to drag Viv's parents into the mess I've created, but I'll swallow my pride and do it if they continue to harass Vivien.

Cassidy freezes for a few seconds, as my threat settles in the air between us, before she swings her gaze to Bianca. My agent ignores her, looking directly at me. Her eye twitches for a fleeting moment, but otherwise, she's as composed as ever.

"No one is suing anybody over anything." Bianca leans her

elbows on the table and presses her face closer to the screen. "Cassidy won't do anything without your permission in the future, but you need to relax and let this blow over. At least we curtailed the damage before it could hurt. I'm sure I don't need to tell you how sensitive the timing is. We're entering the last stage of negotiations for the next two movies, and you can't make a wrong move, Reeve. Nothing is confirmed until you have signed on the dotted line."

"While it's rare for leading men to be replaced," Cassidy cuts in, her snide tone meant to be grating, "if you refuse to play ball, that can be arranged."

"That's fucking crap, and you know it! They have no legitimate grounds to cut me out, and it makes no sense." Cassidy is talking through her ass. I didn't think it was possible to hate her any more than I already do, but she's just proven me wrong.

"Reeve. The studio is the one pushing for this," Bianca says. "They want the 'single man' agenda. Don't underestimate what they can and can't or will and won't do for this project. This is one of the biggest franchises they have backed. They are throwing everything at it because it has that much potential. This could be the biggest grossing movie of all time. Trust me when I say there is nothing the studio won't do to ensure it's a huge success."

If that is true, I am screwed. "My personal life has nothing to do with my professional life. There are plenty of happily married leading men who don't have to appear to be single. This is complete and utter bullshit." I plop down on the couch and prop my cell up on the table.

"You're eighteen years old, Reeve," Bianca continues. "Teenage girls expect hot young guys to be single so they can feed their fantasies. It's not the same situation. You need to appear to be available. You are naïve if you truly believe you can separate your personal and professional lives because you cannot. Not at this stage of your career and not with this project. The studio is already hearing rumors from the set. It's been said you are guarded and closed off since attending prom and moping like a little lovesick puppy. It's why I advised you to break up with her. You're making this so much harder on yourself than it needs to be."

Fucking Nick. He's clearly been blabbing to my agent behind my back, and I hate it. I'm not a little kid. I don't need anyone tattling to Bianca. "I'm doing my fucking job. I'm nailing the scenes, so I don't see how what I do in my spare time or how I behave has anything to do with this. It is no one's business but my own."

"What you do off-screen is just as important for this project. You're a hot commodity, Reeve, and it's going to get insane when the movie releases. The studio wants the buzz to start now, and we'll build upon it during the promo tour. The cast needs to be tight, just like the characters are. You and Saffron need to be close or appear to be close, just like Cam and Abby are. That means you can't shut your fellow actors out, and you need to hang out with them off set. How does it look when all the leading actors are regularly photographed together, and you're constantly missing? It's not selling the story enough, Reeve. I don't think you or Vivien are prepared, and you really need to get a handle on it. Vivien cannot continue to undermine you at every turn. She either plays along or she's got to go. I thought you wanted to succeed, or has that changed?"

"Of course, it hasn't." I rub the back of my neck. I haven't made sacrifices these past few months to walk away now. Nothing about my goals has changed. And that includes keeping my relationship. I'm not sacrificing Vivien for anything or anyone.

"Then you need to ensure Vivien understands. She can't

talk about you to anyone, and she most certainly cannot post anything incriminating on social media. If she believes in you like you say and she is a truly supportive girlfriend, then she won't have any issue with this. Faking shit for publicity is a time-honored tradition in Hollywood. With her pedigree, one would think she'd understand better than most." Bianca clasps her hands in front of her.

"If she doesn't fully understand, make her," Cassidy says with an evil glint in her eye. "You have all summer to drill the point home."

"Ensure you do it," Bianca adds.

<hr>

I take some time out to calm down before I call Vivien because I don't want to take my anger out on her. The more time I've had to consider it, the more I have to reluctantly concede that Bianca is right. I am still so fucking angry with Cassidy, and I will never approve of her methods, but she wants the movie to succeed. If this is a directive coming from the top, only an idiot would ignore it. I think it's grossly unfair, and I don't agree that life has to imitate art, but they call the shots. They can ruin my career before it's even taken flight, so I don't feel like I have much choice.

I hate I have to play their game, but I can't claim to be ignorant of the inner workings of Hollywood. I don't have to like it or agree with it to play my part. I just have to do what's required to ensure the movie knocks it out of the park when it releases. In the future, when I'm more established, I can tell them to take a hike. For now, I have to toe the line.

I'm not sure how I'll get Vivien to reach a point of understanding, but we have all summer to work through it. There are only three more days of filming left, and then I'll be on a plane back to Cali the next day. I can't wait to go home now.

"Do you know anything about my missing graduation post?" Viv asks the second she answers my call.

"I didn't know anything until after the fact." There is no easy way of sugarcoating this, and Vivien will not understand. All I can do is try to keep her calm, and I'll explain better when we're face to face. She's at Butthead's graduation party, and I don't want to ruin her night with this bullshit.

"What did Cassidy do?" she snaps, instantly understanding who is behind this.

Tension seeps into the air. I'm dreading telling her this. There is no way of making this palatable because it's vile. "I'm disgusted, Viv. I just want to put that out there first, and I've already ripped her a new one. It's not going to happen again."

"Spit it out, Reeve," she says as the noise in the background fades with her footsteps.

"She had someone hack into your account and remove it."

"She *what?!*" she shrieks. "She has no right to do that! I'm going to sue her fucking ass. The studio too. Who the hell do these people think they are?"

I'm not surprised her reaction is the same as mine. "I get you're pissed. I am too. It's the closest I've ever come to wanting to hit a woman, but we can't do anything about it."

"You can't, but I can!"

I hear her pacing and can almost see the gears grinding in her head. "Babe. You can't. Not without it affecting me."

"You're almost finished filming."

"There are still reshoots, promo, the premiere, and the potential of more movies. You know this, Viv." I finally admitted there were negotiations taking place for the next two movies, but I didn't make a big deal of it because, like Bianca said, until I have signed on the dotted line, nothing is set in stone. "I can't do anything to rock the boat, and that means you can't either."

"What was her objection this time?" she asks after a few moments. "You weren't even in the photo with me."

Exhaustion shrouds me as every bone in my body feels like it's on the verge of collapse. Shooting this movie has been intense, stressful, and draining, and I'm grateful it's almost over as I need to sleep for like a hundred years. "You tagged me," I admit in a resigned tone. It's preposterous. The whole thing. But I can't keep fighting the machine.

"So, are you saying I can't tag my boyfriend in posts now?"

"No. You can't. They don't want any ties linking us together. They need me to appear to be single." I have danced around this before, but the time for pussyfooting is over.

"I think they'd put a bullet through my skull if they thought they'd get away with it." Pain underscores her words, and it hurts me.

"Don't say that! Of course, they wouldn't. It's just semantics."

"It's not just semantics, Reeve. Don't insult my intelligence."

"I don't know what you want me to say here, Viv." I'm beat, and I don't want to argue with her over the phone. "This is my career, and we both know this bullshit is the norm in the industry."

"I know all that, but you can't let these people manipulate every aspect of your life, Reeve! Are you really sure this role is worth it?"

What the fuck? Not only has she insulted me by suggesting I'm too weak to stand up to these people when I've been fighting them every step of the way, but now she's questioning the validity of my work? My goals? After everything I've been through and everything we have sacrificed as a couple to get to this point? Does she not support me? Is Bianca right? When it comes to crunch time, am I the only one who's prepared to stick to our plan?

Simmering anger lingers in my veins, and I work hard to keep my tone level when I say, "You know how much this part means to me, Viv. This is one of the biggest studios in the biz. This role will make or break my career. I thought you supported me, but I'm beginning to wonder if that's really the truth."

"Now you're being unfair. Of course, I support you, but I didn't realize I'd have to become your dirty little secret!" she screeches.

"Babe, c'mon. You know it's not like that. Who cares what anyone else thinks? You know I'm yours and you're mine. As long as we're solid, it doesn't matter what the press says."

"It matters to *me*, Reeve. Do you think this is easy for me? To have people say I'm not good enough for you? That *she's* more deserving of you? Now, I can't post about us, or talk about us, because I have to pretend like I'm not your girlfriend? In what realm do you ever think I'd be okay with that?"

"It's not going to be forever, and we know the truth, as do our friends and the people who matter. Everything else is industry bullshit, but it's a necessary evil." This is the only way we can do this. She has seen the shit her parents have gone through, so if anyone should understand, it's the daughter of Hollywood's most celebrated golden couple.

"What happened to the guy who spoke so eloquently about wanting to be known for his acting ability, not his celebrity status? What asshole has been whispering shit in your ear, hmm, Reeve?"

"I was naïve to think one existed without the other," I grit out, struggling to rein in my anger. "I have a role to play on-screen and off of it."

"God, Reeve. Do you even hear yourself? You're already indoctrinated."

"I'm doing what I need to do to establish my career!" I yell, losing the tenuous hold on my emotions.

"Well then, you continue doing that. Continue putting yourself first, Reeve, because you're so good at it."

"That is not fucking fair, and you know it. I'm always considerate of you! Why do you think I'm arguing with Cassidy and Bianca so much? It's because I'm thinking of you!"

Silence greets my ears, and I stare at my phone in shock.

She hung up on me.

Viv hung up on me.

Rage, unlike anything I've felt before, batters me from all sides. I'm tempted to throw my cell at the wall, but there's a better way to vent all this frustration. Grabbing my jacket and bag, I tap out a message to Rudy telling him I'm en route to the hotel and I'll meet him at the bar.

Chapter Twenty-Four
Then - Age 13

My hands are clammy as I wait in the treehouse for Vivien to show up. I check my watch again and pace the floor as I rub my hands down the front of my uniform pants. Her creative writing class should be finished by now, so what's keeping her? I'm not sure my nerve will hold much longer if she doesn't appear soon.

"Reeve!" she calls out from below, and my heart starts thumping wildly against my rib cage like it's trying to take flight.

"I'm here," I holler, hoping she can't hear the terror in my voice. It's still so weird hearing myself sound so gruff. I thought my voice would break gradually, but it almost happened overnight. Vivien teases me relentlessly, but I've also noticed her blushing and staring at me with big, googly eyes sometimes when we're deep in conversation. I think she likes it but she's too shy to say.

Which I can't tease her about as I've been afraid to say lots of things for ages now. I'm still too chickenshit to tell her I love her in a way that is more than friendly. If she knew I jerk off every morning and at night thinking about her soft lips wrapped around my dick, she'd be horrified. I'm sure she doesn't have thoughts like that, but I can't help it. I'm like a walking hard-on around her these days, and it's not getting any better. I wanted to ask Jonathon about it, but I can hardly tell him I'm lusting over his daughter, so I was forced to go to Simon. Not that he was much help. All he said was it was normal, which wasn't very useful.

"Sorry I'm late," she says, popping her head in the door. "I asked Dad to make a detour on the way home." She's grinning as she walks toward me, flipping her long dark hair over one shoulder as she hides something behind her back.

I'm not the only one changing. Viv has shot up these past few months, and she's only a few inches shorter than me now. She also wears a bra, and I've tried not to stare at her tits, but it's challenging when I'm obsessed with her and jacking off to images of her naked.

Heat creeps up my neck, and I hope she doesn't notice. I love her for more than her pretty face and body. I love her wild spirit, her twin soul, her intelligence, her kindness toward others, and the ballsy way she defends her friends when they're under attack. I love how she can lift my sadness when Simon has done something to upset me. I love how she's always got my back and how easy she is to talk to. I love that I know her secrets, and she knows mine. I could keep going, but she's staring at me with a faltering expression. "What's wrong?"

"Nothing." I tuck a piece of hair behind her ear, watching the blush stain her cheeks, hoping and praying it means what I think it does.

"I got you something." She thrusts a book at me. "I thought it might help with your audition."

I found out yesterday I have my first audition for a small recurring role on a TV show in two weeks. I don't have many lines, but Viv promised to help me to prepare. It's the reason I've been pacing anxiously waiting for her.

"It's an audition book," she explains as I open it up and flip through the pages. "I've seen Mom with them in the past, and I thought it might be a good idea to get into a routine you can apply with every new part you get because this is only the beginning." She squeezes my hand. "I'm so proud of you, Reeve, and I just know you're going to be a massive star."

Emotion swells in my chest as I flick through the book. It has advice, suggestions, and techniques for various types of auditions and interviews with blank pages for notes. It's perfect.

Just like she is.

I act on pure gut instinct, without nerves or second-guessing myself, as I lean in and press my lips to hers, pouring everything I'm feeling into the kiss. My eyes are closed and I'm basking in the feel of her soft lips against mine and my awe at sharing our first kiss, so I don't realize she isn't kissing me back at first.

When I notice, I jerk my mouth away and straighten up, swallowing over a lump in my throat as I study her still form. Viv is staring at me with wide eyes, but she's as still as a statue, and I'm instantly terrified I've misread everything and ruined our friendship.

"I need to practice kissing," I blurt, putting the book down on the window ledge. "It's part of my audition, and you said you'd help." Butterflies are skating around my chest and I feel a little sick as I try to present a plausible explanation for my actions. If she's not into it, I can just claim it was an experiment. For my audition. It's what I planned to say anyway before I got caught up in the moment and kissed her because I just wanted to. Because I'm fed up with waiting when I have wanted to kiss her for so damn long.

"Well then," she says, moving in closer to me and linking her fingers in mine. The dazed look is gone from her eyes, replaced with excitement, and her cheeks are as red as strawberries, but she's smiling. "We should get to it. We can't have you failing."

My heart is thrashing around my chest, jumping cartwheels, and throwing a party. "Are you sure?" I ask, tipping my head down as my eyes greedily latch on to her lips. They're glossy from my kiss, and it thrills me. Things are stirring in my pants, and I silently beg my dick to calm down. I don't want to freak her out.

"Yes." Vivien lifts her chin, and her eyes are twinkling. "Kiss me, Reeve."

So, I do. This time, I'm no less excited, but I don't just plant one on her. I lean in slowly, maintaining eye contact, as my mouth moves toward hers. This time, she isn't in shock, and she kisses me back when my mouth presses to hers. Our kissing is tentative and clumsy because neither of us has done this before. I know because we talked about it recently. I thought it might have been an opportunity to kiss her then, but I was a pussy and too afraid to make a move.

Sliding my arm around her back, I tuck her in close as I angle my head like I've seen Jonathon do with Lauren when he's kissing her. Viv grabs on to my waist as we kiss, and I'm in heaven. I imagined this for so long, but it's even better than my dreams. I'm tingly all over and so happy I feel like I could burst. We kiss for a little longer, growing more confident, and I never want it to end, but my dick is painfully hard and I don't want to scare her. So, I break away first, grinning at her like the lovesick idiot I am.

"Um." Her cheeks are on fire again, and it's adorable. Vivien is usually confident in everything she does, so seeing her like this, knowing I'm responsible for her blush, makes me feel proud. "That was nice."

"It was." It was way more than nice, but we'll go with that if she likes.

"But you should probably practice more. Like way more so that by the time of your audition you're a pro."

My grin expands. I should tell her I only have to kiss the actress on the cheek, but that would end this early, and I'll take all the kisses I can steal from Vivien Grace Mills.

"Sounds like a plan." I twirl a lock of her hair around my finger. "Meet me here every day at this time?"

"It's a date! Or not!" She's all flustered, and I think it might be because she likes me as much as I like her.

"We should probably do it again one more time before we go in for dinner," I suggest because I'm a greedy little prick. "You know, because we're such novices."

She nods while dragging her lower lip through her teeth. "That is smart. Practice does make perfect after all."

I'm going to enjoy practicing with you, I think as I cup her face and lean in to kiss her again.

Chapter Twenty-Five
Now

"Reeve!" Vivien calls out, racing toward me when I emerge from the private jet and begin descending the stairs. My heart rejoices at the sight of her. All throughout the trip, I've been wondering what kind of reception I'd receive. Things have been extra strained since she hung up on me a few nights ago. We spoke the next day, and she apologized, but there's this wall between us now, a growing divide I'm scared of because we're only at the start of this journey, and it's going to get worse.

Hitting the end of the stairs, I drop my bags and run to meet her, closing the gap as she barrels into my arms. Relief is immediate as her floral scent wafts around me, and the familiarity of her touch grounds me. Our lips meet in a deep kiss I feel all the way to my toes. My arms suction her to me as we kiss, and every brush of our lips melts away months of stress. I'm home now, and I'm going to repair all the cracks in our relationship until we're stronger than ever.

"I love you," I murmur against her mouth when we finally surface for air.

"Not as much as I love you. I'm so happy you're home." Tears well in her eyes as her fingers caress my clean-shaven cheeks. "You look more like you."

I have to maintain my current hairstyle, at least until I know if we're filming more movies, but I purposely chose to shave today because I knew she'd like it. It feels a little weird, like I'm semi-naked after months of wearing a stylish layer of stubble on my chin and cheeks.

"I'm still me, baby." I tuck her into my side as I walk back to grab my bags.

"I know. I know." She's quiet as she wraps her arms fully around me while we walk toward the AMG GT that was an eighteenth-birthday gift from her parents. "I hate everything that went down. Can we just forget it happened, put it behind us, and start over?"

"I don't want to start over." I kiss the tip of her nose. "I never want to forget a single moment of our story, Viv. As much as I don't want to dwell on the horrible shit, we need to discuss it because things are only going to get crazier, and we need tools to handle it better."

"I didn't think it would be so hard," she admits when we reach her car. "But I was naïve. At least we know what we're facing now," she adds, popping the trunk.

I'm not sure we do, but we're certainly more informed than we were three months ago when I left for Boston.

"Love the car." I trail my fingers along the sleek lines of the sporty two-seater Mercedes-Benz. It's my first time seeing it in the flesh, so to speak.

"Good." Grinning, she drops the keys in my palm. "'Cause I thought you'd like to drive us home."

"Now you're talking my language, sexy." Grabbing her ass, I reel her into me. "I hope you didn't make any plans because the only thing I intend on doing tonight is worshiping every inch of your body until we both collapse in a sweaty heap."

Her arms encircle my neck. "Sounds perfect. I love when our minds work in tandem." She stretches up, claiming my lips in a searing-hot kiss. "I already told the folks to forget about seeing you until tomorrow, and they know I'm having a sleep-over at your place."

I clasp her face in my hands. "I love you so fucking much, Vivien. I'm sorry for all the shit, but I promise I'm going to make it up to you."

"I just need you." She grips my waist and smiles. "We're going to have the best summer."

"The absolute best," I agree, swatting her ass before I shuck out of her embrace. "Starting with me behind the wheel of this little beauty!"

"Fucking hell." I tighten my arms around her naked form and press a kiss into her hair as I contemplate everything she just told me. I have no clue what time it is, only that it's starting to get dark outside. We have barely moved from my bedroom since I got home, which suits me fine because I'm feeling pretty antisocial these days. I think it's the consequence of being around busy film sets for months. I'm enjoying the quiet at home.

Most nights, we stay up for hours, eating takeout, watching a movie, and talking and laughing before making love nonstop and catching up on lost time. I veer between exhaustion and falling asleep as soon as we're finished fucking or mad insomnia, which has me tossing and turning for hours. The time zone adjustment is wreaking havoc on my system. I haven't been very hungry either, not even for Lauren's infamous lasagna.

For once, Simon got his timing right. The jerk wasn't even here to welcome me home, but whatever. I'm used to it. Mrs. Thompson was happy to see me, and she's been fussing over me like crazy. Dad is away all this week, meaning we have the run of the house, and we're making the most of it.

Today, we hung out with Alex and Audrey by my pool, but they left early to attend some family dinner, and Viv and I raced upstairs to fuck before indulging in an afternoon siesta. We fell asleep, wrapped around one another, and it was sheer bliss. Or at least it was until we woke, and she finally told me about the stunt Bianca pulled. She accosted her after a yoga session and tried to get her to break up with me. I'm shocked, disgusted, disappointed, and really fucking angry. "She really said those things to you?"

Viv's eyes narrow, and she attempts to wriggle out of my hold, but I don't let her. "I'm not lying if that's what you're implying."

"I know you're not lying. It was just a figure of speech." I run my hand up and down her bare back as I sigh. I'm so done with this crap. I told Bianca and Cassidy I would fix everything with Vivien over the summer, but they just can't stop interfering.

"She said I was insignificant, a stage-five clinger, and she doesn't care if I get my little lovesick heart broken." Viv does a pretty great impression of Bianca's voice and facial expression with an edge that is entirely her own. "She looked at me like I was dirt and not good enough for you."

I'm instantly seeing red. Who the fuck does she think she is to say those things to the woman I love? I am sick of her and Cassidy going back on their word and sick of being undermined in my own goddamned relationship. But my job now is to reassure Vivien. "Well, she got that the wrong way around."

Planting two fingers under her chin, I tilt her face up. "It's always I who has never been worthy of you."

Viv shucks out of my hold and props herself up on one elbow. She traces circles on my chest with her finger. "She's poison, Reeve. I don't like her, and I don't trust her."

Right now, I'm finding I can't disagree. I'm sick of people not listening to me. "I'm not accepting this crap anymore." I sit up and reach for my cell.

"What are you going to do?" Viv sits up beside me, leaning back against my headboard. The sheet drops to her waist, and I'm momentarily distracted by her awesome rack.

I flick her nipple and lick my lips. "I'm going to call her, and if she doesn't agree to apologize to you, I'll terminate my contract."

"You will?" Viv's tone is breathy as I play with her tits. She truly has amazing boobs.

"Yes," I say before burying my head in her chest and kissing her silky soft flesh. "I've missed my girls," I add with a grin, cupping both her tits.

She rolls her eyes, but she's smiling. "Call the wicked witch, and I'll let you fuck them as a reward."

I press a hard kiss to her lips. "No extra incentive is needed, but I won't decline the offer."

I call my agent, leering at my girl the entire time it rings. Blood engorges my dick, and it's almost poking a hole through the sheet. After three tries, I leave Bianca a snotty message, asking her to call me ASAP, and then I toss my phone and claim my girl's offer.

"It's about fucking time," I snap when Bianca finally answers my call the next day. I'm highly irritable after being kept at arm's length by my agent. I have been calling her nonstop since Vivien told me what she'd done. Plus, I didn't sleep well last night without Viv—Lauren insisted she go home because Jonathon's sister was visiting with her family—and I was plagued by weird-ass nightmares, which only heightens my crankiness. I almost caved and took a Xanax, but I promised myself I would stop taking pills when I got home. I only need them on set, and I don't want Vivien to know. She'd be disappointed and worried, and we have enough on our plate.

"I do not appreciate your tone or the insinuation, Reeve. I've been knee-deep in negotiations, and this is the first opportunity I've had to call you."

"Vivien told me about your little ambush, and I'm pissed." I cut to the chase instantly as I swivel on the chair behind Dad's desk in his study. I left my friends and my woman out by the pool, and I want to say my piece and be done with this. My wet swim shorts are stuck to the leather seat, and drops of water cling to the hardwood floor. Simon would throw a hissy fit if he were here. "How dare you say those things to her. I told you I'd handle everything over the summer, and you just shit all over your promise."

"I haven't broken any promises, and I won't apologize for doing what is in your best interests. You're too soft on that girl, Reeve. She needed to hear the truth from someone who is busting her ass trying to make you a massive star."

"You will apologize, or we're done."

"Don't threaten me, boy, and stop being stupid. We're extremely close to finalizing the deal. A deal you have that is vastly superior to the one the rest of the cast has secured."

My breath stutters in my chest. "It's going ahead? The next two movies are being made?"

"Consider it a done deal. The studio commissioned an industry report, and they are predicting incredible things for this movie and the franchise. I have written confirmation of a pending offer for you for the next two movies. I just want to iron a few things out, and then I'll have the final contract paperwork issued to your lawyer within the next couple of days. It's happening, Reeve. Congratulations. This deal will make you a lot of money, and you're going to be a superstar. Hollywood's next golden boy is Reeve Lancaster."

"Wow."

"A thank-you wouldn't go astray."

"Thank you," I say, meaning it, but I can't forget what she did. "That doesn't mean you're off the hook, Bianca. If you pull a stunt like that again, I *will* terminate my contract. Margaret Andre has already expressed interest, and I have options." Margaret is Lauren's agent, and Viv said her mom spoke to her, and she's keen to sign me, so it's no lie. I can't end things with Bianca at such a sensitive stage of contract negotiations, but I want her to know I'm not tied to her. I want her to feel threatened so she'll back off and leave my girl alone. "Vivien is off-limits to you and Cassidy. You have a problem, you come to me, not her. I need you to promise, Bianca."

"You're an ungrateful little shit, Reeve. I should string you up by the balls for the way you've just spoken to me, but I'll give you a pass. This one time. Don't threaten or try to outmaneuver me because you will lose."

"Promise, Bianca. This is a deal-breaker for me."

"I promise I'll leave the thorn in your side up to you."

I scowl into the phone as I swing around on Dad's chair. "Cut it out," I snap. "I am grateful to you for everything, Bianca, but you need to show my girlfriend some respect, or we'll have a big problem. I am sick of sounding like a broken record. Vivien Mills is my life. She is not going anywhere, and you need to accept it."

We spend a few minutes discussing the specifics of the new

movies, timelines for filming, and premieres and promotions before we hang up.

I stay in Dad's study, tapping my fingers on his desk as I try to pluck up the courage to go out poolside and update Vivien. She won't be happy. These movies will occupy most of the next two years of my life. It means I definitely will not be joining my girlfriend at UCLA. College is no longer on my agenda because my career is taking off. I'll need to be available to take up other offers as they arise.

The door creaks open as Alex pops his head into the room. "You done?"

I nod, making no move to leave.

A frown creases his brow as he slips into the study, shutting the door behind him. "Is everything okay?" His slides slap across the floor as he walks toward me and flops into one of the empty seats in front of the desk.

"I got offered the next two movies," I explain.

"Isn't that a good thing?" He arches a brow.

"It is."

"So why do you look like someone kicked your puppy?"

My brows climb to my hairline. My buddy is no dumbass. "Why do you think?"

"Ah." He scrubs a hand through the fluff on his chin. "Vivien."

I slowly bob my head. "I *am* excited. This is going to launch my career into orbit. It's everything I have dreamed of. Everything we have planned for our future is starting to take shape, but I didn't realize how hard it would be being away from her. The past three months have been three of the most stressful months of my life. It was no picnic."

"I don't doubt it. It's a big responsibility, and Vivien has always been more than just your girlfriend, Reeve. She's your family, and you two are more attached than any couple I know.

I could have told you it'd be like this, but it'll get better. You'll weather the storm." His tongue darts out, wetting his lips as he runs his hands up and down his thighs. "Actually, I have something to tell you."

Alarm races up my spine as I sit up straighter.

"Audrey and I have decided to break up at the end of the summer."

I'm a bastard because I was panicking it was something to do with Viv, and now that I know it's not, I relax. Which is shitty, because Alex and Audrey are our friends, and from the tortured expression on my best friend's face, this hasn't been an easy decision. They have dated for two and a half years, but Alex was crushing on Audrey for ages before he asked her out. He wasn't quite as young as I was when I craved to be more than Vivien's best friend, but he wasn't far off it. So, this is a big deal.

"Why?" I ask, wanting to understand why and how they made this decision.

"We're going to be on opposite sides of the country." Alex didn't get a scholarship to play ball at UCLA, so he's moving to Boston to play for the Eagles.

"Same as Viv and me."

"Like I just said, you two are different. If anyone can successfully pull off the long-distance thing, it's you and Viv."

"And you don't think you can?"

"I've seen how hard it's been for you guys, and honestly, I don't think it's for us. I don't want to risk it and ruin what we have. We figure if we love each other the way we do, our love will survive four years of college separation, and we can reconnect when we're both in the same time zone again."

"I think you're making a mistake." I swing back on the chair. "What if she falls in love with someone else?"

He shrugs, but he can't hide the pain in his eyes. "Then we

weren't meant to be, but I would rather we part amicably as friends than see our relationship torn apart by separation."

"Out with it," I say because I know there's more.

"Audrey has seen what Viv has had to handle. She doesn't want to deal with college girls throwing themselves at me. She thinks it's cleaner if we do it like this. I wasn't on board at first, but she's convinced me, and now I know it's the best course of action. *For us*," he tags on the end.

"I don't know how you can do it. The thought of ending it with Vivien makes me break out in a cold sweat. I would die if I ever lost her."

"I didn't say it'd be easy. I get all choked up when I think about summer ending, wishing I could prolong it forever, but the decision is made, and it feels right."

"You might change your mind before August," I say, standing. It's time to break the news to Viv.

He shrugs before climbing to his feet. "Maybe, but I don't think so. Neither of us is the type to change our minds once we've agreed to something."

I clap him on the back. "At least you'll have me in the same time zone. I can't promise I'll have a lot of free time, but I'll do my best to be there for you."

"Thanks, man. I'm going to need you."

Chapter Twenty-Six
Now

"What the fuck do you think you're playing at, Bianca?" I roar through the phone as Carson Park, our family attorney, arches a brow and pretends to shuffle papers on his desk.

"I'm assuming you're reading the fine print in the contract," she pants, sounding a little breathless.

"I'm not signing it unless you get that clause removed." It's one thing to agree to keep my relationship with Viv a secret and quite another to agree to fake a relationship with my costar in public.

"It's not as if I didn't know how you'd react. I have already tried, Reeve, and it's a deal-breaker. Hang on a sec. Let me hop off the treadmill and find some place private to talk."

"I have seen contracts like this before, Reeve," Carson says during the silent pause while Bianca moves somewhere quiet. "It is not that unusual in Hollywood."

"I can't agree to it. It would hurt Vivien too much."

"She's a big girl. I'm sure she'll be fine when you explain."

Everyone thinks because Vivien is the daughter of Lauren

and Jonathon Mills that she'll be okay with the seedier parts of the industry because she's grown up surrounded by it. They are forgetting she's a human being. She can't switch off her feelings just because it's the norm, no more than I can. "This is such bullshit."

"It's not," Bianca says in my ear, and I nod at Carson to let him know the conversation has resumed. "More and more, it's becoming standard practice. The industry report the studio commissioned was very encouraging except in one area. People are not warming to Saffron Roberts as Abby, and that's a cause for concern."

"Maybe they shouldn't have cast her then!" I remember raising concerns early on because she was not a match for how the character is described in the book. Bianca said it was part of a new strategy. Seems like it might have blown up in their faces.

"Look, I've seen some of the footage, and she's weak," she continues. "You easily outact and outshine her. The only way we can fix this is if the public believes the two of you are dating in real life. They will buy into it then and overlook her shortcomings on the screen. This is the difference between success and failure, Reeve. This is bigger than you and Vivien. I argued to get it removed, and they refused. They made it blatantly clear if you won't sign it they'll find another actor who will have no issue faking a relationship with the woman who was just named Playboy's Playmate of the Month for June."

Saffron spent all last month bragging about the feature and how tasteful the nude pics taken were. She believes it's a way to reclaim ownership of her body after her ex leaked intimate photos of her, but I find the whole playboy celebrity tacky and misogynistic. It's not gonna wash for much longer in modern society, and I think Saffron made a mistake doing the shoot. Personally, I think the studio should have forbidden it, but they seem determined to play up the sexual side of the story, and this clause ties into it.

"You've just said her performance isn't good and I'm carrying her. And now you're telling me the studio will cancel me if I don't agree to this crap? Come on. I'm not buying it. It can't be both."

"Reeve, they can do whatever the hell they like. *Cruel Intentions* is going to smash box office records. Every famous actor on the planet would jump at the opportunity to fill your shoes. They'll hire Tom Holland, or Timothée Chalamet, or Jacob Elordi to replace you. You cannot be naïve. You have got to trust that I have your best interests at heart and take my advice. If you don't, your career will be over before it's begun."

"So, what you're saying is they won't remove the clause?" I slouch in my chair as pain slices across my chest. I can't agree to this. It will hurt Viv far too much.

"They won't."

"I'll call you back," I say, hanging up before she can respond.

I fill Carson in on the conversation and ask for his advice. Briefly, I consider talking to Lauren or Jon, but I discard the thought as quickly as it landed. I don't want to run to Viv's parents any time I have an issue. I'm trying to prove to them I'm worthy of their daughter, not some pathetic man-child who can't navigate his way in Hollywood.

"Like I said, I have seen these kinds of clauses in Hollywood contracts before. They are becoming more common. If they won't remove it, maybe they will agree to amend it so you just have to hint at a relationship, rather than go all out to fake one," he suggests.

It's good advice, and I call Bianca back to say I'll sign it with a few minor amendments to the fake-dating clause. No sex under any circumstances. No kissing or making out. I'll agree to a few fake dates and some hand-holding in public. We'll ham it up for the public on the red carpet, but there will be no exaggerated PDAs.

I return two days later to sign the contract with the amended clause, swallowing back bile as I put my signature to paper. I don't know how I'm going to explain this to Vivien, but I've got all summer to figure it out.

Our days are filled with hanging out with our friends by my pool or at the beach. We resume our regular Wednesday night movie and dinner double dates, and Viv and I revert to our normal Friday date night at home. Party invites flow in the doors, and we attend at least a couple a week. Most of our ex-classmates are throwing parties before they leave for college in August.

Things feel normal in my world again despite the few paparazzi who show up on occasion, snapping pics and sniffing for a story. We're careful not to be photographed together, and we've gotten good at spotting when we're being followed or when someone has noticed me out in public. I'm not a big star yet, but it's all going to change when we actively promote the movie starting in November, and life as I know it will be over when *Cruel Intentions* premieres in mid-January.

It means I cherish every second spent with Vivien, and I'm reluctant to do or say anything that will ruin our last blissful, anonymous summer together. So, I haven't told her about the contract yet, and the clock is ticking.

"Is all this cloak-and-dagger stuff necessary?" Alex asks as we hustle from the Harry Winston Beverly Hills parking lot toward the front door wearing ball caps and shades and keeping our heads low.

"Yes," I hiss. "I don't want to get papped heading inside."

There is only a slim chance of it happening, but I'm not taking any risks. I asked Alex to come with as he'll make a good cover story if we are noticed, and I also want him here for moral support. Buying an engagement ring is a big responsibility, and I want a second opinion.

We'll be fine once we get inside as Harry is known as the jeweler to the stars, and privacy is a given. Dad got all the staff on shift today to sign an NDA, just in case. Simon Lancaster won't win any Father of the Year awards, ever, but he came through for me this time by setting up the appointment and ensuring secrecy in advance.

I plan to approach Jonathon before I propose to Vivien, to seek her hand in marriage officially. It's not done much anymore, but I like traditions, and Jon's approval means a lot to me. Not that I'm planning to propose yet. I want to be more established in my career before I pop the question, but I want to be prepared, and I like the idea of buying her ring from the paycheck I received from my first official leading man role. Hence, why we're here today.

We get inside with no issue, and we are quickly led to a private back room where rows of diamond engagement rings are already laid out. Before showing me different styles and shapes, the girl asks me about Vivien and what kind of ring I think she will like.

I know I have found the perfect ring when she removes a stunning princess-cut diamond from a glass case and holds it out for me. The two-carat square-shaped diamond glitters under the bright overhead lights. It's bordered by a rim of small diamonds she calls micropavé diamonds, and there are two matching micropavé bands.

The classic, elegant design is sophisticated and the epitome of old Hollywood glamour. It's perfect for my princess. "That's the one," I say with confidence. "It's exquisite, just like my girl."

"You have great taste," she says. "This is one of my personal favorites."

"What do *you* think?" I ask Alex, looking up at him.

"I think you didn't need me at all, and Vivien is going to love whatever ring you pick for her."

I roll my eyes. "I'm asking what you think about it?"

His brow puckers as he rubs his chin. "It's a sparkly diamond ring. They all look pretty much the same to me."

"Philistine," I quip, and the word takes me back in time. "Remember when that was Audrey's favorite word of all time?"

"Don't remind me," Alex says over a groan. "She drove me crazy saying it all the damn time. I'm glad that was just a phase."

"Should I package it up and process the order, Mr. Lancaster?" the woman asks.

"Yes, thank you."

A short while later, I exit the store with a lighter bank balance and carrying an iconic navy bag.

Back home, I stow the navy ring box in my safe away from prying eyes. Then I join Alex and the girls out by the pool, and I can't keep my hands or my eyes off my woman all day. I wish the timing was right now because I'm dying to propose to Vivien and even more keen to make her my wife.

Someday, I silently promise myself.

One day, we will be husband and wife, content in our dream home, raising a family, and being blissfully happy living our best life.

I can't wait.

Chapter Twenty-Seven
Now

"Have you told her yet?" Alex whispers as we trail the girls around the homewares stores as they ooh and ahh over various bed linens, cushions, and candles. Viv and Audrey managed to snag a two-bedroom suite with a private bathroom and living space on the Hill at UCLA, and they're shopping up a storm before they move into the dorms in a few weeks.

The summer has flown by way too fast, and I don't want it to end. Especially because it means coming clean to Vivien about the fake-dating clause in the contract I signed. Something I still haven't divulged. "No," I admit. "I didn't want to ruin summer. Everything is perfect between us, and it's like our separation never happened at all."

"Dude, you're asking for trouble. If she finds out some other way, it'll all blow up in your face."

"I'll tell her after Laguna, just before I leave for reshoots. That way, she'll have some time to calm down before I return." I'm glad I will be back in time to help her move onto campus.

"I hope you know what you're doing," he says, leaning

against the wall and chewing on a toothpick as the girls disappear from sight.

"Do *you*?" I lift a brow in question. It's not like I haven't noticed how depressed he's getting the closer we get to the end of summer.

"Fucked if I know," he says on a sigh. He removes the toothpick from his mouth. "I thought we were making the right call, but now I'm not so sure."

"Have you spoken to Audrey?"

He looks plain miserable as he nods. "That's why I got the silent treatment those couple of days last week. She says it's unfair to bring it up after we have already decided."

"Do you regret it?"

He shrugs. "I just know I'm really going to fucking miss her." He looks away, but not before I spot the moisture in his eyes.

"I'm sorry, man. Can I do anything to help? You want me to ask Viv to talk to her? Maybe she can get Rey to reconsider?"

He vigorously shakes his head. "Don't get involved. You don't need anything else blowing up in your face."

Truth.

My cell pings in my pocket, and I pull it out, seeing a new text from Saff. She's been checking in over the summer, but I haven't spoken to her. I've been keeping in active contact with Rudy and Jacob to a lesser extent. I type out a quick reply.

"Who's that?" Viv asks, startling me when she materializes in front of me.

"Rudy," I lie, smiling as I send the message and repocket my cell. Inwardly, I cringe at lying to my girl, but she has taken an instant dislike to Saffron, and she'll only read more into it if I tell her the truth, so I choose not to. It's not like I'm doing anything wrong. I'm still utterly devoted to Viv, and what she doesn't know can't hurt her.

"Let me get that," I say, grabbing the overloaded trolley.

"My stuff is in there too," Audrey says, leaning over to separate the items.

"Don't sweat it. It's my treat."

"Squee! I love it, and I'm so excited I could pee!" Vivien twirls around the master suite of the gorgeous five-bed house Alex and I rented for the week right by the ocean at Laguna Beach, looking like a goddess in her pretty pink summer dress. Her hair is wavy and tumbling down her back, she has zero makeup on her tan face, and she's glowing as she dances around the room. Her obvious happiness floods my chest with warmth, helping to distract the nerves hovering in the wings at the prospect of telling her about the contract in a few short days.

But I'm not thinking about that now. We're on a mini vacay, and I intend to make the most of our last precious moments together.

When we all arrived, we tossed for the main bedroom, and Viv and I won. It's a stunning space with a large four-poster bed with flimsy white drapes currently swirling with the breeze floating into the room from the open French doors. To one side is a massive en suite bathroom with his and her sinks, a jacuzzi tub positioned under the window with stunning views of the ocean, and a double rainforest shower. On the other side is a large closet and dressing room.

I follow Viv outside to the balcony, bending beside her with my elbows on the railing. "I'm glad you like it here. We took ages finding this place."

"You did good, babe." She flings her arms around my neck and presses herself up against me. "You did real good. You've been spoiling me all summer."

I have because I need her to know she is everything to me. I continued my weekly flower delivery, only now I hand-deliver them in person. Regular trips to the lingerie store are my favorite, and we're having even more fun in the bedroom. I booked a few spa days for her and Audrey for some pampering, and I've been cooking her dinner, running her baths, and attending to her every whim. Honestly, it's when I'm happiest. I love doting on my woman, and I can't wait for the day when I get to do it permanently for eternity.

"You deserve it, and I love you."

"Reeve." Tears pool in her eyes. "I love you so freaking much. I don't have the words to tell you everything I feel in my heart for you because I don't think they've been invented yet."

I thread my fingers through her hair as I lean down and kiss her tenderly. "I need to be inside you," I whisper, grazing her earlobe with my teeth.

"Again?" she chuckles before taking my hand and leading me back inside.

"I know I'm insatiable, but you drive me wild, baby." I grab her ass and squeeze before picking her up and throwing her over my shoulder.

She squeals. "I'm not complaining. Sex with you is out of this world, and I could stay in bed with you for the rest of my life and be blissfully happy."

"Ditto," I exclaim before tossing her down on the bed and climbing on top of her. "You're so freaking sexy and beautiful, Viv, and all mine."

"Yes." She cups my face as I grind my hips against her pelvis. "I'm forever yours."

We undress one another as we kiss, and I worship every inch of her gorgeous body as I make my way down her torso. Burying my head between her thighs, I devour her with an intensity that is borderline manic. She comes in record time, reaching for my erection, but I push her back down on the bed. "I need to make love to you now." I stare into her gorgeous hazel eyes as I position myself at her entrance and slowly push inside. When I'm fully seated, I lean down and kiss her slowly and passionately until she's moaning and writhing and begging me to move.

Lifting her hands up over her head, I link our fingers as I thrust in and out of her in measured, deep strokes, taking my time as I ravish her with my eyes, my lips, and my cock. Viv's legs wrap around my waist and she tilts her pelvis up as I drive in deep, deep, deep, as deep as I can go. "Fuck, Viv." I release her hands so I can caress her pretty face. "I want to stay buried inside you forever."

"I love how close I feel to you like this," she whispers with tears in her eyes. "I've never felt closer to any other person. You are all I see and all I feel."

"I love you, Vivien Grace. I love you now, and I'll love you forever. In the afterlife, or our next life, or wherever we may end up."

"As long as we're together, I don't care where that is," she agrees.

We kiss and kiss as I slowly pump in and out of her, dragging it out on purpose because it feels too good to race to the finish line. When we're both worked up and clinging to the edge by our fingernails, I flip her over, grab her hips, and pound into her like a madman. I rub her clit and ram in and out of her until we come together, both shattering with loud roars. Sitting back on my heels, I pull her up with me so my chest is plastered to her back, and I'm groping her body as my dick milks our climaxes while I kiss her swollen lips.

The next few days are filled with more lovemaking and bouts of frantic fucking in between exploring the different beaches and coves. We mostly separate and do our own thing as couples, but we rent a boat one day and deep-sea dive while the girls sunbathe on deck. Later, we went snorkeling before enjoying the sumptuous picnic the girls prepared.

Most mornings though, Alex and I rise early to go surfing, and then we return and cook breakfast for our girls. At night, we eat out with Alex and Audrey, returning to enjoy some cocktails on the deck. Much later, Viv and I take moonlight walks, holding hands and stealing kisses. Or we swim in the nude under a starry canvas before snuggling under a blanket on the beach, holding one another as we talk for hours, making plans for the future.

It's heaven on earth until Rudy shows up with Saffron in tow, and he lands me in a world of trouble. Viv is furious, and I have to talk her off a ledge. She doesn't want my costar here any more than I want Nate here.

I haven't seen him since the party at Butthead's place where I threw a few punches his way. To be fair, Nate took it like a man, not even attempting to fight back, and he's avoided me ever since. Alex begged me to let Nate come this weekend. His parents are divorcing, and he's pretty upset, apparently. Alex took responsibility for him and swore he'd ensure he kept out of my way and Viv's. I really don't want him here, and I will never understand their friendship, but Nate was there for Alex during the months I was away, so I agreed to let him come purely for Alex's sake.

I hope I don't end up regretting it.

Butthead's party was a productive one. I managed to kill two birds with one stone that night. I thought I'd handled Marnie Gibson by removing her UCLA place, destroying her relationship with Jennings, and releasing the nude pics Dad found on her phone a few days before graduation. As predicted, she didn't show up to collect her diploma, meaning she couldn't harass Viv. I thought that would be the end of it, but Marnie is tenacious and more than a little reckless. Any other girl would realize when they are beat and walk away before the stakes are raised. But Marnie is her own worst enemy. When she threatened Viv, I decided it was time to lay it all on the line.

I cornered her at the party and spelled that out for her. How, if she didn't drop it, I would haunt her for the rest of her life, ruining every aspect of her life. Relationships. Money. Career. She threatened to go to the police, so I told her to try it. Unlike me, she has no evidence. I told her I'd sue her over the video taken at Viv's party. I explained how all it would take is one post on social media and her life would be a living hell. I channeled Camden Marshall when I explained I have contacts in high places and there is literally nothing she could do to me. I told her it was her last warning and, if she crossed me again, I'd bury her.

It did the trick. She promptly left for Florida to spend the summer at her cousin's place, and there hasn't been a peep out of her since.

I wish there was an easy way to handle the situation between Viv and Saffron. I managed to coax my girlfriend into letting her stay by suggesting we show her how much in love we are in the hopes Viv will see there is nothing to be threatened by. I also had a quiet word in Saffron's ear, asking her not to mention the fake-dating clause.

But the girls have been sniping at one another all weekend, and I'm treading on eggshells. This was a bad idea. I should have told Rudy to fuck off and take her with him the minute they showed up. And I should have told Viv about the contract at the start of the summer instead of being a pussy and keeping it hidden.

So, I have no one else to blame when Saffron throws me under the bus on our last night when we are outside enjoying a few beers before going clubbing. Viv and Saff have been making digs at one another all night, and after a discussion about how sex sells, it is sheer spite when my costar says, "It's why he readily signed his new contract agreeing to fake a relationship with me."

Chapter Twenty-Eight
Now

I race inside the house after Vivien, calling her name as panic mushrooms inside my chest. "Viv. Baby, stop." I catch up to her in the hallway and cage her against the wall so she has no choice but to talk to me.

"Let me go, you fucking asshole. I hate you!" she snaps, pinning me with an expression that is equal parts anger and hurt.

I hate myself. We wouldn't be here if I had just manned the fuck up and told her already. "No. We need to talk about this. Look at me, Viv." I hold her face, forcing her to look at me.

"You lied! You already fucking lied after just promising me you would always be open and honest!"

"I was going to tell you tomorrow when we got home, I swear."

"Your words are empty, Reeve. The same as your promises."

"I knew this would piss you off, so I was trying to find a way of breaking it to you that would cause the least amount of pain."

A bitter laugh erupts from her mouth. "Don't pretend you

care about my feelings. You're more worried about upsetting that ho than you are about hurting me."

She couldn't be more wrong. I knew it would hurt her, and I was trying to give her an amazing summer before I revealed the ugly truth. I see now I was wrong, but at the time, my motivations were driven by the need to protect her. "That is not fucking fair or true." I slam my fist into the wall as frustration surges through my veins. She isn't going to believe a word I say now.

Fucking Saffron.

I am fuming, and I will be having words with her too. She promised she wouldn't mention it, and she's now top of my shit list because she did this on purpose to cause maximum damage. I'm going to rip her a new one for it.

"It was a condition of the contract, Viv!" I explain. "I told Bianca I wouldn't sign it unless that clause was removed, but the studio refused."

"That's bullshit, Reeve, and you know it. You're the star of this movie. The fans are already going crazy for you. If this movie is going to be as big as predicted, there's no way they can recast Camden Marshall. You have leverage, Reeve. You're the one with the power in this situation. All you had to do was tell them that clause was a deal-breaker, and they would've conceded. I bet that bitch Bianca has been filling your head with crap because this feeds into her agenda too," she seethes.

"This is bigger than me, Viv. Fans of the series aren't happy that Saffron has been cast as Abby."

"I don't disagree," she barks, and it's crystal clear my girl and my costar will never see eye to eye. It's an additional headache I could do without.

"It's an issue if they don't get on board. While Saff has her own loyal following, the series fans could make or break this movie."

"More bullshit," she hisses. "This isn't a PG-13 movie. The main target audience will be adults, and most adults don't give a crap about stuff that's said online. And what does some fans objecting to Saffron's casting have to do with you agreeing to a fake relationship?"

"The studio believes the fans will come around if they think we're in a real relationship. That it'll cement us as Abby and Cam. Ultimately, it's for the greater good of the movie. That's why I agreed, and I got it modified so we only need to hint at a relationship in public. It won't go beyond a few fake dates, some holding hands, and suggestive looks. I won't have to kiss her. I made them take that out."

"Well, that makes it all okay then!" she shouts, shoving at my chest. "Get the fuck away from me. I can't even look at you right now." She slams her hands into my chest again, but I'm not letting her push me away until we've talked this through. This is not the sword we will fall on. Not if I can help it.

"I'm not budging until we fix this," I say, letting determination seep into my words.

She snorts as she glares at me. "The only way you can fix this is to get that fucking contract modified."

"You know I can't do that. Please, Viv." I rest my forehead against hers, pleading for understanding that's in short supply, and I truly don't blame her for it. If the tables were turned, I would feel the same way she does. But I've got to try to get through to her. "Please don't make a big deal out of this."

"Are you for fucking real—"

"Oops, sorry," Saffron says, holding Nate's hand as they move past us in the hallway. "I didn't mean to interrupt."

"I'm sure you didn't," Viv scoffs, and I've never seen her look so venomous. If looks could kill, Saffron would be stone-cold dead and buried six feet under.

"Leave us the fuck alone, Saffron," I snap, just wanting her to go. Honestly, at this moment, I think I could wring her neck and feel no remorse. I don't know what's gotten into her that she feels the need to treat my girlfriend like this.

"We'll just be on our way," she says, mouthing "sorry" at me, but I just glare at her.

"I thought she was fucking the assistant director?" Viv asks. So did I, but I haven't paid attention to Saff's love life, and I have no clue what's gone down over the summer.

"We broke up. He was too old and boring. Younger guys have much more stamina!" Saff hollers from the stairs, and Viv flips her off even though she can't see.

"You mean he served his purpose and you're chasing the next victim who can help your brand?!" Viv retorts. I rub at the pounding in my temples as their retreating footsteps echo overhead. This wasn't how I saw our last night here ending.

Viv shoves my shoulders. "Get off me. I mean it, Reeve. If you don't step back, I will not be responsible for my actions. Right now, I hate you. I hate you with the heat of a thousand suns. How could you agree to this?" she cries, and I feel my heart splitting in two. "You didn't even consult me about it. We used to discuss everything, and you never made decisions that impact me without my input." Tears roll unbidden down her face. "What happened to me grounding you, huh?"

Now she's just being cruel. Doesn't she know how much stress I've been under? How much the studio has been pressuring me with this shit? I have been defending her to Bianca and Cassidy repeatedly, and I'm fucking tired of going over the same bullshit all the time. It's my fucking job! Why can't she understand that? Why is she making this so much harder for me? Haven't I proven to her all summer how much I love her? How much I prioritize our relationship and how devoted I am to her? Just because I have to do unsavory things for my job does not diminish what I feel for her, and it also does not give her the right to give me shit when I'm pulling myself apart trying to please everyone!

"What happened to you supporting me?!" I shout, releasing my anger as I step back, creating space between us.

"I have always supported you, Reeve."

I scoff as I lean against the wall across from her, wondering if I've had blinders on this whole time because this bullshit feels nothing like support. "All you have done since I got this role is bitch and whine. I have never given you any reason to doubt my loyalty, yet you hurl accusations at me all the time. I can't handle your insecurities, Viv. Do you have any idea of the stress I'm under? I don't need this shit from you. You know it's not real. It's part of the industry." I push off the wall. "For fuck's sake, more than half the so-called relationships in Hollywood are fake. It means nothing, Viv. It's part of the role, and I am getting sick of repeating myself."

"If I'm that unsupportive, you know what to do." She dries her tears, lifts her head, and fixes me with a pointed look, daring me to do it.

I'm temporarily shocked she's gone there, so I stare at her wondering if I know her at all. How could she threaten that? I would never, ever, consider breaking up, and I'd never use it in an argument. It forces me to calm down though, and the severity of the situation is blatantly clear. I can't do anything to change the situation. All we can do is find a way to move forward and work around it. But that's not up to me. This has just been sprung upon her, so hopefully, with time, she'll find a way to live with it. I know she'll never be happy about it, but surely, she won't let go of us over something I have no control over?

I walk to her and take her hands in mine. "I don't want to break up, Viv. I love you, but you've got to find a way to deal with this."

"And if I can't?"

Pain shatters my heart into tiny shards, and my eyes sting as overwhelming sadness washes over me. I shrug because I don't know what else to say, and I'm exhausted from all the drama.

She yanks her hands back, and mine fall bereft to my side. The pressure in my chest is so intense it's a miracle I can breathe. She closes her eyes for a few seconds, and when she reopens them, I see so much hurt, pain, and fear, and I feel like the biggest piece of shit on the planet.

"I'm calling a car to take me home," she says, breaking the tense atmosphere.

"No, Viv. Please don't do that."

"I can't be around that bitch another second."

"I'll come with you." I can't let her leave by herself when she's so upset.

"I don't want you to." She drills me with a look laced with anguish and resolve. "I need some space to think."

"Don't do this, baby. I don't want to leave for reshoots when we're arguing." I'm heading straight to the airport tomorrow after we check out of here. The plan had been to talk to her in the morning and in the car on the way back to L.A., but that's shot to hell now. We need distance from one another to come to terms with this, but not like this.

"You should've thought of that before you lied to me again," she says before walking off.

Chapter Twenty-Nine
Now

"She's a spiteful, manipulative bitch, and she's definitely got an agenda," Audrey says, handing Alex and me another beer. She drops down beside her soon-to-be ex on the love seat while I'm sitting in a cushioned wicker chair across from them on the deck. Behind us, waves crash against the shore under the inspection of the half-moon. Tonight was a complete shit show. Vivien has gone back home. Saffron and Nate haven't surfaced since they went upstairs. Audrey had been shooting daggers at Rudy, blaming him for inviting Saffron, so he called an Uber and went to a club by himself after apologizing to me.

"I am beyond enraged. What she did was so fucking cruel and deliberate, and if it wouldn't cause more shit, I'd boot her ass out of the house right now." I knock back a healthy mouthful of beer as anger simmers in my veins. I am sorely tempted to storm up the stairs, rip Saffron off Nate's cock, and toss her out on the curb. It's what she deserves for purposely hurting Vivien. No explanation will excuse her actions. I'm mad enough to kick her out, but we'll be back on set in a couple of days, and creating more tension with my costar is not the way to go.

Besides, Saffron is not my priority. My girlfriend is.

"Saffron promised she wouldn't say anything, and I trusted her. Now, Viv is upset, my relationship is hanging by a thread, and I'll be lucky if my girl ever talks to me again." Pain presses down on my chest as I throw a pity party for one.

Audrey leans forward and pokes her finger in my chest. "She wouldn't have been able to get one over on Viv if you'd been honest with her from the start. You are far from blameless, Reeve. This happened because you were keeping a secret from her, and that's not cool."

Alex's pointed look says "I told you so," but he doesn't articulate it, not wanting to earn Audrey's venom when she discovers he knew about it too. Not that it was his responsibility to tell Viv. That was, *is*, all on me. "I majorly fucked up. I know that, but I was scared to tell her and afraid to ruin our summer."

"How could you have agreed to fake date that bitch, Reeve?" Audrey shakes her head as she leans back against Alex. "What the hell were you thinking?"

"I didn't have a choice, Rey."

"You always have a choice," she snaps. Disgust and disappointment drip from her words.

"I would've gotten out of it if I could because I never want to hurt Vivien, and—" I cut myself off and bury my head in my hands as the image of Vivien's heartbroken face appears in my mind's eye. A sob bursts from my mouth. "The look on her face will forever be imprinted in my brain," I admit, lifting my head, uncaring if they see the tears building in my eyes. "I love her so much, and I'm terrified I'm going to lose her. What if she breaks up with me?" Tears spill down my cheeks, and I'm shaking all over. "I can't lose her," I sob. "She's my reason for breathing. I don't want to live without her." The magnitude of all I stand to lose slams into me, and I'm petrified.

"Reeve." Audrey's expression softens a smidgeon as she drops to her knees in front of me and takes my hands. "I doubt she'll do that. You're her reason for breathing too, but she's really hurt." Audrey spent time with Viv when she was packing up her stuff earlier. "You can't keep secrets from her. Especially not relating to that manipulative ho. You need to be honest, or else you'll permanently fuck it all up."

"I feel awful." I sniff, rubbing at my eyes with the back of my arm. "I wanted this week to be special, and now everything's turned to shit."

"Vivien will come around, and she'll forgive you," Alex says as Audrey leans in and gives me a quick hug.

"From now on, tell her everything, Reeve, even if you think it's going to hurt. She won't keep forgiving you if you don't. And you need to trust her instincts when it comes to that woman. I know you have to work with the bitch, but you need to keep your distance. She's up to no good, and now she'll be even more determined to cause problems in your relationship. Don't let her."

"Fuck, now I remember why I don't drink very much," I say over a groan the following morning as I amble into the kitchen with a dry mouth, a sick stomach, and a blinding headache.

"Take these." Rey hands me a couple of pills and a glass of water. After I knock them back, she replaces the glass with a different one filled with nasty, green liquid. I must make a face because she swats the back of my head and says, "Don't make that face. I got up early to drive to the store to buy the ingredients to make it. I knew you two knuckleheads would have the hangover from hell."

"I know it looks like something that spewed from a drainage pipe," Alex says, ducking down when Audrey lifts her hand to slap him, "but it's actually tasty, and it helps. I don't feel half as bad as I did earlier."

"I'll take your word for it." Holding my nose as I open my mouth, I drink half of it in one go. "It's decent." I hug Viv's best friend. "Thanks, Rey. Have you heard from her?" I left Viv a couple of drunken messages last night, which I now regret. I can't remember what I said, and I hope I didn't make it worse.

"I sent her a text earlier, but she hasn't replied yet. I'm going to drop by and see her when we get home."

"I changed my flight to tomorrow," I say, just as Rudy and Saffron walk into the kitchen, carrying their weekend bags.

"You did?" Rudy arches a brow.

"I need time to fix things with Viv before I get on a plane for Boston."

"And here we go again." Saffron rolls her eyes.

"Excuse me?" I snap, in no mood for her bullshit.

"Viv is fucking with your head, Reeve, and you're the only one who can't see it."

"Shut your stupid mouth, you conniving cunt," Audrey barks, pushing past me to square up to my costar.

"Don't get involved." Yanking her back, I hand her off to Alex. I know she wants to protect Viv, but she's liable to swing at my costar, and I don't need additional drama. Besides, this is my mess to handle. "This is my battle." I step up to Saffron and glare down at her. "The only one fucking with my head is you, and if you don't stand the fuck down, we're going to have a big problem, Saffron. How dare you say the things you said to Vivien this weekend. You were a guest—"

"An uninvited one," Audrey pipes up.

"An uninvited guest," I agree. "And you had no right to torment my girlfriend all weekend. You were cruel and nasty, and you purposely baited her. It was disrespectful to Vivien and to me."

"I respect you, Reeve, so, so much," Saffron blurts, cutting across me.

"Right," Audrey drawls as Alex wraps his arms around her from behind, holding her in place. "That was respect. Got it." Sarcasm is thick in her tone, and we all hear it.

"I asked you not to mention it, and you promised you wouldn't. That wasn't respecting me, Saff. You purposely stirred shit. You knew she didn't know yet, so why the fuck would you blurt it out unless you deliberately wanted to hurt her?"

"Vivien is not a supportive girlfriend, Reeve, and you deserve better."

"You don't fucking know her!" I shout as my hands ball into fists at my side. "You have no right to spout that shit about her! She's been a constant at my side from the time she was born! My earliest recollection includes her! Every precious memory I have of my childhood involves Vivien. I spent years fighting my feelings for her, afraid of ruining our friendship, until I was sure we were on the same page. My life was complete the day she agreed to be my girl." I'm all up in her face now, and she's not happy. Her arms are folded against her chest, and her lips are pulled tight. "She's my everything, and what you think of her is not going to change that, but it will change how I perceive you. I don't know what your agenda is, but you need to drop it."

"You don't get to slander Vivien when you don't have a clue about the kind of person she is," Audrey adds, and she's visibly vibrating with anger. "Vivien is worth a million of you, whore, and if you think you're fooling anyone with this pathetic act, think again." Audrey's cutting words and daggered expression tell Saffron exactly what she thinks of her.

Saffron's lower lip wobbles as she drops the hard woman act and stares at me with tears in her eyes. "I'm sorry, Reeve. I really am. You're like a little brother to me, and I care about you."

Audrey scoffs loudly before hissing, "Unbelievable."

Saffron ignores her, focusing only on me. "I've seen how upset you were on set and how you're always bending over backwards to make her happy, and I just don't see her doing the same for you. I shouldn't have said anything. I shouldn't have interfered, but please, please, believe me when I say my heart was in the right place. I was doing it for you. You shouldn't have to deal with all this stress. You should have been easily able to tell her about the contract. She's making life harder, and I hate that for you."

"It's none of your business, Saff, and you were way out of line."

"I'll call her and apologize."

"Like fuck you will!" I yell. I wave my finger in her face. "Stay away from Vivien, Saffron, and if you want things to work smoothly between us, you will keep your nose out of my relationship."

"I don't ever want to add to your stress," she says, wiping at the tears leaking from her eyes. "I won't get involved again. I swear. I'm so sorry, Reeve. I only thought I was helping."

Her eyes plead for forgiveness, and I'm torn. She seems so sincere, and despite what Vivien and Audrey think, she has no romantic interest in me. She hasn't given me the slightest indication she wants more than my friendship. But I vow, here and now, to keep distance between us once we return to the set. I'll do what I have to do in public to fake a relationship with her, but outside of that, it will be strictly professional. I'm not giving Vivien any other reason to doubt me, and Saffron is the biggest elephant in the room.

"Our car is here," Rudy says, breaking the tense silence.

"Do you need us to smooth things over with Nick?" Saff asks, drying her eyes and lifting her chin.

"I already talked with him, and he's fine with me arriving straight to set tomorrow." Initially, I planned to get settled into the hotel today and chill out with the cast before we begin reshoots tomorrow. But staying here to talk to Viv is more important.

"Okay, well, if you need anything, call." Rudy salutes me before grabbing Saffron's arm and leading her toward the door.

She glances over her shoulder at me. "Please try to find it in your heart to forgive me. I was only looking out for you."

I refuse to dignify that with a response, and no one speaks until we hear the front door slam.

"She's a lying piece of shit," Audrey hisses. She shucks out of Alex's embrace and marches up to me. "She's manipulating you, and you need to stay on guard around her. I didn't buy one word of that bullshit."

"Babe, you need to relax." Alex comes up behind her and kneads her shoulders.

"Don't tell me what to do." She pulls away from his touch and rubs at her brow. "I'm going to grab a shower and pack."

I finish the rest of my smoothie in silence as Alex plates up eggs and bacon from the skillet. They're probably cold by now, but my rumbling stomach doesn't care. We eat without talking, both of us stewing in our thoughts. After, we clean up, side by side, and then fix coffees and head out to the deck to drink them.

"What do you think?" I ask him. "About Saffron."

"She did a bitchy thing to Viv, but I think it's just a female rivalry thing. I don't think she's after you. If she wants you, she'd hardly hook up with a guy you can't stand. I think a lot of what she said is bullshit, but she believes it. She's probably jealous of Viv, and that's what's behind this. I think she cares for you, and in some twisted way, she truly thought she was helping. But as you said, she doesn't know you or Viv, so she's not qualified to dole out relationship advice."

"I'm going to keep my distance from her as much as possible. Even if she doesn't have designs on me, Vivien hates her, and it has the potential to cause more issues between us. If she's not planning on breaking up with me, that is." I drain my coffee and arch my back. I slept like shit last night, and I was tempted to take Saff up on her previous offer of a few Xanax, but I'm glad I declined. I have weaned myself off the uppers and downers over the summer, and I'm determined not to rely on them when I return to filming. It's a slippery slope I can't afford to fall down. I'm in enough shit as it is.

"Where is everyone?" Nate asks, and we turn around to face him. He's wearing low-hanging pants and yawning as he scratches the back of his head.

"Audrey is showering, and Rudy and Saffron left," Alex explains.

"She left without saying goodbye?"

His crestfallen expression says it all. He's a fucking idiot. "I bet she's already forgotten your name," I say, brushing past him. "You'd do well to forget hers too."

"There's one thing I don't understand, Reeve," Audrey says, turning around to face me when we're en route home. Alex is driving, she's riding shotgun, and I'm in the back. "You said you had no choice, but why didn't you go to Lauren or Jon or even your father for help? Maybe they could have gotten you out of that clause."

"I can't go running to my asshole father or Viv's parents anytime I encounter an obstacle. I'm an adult now, and this is my career. Simon already believes I won't hack it, and—"

"He actually said that to you?" Alex eyeballs me through the mirror.

"As good as." I settle back in the seat and rub my tender stomach. "He thinks Lauren has mollycoddled me—his words— and that I won't be able to go it alone. He said if I'm going to succeed, I've got to learn to do things for myself."

"No wonder Viv hates him," Rey says, shaking her head. "He's an asshole, and that is crap. There is nothing wrong with seeking guidance from those with more experience, and didn't Lauren tell you to come to her if you needed anything?"

"I don't agree with my asshole sperm donor on much, but I do on this. I can't hang off Lauren's coattails. It's always been important to me to do it on my own terms before I even considered how my relationship with Viv's parents could open doors for me. I want to achieve success on my own merit. I don't want to be like one of those Hollywood brats who uses nepotism to advance. I want to succeed because I'm talented and I've worked hard for it, not because of who I know or what strings were pulled for me."

"That's honorable, Reeve, and you wouldn't be you if you didn't think like that, but it sounds to me like you're cutting your nose off to spite your face. You can seek guidance without compromising your talent or your work ethic."

"That's a valid point," Alex agrees.

"There is no point dwelling over what might have been.

The decision is made. The contract is signed. Talking about the what-ifs is a waste of time."

"It's too late on this occasion, but you may need their help in the future, and you should ask for it." Rey tosses her red hair over one shoulder as she stares at me. "Don't be stubbornly proud, Reeve, or you could end up regretting it."

Chapter Thirty
Then - Age 14

I think I might puke. I asked Vivien to meet me at the treehouse because it's only fitting that I ask her to be my girlfriend in the place where we shared our first kiss. That was over a year ago, and I'm still stealing kisses from her. But neither of us has talked about it. Sometimes it's me grabbing her and kissing her, and other times, she initiates it. When we finish kissing, we pretend like it's never happened and go back to doing whatever we were doing.

It's been driving me crazy.

I want her to be officially mine so I can kiss her at will, and so the asshats at school know she's taken.

I wonder if she's as scared as me to take things to the next level. Is she afraid we might ruin our friendship if it doesn't work out? I'm sure about what I feel. I love her. She's the only girl for me, and she's going to be my future wife, so I'm not scared about that. My main worry is if she doesn't feel the same. What if I ask her out on a date and she says no and then stops hanging out with me at all? Or what if she's crushing on some other guy?

"Fuck." I bend forward, clutching my stomach as nausea churns in my gut. I haven't thought of that before, and now I'm extra worried.

No. No. It's not true. She doesn't like anyone else. I would know if she did.

The few times she's been asked out on a date, she has always said no. Most guys don't ask her out because they assume we're together or I've warned them to back off. I haven't seen her looking at anyone else, so that's not it. She's not crushing on any other guy. I slump back against the treehouse wall in relief just as I hear footsteps climbing the ladder. I left the door open so she knows I'm already here.

We don't hang out at the treehouse much anymore as we've outgrown it, so I'm betting she was surprised when she got my text asking her to meet me here.

Hiding the bouquet of lavender roses and chocolates, behind my back, I will my nerves to hold steady as I brace myself for her imminent arrival.

"Hey." Her pretty, smiling face greets me as she dips her head down and enters the space.

"Hey." I hope she doesn't hear how my voice trembles.

"I'll admit I'm intrigued," she says, plopping down on the beanbag alongside me. "We haven't been up here in ages."

"I know, but I have something important to ask you, and it seemed fitting to do it here."

Her mouth makes an O shape as I whip the flowers and chocolates out and hand them to her. "These are for you."

"My favorites." Nestling her face in the roses from her mom's garden, she inhales the slightly spicy scent.

"I got your mom's permission to take the flowers," I blurt. "And Charles drove me to the French chocolate shop yesterday after school. I can't wait until I can get my learner's permit and drive myself around. I hate being chauffeured. How was your writing class? Did you get your last assignment back yet? And did you hear what happened in advanced world history today? I hate Guy Fenwick, and I'm glad he got in trouble." I'm babbling instead of just asking her. This is what has happened the last few times I've tried to get this out.

Simon is right. I *am* a pussy.

"Reeve, relax." Putting the flowers and chocolates down, she takes my hands and smiles at me, and it's like being bathed in the warmest sunshine. "Take deep breaths until you calm down."

Heat warms my cheeks. I'm getting myself all worked up, and it's ridiculous. This is Vivien. She's my best friend, and she's not going to cut me out of her life even if she doesn't feel the same way. I know her, and she's a good person through and through.

"Thank you for the flowers and chocolates. You are always so thoughtful, Reeve. I'm so lucky you're my best friend."

Gulping back nerves, I decide there will be no better time to broach the subject. "That's the thing, Vivien. I don't just want to be your best friend. I want to be your everything."

She wets her lips as her gaze darts to my mouth. "You need to spell it out, Reeve. Just say it."

"I love you as more than just a friend, Vivien. I want to be your boyfriend. I want you to be my girlfriend. Officially, so the whole world knows we belong together."

Air whooshes out of her mouth before the biggest smile ghosts over her lips. "Thank God! I thought you'd never say it!"

Wait? What! My mouth hangs open. "You knew, and you said nothing?"

"Reeve." She scoots in closer, placing her hands on my thighs. "I've wanted to be your girlfriend from the first time you kissed me. Actually, that's a lie. I wanted it before that day."

"So did I!"

"Really?" Her eyes light up.

I nod.

"I wasn't sure back then, and I didn't want to say anything in case you rejected me."

"Never." I shake my head as I link my fingers with hers, delighting in the shivery tremors that skate over my skin. "I would never reject you. You're all I think about, Viv. When I look into the future and I see what my life looks like, you are always at my side."

"You're all I think about too, and I was going to say something these past few months, but I know you, Reeve. You needed to do this, and I wouldn't take it from you. I knew you'd get here, and I tried to be patient, but it's been so hard because I just want to hold your hand and kiss you all the time!"

I seize the opportunity and lean in and kiss her. Her arms wind around my neck as I angle my head and deepen the kiss. Her mouth opens as I prod at the seam of her lips, and our tongues glide against one another as things get very interesting in my pants. I pull back, grinning like the biggest idiot. "I'm so in love with you, Vivien Grace Mills. Will you be my girlfriend, and will you go out on a date with me tomorrow night?"

"I'm equally as in love with you, Reeve Elon Lancaster, and nothing would make me prouder than to call you my boyfriend. And yes, I would love to go on a date with you!"

We kiss some more, laughing in between kisses and hugs, and I'm floating on a cloud, high on life and love, and happier than I've ever been.

"We need to tell your parents," I say as we leave the treehouse and head toward the house for dinner. Viv is carrying her roses, and we already devoured the chocolates in between kisses.

"No, we don't." She levels me with one of her special Vivien looks. "At least, not yet. Mom will be annoying and come up with all these rules, and I'd rather not deal with it. We'll sneak around for a while and come clean later."

I expected this response, but this is one occasion where I need to stand my ground. "We have to tell them, baby."

She beams at me as she flings her arms around me, still holding the flowers. "Oh, I like it when you call me that!"

"It's not too cheesy?"

"Give me all the cheese, babe. I'm totally down for it."

Holding her flush against me, I lean down and press my lips to hers just because I can now. It occurs to me that it might become a problem because I feel like kissing her all the damn time, and now there's nothing stopping me.

Vivien sways in my arms as we kiss, clinging to me like I'm the only thing keeping her afloat, and I love how strong and manly it makes me feel. "Oh, Reeve," she says, peering up at me with glazed eyes when we finally surface for air. "I love kissing you, and I'm excited I can do it all the time now."

"I know." I thread my fingers through her hair. "But it's why we need to tell Lauren and Jon. They're going to catch us, and I haven't forgotten that warning your dad gave me when we were younger. He said you weren't allowed to kiss boys until you were much older."

Viv giggles. "You're too funny! Dad only said that to scare you off."

"Pity it didn't work," a man with a deep, familiar voice says, and I think I stop breathing.

We both whip our heads around, sporting matching shocked looks as Vivien's parents draw up close to us. We didn't even hear them approaching.

"Stop that, Jon." Lauren loops her arm through her husband's as she smiles at us. "We knew this day was coming."

"Guess the cat's out of the bag now anyway." Viv pouts as she turns fully to face her parents, cradling her homemade bouquet. I chuckle as I wrap my arms around her from behind.

Jon and Lauren share a look as they stare at us, both smiling and not looking too angry. Thank fuck!

"We should talk inside," Lauren says. "Dinner is getting cold."

We chat casually over dinner in the kitchen, where Viv and I sit super close to one another, exchanging loving looks while we eat. I'm giddy, and it's a miracle I can manage to swallow any food as my stomach is jumping constant cartwheels, and I don't feel in the least bit hungry. Eating a ton of chocolate before dinner was not the smartest idea. But Lauren cooked today, and I won't offend her, so I shovel mouthfuls of the delicious chicken parmigiana in my mouth until it's all gone.

After, Viv's parents ask us to join them in the living room for "the talk."

"Prepare yourself," Viv whispers as we trail her parents hand in hand from the kitchen. "This is going to be bad."

"As long as they approve, I don't care what they say." There was a small part of me that thought Viv's parents might disapprove of me as her boyfriend. Simon never wastes an opportunity to tell me what a loser I am, and while I don't want to believe it, sometimes that shit sticks. So, whatever Viv's parents want, they've got it. I will prove to them I'm ideal boyfriend material and the perfect man for their only daughter.

"How long has this been going on?" Jonathon asks when we are seated in front of the open fireplace, each couple on opposite couches.

"It only happened today," I say as Viv blurts, "We've been kissing on and off for ages."

My cheeks redden. "I only asked Vivien to officially be my girlfriend today, but we have shared a few kisses before then."

"He'd make a great politician," Viv jokes, squeezing my hand.

"And has there been more than kissing?" Lauren asks, and I inwardly cringe.

"Mom!" Vivien sits up straight and eyeballs her mother. "You can't ask us that! It's private."

"That's not how this works, princess." Jon puts his mug down on the end table. "Neither of us wants any details, nor would we ever invade your privacy, but you are minors, living under our roof, and it's our job as parents to ensure you are safe and respectful to one another."

"You are only fourteen," Lauren reminds us.

"It's only been kissing," I truthfully reply. They don't need to know how often I jerk off to visions of their daughter naked and on her knees. "I would never take advantage of Viv, and we're in no rush. We just want to be together as a couple and for everyone to know."

"I'm glad to hear it," Jonathon says, nodding in my direction.

"Is a reminder of the sex talk necessary?" Lauren asks with a straight face.

"Hell no." Vivien visibly shudders. "We're not innocent little kids, and you gave us a detailed explanation when we were ten. Neither of us needs a repeat of that talk!"

Truth.

"We've had sex education classes at school too," I remind them. I'm not saying we're experts—clearly, we're not—but we know the dynamics of sex.

"You're not ten any longer, and I want us to be able to talk openly and frankly about sex. It's a big deal at your age, and I want to ensure you are making the right choices for you," Lauren says, clasping her hands on her lap.

"We're aware kids are sexually active from a much younger

age these days, but we're asking you to wait until you both feel mature enough to handle all the emotions that come with being intimate," Jonathon adds.

"Dad, seriously, this doesn't need to be said." Vivien snuggles into my side, and I'm guessing she wants to disappear into the couch as much as I do. "It's not like we've decided to instantly have sex now we're boyfriend and girlfriend."

My dick likes that idea way too much, and I'm praying no one notices the growing bulge in my pants.

"The age of consent in California is eighteen, and we'd like you to wait until then," Lauren says.

"Oh, come on." Vivien throws her hands in the air. "That's like four years away!"

I hear you. I have no clue how we'll manage to abstain for that long, but I can tell this is important to Viv's parents, and I want them to know they can always trust me with her. "We agree," I say, prepared to risk Viv's wrath. "We'll wait until we're legal."

"Reeve!" Viv pokes me in the side and glares at me. "That should have been a joint decision."

"The authorities set the legal age for a reason. It's when they think we're ready for it, and it's what your parents have requested. I don't think it's too much to ask. It will make the wait all the more worthwhile."

"I know girls at school who have already done it," Vivien says, chewing on her lower lip. "We'll be like the oldest virgins in school, and everyone will think we're doing it, but they won't realize I've been cockblocked by my own parents!"

"And this is exactly why you should wait," Lauren says. "It's not a competition, honey. It's a big step. A big commitment, and it is one you should only take when you are both ready."

"That should be for us to decide." Viv scowls.

"Perhaps," Lauren concedes. "We can always discuss it again in a few years. For now, we'd like you both to be responsible. This progression in your relationship is new, and you don't need to rush into anything."

"We'll be responsible," I say, wrapping my arm around Viv and pressing a kiss to her head. "You can trust me with Vivien. I promise."

Lauren and Jon share a look. "We wouldn't trust anyone the way we trust you, son," Jon says. "This isn't about trust. It's about ensuring you remain kids for as long as possible." His features soften as he looks at his only daughter. "Don't be in a rush to grow up, princess. You never get to be a kid again."

"Now that's settled," Lauren adds, "we need some ground rules."

"Told you," Viv mumbles under her breath, and I chuckle as I hold her tighter to me.

"Your bedroom doors must remain open anytime you are upstairs, and while you're welcome to stay over, in your own bedroom, like usual, Reeve, it might be advisable not to sleep over quite so often. The open-door rule applies at nighttime too."

"That means no going into one another's rooms at night, princess." Jon slants a stern look in Vivien's direction, and it's not often he lays down the law with his daughter. Vivien has Jon wrapped around her pinkie, and it's usually Lauren who is the strict disciplinarian. "If you disobey, we'll have to ask Reeve not to stay over anymore."

I'm not sure I'd be able to sleep next door to Vivien and not sneak into her room at some point, so I have already decided I will just sleep at home from now on.

"I'm going to install a camera in the hallway," Lauren adds, and Viv's mouth trails the floor.

"For fuck's sake, you're acting like sex is a criminal activity! It's a loving act between two people!"

"No cursing, princess," Jon says, "and it's a loving act between two consenting adults."

"*Adults* being the most important part," Lauren concurs.

"I'll sleep at home from now on. It's not a big deal."

A funny expression washes over Lauren's face. "Sweetheart, we don't want you to feel like you can't come here. That room is yours for as long as you need it."

I wonder if she's aware of all the random women roaming the halls of my house at all hours of the night or if she wants to make sure I can always escape to her house if Dad is on one of his rants and blaming me for everything under the sun.

"If I need to stay over, I will, but I think it's best I don't sleep over as often as I usually do." I'm fourteen now, and we're no longer little kids.

"This day is starting to suck," Vivien grumbles.

"I love you," I remind her. "And we have the rest of our lives to be together. Four years will pass by in a blip, and sex isn't everything." Okay, I'm lying with that last part, but I mean the rest.

"I love you too, and we're just parking the subject for now."

I kiss her quickly, hoping PDAs aren't off the menu too.

"God, you two are so adorable together," Lauren says, resting her head on Jon's shoulder as she stares at us snuggling on the couch. "I always knew you would be."

"You guessed we would become a couple?" Viv asks.

"It was written in the stars, princess." Jon circles his arms around his wife as he smiles at us. "You and Reeve have always been adorable together. From the time you were very little, you were joined at the hip. We have always known this was inevitable."

"And we're happy for you," Lauren continues. "As long as you remain happy and you take your time. There is no need to rush anything. Like Reeve said, you have your whole lives to look forward to."

Chapter Thirty-One
Now

Viv and I manage to get back on track after the Laguna Beach shit show, but all too soon, we are separated again, and the strain reappears. Viv and Audrey are throwing themselves into college life at UCLA while I'm filming *Twisted Betrayal*, the second book in the series.

Our schedule is as demanding as ever, and I've had to resort to pills to cope. It's fine though. I'm fully in control, and it's helping to keep me levelheaded.

Viv blows up after I have my first official fake date with Saffron, and we have another blazing argument. I'm walking around the set like a miserable fuck most days. It's like nothing I say or do is right anymore, and visible cracks are showing in my relationship, which gravely concerns me. The strategy is working though, and fans are going crazy online. Buzz for the movie is at an all-time high, and they're predicting we're going to break all kinds of box office records.

Filming ceases in late November to make way for the *Cruel Intentions* promo tour, ahead of the premiere in January. While I'm trying to keep the focus on the movie, far too often, interviewers want to know about my private life, asking intrusive questions about Vivien and Saffron, and I'm slowly losing my mind.

"Come with me," Saff says, grabbing my arm and pulling me into her dressing room. "You need to relax. You're wound tighter than a ball of yarn."

She's not wrong. We're in Italy as part of the European promo tour, and the interviewers are especially determined to get the scoop here. With the significant time difference and our punishing schedule, finding time to call Viv has been almost impossible. We have been mainly texting one another. She sent me a scathing message last night while I was asleep with a link to an article showing a picture of Saff and me laughing as we roamed the streets of Milan. I'm not even touching her, and we were with Rudy, Jacob, Jolina, Darren, Ed, and Conrad, but they had cropped them out of the pic to make it appear like a romantic stroll between costars. I'm in a super pissy mood today because of her insinuation. I replied by explaining we were all there, but I haven't received a response yet.

To be fair to Saff, she hasn't said one word to me about Vivien since August, and she's been polite and professional on and off set. Even when we went on our first fake date, she was the one to establish clear rules and boundaries when we were in the car en route to the restaurant. She is trying, and I can't ask for more than that.

Vivien, on the other hand, is like a dog with a bone. She is constantly hounding me about Saffron, checking if I'm with her when we're on calls, and she wastes no opportunity to stick the knife in Saff's back. I wish she'd just drop it because it's exhausting, and I'm sick of fighting about my costar. It feels like it's all we do these days. I'm looking forward to Christmas and spending some alone time with my girl to remind her of who we are.

"Movie star." Saffron snaps her fingers in my face. "You spaced out on me again."

"Sorry." I rub the back of my neck as my gaze locks on a few of the guys snorting lines on the table behind us. "I didn't sleep great, and we've barely had a break all day." This is our last interview, and then we're all heading back to our hotel to grab dinner and a nightcap. Tomorrow, we fly to Paris.

"Aren't you taking the Xanax?" she asks in a low tone.

I nod. "I'm still having trouble sleeping. It's like it's not working anymore."

"You need to up the dose. Take two Xanax at bedtime and then two Adderall in the morning. That will help to balance you out, and I bet your sleep will improve."

"Can you increase my order?" I ask, leaning in close so the others don't hear.

"Of course, but right now, you need a little pick-me-up." She drags me toward the lines of cocaine spread out on the table.

"Nope." I shake my head. "I don't touch hard drugs."

"It's a stimulant, like Adderall, only this will give you a different kind of focus. You look dead on your feet. Trust me, one line and you'll feel on top of the world."

I shouldn't do it. It goes against all of my principles, but I'm exhausted, and I'm feeling hollow and empty inside. Constantly worrying about my relationship is depressing, and I just need to get out of my head for a while, so I do a line, and then we head out for our last Italian interview.

"Reeve." Vivien's troubled gaze peers into mine. "What is going on with you?" Placing her hands on my shoulders, she examines my face with a puckered brow.

"I'm just tired." I'm exhausted and drowsy, and I feel like complete and utter shit. "The promo tour was brutal, and all the travel and different time zones are catching up to me."

"Baby, you almost face-planted into your Christmas dinner yesterday. I'm worried about you."

"Don't be." I wrap my arms around her and pull her into my lap. "This is par for the course. Promo tours are grueling, and the filming schedule is tight." I was only supposed to be home for three days, but Bianca maneuvered a few things so I'm home for five days now. We have more promo before the premiere and for a couple of weeks post release, and then it's back on set to complete the second movie.

"Maybe you shouldn't have auditioned for other roles next summer. It sounds like you need a break. You should come to Europe with Audrey and me."

Yeah, she dropped that bombshell on Christmas Eve, and I'm not a happy camper. But I said nothing because I didn't want to find something else to argue over. We already had a big fight over the shit that's being spewed online. Viv is pissed that the fandom has devised a ship name for Saff and me—Reeveron —and she's getting flak from Saffhards—rabid fans of Saffron's. I advised her to ignore it and stay off social media. We talked about this before, and I don't know what else she wants me to say. We knew this would happen. It's panning out exactly how Cassidy and the studio planned it, so I don't know why she's getting on my case all the time. It's not like I can do a damn thing about it.

I'm not sure where I'll be or what I'll be doing in the summer, but I assumed Viv would come with me. I auditioned for several big parts before I left for the promo tour, and I'm waiting to hear if I secured any of them.

I'm gutted Vivien has chosen to spend the summer with her best friend instead of spending it with me. Audrey is apparently struggling over her breakup and the fact Alex is fucking other girls. It reminds me I need to catch up with my buddy as we haven't had any time to hang out in Boston, and I've only spoken to him a couple times over the phone. It's a typical female thing. Audrey was the one pushing for the breakup. Alex wasn't sure and he tried reopening the discussion, but Rey wouldn't go there. So, she doesn't get to criticize him for moving on already when she pushed him into it.

Vivien said Audrey hasn't been able to move on. She's crushed, and she needs her and can't abandon her.

As if I don't?

As if it's okay to abandon me all summer?

"If I don't land a new role, maybe I'll consider it, but I don't want to gate-crash your girlie trip."

She drags her fingers through my hair, and it feels amazingly good. "You wouldn't be. Audrey won't mind. This trip is to take her mind off Alex, and if it works out, I think I'll be freesoloing it a lot of nights."

I do not like the sound of my girl wandering European streets alone while her bestie is off hooking up with random strangers. Maybe I need to have that chat ASAP with Alex. Get him to get back together with Audrey, and they can scrap the trip altogether, or the four of us can go, provided I'm free. I like that plan way better.

Except I don't get to catch up with Alex because I'm way too wiped out the entire Christmas break, and Vivien and I spend the time holed up in my house, sleeping, fucking, and watching movies, until it's time for me to leave.

Chapter Thirty-Two
Now

"Reeve! Saffron! This way!" I keep my arm up high on Saffron's waist and plaster another fake smile on my face as I turn us toward the photographer calling our names, and we pose for another picture. I don't know how long we've been on the red carpet, but it feels like an eternity since we climbed out of the limousine. Flashbulbs go off in our faces as more photographers hustle forward, clamoring for our attention, and fans scream, cry, cheer, and wave banners from behind barriers that line the length of the road in front of the theater.

Our costars are here too, swallowed up by fans and photographers, but there's no denying the biggest attention and the loudest cheers are reserved for Saffron and me. Cassidy approaches, ushering us toward the crowd, and we spend a few minutes taking pics with fans and signing autographs. I have to push a lot of grabby hands away and twist my head to avoid kisses so many times it feels like my neck is on a rotating pole.

I'm too busy to remember my earlier melancholy. I always thought Viv would be on my arm on the red carpet for my first leading man role, and it's bittersweet. The buzz in the limo on the way here was electric, but I found it hard to partake without the missing part of my soul. I hope Viv liked the earrings I bought her and that they compensate for her having to be snuck in the back door like a criminal.

I didn't stop to think about what my fake relationship would mean for my real one in terms of the premiere. I hate that Vivien can't enjoy this moment with me, and it's hard to truly bask in it when she isn't the one tucked into my side or the one smiling with me for the cameras.

When no one was looking, I snuck an addy, and it's definitely helped to lift my spirits. As much as it saddens me that Vivien isn't walking the red carpet with me, it's still a pivotal moment in my career, and I can't spend the night acting like a depressed freak.

"Oh my God. This is insane!" Saffron whispers in my ear when we are reunited. She loops her arm through mine. "I have never experienced anything like this." Cassidy is urging us to make haste into the theater as we're already behind schedule, and they are waiting for us to begin.

"I know. Can you believe it?" I keep my eyes on her face as we walk, remembering the eyeful I got when she got into the car earlier. She's wearing a silky red dress with lace panels, and it's ridiculously low cut in the front. I'm not surprised she's gone for an eye-grabbing barely there dress, as it's her MO, but I thought she might have gone for something a bit classier for her first major premiere.

We follow the other main cast members and Cassidy into the packed theater. I spot my dad at the front, and a layer of stress lifts from my shoulders. He promised he'd be here, but I wasn't convinced. It's important to me he's here. I want him to see my first big studio movie and to be proud of me. I've seen the film several times now, and I have nailed it. Bianca was right. I have definitely stolen the show, and I'm not surprised I have secured a major part in a big-budget production being shot in Australia over the summer. The cast list is the crème de la crème of Hollywood royalty, and I'm really excited for the project.

It's finally happening for me, and everything Viv and I have planned for our future is coming true.

I scan the lower rows for my love, breathing a sigh of relief when I spot her with Lauren. There is no sign of Jon though, which is weird. Maybe he's at the bathroom or the concession stand.

"This guy asked me to sign his dick," Saff says, reclaiming my attention. I bend down a little so she can talk in my ear. "When I declined, because, hello, cameras, he proceeded to drop his pants and shove his butt in my face so I could sign his ass cheeks." Saffron clings to me tighter as we descend the stairs.

"No way?" I crack up laughing, just imagining it. I had to sign a few chests, which was uncomfortable as hell. "What happened?"

"Security came and hauled him away, but I managed to write my initials on his left butt cheek before he was carted off."

I chuckle as a familiar face locks on mine. My eyes pop wide as Jon approaches, coming up the stairs.

"Reeve." He tosses me a curt nod, completely ignoring Saffron. "We need to talk tomorrow." His terse tone is most unusual, and a trickle of dread tiptoes up my spine. He clamps a hand on my shoulder. "Enjoy tonight and well done. I have heard nothing but exceptional praise for your performance. I'm looking forward to seeing the movie."

"Thanks, Jon," I say, but he's already on the move.

Weird.

"That was rude." Saff smooths a hand down the front of her

dress, yanking it even lower at the chest. "Now I know where Vivien gets it from."

"Saffron," I warn, keeping a wide smile planted on my face. I can't forget we have a nosy audience tonight. Cassidy drilled it into me earlier today when I was being dressed in my Armani tux and having my hair professionally styled. "Don't start this shit again." She hasn't said a word about Vivien in months, and she's not going to rile my girlfriend up tonight. "Behave."

"I will if she does," she says, like she's five, but I have to park my annoyance when we come up to Rudy who has stopped to say hi to Lauren and Viv.

Cassidy warned me not to be seen with Vivien, which hurts, but it's what I signed up for. Still, I don't think there is any harm in stopping to say hi to my neighbors. It would appear rude not to.

"Lauren, Viv." I nod my head respectfully, trying my best not to ogle Vivien, but it's hard because my girl looks so damn beautiful.

Now this is how you dress for a premiere.

Vivien is wearing a strapless lemon dress with sparkly silver beading all over the tight-fitted top and full skirt. Painted toes peek out from behind pretty silver sandals. Her gorgeous hair is teased off her face with the aid of a few sparkly clips, and it falls down her back in soft waves. I love when she wears her hair like this, and I know she did it for me, which only makes me love her more. The diamond earrings I bought her hang from her earlobes, and they perfectly match the outfit Vivien designed and created herself. She is such a talented seamstress, and I'm surprised she didn't pick that as her major instead of creative writing. Makeup adorns her stunning face, way more than she usually wears, but it's tasteful and classy.

She is the epitome of the classical Hollywood princess and I wish I could shout from the rooftops that she is mine.

"Oh my God, it's so amazing to meet you, Lauren. You're my biggest inspiration, and I just adore you," Saffron says, sounding wholly insincere, and I internally grimace.

Lauren gives her a tight smile, which says it all. She's clearly in the anti-Saffron camp, and I know Saff is going to react before she does. Clinging on to me even tighter, she places her hand on my chest and stares up at me with adoring eyes that immediately put me on edge. Keeping the fake smile on my face, I warn her to quit this shit with my eyes.

I glance at Vivien, and my smile fades when I see the expression on her face. It's a mix of pain and anger, and she's gripping the arms of her chair super tight.

"You go on," I say, not looking at Saff. My gaze is firmly fixed on my girl.

"Okay, baby." Without warning, she yanks my head down and moves to kiss me.

What the actual fuck?

Out of the corner of my eye, I see Lauren holding Vivien in place. She's primed to explode.

I tilt my head to the side so Saff's kiss lands on my cheek. She giggles before smiling smugly at Vivien. Jesus Christ. This is the last thing I need. Now Viv is going to be busting my balls all night over something I had nothing to do with. I'm going to rip into Saff for landing me in deep shit again. She just had to act out tonight of all nights and give me an additional headache, didn't she?

"Don't be too long," she says, fake fawning all over me again. "It's just about to start. I can't wait for everyone to see what amazing chemistry we have."

I can't even look to see what expression is on Vivien's face now.

"All that girl is missing is a scarlet A strapped to her chest,"

Lauren says, piercing me with a look that shaves layers off my skin.

"I'm sorry about that. I know she's a lot to handle." And she is, but you just have to know her to understand how to deal with her.

"I hope you know what you've gotten yourself into, Reeve, and I'm not the one you should be apologizing to," Lauren chastises.

I cast a subtle glance around, to ensure no one is paying too much attention, before mouthing "I'm sorry" to Viv.

She lowers her eyes, delving into her purse before handing me a card. Our skin touches in the exchange, shooting a flurry of tremors up and down my arm. Viv's touch is like a supercharged electrical current igniting every part of me.

"You look beautiful," I softly say, glancing around again to ensure we're still under the radar. "Do you like the earrings?"

She nods, offering me a ghost of a smile. "Thank you. You look hot," she adds, but it sounds off. Like she's forcing herself to say something nice to me, and pain bubbles up my throat.

An awkward silence ensues, and I should go, but I can't make myself leave. All of a sudden, everything feels wrong, and an overwhelming sense of doom slicks over my body like a second skin. I don't know what's wrong, besides the obvious, but I need to fix whatever it is. I'm opening my mouth to ask her to meet me in the bathroom, when Cassidy materializes at my side like the wicked witch who just flew in on her broomstick. "Get to your goddamn seat now! People are watching!" she whisper-hisses in my ear.

I grind my teeth to the molars and barely resist glaring at her. We still hate one another. Nothing will ever change there.

"I've got to go, but I'll see you at the after-party," I say, hoping Vivien can see and hear how sorry I am for whatever it is I've done now.

Chapter Thirty-Three
Now

We receive a standing ovation in the theater when the credits roll at the end of the movie. Everyone is in high spirits when we make our way to the hotel where the after-party is taking place. Vivien and her parents were gone by the time I managed to get away from the well-wishers, but they'll be at the hotel. I secured tickets for Audrey and Alex and a couple of the other guys too. I plan to find somewhere private at the hotel to spend some time with my girl, but things quickly spiral out of my control.

Rudy and Jacob booked a suite at the hotel, and the main cast congregates there to drink shots and snort a few lines before we have to make our grand entrance in the ballroom downstairs. I don't hesitate when Saff leads me to the table. I'm already on a proverbial high after the success of the premiere, and one line of blow will hardly do any harm.

I'm buzzing when we make our way downstairs, laughing at some shit joke Ed makes as we enter the ballroom to loud applause. I'm instantly swept up in the crowd, and I only manage a quick hello to Audrey and Vivien as I'm swallowed up by industry heads and some of my idols.

Saffron is by my side as we schmooze with powerful players, knocking back champagne like it's water. I'm introduced to so many people, and I'm on fire, talking energetically about my plans for my future career, how amazing this project was to work on, and how fantastic it is that the whole cast has jelled so well. A couple of producers and the director from the Australian movie I'm filming over the summer are in attendance, and we chat for ages about the project, and I'm even more excited about it.

"We're busy," Saffron sneers at someone over her shoulder. "Go away."

"Reeve."

"Excuse me," I tell the gentlemen I'm talking to and turn around to face Audrey. "Hey, Rey." I beam at her. "What's up?"

"What's *up*?" She plants her hands on her hips and glares at me, slicing the edge off my euphoria. "What's fucking up, Reeve, is we've been here for over an hour and a half, and you have yet to talk to your girlfriend."

"He *is* talking to her." Saffron wraps her arm around my back while I hiss at Audrey, "You can't say that here! You know the score."

Her nostrils flare as she grips her purse. "I know that you're going to lose her unless you take your head out of your ass."

I roll my eyes. Were Audrey and Vivien always this dramatic, or is it a recent development? "Where is she?" I ask in a low voice.

"In the bathroom, and we're leaving then."

"Hey, what's going on?" Alex asks, coming up on my left.

"Your girlfriend is busting my balls for no fucking reason."

"Not his girlfriend," Audrey snaps, not even looking at

Alex, "and it's not for no fucking reason. You're acting like a complete asshole."

"That's not fair, Rey. This is the biggest night of Reeve's career to date, and he's got to work the room."

Audrey straightens up before turning to face her ex. "I'm not surprised you'd take his side. When the chips are down, you've both shown what's important." She leans in, practically breathing fire on both of us. "News flash, it's not Viv or me."

Alex visibly bristles. "Like I said at Christmas, this was your call. Don't blame me for moving on like you fucking told me to!"

"Fuck you, Alex, and stop texting me. As far as I'm concerned, you're dead to me." She turns that scathing lens on me. "If Viv had any sense, she'd do the same to you." She storms off then, shoving her middle finger up before she leaves.

"Wow, man. Think you dodged a bullet there. Who knew Rey was so fucking unhinged?"

"Don't say that." He drags a hand through his hair. "She's not unhinged. She's upset, but I'm upset too. She wanted this. I just went along with it, and now I'm getting crapped on for doing what she wanted. I'll never understand women."

"Tell me about it."

His brow furrows. "Hey, man. Are you okay?"

"I'm fine."

He leans in closer. "Are you on something?" he asks in a low voice. "Your pupils are dilated, and your eyes are rolling like crazy."

"Don't be ridiculous," I lie. "I'm on a natural high. Riding this wave and buzzing off the vibe."

He stares at me for a few beats, as if he's trying to drill a hole in my head and look inside. "We should catch up when you're back in Boston."

"Definitely."

"And you should go check on Viv. Your costar hightailed it out of here when Rey said Viv was in the bathroom, and I'm betting she made a beeline for her."

I whip my head around, only now noticing Saffron is nowhere in sight. "Fuck." I back up. "Thanks for coming, dude. Later."

I manage to evade all the people trying to claim my attention as I make my way out of the ballroom and head in the direction of the bathrooms.

I'm almost at the door to the ladies' bathroom when Viv runs out, slamming headfirst into me. She grabs me as she says, "Oh my God, Reeve. Thank God."

Saffron comes charging out of the bathroom after her, immediately falling to the floor and sobbing as she holds on to her foot. "She attacked me!" she shrieks, and the sound hurts my eardrums.

"You have got to be kidding me." A look of disgust washes over Viv's face. "You really are a piece of work."

Not again. I need this shit like a hole in the head. "Viv. What the hell is going on?" I ask, looking between the two women. Remembering we're in the hallway of the hotel, I remove her hands from my chest and put some distance between us. I can't be seen with her in public. I look around, but no one is around, thank fuck.

"I can explain, but she hurt me first." Her tone is meek because she knows she fucked up. It's about time she's taking some responsibility. I'm fucking pissed she'd start something with Saff tonight of all nights. It's the biggest night of my career, for fuck's sake! But she just has to go and make it about her. I am fucking sick of this shit.

"Dude, what's going on?" Rudy asks, coming up behind us.

"Get Saff out of here. I need to talk to Viv in private."

Rudy helps a sobbing Saffron to her feet. "I don't know if I can walk," she cries, and it grates on my nerves. She was managing just fine when she raced out of the bathroom in pursuit of Viv, so this is dramatic bullshit. Whatever fight they've had is just as much Saffron's fault. She clearly came here to bait her, and I'm not putting up with her shit either. Viv should know better than to fall for it.

"You had no trouble chasing me out of the bathroom," Viv barks, all meekness forgotten, and I see red.

What a pair of selfish bitches! They're trying to ruin my buzz and fuck up my night, and I won't let them. An irrational surge of anger flows through my veins as I lose control of my emotions. "That's enough!" I yell, rubbing my brow.

"Baby." Saffron lunges at me, but I step back. She can fuck off with that shit.

"Go with Rudy," I snap, all out of patience. "And I don't care how fucking sore your foot is. If you go out there and make this into *anything*, I'll walk." I know her MO, and it's clear Saffron will milk this for all she can get. I'm furious with Vivien, but I won't have Saffron targeting her when they are both to blame. A muscle pops in my jaw as I stare at her tear-streaked face. Pity she didn't put as much effort into her role. I cringed at some of her scenes on the screen, and Bianca is right—I am carrying her, and she would do well to remember it.

"Please, Reeve. This wasn't my fault," she pleads, making a grab for me again. "I did nothing wrong. You've got to believe me."

"Fuck off, Saff." I am done listening to her sniveling and am grateful when Rudy takes her away.

One down, one more to go.

Grabbing Viv's wrist, I pull her into a small office down the hallway. "Ow. You're hurting me," she cries.

I gentle my touch and examine her wrist, noticing clear nail impressions in her skin. I wonder if that was retaliation for whatever Viv did to her foot or if it came first.

"She did that, and I only stabbed her with my heel because she wouldn't let go of me." Viv answers my unspoken question.

"What the fuck is going on, Viv?" Releasing her hand, I run my fingers through my hair, still irritated and all wound up as she gives me a blow-by-blow account of what went down, stating how Saffron said she's going all out to get my ring on her finger.

It's fucking ridiculous, and Viv is clearly delusional if she thinks Saffron said that. How many fucking times do I have to tell her it's fake and there is nothing but sibling affection between us? I honestly feel like bashing my head against the wall. I shake my head as I stare at my girlfriend, wondering if I know her at all anymore. She's starting to sound a little crazy. "I know you two don't like one another, but lying about it doesn't help."

"I'm not lying," she shouts. "Why would I do that?"

"Maybe because you want to ruin things for me? God knows you're trying hard to suck all the enjoyment out of this experience." I thump the desk, so fucking pissed at having to deal with this shit tonight of all nights. "You couldn't just give me one night without all this shit? You didn't even congratulate me! I am so sick of the two of you in my ear, and it's got to stop!" I roar.

Her body locks up, and she glares at me in a way I've never seen her glaring at me before. "What the fuck do you think I've been doing all night? I was sidelined so you could have your moment in the spotlight with her. You haven't even spent five minutes with me, so when the fuck was I supposed to congratulate you?! When, Reeve?" She waves her hands in the air. "She's been clinging to your side all night, and I've put up with it even though my heart feels like it's being ripped apart. Do you have any idea how hard tonight has been for me, you self-ish, self-absorbed prick?"

"*I'm* selfish?" I yell, shoving my face in hers.

Who the fuck does she think she is trying to throw this back on me?! What the hell have I done except bend over backwards to get her into the premiere and after-party and I spent a fortune on those diamond earrings. I bust my balls calling and texting her when I get any free time, and I listen to her bitching and moaning about social media and stuff I have no control over. I didn't even cause a scene when she told me she was ditching me in the summer for Audrey. The fuck she gets to call me selfish! I have never thought Vivien was an ungrateful little bitch, but it's beginning to look like that.

"That is fucking rich, coming from you," I sneer. "Your self-ishness is ruining my career!"

Her eyes pop wide. "You're on something. You did drugs with her!" She covers her mouth as shock splays across her face. "My God, Reeve. What is she doing to you? What are you doing to yourself?"

Yeah, nope. She's not going to sit in judgment on me when she has no idea of the stress I'm under and how I'm being pulled in all different directions trying to please everyone. "So, what if I did?" I shrug because it's no biggie. "We all did a line after the premiere. It's not a big deal."

"Maybe not to you. But it is to me." She moves to leave. "I don't even know who you are anymore, Reeve."

"I could say the same thing to you."

"Then I guess we both know what to do."

Chapter Thirty-Four
Now

"Movie star, come on." Saffron perches on the side of my chair, pleading with me again.

"Fuck. Off." I take a few puffs of the blunt before passing it over to Darren while I ignore my other costar. I've been seriously pissed off since the argument between her and Vivien downstairs, and I'm doing everything to get out of my head so I can't think about that shit anymore. Viv's final words were a challenge, but she can fuck off too if she thinks I'm going to ditch the after-party to run after her. Is it too much to ask for her to bite her tongue on a night that's important to me? Could she not have made it about her for once?

Grabbing the bottle of whiskey at my feet, I guzzle it down, relishing the burn as it glides down my throat. Rudy chuckles as he swipes it from my hands. "Leave some for the rest of us." He waggles his brows before bringing the bottle to his lips.

"Reeve. Puh-lease." Saffron lands in my lap, and I instantly push her off. Laughter bounces off the walls as the guys snicker. Oh, she really doesn't like that. I smirk. She scowls at me from the floor. "Don't be such a dick."

"Don't be such a bitch."

"You're a nasty drunk."

"And you're a jealous ho."

"Fuck you." She climbs to her feet and glares at me. "For the hundredth time, I said none of those things to your prissy princess. She's lying. God, when are you going to wake up?! It's so goddamn frustrating to watch her taking advantage of you! Go take your sour mood out on her, because all I've done is have your back, you naïve prick!" she hisses, kicking at my shin with her high heels.

I barely feel the pain, flipping her the bird as I take the blunt back from Darren.

"I know something that will put you in a better mood," Jacob says, grabbing his crotch and leering at Saff. "Want a spin on my dick?"

Saffron glowers at me before her lips kick up. "You know what, Jacob?" she says, still looking at me. "That sounds like an offer I can't refuse."

Saff appears to be doing the rounds of the male cast members, and she doesn't seem to care they all trade bedroom stories about her. It's all a bit...seedy, but bed-hopping on movie sets is not a new thing. I just hope she hasn't added me to her list of potential conquests. I wouldn't touch her if she was last woman on Earth. She shrieks as Jacob picks her up and tosses her over his shoulder before frog-marching her into one of the bedrooms.

Good riddance. Now I can get trashed in peace.

I wake hours later with daylight streaming through the windows of the suite. I'm lying at an awkward angle on the couch with my face pressed into the leather and a pool of drool under my cheek. My mouth is as dry as the Sahara, and I'm dying to take a piss. Darren and Conrad are passed out on the floor, the latter snoring like a freight train. The suite is a mess with empty bottles littered on the floor, remnants of blow and MJ evident on several hard surfaces, overflowing ashtrays, and broken glasses. Half-eaten trays of food add to the obnoxious smell in the room, and my stomach lurches as bile travels up my throat.

I make it to the bathroom in time to vomit the contents of my stomach. My head is thumping, my brow is sweaty, and I stink to the high heavens. Fuck, why did I think it was a good idea to get so fucked up?

Yeah, now I remember.

Gripping the edge of the sink, I stare absently in the mirror while remembering the harsh words Viv and I exchanged last night. I don't remember everything we said, but I remember enough to know I'm majorly in the doghouse. Especially if she realizes I partied all night with Saffron and my other costars.

Damn it. I need to get home before she realizes I stayed out all night.

I take a piss and rub some toothpaste on my finger and around my mouth before rinsing with water. Then I leave the bathroom to look for my things. I'm unsteady on my feet as I make my way around the suite, searching for my shoes and my dress jacket. When I find my stuff, I grab my cell, relieved there is still some battery life, and I call a town car to come pick me up. Then I down several glasses of water while I hunt, unsuccessfully, for some pain pills.

When I get home, I pop a couple of pain meds, collapse on my bed, and pass out immediately.

When I wake a few hours later, I still feel like shit but not quite as shitty as earlier. I rub a hand over my stomach as I lie in bed, staring at my cell phone like I can magically conjure missed texts and calls from Vivien because there are none. "Fuck." I curl my body around a pillow as fear sets in. I might have really messed up last night. She knows I took drugs, and she wasn't happy. I also didn't take her side in the argument with Saff, but it was hard to know who was lying and who was telling the truth.

In the cold light of day, I know Vivien wouldn't make everything up, but if Saff really did say those things, then she only said them to get a rise out of my girl and it worked. Vivien will have to toughen up and stop letting Saffron get to her so easily.

But I shouldn't have gotten angry. I should have taken her side, even if just to keep up appearances. It seems obvious to me now that Saff wants to break Viv and me up because she believes she isn't good enough for me.

I'm still pissed they both tried to ruin the night, but what's done is done. Now, I need to grovel like I've never groveled before. Swinging into damage-control mode, I drag my weary ass from the bed, take a long, hot shower, and head to the kitchen to make some food. I'm not feeling overly hungry, but my stomach is rumbling like a volcano about to erupt, and I figure some soup and bread might settle it.

"Looks like it was some night if you only rolled in this morning," Simon says when I enter the kitchen in jeans and a clean shirt and in my bare feet.

"It was a long one," I say, not willing to divulge details. We don't have that kind of relationship. And I'm pissed because he skipped out after the movie with only a nod in my direction. I move to the coffee machine. "What did you think of the movie?" Acid churns in my gut as I wait for my cup to fill.

"As teen dramas go, it wasn't bad, but some of the casting decisions are extremely questionable. Saffron Roberts is sexy, and she's got a great rack, but she's a talentless bimbo, and she really drags your performance down. I don't know what Ken and the other execs were thinking in hiring her."

"They were thinking she'd bring buzz, a large social media

following, and entice a greater male audience, and they were right," I retort.

"Everyone knows it's teen girls and young women who will make or break a project like this. They made a mistake casting her, and they know it."

I add cream and sugar to my coffee and turn to face him. I lean back against the counter. "What did you think of my performance?" I ask even though I shouldn't.

He props his elbows on the island unit as he stares at me. "It was decent, but there's always room for improvement. What matters is industry gossip, and they like you." He finishes his coffee and stands. "Be careful which future projects you choose. They'll make or break you." With those words of wisdom, he exits the room, leaving me stewing in a rancid broth of my own making.

The doorbell chimes, and I tell Mrs. Thompson I'll get it, assuming it's the flower delivery I ordered. There's no way I'm showing up on Viv's doorstep without a peace offering. She still hasn't reached out to me, which means she's really mad. My eyes pop wide when I find Jonathon outside my house. "If you're looking for Dad, he left a couple hours ago."

"I was looking for you."

"Okay." I step aside to let him enter. "Want a coffee?" I inquire as he follows me down the hallway.

"I'm good. I'm taking Lauren out to dinner, so I won't be staying long."

"Okay. What's up?" I ask, flopping down on the couch in the main living room.

Jon claims one of the high leather-backed chairs in front of the fireplace. "What's up is the way you're treating my daughter, Reeve."

I bolt upright as instant panic bubbles in my chest. Did Viv tell him about last night? Fuck! I hope she didn't say anything about the drugs!

"I know things have been strained between us, but we'll work it out, and not to be rude, Jonathon, but my relationship with Vivien isn't anyone's business but our own."

"It becomes my business when I see how much she's hurting because of bad decisions and thoughtless actions on your part."

Bad decisions? Thoughtless actions? What the fuck? "I'm not sure what she's said, but I never intentionally set out to hurt Vivien, and I'm doing my best to juggle the demands of my role with her needs and prioritizing our relationship."

"Vivien hasn't said anything, Reeve, but Lauren and I have eyes. I don't know what the hell is going on with the studio or what's happening on set, but what happened last night was rude, disrespectful, and downright hurtful. The young man I know would not have been happy to see his girl shoved in a corner like some afterthought. The Reeve I know would have fought to have the woman he loves by his side on the red carpet; instead, she was shunned and made to feel invisible and unwanted. And I know something went down with that nasty costar of yours, but Vivien wouldn't tell us anything. She remains loyal to you even though you're treating her poorly. All I know is my princess cried herself to sleep last night, like she's done plenty of times since you began filming these movies, and I'm done sitting back and saying nothing. It's not right, Reeve, and you need to step up and protect her."

The thought of Viv crying herself to sleep guts me, and guilt slaps me in the face. But the other stuff he's said confuses me. "I don't understand. Vivien wasn't shoved in a corner. I ensured she was close to the front, and it sucks that I couldn't sit with her, but—"

"Reeve, Vivien wasn't assigned a seat in the front. She was

assigned a seat in the very back row, right over in the dark corner where no one could see her. The only reason she wasn't sitting there is because I refused to let my princess be hidden away like she's something to be ashamed of. I took her seat, and she sat in mine."

I'm dumbfounded. "I had no idea, and I didn't request that." I gulp over the lump wedged in my throat. "I would never put Vivien in a corner, and I could never be ashamed of her. I love her."

"You need to start acting like it, son." Jonathon stands. "Whoever has a vendetta against Vivien needs to be dealt with once and for all, and you need to man up and handle it." His eyes bore into mine, and I instinctively prepare myself for what's coming next, already knowing it's going to hurt. "I'm disappointed in you, Reeve. We both are. We know you are capable of doing better. If you need help, if that's what this is really about, you only have to ask us."

I'm sweating under my clothes as he stares at me like he knows more than I'm saying. He has already admitted Vivien hasn't told them anything, so I think he's just fishing for information. I didn't want to involve Jon or Lauren before, and it's even more important I keep them out of this now. They are already disappointed in me, and if they knew everything, they'd probably wash their hands of me. It can't come to that. It won't. I'm going to fix it.

Jonathon sighs as he rubs his hands down his face. "You're as much our son as Vivien is our daughter, Reeve, but that might change if you don't get your shit together. We won't allow you to continue hurting our daughter, and I won't hesitate to step in and protect Vivien if you fail to prove you're the man we believe you to be."

I spend the next hour on the phone with Bianca and Cassidy, screaming at them repeatedly and threatening to quit. Cassidy readily confesses to altering the seating arrangements, explaining Bianca had nothing to do with it. Cassidy shows zero remorse, instead telling me I'm lucky Vivien was allowed to attend and I should be grateful she squeezed her in because the studio didn't want her there at all. I go to town on the bitch before threatening Bianca with termination of my contract, and then I hang up. Anger is rampaging through my veins like an out-of-control bull, so I go for a run in an attempt to calm down before I head over to see Vivien.

It's getting dark by the time I land on Viv's doorstep, and I'm anxious as I enter the hallway and call her name. I perform a quick check downstairs before taking the stairs two at a time, and heading toward her bedroom with the flowers in my hand.

"Viv." I rap on her bedroom door. "It's me." Nerves fire at me from all angles because I truly have no idea what kind of reception I'll face. But I'm not letting her break up with me. I hear the TV on, so I know she's in there. "Viv, please." I rest my forehead against the door. "I'm so sorry. Please let me in so I can explain."

"You can come in," she calls out after a few more tense beats.

She's lounging on her couch in yoga pants, a top, and a hoodie with fluffy socks on her feet. Red-rimmed eyes meet mine as I approach, and her skin is all blotchy from crying. "Took you long enough," she says, pulling herself upright and hugging her knees to her chest. "You didn't even call or text me. Too busy having fun with all your fake new friends?"

Ignoring her sneering tone, I sit beside her and set the flowers down on the coffee table. "After how we left it, I didn't know if you'd want me to call or text. I had a late night and slept most of the afternoon, and then I spent an hour screaming at Bianca and Cassidy after your dad told me what they did." Remorse courses through my veins as I pin her with pleading eyes. "I didn't know they did that to you, Viv. I'm so, so sorry. I understand now why you were so upset."

"It wasn't only that." She sniffles, dabbing her nose with her sleeve. "It was how you seemed happy without me. How little I seemed to matter because you couldn't even find more than a few minutes to talk to me. You didn't even look for me at the after-party. Instead, you let that cunt-face whore drape herself all over you." Tears spill from her eyes. "But mostly, it's how you didn't believe me." She sobs. "I told you the truth, and you dismissed it. You were so cruel, Reeve. You didn't believe *me*." She thumps her closed fist over her chest. "You never do when it comes to that bitch, and that hurts the most." She swipes angrily at her tears. "That and you're doing drugs. Like what the actual fuck, Reeve? What are these movies doing to you? The Reeve I know would never take drugs."

"I'm still the same Reeve."

"Are you though?"

"I am still *me*, Viv. I'm evolving, adapting to my new environment, and I don't always make the right decisions, but I am still the same person you know. The one you've grown up with. The one I hope you still love."

"Of course, I still love you, dumbass." Tears stream down her face. "This would be so much easier if I didn't." She breaks down then, and I can't hold back. Scooting over, I pull her into my arms and try to comfort her. Her body is wracked with heart-wrenching sobs, and I feel every one of them. I feel like the shittiest boyfriend in the world. We're both at fault for different things, but it's my job to protect her, care for her, and make her feel cherished, and I've failed. I've got to do better.

"I'm so sorry, Viv. I hate seeing you in pain, especially knowing I'm the cause of it."

"I should break up with you," she says, lifting her tearstained face to mine. "This seems too painful for both of us."

"No, babe." I brush damp strands of hair off her face, fighting a surge of panic. "I know it's hard, but please don't break up with me. I'll do better, I swear. I'll make more time for you, and I won't let Bianca or Cassidy or the studio do anything like that to you again."

"No more drugs, Reeve."

"No more." I nod because I've got no intention of doing cocaine again.

"How bad is it?" she asks, scrutinizing my face. "And don't lie to me. How often have you done that?"

"That was only my second time, and I swear it was my last." I press my hand over my heart. "I promise." I don't mention the other pills because they're not the same. They help me with my sleep and anxiety issues, and it's not like I'm doing blow every day.

Suspicion ghosts over her pretty face. "Is that the truth? Because if it's a problem, I want to know so I can help."

"It's not a problem," I rush to reassure her. "I swear I've got everything in hand."

She stares at me for a few tense moments, and I'm beginning to think she doesn't believe me. A bead of sweat rolls down my back as I wait her out. "If it becomes one, you can always talk to me. I'm worried."

"Don't worry." I take her hand and kiss the back of her knuckles. "I promise I'm good."

"Okay. I won't break up with you, but you really hurt me, Reeve. Worse than any other time before."

I brush my lips against hers. "I'm really sorry, baby. I hate that I upset you so badly. You know how I hate seeing you cry."

I sweep my thumbs under her eyes, collecting the moisture gathered there.

Crawling into my lap, she wraps her arms around me, and we hug for ages. Gradually, I feel the stress leaving my limbs. I was more scared than I realized. "Things have been rough, but we'll try harder," I whisper in her ear. "We mean too much to one another to let what we have go."

Tipping her head up, she clasps my face in her hands. "You've got to be completely honest with me, babe, and I know you're sick of me mentioning *her*, but I don't trust her, Reeve. She's up to something. Please open your eyes and see what's in front of you. I wasn't lying to you. I was telling the truth."

Saff has been blowing up my phone all day, leaving teary messages and apologies, and I haven't responded. "I believe you." I do, but I still believe Saff was just saying all that shit to rile Vivien up. That doesn't excuse it though. I've asked her not to interfere, and she's not listening. That's a red flag for sure. "And I have been keeping my distance from her as much as I can." It's hard when we're traveling the world promoting the movie, staying in the same places, and hanging out at night, but I will make a greater effort as I'm not going to let her come between us anymore.

Chapter Thirty-Five
Then - Age 15

"I want to try something," I say, pulling Viv to the edge of my bed. Lauren doesn't know she is here. She thinks she's over at Audrey's, but we're all hanging at my place today because Simon is away on business again and not due home until late tonight. Audrey and Alex just started dating exclusively, and they wanted alone time as much as we did. They are in one of the guest bedrooms getting up to similar stuff, I'm guessing.

"What are you up to?" Viv giggles as I spread her thighs and run my hands up under her skirt. I love how soft her skin feels.

"I want to taste you." My eyes lock on to hers as she catches her breath. We are respecting her parents' wishes and refraining from full sex even though tons of our friends are no longer virgins. Instead, we are finding creative ways to touch one another, and I got a few ideas from some porn we watched together a few nights ago.

"Like in the movie?" she asks, and it's cute she calls that sex-fest a *movie*.

"Yes." My fingers brush against the crotch of her panties. "Can I?"

Her cheeks flush red, but she's nodding eagerly. "Yes, but only if I get to taste you after."

My dick roars to life behind my zipper, more than loving that suggestion. "Only seems fair." I'm grinning as I hook my thumbs in her panties and shimmy them down her legs. Bunching the crisp white panties in my palm, I bring them to my nose and sniff.

"Oh my God," Viv splutters over another giggle. "You're so dirty."

"You bring out that side of me." My grin expands as I stuff her panties in my pocket to add to my collection.

"Mom is going to start asking where all my underwear is disappearing to." She arches a brow.

"I'll give you money to buy more," I suggest as my hands wander up her smooth, bare legs. "Now lie back and let me show you how good my tongue is." It's total bravado, and we both know it because I've never done this before. But Vivien loves my fingers inside her, and we're both experts at getting one another off by now. Some days, she only has to look at my cock and I'm leaking cum.

I remove her skirt next and sit back on my heels to admire the view. She has such a pretty pussy, and it's always glistening and ready for me. My dick is painfully hard now, and butter-flies are swooping around my stomach as I lean in and press my nose to her smooth cunt. I look over her flushed face and lust-filled eyes with pride. I love putting that look on her face. Parting her pussy lips with my thumbs, I keep my gaze locked on Vivien as my tongue darts out, and I lick a path up and down her slit.

Viv moans and her hips jerk when I do it again. She tastes sweet but tangy, like lemons, or maybe I'm tasting the citrusy shower gel she uses. Either way, I love it. My hands hold her thighs in place as I dive in, driving my tongue inside her, and I almost come on the spot. Holy fucking shit. She's clenching around my tongue and writhing on the bed, and I'm already addicted. I feast on her, lapping at her juices and gently sucking on her clit as she grabs handfuls of my hair and urges me to come closer.

My face is buried in her pussy when she comes all over me, and it's the most delicious, most precious, most intimate thing, we've ever done.

"Reeve," she cries as her back arches, her hips swivel, and her thighs quiver. I stay with her—my lips and tongue continuing to coax the orgasm from her—as I grip my dick hard to stop myself from coming. "Oh my God, Reeve!" she pants, collapsing flat on her back when her thighs stop shaking and she basks in the afterglow of her O. "Come here," she demands, curling one finger, and I climb up over her.

"Was that good?"

She grabs my face and smashes her lips to mine, swallowing my tongue and groaning into my mouth. "I can taste me on you."

"Now who's dirty?" I tease, peppering little kisses all over her face.

"Reeve." She sounds serious, so I stop what I'm doing to look at her. Emotion swirls in her gorgeous greenish-brown eyes. "That was fucking incredible. Like seriously, how are you so naturally good at this?"

My chest swells with male pride. "It's easy when I'm with you. I'm driven by the need to make you feel good. I want to learn all the things you like so I can keep making you feel good."

"It's working." She laughs, dragging her fingers through my hair. "I'm going to need you to do that every day."

Now it's my turn to laugh. "That won't be an issue. I'm already addicted."

She sits up abruptly, pushing me down on my back. "My turn." Her eyes flash with want as I reach out and cup one of her tits through her top. "These are getting bigger."

"Thank fuck." She's felt self-conscious at school because a lot of the girls have bigger tits, but it's never bothered me. Her small tits were as perfect as the rest of her, but they are definitely growing, almost fully fitting my hand now.

"I love them no matter what size they are," I remind her, fondling them and rubbing my thumbs across her taut nipples.

"I know, and I love you for that." She leans down and kisses me softly. "I just love you."

"Not as much as I love you."

The guys are always giving me shit for how sappy we are, but I couldn't give two shits. I always want my girl to know she is worshiped and adored and so fucking loved. Some days, the magnitude of my feelings for her almost feels like it's too much. Too intense. Too consuming. Overwhelming when we're still only teenagers. But I don't know any other way to be, and I don't ever want it to change.

I love loving her, and I love how her love fills me with confidence. With Vivien in my life, it feels like I can overcome any obstacle or challenge as long as she is by my side.

Man, the guys would give me so much shit if they were privy to my inner thoughts.

Thank fuck mind reading isn't a common skill.

I think I was put on Earth to love Vivien Grace Mills with my whole heart, and I intend to fully deliver on it.

"Get down here," Viv says, yanking me out of my head. She's kneeling at the end of the bed and licking her lips. "I've been dying to give you a blowjob."

"Now she tells me," I quip, scooting down the bed and

lifting my hips as she pulls my shorts down my legs, and my cock springs out, fully erect and greedily anticipating the feel of her hot mouth.

"My boobs aren't the only thing growing," She wraps her hand around me. "Look, I can barely fit my fingers around it now."

"Babe, please," I plead, tangling my fingers in her long hair. "I need you to take me in your mouth now." I'm already primed to explode, so I doubt this will last long.

She gives my cock a few tugs, in practiced strokes, that have me seeing stars. Viv is extremely good at handjobs, and if she matches that skill with blowjobs, I'll be in perpetual heaven.

"I'm not sure what to do," she says, dragging her lower lip between her teeth. "I should've paid more attention to the movie."

This girl.

She slays me in the best way.

"Hold me at the base, and then slide your lips up and down."

Her fingers tighten around me as her tongue darts out, swiping the bead of precum at the tip. "Holy fuck," I groan, digging my hands into the comforter. "I don't think I'm going to last long."

"It doesn't matter," she murmurs before licking the underside of my dick. "I can do it again."

Viv nibbles on my throbbing flesh, grinning with pride when she takes me into her mouth, letting me hit the back of her throat, and I lose control instantly, ejaculating into her mouth without any advance warning. Streams of cum launch from my cock as I come with a loud groan. "Shit." I laugh to hide my embarrassment as I pop out of her mouth, but my girl is having none of it.

"That was so fucking hot." She licks her lips and ravishes

my dick with her gaze. "And I don't mind the taste of it. I actually quite liked it."

And my cock is already hardening again.

"Cassie Harrison was telling the entire cheerleading squad the other day how she blew Guy," she continues, "and he came in her mouth, but she spat it out 'cause it tasted salty and gross."

"Ugh, babe." I run my fingers through her hair as I come down from a high. "I *do not* want to think about that fuckface when we're in bed."

"Guy who?" she jokes, but she wouldn't be laughing if she heard the things that asshole says about her. We are still constantly butting heads, and one of these days, I am going to knock him the fuck out.

"I need more practice." Her smile is wickedly sweet as she cups my balls and strokes her finger along my taint. "Can I blow you again?"

As if she needs to ask! My cock is now rock hard, and it seems we're all ready for round two. "You'll never hear me complaining, babe. I'm game if you are."

I'm on such a high after oral sex that I'm still wide-awake hours later, tossing and turning in bed. I can't stop reliving it, and my hand is sore from jerking off so much. Even now, my dick is semi-hard as I climb out of bed to get some warm milk. I've had bouts of insomnia on and off for years, and Viv is constantly researching options to help. She printed out a recipe for warm vanilla milk a couple of days ago, and though it recommends you drink it thirty minutes before bed, I figure it can't hurt to try it.

I pad downstairs in my bare feet wearing only cotton sleep pants, yawning as I run my fingers through my messy hair. I heat some milk in a pan while I fetch the honey, vanilla, and nutmeg from the pantry. I have just assembled my drink in a mug when the sound of approaching footfalls has me lifting my head.

Jesus Christ. Are you kidding me? Irritation instantly flares as I recognize the woman approaching me.

"Hey there, honey," she slurs, flashing me a flirty smile as she ambles into the kitchen barely dressed. My father's half-buttoned shirt is way too big on her slim frame, hanging off one shoulder and barely concealing her chest. It hits mid-thigh, but I'm guessing she has nothing on underneath. Blech. Her hair is a tangled mess, and her face has that freshly fucked flush. Unfortunately, I've come to recognize the look because my father has an endless line of random women rotating through the front door, and this isn't the first time I've bumped into one of his conquests in the house.

"Whatcha doin', sweetie?" she asks, rounding the counter and coming up alongside me.

From this angle, I can see the swell of one tit, and I look away in disgust. I know who she is too.

Maritsa Fenwick.

The very married mother of my archnemesis.

I don't know if she realizes I go to school with her son, but she is definitely his mother as I have seen her frog-marching him from the principal's office in the past.

"I'm just going to bed," I say, trying to back away from her, but she's fast for a drunken cheating whore.

"Stay." Grabbing my arm, she pushes me back against the counter and plants herself right in front of me. Her tongue darts out, and she licks her lips as she slowly peruses the length of my body, lingering on the outline of my semi through my thin pajama pants.

"You got a girl?" she slurs, pressing up against me.

"Get the fuck away from me," I say through gritted teeth, my fingers tightening around my mug. "And yes, I do. Not that it's any of your business."

"I'm not surprised to hear that." She moves her hand from my biceps to my chest. "A sexy guy like you has girls crawling out of the woodwork, I bet."

"Don't touch me," I snap when both of her hands begin roaming over my abs.

"You're the younger, sexier, hotter version of your dad." She giggles as her hands continue exploring, and panic is charging through my veins. She rolls her hips and presses her groin against mine, and I'm frozen in place, hoping I'm in bed and having a nightmare and this isn't real.

A few of my dad's fuck buddies have flirted with me in the past, but none of them ever touched me.

I feel sick, and I don't know what to do.

Some guys might get off on this, but I'm not one of them.

I don't want her touching me or flirting with me. I want her to leave me the fuck alone.

The shirt slips down her arm, fully exposing one boob, and I'm close to puking. I'm shaking as I'm rooted to the spot, panic doing a number on me. I want to push her away, but I'm terrified of touching her when she's basically semi-naked. Women have cried rape for less.

"Don't be shy," she adds, rubbing her palm up and down my dick through my pants. "I know you want me. Your body speaks volumes."

"That's not for you," I hiss. "You make me sick." Her hand tightens around my swelling dick, and nausea swims up my throat. I finally snap out of my panicked daze and push at her bare shoulder, shoving her back a little. "Stop fucking touching me! I'm fifteen, you sick bitch! I go to school with your son!"

Her face pales as the truth sinks in. Yeah, bitch, you didn't consider that when you put yourself all up in my space.

"What the fuck is going on?" Dad strides into the kitchen wearing a thunderous expression.

Panic splays all over Maritsa's face, but she quickly composes herself, which might be impressive for someone so drunk if I didn't loathe everything about her. She schools her features into a neutral line, looking like butter wouldn't melt in her mouth. It's a skillfully manipulative look and creepy as fuck. I can't even breathe a sigh of relief when she takes several steps back because the look on Simon's face is scary as shit.

"Hey, darling." Maritsa stumbles as she makes her way to my father, falling into his chest. "I was just saying hi to your son. It's like looking at a younger version of you," she slurs, circling her arms around Simon's bare torso and snuggling into him.

"You better not have been doing what I think you were doing!" he says, his gaze lingering on the obvious bulge in my pajama pants before he lifts his eyes to glare at me.

"I didn't do anything!" I shout, pushing off the counter. "She fucking hit on me! I told her to stop, but she just kept groping me!"

"Don't fucking lie to me, boy." Simon wraps his arm around her back, tucking her into his side, but he sways a little on his feet, confirming he's had too much to drink too. "I know exactly what this is. You thinking you're a man now because your balls have finally dropped and you're getting some action from that sweet little piece next door."

"Don't you fucking talk about Vivien like that!" Red-hot rage swirls through my veins as I jab my finger in my father's direction.

"Do you honestly think any woman would hit on you when they have me? You're pathetic, Reeve, and a constant embarrassment. I should have sent—" He stops whatever he was about to say and pulls the shirt up to cover his fuck buddy, only just now realizing she was flashing his underage son. "That's enough with your lies." The icy tone of his voice matches the cold expression on his face. "Get the fuck up to bed. After you've apologized to Maritsa for disrespecting her."

"What the actual fuck?" I shriek, close to losing it altogether. "I'm not lying, and I'm not apologizing to that pedo whore! I just came downstairs to get some warm milk because I couldn't sleep, and *she* attacked *me*!"

"Warm milk?" he sneers before a harsh laugh rips from his chest. "Oh, I get it now. It's not surprising you have mommy issues. Did you ask her to tuck you into bed and feed you your drink? Or maybe you asked her to play with your pee-pee?" His mocking tone is like waving a red flag in front of an angry bull.

Shock splays across Maritsa's face as she stares at me, but the bitch says nothing, content to let me take the fall.

"Fuck you, asshole. It's not my fault she came on to me because you can't satisfy her!"

I don't see the punch coming until I'm falling on my back to the tile floor, lukewarm milk splashing all over my chest and pants. My jaw throbs, my back aches, and something comes loose inside me. I barely feel any pain as I hop up and lunge at my father. Maritsa shrieks and quickly unhooks herself from around his body. My clenched fist lands squarely on his nose and blood instantly spurts from his nostrils. "You can't ever take my side! You always blame me when I do nothing wrong!" I slam my fist into his gut next before I kick out with my foot, sending him flying to the floor.

I hover over him, enjoying the shocked expression on his face. Yeah, jerkface. You can't knock me around anymore because I'm younger, fitter, taller, and stronger than you. I'm tempted to unleash all the pent-up emotion rampaging through me on him, but he's not worth the effort. "That's the last time you hit me," I warn, pressing my foot down hard on his chest and keeping him trapped on the floor. "Next time, I won't stop. Not until you stop breathing."

I walk off with a sore jaw, bruised back, aching knuckles, and a pain in my heart.

But it's the last time he ever physically abuses me.

And the last time that woman is in our house.

Chapter Thirty-Six
Now - Age 19

We return to the set in February, after the promo tour ends, to resume work on *Twisted Betrayal*, and I try to keep my head down and focus on my role. Saffron has gotten the hint I don't want to hang out with her outside the set, and after initially acting like a total bitch, she's now resorted to apologies and sweet smiles and blatant flirting. Whatever she's planning, it won't work. I remind her repeatedly I'm not interested in her as anything more than a friend. I promised Viv, and myself, I would keep my distance from her, and I'm determined to do that. I'm not rude to her. It's amicable on set, but I've made it clear us hanging out together or in a group, outside of work and fake-dating commitments, is a big no-no. It means I spend less time with the guys too, but if that's the sacrifice I must make to fix things with my girl, I will do it.

Things are strained with Vivien, and there's a divide between us that's never been there before. I hate it, but it's almost impossible to resolve when there are thousands of miles separating us. For the first time, I'm worried I might lose her, and that thought has me panicking a bit.

Jacob hooked me up with his supplier, so I don't have to rely on Saffron for my pills. I've had to increase my dosage again, but it's cool. I'm not addicted. I could stop at any time, but I don't because I need them to keep the insomnia and anxiety at bay. And it's working. I'm more focused than ever.

Viv and I have our first argument in weeks when pictures of me on a "date" with Saffron are splashed all over the media. I'm guessing Cassidy is tipping them off because there was a virtual stampede outside the restaurant when we left after our meal. It's the first time I'm glad the studio insisted on hiring body-guards for us. Interest in our supposed relationship is insane, and I have stopped checking social media because we are plas-tered all over it.

So, I understand why my girlfriend is upset, but she knows there is nothing I can do about it. It's not like I even enjoy spending time with Saffron.

It's torture, pure and simple.

Although Saff is nothing but civil and friendly, I'm begin-ning to see what Vivien has been saying.

She's fake.

And I'm starting not to trust anything that comes out of her mouth.

It's all an act, and having to pretend to be in love with her makes me wanna puke. The feel of her hand in mine makes my skin crawl. The scent of her overpowering perfume makes me gag. Her girlish giggle hurts my ears. The way she hangs on to me, staring with a faux adoring smile, conjures images of a bloodsucking leech siphoning vitality from my body.

I'm fighting constantly with Bianca and Cassidy over plans for fake dates, refusing to do anything but the bare minimum.

All of it is exhausting, and I'm clinging to my sanity by my fingernails.

Throwing myself into work is the only thing that stops me from losing it completely.

Summer arrives, and I move to Australia to film a new project. The cast is mostly older in this movie, and the experience couldn't be more different. My character is a young man having an affair with an older married woman. It's an emotionally complex plot full of moral dilemmas. I'm enjoying flexing different artistic muscles and really enjoying the character-driven role.

While I get on famously with my costars, they are all either in committed relationships or married with families. Everyone has their significant other with them, and I'm feeling more lost and left out than ever. I am missing Vivien badly. Talking on the phone is virtually impossible with the large time difference between Australia and Europe, so we are mostly communicating via messages and emails. She sends me pics of the different places she and Audrey visit, and it looks like she's having a blast.

I'm glad she's enjoying herself, but I won't lie; I'm still bitter she ditched me this summer for her female bestie.

I *need* her.

I'm a mess without her.

And I'm resentful she's left me out here all alone. That she can't even find some time to come be with me. I'm lonely and resorting to popping more pills and drinking by myself to numb the ever-present pain in my heart and quiet the constant thoughts bouncing around my head.

When I envisioned a career as a famous actor, I did not picture it like this. In all my dreams, Vivien was by my side. I'm not sure I'm cut out for this if she isn't with me. More and more, it feels like we are being ripped apart, and I'm worried about our future.

If I could go to her, I would, but I can't. The schedule doesn't permit it. I've booked flights to Cali for August after filming ends, and there should be enough time to hang out for a few days before I have to return to Boston and Viv resumes her studies at UCLA.

On rare days off, I wander the streets of Sydney alone, enjoying the relative anonymity. While *Cruel Intentions* broke box office records here, people seem more chill in Australia, and they don't bother me. I'm not hounded by paparazzi either even though they are around. Some pics and articles have appeared online and in the media, but it's lowkey compared to the hysteria I was dealing with in the US.

On that score, Australia is providing a much-needed respite. Maybe we'll buy a place here at some point. A sanctuary we can escape to when we need a break from all the madness in L.A.

Some mornings, when I can drag my ass out of bed super early, I go surfing on Bondi Beach, enjoying the peace and quiet as day breaks. Alex comes to visit for ten days, and I manage to get a few days off. I have missed my buddy too, barely having any time for him this past year. We have fun catching up and hanging out, and it's hard when he leaves.

I'm in regular contact with Rudy, and he keeps me updated on happenings with the crew and stuff in the US. He's been hanging out with Darren and Jacob most of the summer. The separation from Saffron is welcome. I'm tempted to block her number when she continuously texts and calls me, but I can't. We still have one more movie to film, and there's promotion for both movies to come too. So, I respond to some of her messages and take the odd call, purely to keep the peace.

Cassidy was trying to arrange for Saffron to come visit me

on set, to keep up the fake-dating charade, but I put the kibosh on that. Of course, it caused World War Three, yet both our schedules didn't align, so it was a moot argument anyway. Speculation online about the state of our relationship is ongoing, so it's keeping us in the spotlight regardless, just how they wanted. I don't see that the studio has any cause to complain.

I surprise Vivien when I show up at her house in August six days before I have to hop on a plane to Boston.

"I'm so happy you're here," she says a couple of hours later after we've caught up casually over dinner with her parents. "I have missed you so much."

Wrapping my arms around her, I hold her tight to my chest and close my eyes, savoring the feel of her back in my embrace. Warmth seeps into my limbs, comforting me, but the strain isn't completely gone. "I missed you too. I hate all these long separations." Inhaling her familiar floral scent, I fight a sudden stab of tears.

"You're shaking, babe." Viv eases back a little, tipping my chin up and peering at me with concerned eyes. "Are you okay?"

It takes me a few seconds to force words out through my mouth over the lump wedged in my throat. "I didn't think it would be this hard. I hate being apart from you."

Soft fingertips brush my cheeks. "I know," she whispers. "It's killing me too." Hurt and pain flicker in her eyes, and I force myself to get a grip. I didn't come here to make her feel bad or to worry her. I don't want to spend these precious few days focusing on all the depressing stuff. If this is all I get with her for some time, I want to make the most of it.

"I love you," I say before claiming her lips in a tender kiss.

"I love you too, Reeve," she says a few minutes later when our mouths part. Her hands land on my hips, and she presses her pelvis into mine as she waggles her brows and shoots me a flirty smile. "Let me show you how much?"

We fall into bed, slowly undressing one another, taking our time as we get reacquainted. It's been so long since we've been intimate, and though I'm eager to make up for lost time, I don't fuck her hard the way my cock demands. I make slow, sweet love to her, enjoying the feel of her around me and under me, and I can't stop kissing her as I thrust in and out of her warmth.

I never want to lose this with her.

Desperation drives me to push deeper inside her, and we both moan while maintaining eye contact. A myriad of emotions shines in her eyes, and she's feeling all the same things I'm feeling.

After, we lie sated, naked in each other's arms, and it's the closest to happiness I've felt in months. "Tell me about your summer," she says, turning into me on her side and propping up on one elbow.

"What do you want to know?" I ask, trailing my fingers up and down her arm.

"Everything. What were your days like? And did you like Australia?"

I talk for ages, filling her in on the experience. Of course, she's aware of some stuff from our communications, but I go into detail about everything I did from the time my plane landed on Aussie soil. I purposely leave out the parts where I was lonely and close to throwing in the towel because I missed her so much. What is the point of bringing that up now? I haven't said anything before, despite my irritation, because I didn't want her to feel guilty, and that hasn't changed.

Then we talk about her trip to Europe, and she expands on stories she briefly mentioned previously. We share photos and drift off to sleep, tangled in one another, and having her back in my arms helps to settle some of my concerns.

The following morning, we exchange gifts, and it reminds me of birthdays and Christmases when we were little, when we tore at the packaging and enthused over the gifts we had carefully chosen for one another. Like me, Viv picked up little souvenirs while away, and it soothes something inside me to know she was thinking of me like I was thinking of her. "These are cool," I say, holding up a pair of reddish-purple board shorts with a small circular pattern.

"They represent pomegranates," she explains. "The fruit is a symbol of good luck in Greece." She shrugs, looking a little shy. "I just thought of you when I saw them and picked them up."

I lean in and kiss her. "They're perfect, thanks."

"Thank you for my Uggs, and I love the bracelet," she says, admiring the pretty gemstones on her wrist.

"Opal is Australia's national gemstone, and over ninety percent of the world's opal supply is shipped from Oz. We had a tour of a local factory, and I wanted to buy the whole place for you but figured that might be overkill." I have a matching necklace and earrings I'm keeping aside to give her for Christmas.

Talking about jewelry reminds me of the engagement ring sitting in my safe. I wonder if I should propose now. If a sign of my continued commitment and a concrete promise of that future we have planned might paper over the cracks in our relationship. But I dismiss the idea. I don't want to rush to get engaged when I haven't had the time to plan an elaborate proposal.

One day, it will happen.

This is just a stumbling block.

Every couple has them, but we'll get over it.

Viv and I are lifers. Of that, I'm sure.

We spend a blissful week together, mainly staying at home to avoid fans and paps. We are joined at the hip every second of every day, and we get lost in one another's bodies, both of us eager to reconnect at the most intimate level. It helps, but neither of us mentions the divide that exists now and how we're both purposely avoiding talking about the tough stuff.

When I get on the plane, my heart is heavy, already missing my woman and praying we are tough enough to ride out the rest of this storm.

Chapter Thirty-Seven
Now

Things are different on set this time. Reshoots are finished and we've started filming *Sweet Retribution*. Although this is the last movie and I should be happy now the end is in sight, I'm not. I really don't want to be here, and I'm sinking further into a dark hole that is sucking all the joy from my life. Some days I feel hollow inside. Completely empty. Like I'm just a shell, and it's hard to care when I feel like this.

Things are still strained with Vivien, and some days when we talk, we are like two strangers. Distance is destroying our relationship, and I have days where I wish I had never signed up for this project. Everything I've dreamed of for the future feels like it's slipping through my fingers, and I'm anxious and on edge. I'm also irritable and short-tempered, snapping at everyone because all they do is annoy the fuck out of me.

And my insomnia is back with a vengeance. I've lost count of how many pills I'm taking daily, but I don't care. The only solace I get from the tortured thoughts racing through my mind is when I'm in a numbed drug-induced bubble, and I welcome it.

But I'm fucking up on set some days, fluffing lines and turning up late. Nick is on my back all the freaking time. Our trainer is also busting my balls because I've lost weight and muscle. It's not my fault my appetite is in the toilet. To shut him up, I shovel protein down my mouth despite not wanting to eat. I also increase my intake of Adderall, and it helps me to feel more like myself and to feel more confident on set.

Gradually, I get a handle on things, but I'm on autopilot mode most of the time and hiding my pain behind a skillful mask.

Saffron and I go on several fake dates to generate more media coverage, and I go through the motions, like an alien has inhabited my skin. My costar is very touchy-feely on these dates, and it's a miracle I have any teeth left as I'm always grinding them to stifle my frustration. When Saff tries to pull that shit in private, I remind her I am not interested in her like that. She proclaims it's only friendly flirting, but I'm not fooled. She's definitely up to something, and I'm now wary being around her. In public, I can't do anything when she drapes herself all over me, and I'm losing my integrity and my will to live. I'm not sure how much more "fake dating" I can handle.

Viv has stopped mentioning it, but I know she is aware. I wish I had never agreed to it because I hate upsetting my girl. At least, it's almost at an end. As soon as *Sweet Retribution* is in the bag, I'm calling the whole thing off. Fuck waiting until all the promo is done. The studio can try to sue me for breach of contract if they like, but I doubt they'd go that far. It would only expose the whole shit show, and it would impact negatively on all of us.

"Dude." Rudy leans against the door of my dressing room, looking troubled as he rubs at the back of his neck. "I think you might need to go easy on those." He stares pointedly at the bag of pills sitting on my dressing table. "I'm worried about you."

"Don't be," I say, tossing the baggie in my duffel bag and grabbing my wallet and hotel key card. "I'm fine."

"You're not fine. You haven't been yourself since you showed up after summer. I'm only sorry I didn't say anything before."

"Me too," Cora says, adding her pennies' worth. Cora joined the cast toward the second half of shooting *Twisted Betrayal*. She plays Shandra. Shandra is a friend of Abby's and Drew's on-and-off love interest. At twenty-eight, she's the oldest of the main gang, and she's adopted a bit of a motherly role on set. Might be something to do with the four-month-old baby at home with her husband. "You need to go easy on those things. They don't help in the long-term."

"I've got it under control," I hiss through gritted teeth. I do not need a fucking lecture from the only two people I actually like on set these days. Swinging my bag over my shoulder, I glare at my two friends as I walk toward the door. "I'm doing what I have to do to get through this shoot."

Rudy and Cora exchange a look.

"We just care," he says when I come up to them.

"If you need to talk, I'm always here for you," Cora adds.

"Can you move?" I drill Rudy with a look until he steps aside.

"You need to stay away from Saffron," Cora adds, following me out into the hallway. "I know she's the one supplying you with that shit."

I had been using Jacob's supplier until his operation got busted, so I've had to resort to going through Saffron again. It's not ideal, but I don't exactly have the right contacts to find my own supplier.

"Butt out, Cora. Go home and mother your actual baby."

"Reeve." She tugs on my arm, forcing me to stop. "We don't know one another well, but I can tell this is not you. We want to help. Don't push us away."

Rudy appears behind her. "We're your friends. Saffron is not."

"You've changed your tune." I quirk a brow. He always seems quite happy to party with her.

"She's turned you from someone who was anti-drugs into an...someone who needs them to cope. I think she did that on purpose. She's up to something. I don't trust her, but I'm continuing to play her game so I'm there if she pulls any shit. Keeping your enemies close, etcetera."

"I can handle Saffron Roberts." I push through the door and out to the parking lot.

"Not like this you can't." Rudy keeps pace with me. "You're too talented to go down this path, Reeve. Think about it," he adds. "You know we're talking sense."

"Reeve." Nick calls to me where I'm waiting at the side of the set to begin filming the next scene. "Bianca is here to see you. It's some kind of emergency. You have thirty minutes, tops."

I frown, wondering what the fuck is up now. Bianca rarely shows up on the set. "What's going on?"

He shrugs. "I have no clue."

I look around for my assistant Wen, but of course, he's nowhere to be found. He's still a useless piece of shit.

"Reeve." Nick calls out again as I turn around and move to walk away.

I look over my shoulder at him.

"You're doing good work this past week. Whatever has changed, keep it up."

I nod and smile to myself as I walk off. Fuck Rudy and Cora and their attempt at an intervention last night. I knew I was fine. Correcting the balance between Xanax and Adderall has me more focused. Okay, yes, I'm not sleeping as well now I've lowered my Xanax intake and I'm feeling more anxious, but the Adderall gives me back lost confidence, and as long as I'm outwardly okay and delivering a stellar performance, that's all that matters. Makeup hides the shadows under my eyes, and I have a lifetime's experience of shielding anxiety from the outside world.

Bianca comes toward me wearing her "damage control" expression, and I'm weary of what the fuck has happened now. I am not in the mood for more bullshit. She drags me into a meeting room where my least favorite person is waiting.

"Cassidy. I'd say it's good to see you, except that'd be a lie," I drawl, sinking into one of the empty seats.

"Don't fucking start with me, Reeve. I warned you that girl would get you in trouble, and I was right."

I'm instantly on high alert. I look over at Bianca, who has claimed the seat beside me. "This is about Viv?"

Bianca nods tersely as Cassidy turns the screen of her laptop around. "I hate to say I told you so, Reeve, but—"

"We told you so." Cassidy's smug expression is begging for my fist in her face, and I only barely restrain myself.

"This will hurt, Reeve," Bianca adds. "But the truth always does."

I grip the arms of the chair hard as I watch the video unfolding before me with mounting horror and anger. On the screen, a drunk Vivien is pouring her heart out to some nerdy asshole while a party rages in the background. She tells him the truth. That she's my girlfriend, but she's been sidelined by me and the studio so that Saffron and I could pretend to date. She talks about the engagement news—whatever the fuck that is—

and how she hardly ever gets to talk to me or see me anymore and all we seem to do is fight these days.

"Jesus Christ." I prop my elbows on the table and bury my head in my hands. Viv has just blown the strategy out the window, not that I really give two fucks about that, but she's made me sound like a weak idiot, and she's presenting me as some kind of cruel, heartless prick who doesn't give a shit about her when she knows that is not who I am. "She's fucking hung me out to dry."

"It gets worse." Cassidy gloats.

"Lose the grin, bitch, or I'll gladly wipe it off your face."

She gasps, appearing outraged as she opens her mouth to retaliate, but Bianca silences her with one of her signature sharp looks.

"I don't know about you," Bianca says, tipping her head toward the screen. "But it looks to me like your girl is not very loyal, Reeve."

"She's cheating for sure." Cassidy flips me the bird, grinning again, and one of these days, I am going to take that bitch down.

I return my attention to the screen, and my heart plummets to my toes as I watch Vivien dance with several different guys. Some paw at her, but she eventually pushes them away. Others grind up against her, and she seems to enjoy it. My hands clench into fists as red-hot anger sweeps through me.

This is not the Vivien Grace I know. That girl would never embarrass me so publicly. That girl would never let another guy touch her, let alone grind all over her. It makes me wonder if that kiss with Nate went down the way I was told it did. Did she welcome that too?

I jump up, knocking my chair over in the process.

"We need to contain this," Cassidy says.

"The damage is already done," Bianca adds as I pace the room, yanking handfuls of my hair.

"With the right strategy, we can turn this our way." Cassidy drills a hole in the side of my head. "Sit down, Reeve, so we can make a plan."

"Fuck. You." I slam my hands down on the table and lean into her face. For a second, she looks scared, and I revel in the expression. She leans back, pressing her spine into her chair. "This is all your fault! You started this bullshit, and now look where we're at!" I yell.

"You need to calm down, Reeve." Bianca tugs me back and forces me into a chair. "Shut up and listen."

I grind my teeth to the molars.

"We will work to get that video taken down, but it's out there already, and the damage is done. You must properly distance yourself from Vivien. You need to publicly refute her claims and make it very clear it's all lies and a knee-jerk reaction to the news of your engagement to Saffron."

"What the fuck?" My gaze bounces between them. "What fucking engagement?"

"It's bull. Obviously," Cassidy says, straightening up in her chair. "And I've no idea where it came from," she lies. "But it was all over social media yesterday. Reeveron is still trending." She can't keep the delighted grin off her face, and I grip the arms of my chair hard, digging my nails in.

No wonder I had so many missed calls from Vivien last night. I intended to call her back when I got to the hotel, but I collapsed on the bed the second I arrived and fell asleep in my clothes. When I woke, it was the middle of the night in Cali, and it was too late to call her. Now, I wish I had. I understand what prompted this behavior, but it doesn't excuse it. Vivien knows I would never get engaged to Saffron. She knows the whole thing is fake. She has landed me in a whole world of hurt because what? Her feelings are bruised? She couldn't wait one fucking day to ask me about this before she got drunk, blabbed to some money-grabbing leech who sold her out, and made a show of herself dancing with drunken frat boys?

I have never been more disappointed in her, but I'm not badmouthing her to my agent or that bitchy publicist. I work hard to calm down before I speak. "I'll talk to her. I'll get her to retract everything, and I'll go on a date with Saffron this weekend to shut everyone up."

"That won't work." Cassidy drums her fingers on the table. "You need to categorically state she is lying and it's the ramblings of a bitter ex, jealous because she's been replaced with someone hotter."

Anger returns full force at her nasty words. As mad as I am at Vivien, and I'm going to let rip at her, I am not letting that slur go. Leaning across the table, I glare at Cassidy. "Saffron is *not* hotter than Vivien. They don't even compare. Vivien is fucking beautiful in a way Saffron will never be. Do not insult my girlfriend again, or I will not be responsible for my actions."

"I doubt she's your girlfriend any longer," Bianca coolly says, inspecting her fingernails. "Open your eyes, Reeve. Vivien is cheating on you, and you can't let that go." She stands and hands me my phone, which she must have gotten from that imbecile Wen. "Call her and break up with her. Let's be done with this once and for all."

"No." I snatch my cell and curl my hand around it. "I'm livid over this, but I'm not breaking up with her. I know Vivien, and she'll be inconsolable."

"Oh, really." Bianca cocks her head to the side and an ugly sneer ghosts over her mouth. "Where are all the missed calls and tearful apology texts? I spotted none on your cell. All her messages were prior to that party. None after. That's not exactly screaming remorse now, is it?"

"She's probably fucking asleep!" I roar. "And don't fucking look through my cell. That's a complete invasion of my privacy and above your pay grade, Bianca."

"Watch your tone with me, boy." She grips my arm, digging her nails in as she fixes me with an acidic look that hints at the true nature of the person hidden behind mountains of plastic surgery, false smiles, and fake reassurances. I think Bianca and I will definitely be parting ways when my contract comes up for renewal. I am sick of her shit.

"You're pathetic," Cassidy snarls, and that word sends me hurtling into the past, but I snap out of it fast.

"The only pathetic one will be you when I'm finished with you," I threaten, pushing past Bianca and leaving the room with both calling after me. They seriously give me a headache, and I can't wait to be rid of them.

I call Viv's cell nonstop until Audrey finally answers confirming Viv is still asleep. Then she lays into me, and we volley arguments back and forth. Audrey says I'm way out of line and, of course, Vivien hasn't cheated. She calls me out on the engagement news, refusing to believe me when I say I didn't know anything about it. I end the call when I'm summoned back to work, and it takes enormous willpower and concentration to get my head in the game, but I do it.

A few hours later, we have another short recess, and I storm off the set to try calling Vivien again. Saffron races after me, the click-click of her heels giving her away. "Not now," I hiss over my shoulder as I stalk toward the side where a couple of small private rooms are.

"Reeve, wait up!"

Ignoring her, I forge ahead.

"I heard what happened, and I'm so sorry."

I snort as I slam to a halt and spin around. "Why would you be? Isn't this what you've been telling me all along?"

"I'm not going to say I told you so if that's what you think." Concern flares in her eyes. "I care about you, and you're hurting. Can I do anything to help?"

"Just stay away. I need space."

Hurt splays across her face, but I can't handle her emotions right now. Without another word, I walk off and enter one of the empty rooms to make my call. Thankfully, it's answered on the first ring. "Viv?" I ask.

"It's me."

Her voice is flat, uncaring, lacking emotion, and it stokes the embers of rage to a roaring crescendo inside me. I detect no hint of regret or remorse in her tone, only resignation, and I'm stunned. Hurt. In disbelief. Does she not care about me at all anymore? Is this really what it's come to? I'm over here busting a nut to create a life for us, struggling to keep my shit together, and barely holding on to my sanity while she's on campus partying it up and bitching me out to random strangers.

How fucking dare she!

What gives her the right to just throw me to the wolves?

After everything I have sacrificed for her? The fucking nerve of her!

I lose it, spectacularly. "What the actual fuck is going on with you? I can't believe that video. I have never seen you like that! If you wanted to hurt me, you've definitely succeeded. Did you cheat on me last night?" I shout.

She laughs. Repeatedly. And it only cranks my rage to the max.

"Vivien, what the hell? Stop laughing. This is fucking serious. You've landed me in a world of shit today. This will damage my brand and my rep. How could you do this to me? You have made me look like a laughingstock. Like a selfish prick who doesn't give a shit about anyone but himself. The studio is going crazy, and this could do real damage to the movies. You need to issue a statement saying you lied, that you were hurt after those fake engagement rumors surfaced, and yes, they are fucking fake, as well you know and..."

I realize I've been talking to silence for minutes. "Viv. Are you still there?" I snap.

"Are you done?" she asks in an icy tone that is not her.

"No, I—"

"I'm not in the mood to argue today," she adds. "And I give zero fucks how this impacts you. That bitch of a costar or that bitch of a PR person or that bitch of an agent orchestrated this whole situation, and I'm done pandering to all of you. I am done being the punching bag." Her voice cracks "I am done coming last all the time." A heavy sigh filters down the line. "I am just fucking *done*," she shouts. "Do you hear me? I'm done, Reeve. Fuck you. Fuck Saffron. Fuck Cassidy, and fuck Bianca. Fuck you all."

I am shocked speechless at the pure hatred lacing her words. How the fuck is she turning this around on me when she's the one who caused all of this?

"Don't call me again," she says before the line goes dead.

Chapter Thirty-Eight
Now

Three nights later, I ask Cora and Rudy to come to dinner where I apologize for the shitty way I've been treating them and request their help. I come clean about the stuff I'm taking, and to say they are shocked is mild. Since then, I am cutting down on my usage, but it's only adding to the torment Viv's silence brings. Despite extreme fatigue, I'm still struggling to sleep. When I do, I have nightmares. Other nights, I have hallucinations, and it feels like I'm losing my fucking mind. Headaches are my new norm along with bouts of nausea, shivering, and sweats, and this is hell on earth.

But I persevere because I'm at real risk of losing the only woman I love and I need to get my shit together and fight to get our relationship back on track.

"I got you a coffee, *movie star*. Just how you like it." Saffron thrusts a paper cup at me, waggling her brows and grinning. "You can thank me later," she adds, pressing up against me and smirking suggestively as we stand to one side of the set, waiting for the director to call us.

"Thanks," I reply, faking a smile and purposely ignoring her blatant innuendo. We have been on set since six a.m., over nine hours so far, and I'm in a shitty mood. It's been a long day, and we still have two scenes left to shoot. I'm dying to call it a wrap and head back to my hotel to sleep. I sidestep her, leaving a gap between our bodies. Since all that stuff went down a couple of weeks ago with Viv and the drunken video, Saff is getting more touchy-feely with me. I have told her to quit with the flirting and reiterated I am only interested in her as a friend, but I'm not sure the message is getting through to her.

Taking a sip of the lukewarm black coffee, I almost spit the bitter-tasting liquid back into the cup.

Just how I like it, my ass.

Most everyone on set knows I take my coffee with cream and sugar.

"Don't tell me you're still moping over your ex?" Closing the distance, she sidles up close again. "I know you're hurting, but you'll see it's for the best." She bats her lashes at me as she clings to my arm. "Vivien doesn't belong in your world. Your breakup was inevitable."

I grind my teeth to my molars as I step away from her again. "For the last time, we haven't broken up."

I think. I hope.

I haven't talked to my girlfriend since it went down because Viv is ignoring my calls and my heartfelt texts. I even tried calling the house, but Lauren told me in no uncertain terms to back off and give Viv some space.

She laid into me, and I could do nothing but listen and accept it. I have made a mess of things, but Viv hasn't exactly helped either. It wasn't on purpose, but she knows better than to entrust intimate details of our relationship to anyone outside our inner circle. What was she thinking getting drunk and blabbing to that asshole?

Still, it's behind us now, and the media has already moved on to another scandal. It's made me realize I need to protect Vivien more with the press, and I've decided to hire my own publicist. His or her role will be to look after my interests, and that includes Viv.

We can fix our relationship and get it back on track, but we need to talk for that to happen.

Our last call was eighteen days ago, and it was painful. I overreacted. I'm ashamed that I lashed out at my girlfriend before giving her a chance to explain, but in my defense, the video was pretty damning. Bianca and Cassidy gave me hell, and I got some heat from the studio. After a grueling day on set, the last thing I needed was to deal with that shitstorm. I was also majorly pissed watching Viv dancing with other guys at the frat party. She gives me hell if I'm even sitting beside Saff in a photo, yet it's okay for her to dirty dance with random strangers?

That is still a touchy subject for me.

I shouldn't have accused her of cheating on me though. That was a low blow. Viv would never do that to me, like I'd never do it to her.

We are just going through a rough patch. It happens to all couples in long-term relationships. These movies put a big strain on our relationship, but I can't lose Viv. I won't. I'll be home soon for Christmas, and my sole mission is to make things right between us. This has been hard on Vivien. My pretending to be in a relationship with Saff has hurt her, but it's only temporary, and she knows it's fake. I have zero interest in Saffron outside of friendship, and lately, I've even begun questioning that. I'm starting to see a side of her I really don't like.

I think Viv was right, and she's had an agenda all along.

"Movie star!" Saffron pinches my arm before waving one hand in front of my nose. "Don't ignore me when I'm talking to you!"

"Back off, Saff." Removing her hand from my arm, I side-step her again. "And cut me some slack. I've got a lot on my mind."

"I know you do." She tilts her head to one side, piercing me with puppy-dog eyes. "I just want to help." She glances around before stepping up closer, shoving her tits against me as she presses the front of her body into mine. "I know you're not sleeping, and it's showing on set." She slides something into the front pocket of my jeans. "These will help."

Grabbing her wandering hand, I remove it and the small packet of pills from my pocket. "Quit with that shit," I hiss, stuffing the packet in her hand and taking two steps back. "I told you I'm done with that stuff. And stop crowding me."

"Hey, man," Rudy says, coming up on my left. I'm surprised to see him as he has no filming today, and I know he went partying last night. Although it's after three, I didn't expect him to surface on set at all today. The fact he is here instantly raises my hackles. He must have sought me out for a reason, and I'm immediately wary. His gaze bounces between Saff and me. "Am I interrupting?"

"Wouldn't you like to know?" Saff says, licking her lips and grinning at our costar and my best buddy on set.

Rudy barks out a laugh as I scowl.

"You're not interrupting. What's up?" I ask.

"Can we talk in private?"

Saffron giggles. "Reeve and I have no secrets from one another. Isn't that right, movie star?" She waggles her brows and links her arm in mine as if I haven't just told her to quit that shit.

"Stop insinuating there is more between us." I rub a tense

spot between my brows. "I sound like a broken record around you all the time, and it's exhausting."

Saffron feigns hurt before throwing her hands in the air and moving away from me.

Finally.

"Everyone knows I'm a big flirt and I mean nothing by it. You are seriously tense, Reeve. You really need to get laid." She winks at Rudy before flouncing off.

Rudy chuckles. "She's not wrong on all scores."

I'm not even touching that. "What's going on?"

"Not here." Rudy lifts one shoulder. "Director's office is free. Let's talk in there."

We walk silently side by side to the small office off the set, and I close the door when we're both inside the room.

"I know you haven't been online, so I wanted to be the first to show you this."

Goose bumps sprout on my arms as trepidation instantly sets in. Social media is a curse. It's an evil necessity in my line of work and something I have come to dread. "What now?" I ask, accepting his cell when he hands it to me.

"It's Viv. The reports aren't substantiated yet, but if what they are saying is true, she's been attacked."

All the blood drains from my face as I silently listen to the woman from CNN reporting from a dark alleyway beside the yoga studio Viv attends. The reporter claims a woman was attacked there last night and a source in LAPD has suggested it was Vivien Mills. "Fuck!" I toss the cell at my friend and storm out of the office, searching for my assistant.

I need to use my phone, and Wen holds it for me when I'm on set. I had no messages or missed calls when I last checked it at five thirty this morning, which is strange if the reports are true and this happened last night.

Maybe it wasn't Viv. Perhaps the media got it wrong.

I hope so because the thought of anything happening to her terrifies me. Pressure sits on my chest, making breathing difficult, as I stalk around the set, seeking out my assistant. From the corner of my eye, I spot Saff trailing my movements with an intense, off-putting gaze.

I find Wen flirting with one of the set engineers in the coffee area, and I'm ready to rip into him. Why is my friend the one to bring this information to me? Wen should have been all over this. He's a lousy assistant, and if it was up to me, he'd have been fired in the early days. But the studio hired him and they pay his salary, so I'm forced to put up with the moron.

"Phone," I snap, holding out my palm.

"Has something happened?" he asks, his brow puckering when he notices the look on my face.

"Shouldn't you be telling me that?" I bark, grabbing my cell from his fingers and opening it. Or Cassidy, for that matter. Or my agent. Why has no one thought to contact me on set if it's true?

Just as I've convinced myself it must be a case of mistaken identity, I spot the slew of missed calls from Lauren and Jonathon, and I curse.

Ignoring my idiot assistant as he shouts after me, I race back into the director's office where Rudy still waits. He sits patiently in a chair in front of the desk while I call Vivien's dad. Jon picks up on the fourth ring as I pace the floor. "Is it true? Has Viv been hurt? Is she okay? Where is she? Can I talk to her?"

"Calm down, son. Breathe. Vivien is going to be okay. We're at Cedars-Sinai, and she's getting the best medical care."

Air whooshes out of my mouth in strangled spurts. "What happened?" My voice cracks, and pain lays siege to my insides. It must be bad if she's at the hospital.

"We don't have the specifics as Vivien hasn't woken yet, but she was found last night by the owner of the yoga studio unconscious and lying bloody and bruised in an alleyway that leads to the parking lot."

An inhuman sound tears from my throat, and Rudy sits up straighter in his chair. "How badly is she hurt?"

"She has a concussion, three broken fingers, and a broken wrist, and a couple of her ribs were fractured."

"Oh my God. That sounds serious." I rub at the shooting pains spreading across my chest, and knots twist in my gut at the thought of the agony my girl must be in.

"The doctor has said her injuries are not life-threatening and she'll make a full recovery."

"If this happened last night, why hasn't she woken yet, and why didn't you contact me yesterday?" I could've been there with her now if I'd been informed immediately.

"She woke briefly, but we weren't there, and she fell back asleep quickly according to the doctor. He's not concerned. He said the CT scan shows no permanent brain damage and sleep is the body's and brain's way of healing. As for your second question, Lauren and I weren't sure if Vivien would want us to call you, so we held off, waiting for her to wake up. When the media broke the story this morning, we called."

"I want to see her. I need to be with her. I'm on set, but I'll make arrangements straightaway." It's almost a seven-hour flight to L.A. Which means it'll be tonight before I reach my love, so there is no time to waste.

"Do what you must," Jon says, "but if Vivien doesn't want to see you, Reeve, you know we'll have to respect her wishes."

"I understand." That doesn't mean I won't pull out all the stops to see her, and it's not something I need to worry about now. "I'll see you soon," I say before hanging up.

I fill Rudy in and then call my dad. I hate asking that bastard for anything, but he's my best hope of getting to L.A.

quickly. Studio 27—the production company he co-owns and is the CEO of—has a fleet of private jets at their disposal. Dad promises to find me a jet and tells me to make my way to Logan International and he'll text me the details as soon as he has them.

Then I talk to Nick, telling him I need to go. He refuses to release me before I've filmed the last two scenes, citing a whole slew of reasons why I can't just walk off the set.

"I don't care," I say, crossing my arms and leveling him with a dark look. "My girlfriend is lying unconscious in a hospital bed after a brutal attack. I need to go to her now."

"I'm not unsympathetic, Reeve, but you can't hold up production like this. You know how tight our schedule is."

"Just add the scenes to the last day of shooting." They aren't anything special so they can easily be moved. "I'll pay whatever it costs to reschedule them."

"I know you're worried, Reeve," Saffron says, walking forward from the spot where she was clearly eavesdropping. "We all are. What's happened to Vivien is terrible, but surely, she wouldn't want you to relinquish your responsibilities? She's probably sleeping anyway, and she won't miss you if you're a few hours late."

"Saffron makes sense," the director says. "My assistant will organize a car and a flight while we get these scenes down, and you can leave the instant we are done."

"No." I shake my head and drag my fingers through my hair, grabbing handfuls. I continuously shake my head as I pace the floor in front of them. "I couldn't concentrate even if I wanted to stay, which I don't." Alarm races through my veins as I take a step back. "I'm sorry to let you and the crew down, but Viv needs me. She's the love of my life, and I won't forgive myself if anything happens to her and I'm not there. I've got to go now."

"You can't just walk off without consequences," the director hollers after me, but I ignore him, heading across the lot toward the exit.

"Reeve!" Saffron's heels tap noisily on the floor as she runs after me. "You're making a mistake. They're going to punish you if you do this!" She tugs on my elbow, slowing my progress.

"Do I look like I care?" I shuck out of her hold. "It's not like they're going to fire me this late in the game."

"They will hit you in the pocket. You know that's how they do things."

I shrug. "They can take every penny they have paid me for all I care. Getting to Viv is the only thing that matters."

She scowls, planting her hands on her hips and thrusting her tits up. "She doesn't deserve you, and you're making a mistake. She's going to ruin your career, Reeve, and you'll have no one to blame but yourself."

The driver drops me off at the entrance to Cedars-Sinai, and I hop out, pulling the hood of my black hoodie up over my head to avoid detection. But it's a feeble attempt. A throng of paparazzi, at least three rows deep, surges behind the barricade facing the entrance to the hospital, jostling and pushing one another as they vie for the perfect shot. "Reeve! Is it true Vivien was attacked by Reeveron fans who want her dead?" some asshole shouts just before the doors glide open, and I step inside, shutting the vultures out.

I checked my feed in the car en route from the airport, and I'm up to speed on the latest speculation. The LAPD has made no comment except to confirm a young woman was attacked in the alleyway behind a yoga studio on Saturday night, but shit is blowing up online with plenty of commenters stating the attack was made by my fans and Saffron's fans. I am waiting to speak to Lauren and Jon before jumping to conclusions, but if the reports are correct, I will never forgive myself for putting Viv in the line of fire.

A woman with a pixie cut and an austere black skirt suit steps out in front of me, introducing herself and offering to escort me to the private suite where Viv and her parents are.

We ride the elevator in silence with only my frantic thoughts for company. I didn't get a wink of sleep on the plane because I couldn't stop worrying about Viv. Worrying about how much pain she's in and torturing myself trying to figure out how this could happen and who would want to hurt my girl. I panicked constantly wondering if she is awake or still unconscious. Terrified the doctors got it wrong and there is permanent brain damage, and that's why she hasn't woken up.

Trailing the woman out of the elevator and along a corridor, I ignore the heated stares and excited whispers that follow me. She swipes a card at a set of double doors and ushers me inside a large private suite. Jon is standing in front of a large window, looking out over the views of the city at night. He glances over his shoulder when he hears us enter. The bruising shadows under his eyes match my own and are a testament to his lack of sleep too.

The woman leaves while my eyes skim over the luxurious waiting room with a cream leather couch, glossy black coffee table, and a small matching dining table with three chairs. To the left is a small hallway, which leads to the guest bedrooms, I'm guessing. Details of these luxury suites have been widely documented in the press, thanks to its celebrity clientele.

"You're here," Lauren says, closing the sliding door to Viv's room behind her as she slips out.

I move toward Viv's room. "I want to see her."

"We need to talk first," Viv's mom says, narrowing her eyes. "And she's sleeping."

"She's still sleeping?" Lowering my hood, I drag a hand through my messy hair. "That's over twenty-four hours. That can't be good. Not with a concussion."

"She woke earlier for a few minutes," Jon says, moving around to the coffee machine.

"It's a misconception you shouldn't sleep with a concussion," Lauren adds. Her eyes rake over me, and her features soften. "You look like shit. When did you last sleep or eat?"

"I ate on the plane, and I couldn't sleep."

Lauren pulls me into a hug. I cling to her like a lifeline, feeling drained and overemotional and completely wound tight. She eases back, momentarily gripping my arms as she inspects my face. "What are you doing to yourself, Reeve? What are you doing to my daughter?" She chokes up at the end, and Jon slings his arm around her shoulders as he hands a mug of coffee to me and gives one to his wife. "I'm so mad at you," she adds, letting her husband steer her to the couch. "But that doesn't mean I don't worry about you."

"You shouldn't worry about me. I'm fine," I lie. I'm the furthest from fine a person can be. "Reserve your energy for Viv. She's the one who needs it." I take a sip of my coffee, and it's perfect, exactly how I drink it.

"Sit down, son," Jon says. "You look dead on your feet."

I walk silently to the couch, sitting on the other end. "Tell me what you know."

"This wasn't a random attack," Jon says. "Vivien was targeted."

I gulp over the messy ball of emotion clogging my throat, and it's an effort to force the words from my mouth. "Targeted by who?"

"Who do you think?" Lauren snaps, and Jon tugs her in tighter to his side.

I hang my head in shame, squeezing my eyes closed as my hands circle my mug, and I try to siphon some warmth into my icy bones. Tears prick my eyes when I open them. "Fans of the movie did this?" I quietly ask, needing them to confirm it so I can add it to the list of my sins against the woman I love.

"Viv said they were Saffhards. Young girls, but they were vicious." Lauren's voice cracks. "They scratched her face, pulled out clumps of her hair, kicked her, and spit on her. One of them even stood on her." She bursts out crying, burying her face in Jon's chest as she sobs.

"Please tell me they have them in custody?"

Jon shakes his head. "Viv was found alone at the scene, and the cops are investigating, but we have heard nothing so far."

Pain rushes through me, filling every cell, nook, and cranny until it's all I know. Thinking of my Viv, lying unconscious on the cold hard ground, beaten and broken, destroys me. It's killing me inside to visualize her like that. How could someone who claims to be a fan of me or Saffron do this to an innocent woman and just leave her there? When I get my hands on them, I am going to reenact everything they did to my love and see how they like it. My heart hurts as pain lays siege to my body. This happened to Viv because of her association with me, and I am so ashamed my decisions have led us here. "This is all my fault."

"Damn straight it is." Lauren lifts her head and glares at me. "Your actions have led to this. You never should have signed that bullshit contract or agreed to any of those awful terms. You haven't done right by Vivien, Reeve, and I'm so disappointed in you."

"I'm disappointed in myself," I truthfully admit.

"You need to fix this," Jonathon says.

"Or the next time, they might kill her." Anguish is etched upon Lauren's face.

"I'll hire her a bodyguard. A whole team of bodyguards, and I'm already in the process of hiring my own publicist." I take another mouthful of my coffee as my brain conjures up ideas of how to proceed from here. I know what I need to do. Something I should have done that summer when we were negotiating the second contract. Something I was too stupid to insist on. I've been so naïve, and it's time I grew up and showed I have balls.

"Good, that's good, son."

"You need to do more." Lauren straightens up as she swipes at the moisture under her eyes. "You need to put that Roberts bitch in her place, and I really think you need to cut Bianca loose. She's not a good person, Reeve. I know you don't want to hear this, but she has manipulated you and the entire situation. She does not have your best interests at heart. All that self-serving bitch cares about is herself. Just say the word, and I'll talk to Margaret. She'll take you on, and you will be in much safer hands."

"I'll handle Saffron, and I'll think about Margaret," I say, setting my coffee down and standing. "But now I need to see Viv. Please." I pin pleading eyes on her parents, praying they are not going to block me from her. I need to see my girl with my own eyes to know she's okay. I need to hold her and tell her I love her and beg her to forgive me.

"Don't do anything to upset her," Lauren warns, narrowing her eyes on me again.

"That is the last thing I would do, and you should know that. You know me."

"I used to think we did," Lauren says. "But I honestly don't know anymore."

"No heavy talk, Reeve," Jon says. "Vivien can't handle

anything like that right now. She's already in a lot of pain, so just let her know you are here for her, but don't pressure her to talk about anything she doesn't want to talk about."

"I won't. I promise," I say, curling my fingers around the sliding door and pushing it back.

Entering the room, I close the door softly behind me. Lifting my head, I stare at my love with a mix of relief and anguish. Pain rattles around my chest as my gaze roams over her. Viv is sleeping, lying perfectly still in the elevated hospital bed, looking tiny and vulnerable under the sheets with her dark hair fanned out on the pillow. She is hooked up to a drip and a machine, and she looks so young and so broken but still so beautiful. My heart pounds painfully behind my rib cage as I drink her in, hating to see her like this. Guilt slaps me in the face.

I did this to her.

My failure to protect her, to put her first like I always promised I would do, led us to this moment.

As long as I live, I will never forgive myself for letting her down.

Scratch marks mar her pretty face, and bruising is evident on her exposed lower arms, hinting at what she's endured. I sway on my feet as my legs threaten to go out from under me. A lump the size of a ball wedges at the back of my throat, and tears sting my eyes as I walk toward the bed.

Pulling the seat up close to her right side, I sit down and take her hand gently in mine. It is warm to the touch as I lift it to my lips, pressing a soft kiss there. "I'm so sorry, baby," I whisper, not wanting to wake her but needing to get this out. "I'm so sorry for failing you. I swear I will fix things. I will do what I should always have done." Lowering her hand back to the bed, I stare at her gorgeous face as my heart swells with a mixture of pain and longing. "I love you so much, Viv. I hate that you haven't felt that recently, but I promise I will do everything in my power to rectify that. You are my everything, and I let you down, but never again."

She stirs ever so slightly in the bed, and I hold my breath, waiting to see if she wakes, but she doesn't. I don't whisper to her after that, letting her sleep, hoping she is finding some peace in slumber. I stare at her while holding her hand and making plans and promises in my head. I guess at some point I must have nodded off because I wake later as slivers of buttery sunshine trickle through the blinds in the room.

I don't want to leave her, but I need to take a piss, so I head to the adjoining bathroom and attend to business. When I return, Jon is by her bedside, crouched over Viv as he presses a soft kiss to her brow. He glances up at me. "Lauren is showering," he whispers. "I'm going to order breakfast. What would you like?"

I shrug. "Order me whatever," I say, glancing at the time on my watch. It's a little after seven.

Jon squeezes my shoulder before exiting the room. I sit back down by Viv's side and retake her hand.

A few minutes later, Viv moves onto her side, murmuring quietly, and I sit up straighter, clutching her hand a little tighter. Her eyes blink open, and she winces at the light filtering into the room.

"Viv. I'm here," I say.

She turns around, whimpering, and her face contorts in pain.

It kills me. "Baby, I'm so sorry." I kiss the back of her hand as tears fall silently down my face. I don't try to stop them. I want her to see how devastated I am. "Sorry this happened to you, and sorry I wasn't here immediately. I got here as soon as I could. The plane ride was the most excruciating journey because I was terrified, Viv." Raising our conjoined hands to my cheek, I lean into her warm touch. "You were still unconscious when I got on the plane, and I didn't know what I'd find when I arrived."

I quietly sob as she watches me, saying nothing, and I wish I was a mind reader so I could hear her thoughts. She probably hates me. I know I would if I were in her shoes. Shame washes over me as I recall the last words I spoke to her on the phone. And now this. She knows this is all my fault, and I have never hated myself more than I do at this moment. I need her to know I'm sorry and I love her, and I can only pray I haven't fucked us up for good.

"I was so scared you were dead, Viv. Scared I would never get to hold you again or tell you how much I love you. Scared I wouldn't get the chance to apologize for all the ways I have let you down. Scared I wouldn't get an opportunity to make up for all the wrongs."

Her chest heaves, and pain engulfs her bruised, scratched face. "Your fans hate me, Reeve. They want you with her, and it seems they'll stop at nothing to make that happen." Tears stream down her face, and I hate seeing them.

I hate that she's hurting, and it's my fault. "Your parents filled me in." I grind my teeth, my tears quickly transforming to anger. "I know this is my fault. I haven't prioritized you or your needs, and I've been a selfish asshole, but it stops now." I peer deep into her eyes, hoping she can see the resolve there. "I'm going to make this up to you." Carefully, I reach out and touch her cheek, mindful to avoid her injuries. "They will pay for what they did to you, and I'm going to make sure no one ever touches you again."

Leaving the hospital for home is a shitshow. The entrance to the hospital is swamped with reporters, paparazzi, and my fans. Lauren tells me my presence here is making things worse, which only adds to my guilt. I know she's right. Like I know she is furious with me. Viv isn't the only one I have hurt with my careless actions. Lauren and Jon mean the world to me too. They have been there for me when my father wasn't, and this has been a shitty way of repaying them for their love and affection.

I have a lot of groveling to do, and I intend to do it.

Back at the house, after I carry Viv to her bedroom, Lauren shoves me toward the kitchen, telling me to fix something for Viv to eat while Jon goes to retrieve her bag from the car.

Lauren pulls out a tray table and gives me instructions on what to prepare. I don't argue, doing what she tells me because I'm in the doghouse and I don't have a leg to stand on. She fills a glass with water and strides out of the kitchen a couple of minutes later.

I heat up some chicken noodle soup and cut a few slices of crusty bread before adding them to the tray table. I head upstairs and enter Viv's room for the first time in months, a rush of nostalgia slapping me in the face. I have so many happy memories of time spent in this room. Viv is tucked into bed, sitting up, propped against a mountain of pillows, as I place the tray table over her lap.

"It's good to have you home, princess," Jon says, coming into the room behind me. He drops Viv's bag on the floor and smiles softly at his daughter.

"It's good to be home, Dad." Viv offers her dad a smile in return, but her face is tense with pain, and she looks pale and exhausted.

Lauren and Jon leave, shooting me abject warning looks on their way out. As soon as the door is closed, I kick off my shoes and carefully climb onto the bed beside my love. Lying on my side, I face her, my eyes flicking to the tray. "Eat, babe."

I watch her sip her soup, looking like she has the weight of the world on her shoulders. There is so much I want to say to her, but this isn't the time. She's tired and hurting, and her dad wasn't wrong when he warned me about keeping things light. Viv can't handle any of the heavy right now, and I won't add to her pain.

When she finishes eating, I lift the tray off her and set it down on the floor on this side of the bed. Viv lies down, and I crawl under the comforter and reach for her hand. The instant my fingers link with hers, a comforting warmth seeps into my bones. Without stopping to think about it, I press a light kiss to her lips. It's been too long since I felt her mouth and her body moving against mine. I scoot closer, happy when she rests her head on my chest.

Very carefully, I run my fingers through her hair, closing my eyes and savoring the moment. Viv is back in my arms where she belongs, and everything feels right with the world. Her familiar scent and touch wrap around me, and when we are together like this, I feel invincible. Like I can fix everything I have broken and get us back to the place where our love was everything and nothing else mattered.

Her eyelids flutter, blinking open and shut, and I can tell she's fighting sleep. "I love you, Viv," I whisper, pressing a feather-soft kiss to her damaged cheek. "I know I've done a piss-poor job of showing you recently, but I'm going to do better. Almost losing you has put everything into perspective. I can't lose you, Viv. I won't. You're the other half of my soul, and nothing matters more to me than you."

She falls asleep, and as I feel my eyelids drooping, I set my alarm for later so I don't miss my flight.

I don't want to return to the set.

I want to stay here with her. To nurse her back to health and care for her as she heals.

But I've been fielding angry calls all day, and everyone is livid with me. Filming ground to a halt today because I wasn't there, and the studio threatened to bring in the lawyers if I'm not back on set tomorrow. I spoke to Lauren about it earlier. I asked for her advice, and she told me to go back. Viv wouldn't want me jeopardizing my career, and there isn't much I can do to help. Viv needs rest, and her parents will be here to take care of her.

I hate having to leave her.

I don't want to return.

I want to stay here where I belong, but I'll be home shortly for Christmas, and I will be spending every single second with Viv then. It's the only way I'm able to convince myself to return to Boston.

My alarm goes off way too soon. I forgo a shower to stay in bed, not wanting to waste a second of precious time with the only girl who has ever mattered. I can shower on the plane later before we land. When I can't leave it any longer, I dot soft kisses into Viv's hair before reluctantly getting out of bed.

I take a piss and brush my teeth before coming back into the bedroom.

I'm bent over her, gently sweeping hair from her face when she stirs. I don't like waking her, but I won't sneak out without saying goodbye. Her gorgeous hazel eyes are soft and unfocused as she blinks them open. "I've got to leave, baby," I whisper. "But I meant everything I said. I know we need to talk too, and I promise we'll do that when I come home for Christmas." I kiss her plump lips, wishing I didn't have to go. "Don't give up on me yet. Let me make this right, and everything will go back to the way it was. I promise."

"How?" she asks, disbelief threading through her tone.

It guts me, but what did I expect? "I am hiring my own publicist, and I'm issuing a video statement later today. When I return to the set, I'm telling the studio I'm publicly 'breaking up' with Saffron. And I'm setting her straight too. I know she harbors ideas of us, but I'll tell her again that it'll never happen." I have told her countless times, and the message isn't getting through, but I'll just have to drill it home. Saffron needs to back off and stop interfering in my relationship.

"That will only make her more determined," Viv murmurs.

She isn't wrong. Saffron is like a dog with a bone when she wants something, but she can't have me. I have let her get away with too much shit. Been too trusting and too blind. That stops now. I never should have let her manipulate me into doing drugs, as it only compounded the situation. But I'm not holding her responsible for that.

That's all on me.

I have lost sight of who I am.

The old me would never have gone down this road, and I'm so fucking angry at myself.

For so many things, but especially for letting myself get manipulated by Saffron Roberts. I didn't listen to Viv before, but I'm listening now. If Saffron won't back down, there will be no room for her in my life in any capacity. The movie is wrapping up soon, and I won't have to deal with her for much longer. I have no problem cutting her loose. If that is what Viv needs, she's got it.

I don't belong to Saffron, and I never will. Viv is the only woman who will ever have a claim on my heart. "It doesn't matter. I love you. I know I've let her come between us, and it ends now."

As I walk out of the house, I am more determined than ever to reset my life and restore my relationship with the woman I love.

Chapter Thirty-Nine
Now

"Edwin Chambers is a good guy and a great publicist," Lauren says as we FaceTime. "I had a brief call with him, and he's interested in signing you. I can arrange a meeting for after Christmas, before you have to leave, if you like."

I haven't had much success hiring my own publicist. None of the meetings I set up directly went well. I didn't like a single one of them. I want someone who will respect me as a person, not just a celebrity. Someone who will fight to protect my privacy and Vivien's, and I haven't met the right publicist yet. I reached out to Lauren a few days ago, and she's already come through for me. I should have just asked her in the first place. "That would be great. Thanks, Lauren."

"And Margaret is happy to have a hush-hush meeting now to provisionally start lining things up before your contract with Bianca expires in May."

"Set that up too."

"Consider it done. We can't wait to see you. Do you need us to pick you up tomorrow from the airport?"

"I have already booked a car, so I'm good." Usually, Vivien would pick me up, but she's still recovering. "I'm looking forward to seeing you all and chilling out for a bit."

We've been on the promo train for the past few weeks, and I'm exhausted. We are back in Boston today for official photographs for the *Twisted Betrayal* release in a few weeks, and I let Rudy and Jacob coax me into partying with the gang tonight. I haven't socialized with them in months, and it's Christmas, so I figure a few drinks is just what the doctor ordered.

Although I've been worried about Vivien, most everything else is going well. I have weaned myself off most of the pills, and I seem to be over the worst of the side effects. I'm still having issues sleeping, but that's a problem for a different day. I'm starting to feel good, and I'm going to get my life back on track. That's all that matters.

"Have a safe flight, honey," Lauren says before we hang up.

"I'm glad you came out tonight," Rudy says a couple of hours later when we're seated in a booth in the VIP section of the club. The entire place is decked out for Christmas, and everyone is in a festive mood. "You deserve one night to let loose." He presses his mouth in close to my ear. "I'm proud of you, man. I know it's still rough, but hang in there."

"I'm doing good," I say, tipping back more beer. "And being home with Viv will help." I can't wait to see her. I plan to have a long conversation with her about bodyguards. Jon told me she is not keen on the idea, but I intend to convince her. It's not safe for her without one, especially when the police have not apprehended the girls who attacked her, and they have no leads. They could return for round two, and there are plenty of other crazies in the world. It's why I have already reached out to Morgan Security, and I have a meeting lined up in January with the owner, Devin Morgan. They are making a name for themselves in celebrity circles, and I only want the best watching over me and mine.

A few more beers later and I'm nicely buzzing. We're all up dancing when I spy Rudy slinking off with some brunette in the direction of the bathroom. Dirty Dog.

"Hey, man." Jacob slings his arm over my shoulders, leading me to the side of the dance floor where it's more private. "I have an early Christmas gift for you." He waggles his brows and flashes me a wide grin. "Something to really get you in the party spirit." He tucks something into the palm of my hand.

"No thanks, dude." I move to hand the pill back to him. "I don't take that shit anymore."

"You haven't done this before and, trust me, you'll want to." He shoves his hand in the pocket of his jeans so I can't give it back to him.

"I don't want it."

"Relax, buddy." He squeezes my shoulder. "It's not addictive. It'll just give you the most amazing buzz. Man, if I could let you into my head right now, you would not question it."

My curiosity is piqued. "How come?"

He grins at me, smacking a loud kiss off my cheek. "I'm happy, dude." He raises his arms in the air and whoops. "So fucking happy." He pulls me into a hug. "I love you, man. You're the fucking best. When you're this massive superstar, I'll be able to say I was there when it all started. You're the man, Reeve." He waggles his brows and shimmies his hips, and I chuckle. "Go for it, dude. It's only molly. One little taste won't hurt you."

Oh, what the hell. I'm in control now. I've stopped with the other pills, like I knew I could if I wanted. He's right. One little taste is not relapsing, so I think nothing of it when I drop the circular pink pill in my mouth and wash it down with a mouthful of beer.

Sometime later, I'm wandering around the room, talking to people, laughing and joking, and feeling happier than I have in ages. More than that, I'm excited, high on life, feeling like I could climb mountains, and this party is the best fucking party ever. I grab some tinsel from the bar and wrap it around my neck, belting out Christmas songs as I flit around the room.

I throw myself into the middle of the dance floor, and my friends whoop and holler. Someone hands me another beer, and I knock it back. There's a vibrant buzzing in my veins, and I've never felt more alive! Warmth crawls all over me, and I roll my shirt sleeves to my elbows before making my way to the bar to grab another beer and some water. I'm thirsty from all the dancing.

My head is spinning, along with the room, but nothing can take away from my good mood. I swirl around the dance floor, bumping into faceless, nameless people, laughing and singing. My blood is on fire, and I feel like I'm king of the world! Time ceases to have all meaning as I work up a sweat on the dance floor. Nothing can dampen the euphoria I'm feeling. It's like I'm floating on air with an injection of pure bliss connecting straight to my veins.

"Come here, baby." A soft hand curls around mine, and the biggest grin spreads over my face.

She's here! My baby is here. "Viv." I reel her into my chest, swaying a little on my feet as I try to focus my vision. Woah. When did that get so blurry? "You're here." I bury my head in her neck, nuzzling her flesh as I cling to her. "I've missed you so much," I mumble, pressing a slew of kisses along her neck and jawline.

Her hands roam the length of my back before she grabs hold of my ass and squeezes. It's like a shot of liquid lust, and my dick instantly hardens to the point of pain. I'm horny, and I need to fuck my woman. Desire charges through my veins, and I don't waste a second, grabbing her head and pulling her mouth to mine. I bundle her in my arms as I ravage her lips, pulling her as tight as humanly possible, my dick poking her through the stomach as I kiss her passionately. Every nerve ending in my body is on fire, and I need to fuck. Rotating my pelvis, I push my erection against her, and she moans against my mouth.

"I need you to fuck me now," she rasps in my ear as a waft of perfume tickles my nostrils.

Something rattles around my brain.

Wait.

That voice is all wrong. The smell too.

I pull back, pushing her away as I grab the back of my head and try to make sense of it. My confused brain struggles to catch up with my vision as it clears. I sway on my feet, stumbling into someone.

"I've got you." Strong arms hold me up as Rudy rides to the rescue.

I look from Saffron to Rudy and back again, still confused. I glance around the packed room, but I don't see her. "Where's Viv?"

"Viv isn't here, but I am, and I'm everything you need," Saffron purrs, pushing her tits against my chest.

"You bitch," Rudy hisses, glaring at Saffron.

"Fuck off, Rudester. You're interrupting." Saffron grabs my dick as I struggle to work out what the fuck just happened. "Come on, baby. Let me take care of that for you."

"Get the fuck away from him." Rudy yanks me away from her, and I'm grateful.

"You, I, we ..." Pressure sits on my chest as I frantically scan the room. "I need Viv. Where is she?"

"Vivien is back in L.A., Reeve," Rudy says. "And I'm getting you out of here."

"This is none of your business." Saffron grabs my hand. "Reeve wants to stay here with me, don't you, baby?"

Tugging my hand back, I slowly shake my head.

No! No!

I can't have. I couldn't...

Viv's beautiful face swims in front of my eyes, and even in my fucked-up state I know I just seriously screwed up. My stomach twists painfully, and I bend over and throw up on the floor. I think Saffron shrieks. I might have puked all over her, but I don't remember much after Rudy drags me out of the club.

When I wake the next morning, I almost retch at the icky smell in the room that matches the gross taste in my mouth. I don't even remember getting to bed. Loud snores stab me in the ears as I haul myself into a seated position, glancing at where Rudy is passed out on the couch in my room with a small blanket covering him. What's he doing here? I look down at myself, and I'm still wearing the clothes I went out in last night.

"What the fuck?" I mumble to myself when I spot copious vomit spatters all over my shirt and jeans. Ugh. A shudder works its way through me. It's so gross. I'm dying to take a piss, and I'm in desperate need of a shower, so I climb off the bed on shaky limbs and make my way to the bathroom. I'm sweating and shaking and struggling to remember what happened last night.

I take a piss, frowning at the dark pool of urine in the toilet.

It's almost brown, which is not normal. Neither are the chills that overtake every inch of my body and even after I strip off my soiled clothes and step under the hot spray of water from the shower, I can't warm up. I clutch the wall as my vision blurs in and out and my stomach churns violently.

Panic crawls up my throat at the realization this is not just an alcohol hangover. Puzzle pieces start slotting into place as I get out of the shower and dry off before wrapping a towel around my waist. Wiping condensation from the mirror, I stare at my reflection as a sense of dread overtakes me. I look like complete shit, and it mirrors how I feel inside. My gaze lowers to my mouth, and suddenly, it all comes back to me.

Taking molly.

Thinking Viv was there.

Kissing my costar.

Horror, unlike anything I've ever felt before, slams into me like a wrecking ball. Dropping to my knees, I heave the remaining contents of my stomach into the toilet. Flashes of last night replay in vivid Technicolor in my mind, and I repeatedly gag even when there is nothing left in my stomach to expel. Silent tears stream down my face as it all returns to me, and I want to die.

The door opens, and I see a yawning Rudy out of the corner of my eye. I stare up at him. He looks as bad as me. He plants a hand on my shoulder as he walks to the sink. Wetting a cloth, he silently hands it to me before leaving. I flush the toilet and scrub at my face before rinsing with mouthwash.

I hate the sight of myself.

I'm disgusted, ashamed, and terrified.

"What time is it?" I ask when I emerge from the bathroom. If I've missed my flight, I'm liable to throw myself off the roof.

"Late, but don't worry. I contacted your dad, and he rearranged your flight. I knew you'd be in no fit state to get on a plane first thing. You can't go home looking like that." His eyes lock on to mine. "We've got a few hours before you need to be at the airport." He drills me with a look that is a mix between frustration and pity. "You should probably message Viv."

Mention of her name undoes me, and I sink to my knees on the floor, bury my face in my hands, and cry. My shoulders shake, and I don't even care that I'm losing it in front of Rudy. That is the fucking least of my worries.

The air stirs as he sits down beside me, but he says nothing, letting me fall apart. The pain in my chest is so intense it's a miracle I can breathe. My cries bounce off the quiet walls as my heartache seeps from me in loud, anguished sobs. I'm quaking, and I don't know if it's the aftereffects of taking molly, the severe emotional pain I'm crippled with, or a combination of the two. After some time, I rub at my eyes as my tear ducts finally dry, accepting the tissue he hands me. I blow my nose and scoot back against the side of the bed, leaning my head back and staring at the ceiling. "I'm going to lose her," I croak, and the motion hurts my dry throat.

Rudy hands me a bottle of water as he mirrors my position, sitting on the floor alongside me. "I feel partly responsible."

And so he should. I haven't been partying for a reason. I would never have gone out last night if he hadn't convinced me. "I should never have gone out." I uncap the bottle and chug water until the bottle is half empty. Turning my head to the side, I eyeball my friend with a sharp look. "Where the fuck did you go last night?"

"I hooked up with a girl in the bathroom. She was hot, and her place was only around the corner. We went back there for a while." He cleaves a hand through his hair as he lifts his knees to his chest. "I shouldn't have left you alone."

"No shit, Sherlock!" I hiss.

A muscle clenches in his jaw, and his tone is cutting when

he says, "I'll accept some responsibility, Reeve, but this isn't all on me. I wasn't the one who took molly, and I wasn't the one who played right into Saffron's hands." He glares at me. "What the fuck were you thinking? You've been doing good, and you just undid all your hard work!"

"I don't fucking care about the drugs. It was only one pill. Just a one-time thing. That's not what matters. What matters is..." I choke over the words. I can't even say it. It will only make it more real.

"You cheated on Vivien with that cunt." Rudy says what I can't.

I briefly hang my head as more tears threaten. "I thought she was Viv. I was fucking out of it, and I thought she was my girl." I swipe angrily at the hot tears leaking from my eyes.

"I got that much, and I'm guessing she was happy to let you believe it." He stretches his legs out. "She's a piece of work. Jacob admitted she asked him to convince you to take the molly. She planned this, Reeve, and I think it would've been worse if I hadn't come back when I did."

"I'd pushed her away. I was still confused, but I knew she wasn't Viv. I would never have fucked her. I would never fuck another woman."

"You just kissed another woman!"

"I know! I don't need the fucking reminder!" I yell, yanking on my hair as frustration trundles through me. "Why the fuck are you getting angry anyway?!" I add, fighting a wave of shivers. "It's not like she's your girl. You're not the one who stands to lose every fucking thing because of one stupid drugged-up mistake!" My hands tremble as I raise the bottle to my lips and drain the rest of my water. I'm so fucking thirsty.

"I don't want to argue with you, Reeve. I want to help. You can't change what's happened, but you've got to stay away from that bitch. This will only make her more determined. She wants to split you up to get payback on Viv."

"We're not breaking up." I grab another bottle of water from the mini refrigerator before snatching clean clothes and getting dressed.

"You're not going to tell her?" Rudy arches a brow as he climbs to his feet and stretches his arms over his head.

"How can I?" Bile swims up my throat. "Viv won't understand. She hates Saffron. It doesn't matter that Saff tricked me. Viv won't forgive me."

"I don't know, dude." He scrubs his hands down his tired face. "Hiding it doesn't seem like a smart idea. If Viv finds out and you haven't told her, she'll never believe you, and it'll definitely be over."

———

I am mulling over Rudy's words the entire plane journey home. It is, hands down, the worst plane ride of my life. I alternate between chills and sweating. Even though my stomach is painfully empty, I have no appetite, and I'm feeling constantly nauseous. I must have drunk at least four liters of water by now, and my pee is finally back to normal. Despite extreme fatigue, I'm just lying in bed on the private jet, staring at the ceiling, wondering how I'm going to tell the love of my life I made out with her archnemesis.

Every time I think of it, I'm glad I haven't eaten anything because I've no doubt I would puke if I had.

I am so disgusted with myself.

How the fuck could I think that slut was my girl? How did I not realize she was too short, the wrong shape, or how her lips tasted all wrong? How could I have been so stupid? And why did I even take that fucking molly? I'm stronger than this, and I've let myself down.

I don't want to tell Viv. There's a very strong chance she will end things between us because she hates Saffron that much. But that might also work to my advantage. She won't want me single and fully at Saffron's mercy. Either way, I have to come clean. Rudy is right, but it's more than that. I couldn't live with myself if I carried that secret around with me.

I'm shaking all over as I consider how to even start this conversation with my love. Tears prick my eyes, and I want to slam my head into the wall for being so fucking naïve. I curl into a ball, hugging a pillow to my chest. I feel sick. That bitch had her mouth on me, her tongue in me, and she groped my ass and my dick through my jeans. My eyes shutter as shame and remorse wash over me.

Although I've made a public statement confirming I'm not in a relationship with Saffron Roberts, and the fake-dating responsibilities are no more, I still have two premieres to attend with that bitch. We also have some scenes to film in a few weeks. It's going to be hell on earth. Having to touch her on-screen after what happened will be momentously hard because I want that bitch nowhere near me.

Vivien was right all along, and I was a fool not to believe her.

I hope I don't pay the ultimate price for my naivety.

Chapter Forty
Then - Age 16

"What's all this?" Viv's eyes are out on stalks as she walks into my bedroom and spots all the lit scented candles dotted around the space. Lavender rose petals cover the bed, and romantic music plays in the background, courtesy of the playlist I compiled during the week especially for tonight.

Taking her bag, I dump it on the floor and pull her into my arms. Exactly where she belongs. "I wanted to make tonight special." If I didn't think her parents would throw a hissy fit, I would have booked a cabin at Big Bear, but I didn't want to advertise the fact we were planning to have sex and break their rules. Jon and Lauren wanted us to wait until we were legal, but I need to be inside my girl. I'm so hot for her. So completely in love with her, and I can't wait any longer. Thankfully, Viv is on the same page, and here we are.

About to fuck for the first time.

I nearly come in my pants just thinking about it.

"You're the best boyfriend ever." She snakes her arms

around my neck and bites the corner of her lip in an obvious tell.

"Are you having second thoughts?" I ask. Please don't be having second thoughts. Please, please.

Her hair falls around her shoulders as she shakes her head. "No. I want this with you. I'm just nervous."

"Me too." I press kisses all over her beautiful face. "But I promise I'll be careful, and if you want to stop, we can."

"You'll look after me." She stretches up and presses a kiss to the underside of my jaw. "You always do."

"I love you." I rub my nose against hers.

"I love you too. You're my person, Reeve. For now and forever."

I kiss her slowly and deeply, trying to contain my excitement before I blow my load in my pants.

"You have chocolate strawberries and champagne," she pants when she breaks our lip-lock a few minutes later, noticing the silver bucket, glasses, and bowl on my coffee table.

"I raided Simon's stash." Of champagne. I bought the strawberries on my way home from drama class. I could have asked dear old dad before swiping the bubbly, and he would have said yes anyway. He doesn't give a shit if I drink.

He doesn't give a shit, period.

Holding her hand, I walk us over to my bed. I put fresh bed linen on it before she came over and cleaned up my room. Pouring two glasses of champagne, I hand her a flute and make a toast. "To us."

"To love." We chink glasses.

"And sex." I waggle my brows.

"And our dream home," she adds, trailing her fingers over the drawing on my bedside table. Viv sketched it a few weeks ago after we talked endlessly for months about our dream home. She wanted to visualize it. I snagged the drawing for safekeeping. Someday, we're going to build it and raise our family there.

A lump forms in my throat as I lean in and kiss her softly. "My life would be so empty without you in it. I hope you know that." I sweep my fingers across her cheek.

"As mine would. You make me so happy, Reeve, and I will only ever have eyes for you."

We drink champagne, and then I put the glasses down and reel her into my arms. We dance around my room, and she giggles when I twirl her around. She's so beautiful, and I can't believe she's mine. I still have to pinch myself most days. We kiss and make out as we sway to the music, and then I lead her to the bed, gently pushing her down. Picking up the gold bottle from the bedside table, I hold it out and waggle my brows. "I thought I'd give you a massage to help you to relax. I ordered this online."

I've been on a countdown to this night since we first made things official, so I've had plenty of time to prepare, and I've gone all out. I want it to be a night we both remember forever. Another precious first we share.

"Um, let me get changed first," Viv says before crawling over the bed, grabbing her bag, and racing into the bathroom. I was going to tell her clothes really are not necessary, but I'll do whatever she wants to make her more comfortable.

When she emerges a few minutes later, my mouth hangs open as I rake my gaze over every delectable inch of her. She's wearing a sexy red silk and lace negligee that barely covers her tempting body. "Is it bad I want to rip it from you and devour you with my teeth?" I blurt, unable to stop my thoughts from spewing from my mouth.

Her smile is sweetly anxious as she walks toward me. "You don't like it?" She playfully cocks her head to one side.

"What's not to like?" I say in a gruff voice as my dick swells to bursting point behind my thin pajama pants. Quickly peeling my shirt off, I toss it on a chair and close the gap between me and my girl. My fingers smooth over the soft material of her nightie, and I trail a path from her thigh up over her hip and along her waist, brushing the side of her breast as I move to her collarbone. "You look so sexy, and I'm dying to fuck you."

"Then what are you waiting for?" She grabs my dick through my pants, and a groan rumbles from my mouth.

I graze her earlobe with my teeth. "I need to get you ready, my love."

Alex said to make sure she's really wet before pushing in. Audrey and Alex lost their virginity to one another six months ago, and I asked him for a few tips because I want this to be pleasurable for Viv, and I know the first time can be painful for girls. I don't want to hurt her. I want her to enjoy this like I know I will. Cupping her gorgeous tits through the flimsy material, I flick my thumbs against her nipples, instantly hardening them.

"I'm ready," she rushes to reassure me.

"Humor me." I pepper kisses along the elegant column of her neck as I fondle her tits.

Leading her over to the bed, I position her on her stomach and settle between her legs before opening the massage oil. I warm it up on my hands before applying it to her back. The little whimpers she makes as I knead her tense muscles are like an aphrodisiac, and it'll be a miracle if I don't come the second I'm inside her.

Slowly, I work her taut muscles, lowering the nightie as I work my way down her back. She sits up to let me take it off completely, and I can't help bending down and sucking her nipple into my mouth.

"Reeve," she pants, squirming on the bed. "I need you to

fuck me now."

"Patience, my love." I kiss her pouty lips. "Don't rush me. I want to do this right. We'll never get this night back, and I want it to be memorable."

"Fuck, I love you so much." She drives her hand down my pants and grips my erection. "Even if you're currently the biggest pussy tease on the planet."

I chuckle as I push her back down on the bed on her stomach and make my way up from her feet, over her calves, and toward her thighs, kneading her silky flesh as I work the sweet almond oil in. My fingers brush against her glistening cunt, and she almost arches off the bed. I can't contain my smile as I alternate between massaging her inner thighs and teasing her pussy lips with my slick fingers.

Finally, I slide two fingers inside her, stroking them slowly.

"You're killing me," she mumbles with her face half-buried in the comforter.

"Turn over, babe." I chuckle at the speed with which she flips onto her back.

My dick is painfully hard as I massage her front, pouring oil over her tits and stomach.

"Reeve, please." Viv squirms on the bed, and I take pity on her—and me—'cause I'm close to combustion and lower myself in between her legs. My lips latch on to her pussy and I tongue fuck her in the way she likes.

"Reeve!" she screams, shoving her pussy in my face as she starts coming. Grabbing her ass, I hold her lips to my mouth as I lick and suck and bite while she rides out her orgasm. As Viv is coming back down to earth, I stand and get rid of my pants, holding my cock and silently warning it to behave as I retrieve a condom from the drawer of my bedside table. I wish Viv was on the pill or had an IUD so I could fuck her bare, but she didn't want to go on birth control behind Lauren's back, and I respect that.

Viv watches me as I roll on the condom and then haul ass back on the bed. She spreads her legs in invitation as I crawl up to her, and it's the most glorious sight. Her cunt is dripping and ready for me. "How was that?" I purr, nipping at her jawline before I brush my lips against hers.

"Epic. Like always." She tugs me down on top of her. "I love you so fucking much, Reeve, but if you tell me I'm still not ready, I'm liable to get all stabby."

I chuckle as I sweep her messy hair back off her pretty face. "I can't hold off any longer, and I gotta warn you I'm liable to come the instant I'm inside."

"We both know you can go again."

I nod, studying her face for any signs of nerves, but I don't find any. "You good, baby?" I say as I move down and settle between her thighs.

"I'm good." Her voice wobbles a little.

I position my cock against her entrance, rubbing it up and down her slit. "I will stop if you need me to."

"I know, like I know the pain is inevitable." Tears sheen in her eyes. "Fill me up, Reeve. I want to feel you inside me. I want to feel what it's like to be joined together in every way that counts. I want you to bury yourself so deep inside me I always feel you there."

Fucking hell. I swear my cock is leaking cum now. "Spoken like a true writer," I tease as I hold my cock to her pussy and slowly edge in. Her walls grip my crown, and her body is wound tight, every muscle strained and tense. Leaning down, I kiss her softly. "Relax, Viv. Just relax. We can take our time."

Internally I'm laughing because I'm seriously struggling to stop myself from coming and only the tip of my dick is in her.

When I feel her muscles loosening, I ease another inch

inside, kissing her mouth as we slowly become one. "Okay?" I whisper, peering into her eyes when I'm halfway inside. My dick is giddy, excited, and hungry for more, and my muscles are trembling with the effort involved in going slow when all I want is to ram inside her and pound her into the bed.

"I'm okay," she says, her voice elevating a notch.

"This is the part that will hurt." At least that's what all the articles I read said. They also said to do this part in one thrust. "Ready?"

She nods, and I maintain eye contact as I drive my dick the rest of the way inside her.

I feel her tensing beneath me, and a tiny whimper flees her lips. I hold myself steady, and holy fucking shit, I'm inside her. I'm as close to Vivien as humanly possible. Blissful warmth bubbles in my chest, surrounded by love, so much love. "I love you." I kiss her passionately, holding myself still even though it's killing me. A bead of sweat rolls down my back.

"I love you too, and you can move."

I lift my head. "You sure?"

She nods. "Audrey said this part would hurt, but as I relax it will lessen and I'll start to feel good. I trust you."

Slowly, I pull out and push back in. Pain glides across her face and I stop.

"Don't stop, Reeve, just keep going unless I ask you to stop."

"I don't want to hurt you."

"You won't. Just keep going until my body adjusts to the feel of you." She must not be convinced 'cause she reaches up and touches my face. "You couldn't ever hurt me. You love me too much."

"I do," I say, beginning to move again. "I love you more than I thought it was ever possible to love another person."

We kiss languidly as I move carefully inside her, and just as

I feel her muscles relax, she wraps her legs around my back and grabs my ass, and I fucking come, roaring out my release as I fill the condom with my cum.

"Oh my God, I'm so sorry." My cheeks are enflamed as I look at her.

"Don't be. You were all worked up when you were readying me." Her eyes glisten with emotion. "Pull out and come up here so I can suck you off, and then we can do it again."

"You're not too sore?"

She shakes her head. "Nope." But she winces a little when I pull out, and I eyeball her.

"I'm fine, Reeve. I know my own body. Now get your sexy ass up here so I can lick your dick."

I get rid of the rubber, and it doesn't take her long to get me all worked up because her mouth is just that good. One positive to come from abstaining from penetrative sex is how skilled we both are at oral sex and getting each other off with our hands.

Then I roll another condom on and push slowly inside her again. This time is much smoother, and we get into a rhythm, moving against one another in tandem, as we kiss and caress, and it's everything I had hoped for and more.

I have never doubted Vivien is my soul mate, but if I ever needed confirmation, this moment proves it. I have never felt closer to her nor been more sure that my love for her is the once-in-a-lifetime kind.

Chapter Forty-One
Now

I dot kisses into Vivien's hair as she lies unconscious in my arms, unable to sleep because I'm terrified these moments are ending. I'm not sure why I've been thinking about the night we lost our virginity to one another. Maybe because the way we made love earlier reminded me of our first time. Or perhaps I need to remember we are soul mates and destined to be together forever to find the courage to tell her what I've done. It's Christmas tomorrow, but this is the first night we've spent together since I came home because she was taking online exams. I have seen her, of course, but only for fleeting moments at a time, so there hasn't been time to properly talk.

Besides, I don't want to ruin Christmas and forever have her sad over the holidays. So, I'm waiting until a couple of days after Christmas to fess up.

I've decided I'm going to propose to her tomorrow. If she's wearing my ring on her finger, she's not likely to break up with me, right? I had intended to plan a huge romantic proposal, but

I can't wait any longer. This situation requires a grand gesture, and what better one than this?

Vivien is my future wife, and nothing is going to change that.

Asking her to marry me will confirm my commitment to her, and we'll get through this like we've gotten through all the other hard times in recent years. I mean, she kissed Nate and she danced with those frat guys at the party, so she can't get mad at me because that would be hypocritical. She was drunk both times and used that as her excuse. I was drunk and high and didn't know what I was doing, and that's no lie.

She'll understand.

She'll forgive me.

She's got to.

My arms tighten around her, and I'm careful not to press against her cast. Dusting more kisses into her hair, I manage to convince myself it will be fine.

Eventually, I fall asleep just before daylight breaks.

"You look beautiful," I tell her, standing in her bedroom doorway the following morning. She is stunning in a gorgeous black, gold, and red dress, and she takes my breath away, like always. She's wearing the opal earrings and necklace I gave her for Christmas and the matching bracelet I gave her in August. After we exchanged gifts earlier, I went home to get showered and changed before returning just now with Simon for Christmas lunch. Spending Christmas Day with the Millses is our regular Christmas routine, and one I always look forward to. Except this year, I can't shake that thundercloud hovering over my head, and I'm on edge.

"Thanks. You don't look so bad yourself." She looks me

over from head to toe, lingering on my clean-shaven jawline, and I'm glad I took the time to get rid of the stubble I wear for the movie.

I want Viv to remember I'm still *me*.

The same man she's loved her entire life.

It's important she remembers that when I tell her how I've failed her. One bad decision shouldn't override all the good memories we share. Sweat gathers at the nape of my neck, and my stomach churns violently, like it's been doing every day since I woke in that hotel room with the recollection of how badly I fucked up.

Shoving my anxiety aside, I move across the bedroom and take her in my arms, needing to hold her, touch her, kiss her. My lips slam down on hers, and I kiss her like I'm a dying man and she's the oxygen I need to breathe. Desperation laces each stroke of my tongue, and my heart is racing incredibly fast, thumping wildly against my rib cage.

Viv breaks our kiss, easing back to look at me. Her brow is creased in concern. "What's wrong?"

Shit. I've got to get a grip. "Nothing is wrong." I smile, hoping she'll just drop it.

Her hazel eyes turn somber. "Just tell me."

"It's nothing." I hate lying, but I won't ruin Christmas Day for her.

She levels me with one of her serious looks. "Don't lie to me, Reeve. I don't want to get into all our shit on Christmas morning, but I don't want you keeping more secrets from me. Something is obviously on your mind, so spill."

Fuck, fuck! I quickly wrack my brain for something to say that will appease her. "Saffron keeps messaging me," I say. "I've told her nothing will happen between us, and I can't hang out with her anymore, but she's not giving up without a fight." None of that is a lie, so my conscience isn't too conflicted. I kiss the tip of her nose. "She's going to be difficult. I'm sorry."

That's an understatement. I am dreading returning to the promo tour in January, and then we've got the premiere too. It's going to be a shit show.

A grimace crawls over her face. "I'd like to say I'm surprised, but I'm really not. She's a scheming bitch, and she's not going to let you go easily."

I thread my fingers through my hair. "You know I love you, Viv, right? No matter what she says, you know you're the only one I love," I blurt, then panic.

Why the fuck did I just say that?!

It's not like I haven't considered Saffron might call Viv to gloat. It's definitely something she would do, but I've already covered that base. I opened Viv's phone while she was sleeping and blocked Saffron's number. I blocked Jacob's too after Rudy told me he's her little bitch boy. Fuck that guy. I'm done with him as well.

Fear splays across her face, and I silently berate myself for being an idiot. "Are you telling me everything?"

I look away as I nod. I can't lie to her face, but she knows I'm not being truthful. I'm bracing myself for her next question, wondering how I'm going to get out of having this conversation now when Jonathon saves me. He comes up to get us for mass, and I've never been more grateful to go to church on Christmas Day.

I'm not religious, but I pray like hell during the ceremony.

Back at the house, Lauren and Viv prepare dinner while I enjoy a whiskey with Simon and Jon in Jon's study. I'm laughing at something Jon says when my phone vibrates in my pocket. Who the hell would be calling me on Christmas Day? Removing my cell from my pants pocket, alarm sets in when I see it's Rudy calling.

"Excuse me, I've got to take this," I say, before hightailing it out of there. The call ends, and he texts me a message to call him back ASAP. I lock myself inside the downstairs bathroom before I return his call. "What's wrong?" I blurt before he's even said hello because he would not call on Christmas Day to just shoot the shit.

"You'll want to sit down for this."

"Just tell me," I say through gritted teeth.

"Saffron went to the media," he says, and all the blood drains from my face. I don't need him to elaborate to know what he's talking about. "E-News is breaking it within the hour. Please tell me you've already told Vivien?"

"There wasn't time." My voice sounds hollow, which is weird because inside I feel anything but empty. My stomach is in knots, my heart is trying to beat a path out of my body, and nausea glides up my throat.

"Shit, Reeve!" His panic spurs mine.

"Fuck, Rudy. Fuck. Fuck." I rest my head against the wall as my breath comes out in exaggerated spurts. Pain shuttles through my chest, and I double over, clutching my stomach as potent fear infiltrates every part of me.

"Reeve, you need to go out there and tell her now! She can't find out from fucking E-News!"

"I know." I gulp back bile. "I've got to go."

"We'll get that bitch back for this," he says, but I hang up. Revenge is the last thing on my mind now.

I splash water on my face and try to calm down before I go back out there. Pulling the ring box from my pocket, I pop the lid, staring at the glistening diamond, hoping it's enough to convince Viv I love her. Although I made a big mistake, it doesn't have to spell the end.

I return the box to my pocket and head outside, hating I have to do this now. I pass the dining room, heading for the kitchen when Viv calls out to me. "We're in here," she hollers. "Dinner is served."

Fuck. Fuck. Triple Fuck.

I can't drag her away from the dinner table. It'll have to wait until after we eat. Except I can't stomach any food. I'm liable to puke it back up, so I shove the meat and veggies around my plate, trying to smile even though it feels like I'm dying inside.

I jump when Viv's hand lands on my thigh. "What's wrong?" she whispers.

"I need to talk to you," I say over the rock lodged in my throat. My cell buzzes in my pocket as my knee bounces on the ground. I'm wound up tighter than the ballerina on Viv's old music box.

"We're in the middle of dinner, Reeve. It'll have to wait."

Sweat beads on my brow and I honestly think I'm going to be sick. This can't wait. I need to tell her now!

"What did you do?" she asks, clearly reading my body language and knowing something is up. She knew it before mass too.

"Not here." I swipe at my clammy brow. "Please, can we go to your room to talk?"

"Turn on the TV," Lauren yells, shocking the shit out of everyone. She is holding her cell to her chest and glaring at me.

Oh my God.

She knows!

"Turn on E-News, Jonathon," she instructs, and I'm fucked.

I am so fucking fucked.

I should have dragged her out before dinner and told her. I wipe my damp palms down the front of my pants before I grab Viv's hand. "It meant nothing. Just let me explain."

"Turn it on, Daddy," she says while maintaining eye contact with me.

"No!" I stand, holding onto her hand. She can't find out like this. "Don't look at that. Please, Viv. Come with me and I'll explain."

She yanks her hand away and turns to face the wall-mounted TV just as Jon turns on E-News.

I shatter inside the instant I read the heart-sickening head-line, and I know. Deep down, I know this is it. This is the end. She will never forgive me for humiliating her like this.

REEVERON HOT KISS! WE'VE GOT THE EXCLUSIVE VIDEO THAT PROVES THEIR LOVE IS REAL!

Chapter Forty-Two

I'm shaking as I stare in horror at the video playing on the screen. That fucking bitch! She had someone record us on the dance floor. Most likely her little lap dog, Jacob. I am going to kill that guy when I next see him. Saffron completely orchestrated the entire thing, and I am the biggest fool! She always planned to go to the media because she wants to break us up. This is payback. Pure and simple.

"Baby, please. Don't look at that," I beg Viv, falling to my knees before her. "It looks worse than it is."

She ignores me, and pain spreads across her face as she watches the brutal evidence of my betrayal. I want to reach inside my body and rip my beating heart from my chest when I see the tears rolling down her face. She's unsteady on her feet when she rises, rushing out of the room with her hand covering her mouth.

I race after her, calling out for her to stop. "Vivien! Stop, please! Let me explain! I love you!"

She grinds to a halt in the hallway and swings around, glaring at me with so much venom I'm stunned speechless.

"Stop fucking lying!" she screams. She's visibly shaking, and it matches how I feel inside. "Stop saying you love me when your actions prove you don't! How could you do this to me?" A sob bursts from her mouth. "Haven't you humiliated me enough?"

"I was high," I rush to explain as desperation clings to me like a second skin. "It was stupid. I never should've taken molly, but everyone was doing it. Filming was over. I was coming home to you, and I was happy."

She laughs harshly. "Yeah. I saw how happy you were." She pushes me with her uninjured hand. "How long has it been going on, and have you fucked her?" She leans forward, looking like she might be sick. "Oh God. We had sex last night. That slut is probably riddled," she yells. "Now I'll have to get tested!"

"I didn't fuck her, and that was the only time I've kissed her. I swear."

She waves her hands around. "Like I believe a single fucking word coming out of your lying mouth!" she shrieks.

She seriously can't believe I would fuck another woman and then have unprotected sex with her? I know she's upset and angry, and she has every right to be, but she knows I would never do that. "Baby. I know you're upset. I'm upset too. I'd never taken molly before. It made me horny as hell, and she pounced on me when I was wasted. I didn't push her away at first because I was confused. I thought she was you!" I touch her gently, pleading with my eyes. "As soon as I realized who I was kissing, I pushed her away."

"A likely fucking story."

Panic is a charging bull rampaging through my insides and I'm desperate. I'll do anything to prove myself to her. I take out my cell and offer it to her. "Call Rudy if you don't believe me. He'll confirm it."

She shoves my phone away, continuing to glower at me. "I don't care if he does. I don't care if you were high. You promised me you were done with drugs, but that was obviously another lie, and it's not an excuse." Pain splays across her face, and she rests her head against the wall. She's trembling all over, and I hate I did this to her.

I need to go big or go home. I'm not getting through to her, so I offer to do something I think will speak volumes. "I'll quit the movie." I mean it. If that's what it takes, I'll do it. I approach her slowly, not wanting to startle her. "They can sue me. I don't care."

"What about your career?" she hisses, staring straight at the wall instead of looking at me.

"I don't care about my career!" I place my hand tentatively on her back. "I only care about you."

She sidesteps me and wraps her uninjured arm around her waist. "You don't care about me. If you did, you would've pulled out a long time ago. You only care you got caught."

"That is not true." How can she believe that? I know I fucked up. Badly. But it doesn't negate how I feel about her.

A muffled sound escapes her throat as she turns to face me. Unadulterated hurt is etched upon her face, and it slays me. "It seems you need a little history lesson, so let me enlighten you. From the very start, you have refused to see what is blatantly obvious. That bitch, Bianca, and Cassidy have conspired to make my life miserable. They're behind it all, I'm sure of it, but you still don't believe it. That"—she points in the direction of the dining room, and I notice our parents watching for the first time—"was carefully timed to inflict the worst pain on a day that should be special. A day that will now be forever tarnished for me. But I'm sure you'll find some way of defending that bitch and blaming the press. Or better yet, why not turn it around on me? Because you're so good at that!" she screams.

I've no doubt Saffron timed it to hurt the most. I agree with her there, and it seems likely now that Saffron is at least in cahoots with Cassidy, but why the fuck would I defend her and turn it around on Viv? That is a completely unfair and unfounded accusation.

"Go on!" she yells. "Tell me how selfish I am for not supporting you! How much I'm adding to your stress because I won't get with the program and endorse your so-called fake relationship. I am the only one who has suffered for your dreams. *Me!* Not you!"

If she thinks I haven't suffered, she is sorely mistaken. I guess I don't blame her for thinking it because I hid most of it from her. I didn't want to worry her, and I was only trying to protect her. It seems that has backfired on me too.

She covers her chest with her hand. "I have been humiliated and vilified at every turn. I was attacked, and I know that bitch orchestrated it, and there you go kissing her in public without any regard for my feelings! You did that days after professing undying love for me and promising to fix everything! I have tried to love and support you, but you continuously shut me out. You refused to accept Mom's help. You refused to believe me. *Me!* The person you profess to have loved for nineteen years. Instead, you believe that conniving slut. You—"

"It wasn't that I didn't believe you, Viv!" I yank on my hair, trying to find the right words to make this right. "You were so irrational when it came to her that it made it difficult for me to believe it wasn't jealousy driving your behavior, but I see it now."

And those clearly weren't the words.

"Well, that makes it all fucking right then, doesn't it?!" She prods me in the chest as she screams, and I have never seen Vivien this angry. "Tell me one time I was irrational!? One time I said something that hasn't turned out to be true?" She puts her hands on her hips and levels me with a glare.

"Rehashing that shit won't do either of us any good." I'm

not disputing I've made a mess of things, but she is overreacting, and going over all that won't resolve this situation.

She barks out a bitter laugh. "Bullshit. You can't think of even one thing because you know I'm right!"

"I'm not disagreeing with you!" I shout, seeing red because she's not fucking listening to me!

"Don't you dare shout at me, you two-timing bastard! You have no right! I'm entitled to my anger! *I'm* the one who looks like a goddamn fool in front of the entire world. Not you or that man-stealing whore! So don't you fucking shout at me." She slams her fist into the wall, and I stare at her in shock. "Ugh." Lauren runs toward us, but Vivien holds out her hand. "Stay back, Mom. I'm getting this all off my chest, and then Reeve is leaving."

I am going nowhere until I get through to her.

"This isn't on me," she says in an eerily calm voice as she eyeballs me. "This is all on you. You've messed up everything, *movie star*. Your selfish pursuit of your dreams at all cost has destroyed what we once shared."

"No, Viv. Please don't say that. We can get through this. I will do whatever you want to make this right. Anything. I'll do anything, but I can't lose you. Please, Viv, I'm begging you." My anger is gone again, replaced by complete and utter desperation. She can't mean what I think she means. This isn't the end of our story. I won't let it be. Dropping to my knees, I hug her legs and cling to her. I'm not letting her go. I love her, and I know she loves me. There's got to be a way to fix this.

She shakes her head as I look up at her. The desolation in her eyes is a mirror of what I feel. "You've already lost me, Reeve. I might as well be single, because I never see you. I'm lonely, and I'm heartsick, and I can't do it anymore."

"Vivien. I love you. I know I've fucked up, but please give me another chance."

The ring!

I had almost forgotten.

Lowering my arms and scooting back a little, I remove the box as I go up on one knee and pop the lid. Please God, let this be enough. "I was planning to ask you to marry me tonight. It's always been you, Viv. Deep down, you know that. Don't let her come between us anymore than she already has. I'm begging you. Please forgive me, and say you'll be my wife."

Tears cloud her eyes, and for a second I think they're tears of joy until I see the pain flitting across her face. "There was a time I would have jumped into your arms and screamed yes, but we are so far removed from that now." Her voice cracks as tears flood her eyes. "How could you even consider asking me to marry you when our relationship is in tatters?"

"We've lost our way, but we'll get it back. I'm still committed to you, and this was my way of proving it. I wasn't expecting us to get married any time soon, but I hoped you would see how much I love you and know I'm still serious about spending the rest of our lives together."

Please believe me. Please let it be enough. Please let me not have fucked it all up.

I will die without her.

I cannot live without her.

We belong together.

She knows that.

"This is the action of a desperate man. It's nothing more," she whispers, her voice drenched in sadness. "I don't even understand why you claim to want me anymore."

"Because I fucking love you!" I shout. "I made a mistake. Lots of them, but my love for you has never wavered. Not once. You're the other half of my heart and soul, Vivien. Please say you believe that? Please, baby. Please, please, believe me. I can't lose you. I'll die without you."

She holds on to the wall behind her, looking like she might collapse. "I don't believe it, Reeve." She sniffles as tears spill over onto her cheeks. "I don't believe a word that comes out of your mouth anymore. I can't marry you. I *won't* marry you, so put that ring away." Her expression is resigned when she adds, "Actions speak louder than words, Reeve. And your actions confirm I don't matter."

"I'll put out another statement. I'll tell the world it was a mistake. I'll stop taking drugs. I'll pull out of the movie." I'm frantic and panicking on several levels. I thought the ring would do it, but I think I've only made things worse. I climb awkwardly to my feet, my limbs heavy with sadness. I put the ring back in my pocket as a sharp pain splinters my chest. It feels like I'm dying. This can't be happening. It can't be the end.

"You have pushed me away, downplayed my feelings, scoffed at my concerns, and let yourself be manipulated," she says in a choked voice. "We should have broken up like Audrey and Alex and protected our past because everything is tarnished now. All my memories include you, Reeve. Every single memory I have of my childhood, you are in it, and now they are all tainted!" She cries out, and I want to comfort her, but her expression tells me I can't. "She hasn't just stolen you from me. She's stolen every good memory. I will never be able to look at our past with anything but pain in my heart."

"She hasn't stolen me, Viv. I don't want her. I only want you." I sound like a hollowed-out broken record even to my own ears.

"I thought we meant everything to one another. I thought you were the one person I could trust with my life. But you've trampled all over my heart. You have shattered my soul and broken my spirit. I hate who I've become. I don't even know who I am anymore. I'm in so much pain, and I'm so lost, and you didn't even see. You didn't see or you chose to ignore it."

I hang my head as her words penetrate deep. Everything I've refused to confront about our relationship is laid bare in her words. Along with the resolve that threads behind every sentiment. I truly believe there is nothing I can say or do to get her to change her mind.

I want the ground to open up and consume me. For the earth to fill every orifice and snuff out my life because I don't want to live if I've lost the only person who has ever loved me unconditionally.

"What if the roles were reversed and you were the one in my shoes?" she asks. "Have you ever considered that? How hurtful would it be if I were the one parading another man around in public as my boyfriend, shunning you and relegating you to the shadows in case anyone discovered the truth? Being victimized online and attacked when you have done nothing, abso-fucking-lutely nothing, but try to be a supportive partner? How would it feel to watch me kissing another man in public, knowing the entire world is watching and laughing at you for being such a gullible fool to believe I was faithful?"

Her words drive the point home. I can't say I have thought about it like that and it only makes it worse. I raise my head as she wraps her arms around herself. "You cheated on me with her." Tears stream down her face. "You have publicly betrayed me. Slain me as skillfully as if you'd taken a sword and sliced me wide-open."

I don't even realize I'm crying until the tears drip down over my chin. All I can do is stare at her, knowing there is nothing else I can try to fix this. How did it come to this? How did two people who love each other so much, who have shared their entire lives and mapped out their forever, end up in this mess?

"It's time I put myself first," she says, lifting her shoulders. "I need to protect my heart and my sanity, and you're just not good for my health. I can't be with you anymore."

"No, baby." I find my voice and take a step toward her. I need to try again. "Please, Viv. Please give me one more chance."

"You're all out of chances, Reeve. I don't want to be with you. I don't want to see you or speak to you. I want you out of my life," she sobs.

"I think it's time for you to go, Reeve." Lauren pulls Viv into a hug, and it hurts to see her sobbing and clinging to her mother, a shell of the person I know her to be.

I did this and I have never hated myself more. "I'm sorry, Viv. More than you can know. I'll give you some space, but I'm not giving you up." Although I don't believe any more time apart will help, she needs space to think about it. This has been a bombshell, and it's no surprise she's reacted like this. Maybe all isn't lost. There is hope yet. I just need to back off and give her the time she needs to work through her emotions. Then I'm going to prove she's my priority.

"You don't have a choice." Her red-rimmed eyes stare at me. "You gave up on us a long time ago—you just didn't realize it."

That is not true. I have never given up on us. I let myself get distracted, and I fell down a dark hole, but I didn't want this. I have only ever wanted her. I want to say this, but it won't help. She's not hearing me now.

Dad walks up, looking awkward as all get out. He rubs the back of his neck. "Thanks for dinner, Lauren, and I'm sorry for all of this."

Lauren narrows her eyes at Simon. "Perhaps, if you were around more for Reeve, he wouldn't feel like he needs to sell his soul to be a success just so you'd be proud of him. You're not innocent in this either, Simon."

Dad says nothing as we walk toward the door. I cast a glance over my shoulder, watching Vivien's parents hug her and surround her with their love, before I walk out the door leaving my heart behind.

Chapter Forty-Three

"I'm trying not to panic," I tell Alex as I stare out the living room window, "but it's been five days, and she still won't talk to me." I turn around on the couch to face my best friend. He's been checking in with me most days since everything went down on Christmas Day. "I'm sending gifts, flowers, and letters, and leaving messages and texts on her cell, but it's complete radio silence. Lauren and Jon won't let me into the house, and I'm really starting to freak out."

I can't eat, and I am barely sleeping—that's nothing new—and I spend most days hiding inside because swarms of paparazzi are outside the gates of North Beverly Park, hoping to catch a glimpse of Viv or me.

"Audrey says she is devastated."

"You've spoken to Rey?" Last I heard, they still weren't talking, but it's no surprise I'm out of the loop. I haven't had much time to catch up with him since we hung out over the summer in Sydney. Audrey dropped by the day after Christmas to lay into me. I've never seen Viv's bestie so angry she actually punched me.

I deserve it. I know.

"Only briefly." He crosses his ankle over one knee. "I wanted to test the waters, see if she'd help you out, but you're on your own, buddy. She's firmly in Vivien's camp and—" He chews on his lip, stopping whatever he was about to say.

"Just spit it out."

"She says Viv is determined not to get back with you."

My eyes shutter as a fresh wave of pain rips through me. "I can't accept that," I quietly say, forcing my stinging eyes to open. "I can't have lost her, Alex. What am I going to do?"

"Just keep doing what you're doing. Reminding her how much you love her while trying to give her space."

My cell pings with a message, and I glance at the screen, my mouth instantly pulling into a grimace as I all but growl at the phone.

"Is that bitch still harassing you?"

"Yep." I delete Saffron's latest message, and this time, I don't hesitate to block her number. At least that's one less thing to worry about. I toss my cell on the couch and lean my head back, sighing. "I think someone will have to restrain me tomorrow because I honestly think I could murder the cunt."

"Is she still proclaiming innocence?"

I nod. "She might have fooled me in the past, but I'm wise to her now. I don't believe a word of it." Saffron has left me tons of teary messages stating she had nothing to do with the leak and it was obviously someone else at the club who took the video.

"You need to avoid her at all costs, because if Viv sees any sign of you together, all hope is lost."

"Tell me how I do that when I'm back on the promo tour soon, and we've got the premiere after that? I can't avoid her, Alex, even though I'd punt her back-stabbing ass to Mars if I could. Multiple interviews are lined up for us, and we'll be expected to pose for photos together on the red carpet." I bury my face in my hands. "It's a shit show."

He leans forward on his elbows, and strands of sandy-blond hair fall over his brow. "So do what you were threatening to do. Say you'll quit unless they separate you for the tour."

"It's too late for the tour. All the arrangements are in place, but I can demand to be kept apart from her at the premiere, and I'll ensure we are sent to separate locations to promote the final movie."

"Meet that guy you were talking about. The owner of the security company. Hire your own bodyguards and tell them their number-one agenda is keeping that bitch away from you."

"That's a good idea." I grab my cell. "I'll see if he can fly to New York to meet me." I type out a message to Devin Morgan and press send before repocketing my cell. I climb to my feet. "I'm going to talk to Lauren and Jon about a bodyguard for Viv. She needs one now more than ever."

"I doubt she'll let you do that for her, but it can't hurt to try."

Twenty minutes later, I'm standing outside Vivien's house trying to calm my nerves. The housekeeper answers, and she refuses to let me inside the house while she goes to get Lauren. Jon isn't at home apparently.

Standing outside their door like a stranger is a reminder of all I stand to lose if I can't win Viv back.

"Reeve, you shouldn't be here," Lauren says the instant she opens the door, folding her arms and leveling me with a look that is missing her usual warmth.

Of course, they would side with their daughter. I expect nothing less. I'm persona non grata.

I'm the enemy.

The man who has hurt their little girl.

I don't know if they'll ever forgive me either.

"I can't stay away," I truthfully reply. "I love her, Lauren. You know I do. I'm more sorry than I can explain. It was a mistake—one I will regret forever. But we can't let Saffron split us up. That's what she wants. If Viv would just give me another chance. If you would just let me in so I can talk to her."

"You heard Vivien, Reeve. She doesn't want to talk to you. You're all out of chances, and honestly, hounding her like this is not doing you any favors. You broke her heart. You have humiliated her and made it so she can't even leave her own home." She flicks her head in the direction of the gate. "Every time Jon or I leave, we are besieged. Imagine how bad it'd be for Viv?"

"Tell me how to fix it," I plead. My voice is laced with desperation.

"I don't know if you can." She shakes her head. "I never saw this coming for you two, but I support Vivien's decision. She has to prioritize herself, and you should too. I don't know how bad things have gotten, but you don't look good, Reeve, and you should work on yourself before you give any thought to reconciling with my daughter. I think you need time apart. If it's truly meant to be, you will find your way back to one another."

"You told me my heart would never steer me wrong when we had a conversation just after I got the part. I should have listened better. Vivien is my heart, and if I'd only listened to her, we wouldn't be here."

"I wish you had listened too, but it doesn't change anything now, Reeve. You've got to accept this. Stop sending her gifts and flowers, and stop bombarding her with messages. You're only adding to her anxiety, and she's distraught enough."

"I need her to know I still love her."

"It won't change her mind, Reeve. All you are doing is prolonging both your agony. You need to accept it and move forward with your life."

"I can't, Lauren." I shove my hands in my pockets and rock back on my heels. "I don't know how to live without her."

"It's a pity you didn't remember that when you were doing drugs and making out with that little bitch." Lauren gives me the evil eye, and it's clear I'm not getting through the door today.

"I know." All fight leaves me as I stare at the woman who is the only mother figure in my life. Seeing her so angry and upset makes things even worse. I haven't just let Vivien down. I've let all of them down. I stand to lose the only real family I've ever had, and the thought devastates me. If I can't repair things with Viv, I have lost them all, and I...I can't contemplate losing Viv, Lauren, and Jon. They mean everything to me. They are my parents in every way that counts, and if I lose them too, I don't know if I'll survive.

A crushing weight settles on my chest. What have I done?

"Reeve?" Lauren prompts me to continue.

Get a grip, Lancaster. I clear my throat and lift my shoulders. "I came over to see if Vivien would agree to a security detail. I have a meeting with Devin Morgan in New York, and I intend to fast-track the paperwork and hire bodyguards for both of us. Do you think she'll agree to it?"

Lauren immediately shakes her head. "She won't accept help from you. I doubt Jon and I will have much luck convincing her to let us pay for one either."

"I need her to be safe. The vultures are circling worse than ever, and I'm worried about her."

Her features soften a smidgeon. "That's not your concern anymore, Reeve. You need to let it go."

"I can't."

"Try harder." She straightens up and opens the door behind her. "I need to get back."

I nod as a veil of sadness crests over me. "If things change with the bodyguard, let me know. The least I can do is pay for her protection."

"I wouldn't hold my breath if I was you."

"Thank you for talking with me," I say, moving to walk off.

"Reeve," she calls out after me, and I look over my shoulder. "Please look after yourself. I meant what I said. You need to take better care of yourself, and you need to stop taking drugs."

"I already have."

Her eyes penetrate mine. "Good. Keep it that way and take care." Then she closes the door, leaving me all alone.

"Please, Reeve. I'm begging you. I didn't do this." Saffron grabs my arm as we leave the Fox5 studio in the city after our interview.

"Ma'am, you need to step away from my client," Bobby—one of my new bodyguards—says, sending my costar a ferocious look.

"Fuck you," she snarls as her fake tears instantly disappear. "I'm only trying to talk to him."

I remove her hand from my arm and step sideways in between Bobby and Leon. Devin Morgan instantly stepped into action, and I had two new bodyguards on my payroll three hours after our meeting. The guy truly is impressive. As are the men on his team. Saffron has been trying to get alone time with me since we landed in The Big Apple and my bodyguards are blocking her every attempt. She's starting to lose her cool and I'm enjoying seeing it.

I drill her with a venomous look. "Again, I don't want to talk to you, and I don't believe you. I know you did this, and nothing you say will convince me otherwise."

"I was doing you a favor, but you're too fucking naïve to see it," she snaps, finally showing her true colors. "Vivien is an uptight snooty bitch, and she had it coming."

"Get her the fuck away from me," I bark at Leon. "Before I'm up on a murder charge." This really doesn't bode well for the three weeks of filming that is yet to come on *Sweet Retribution*, but right now, I need that bitch out of my hair.

Bianca refused to relay my threat to quit to the studio, so I called Simon. Dad loves turning the screws on anyone, and I knew he would help. Through his contacts, he got me on the phone with Ken Cooper, one of the studio execs, and it was a very interesting call indeed.

Although I've already made the decision to terminate my contract with Bianca in May when it expires—because I've realized she doesn't have my best interests at heart—it was still a shock when Ken told me the studio hadn't issued any of the directives about Vivien or fake dating Saffron. He says those requests came via my agent, and they thought I'd requested them to enhance my profile and build my brand.

Viv was right. I feel so stupid. Vivien wasn't even there, and she could see right through them. Yet I fell for their games time and time again. Bianca and Cassidy were behind this all along, and I suspect they were in cahoots with Saffron. I don't know why, but I intend to find out. Devin knows a few PIs, and he's going to schedule a meeting for me with one of the best guys in the business. I want to get to the bottom of everything, and then I'm going to ruin all three of them.

I can't put anything in motion until after the premiere because I barely have time to breathe right now, but I'm determined to get payback. Especially if they've permanently fucked up my relationship. I haven't given up hope yet, and I'm trying to remain optimistic. The alternative doesn't bear thinking about, and I can't afford to fall apart, so I'm treating this like it's just a break. Viv will come around. I know she will. We love each other too much to walk away from years' worth of history. I know I hurt her deeply, and I hate myself for it, but I will make it up to her.

This isn't the end.

I won't let it be.

Chapter Forty-Four

I watch the gardener trimming shrubs in the garden from the sunroom as I demolish the scrambled eggs, bacon, and toast Mrs. Thompson made me for breakfast. Swallowing the last bite, I lift my mug to my lips, drinking the dregs of my coffee as I stare at my cell, willing it to ping with a call or a message. I returned from the promo tour last night and immediately texted Viv to tell her I was home. I also invited her to the premiere tomorrow night.

Unlike the first one, I want her to walk the red carpet by my side this time. Cassidy threw a hissy fit when I informed her of my plans, but she had to back down when I threatened to go directly to the studio about it. Neither she nor Bianca knows I've already spoken with Ken or that I'm on to them. It's the way I prefer to keep it for now until I get all my ducks in a row.

Finishing my coffee, I grab my cell and walk off, wondering if I should drop by Vivien's house. If she doesn't respond by lunchtime, I'm going over there.

Or not.

My lips curl into an instant smile when I open the door and

there she is. Standing motionless in front of me with her eyes closed, looking so beautiful I could cry.

Sensing me, her eyes pop open, and we stare at one another. My heart is skating around my chest, ready to throw a party, but the look of anguish on her face is enough of a warning to withhold the premature celebration.

But at least she's here.

She must be ready to talk.

It's progress and the opportunity I've been seeking to fix things.

Every emotion I've been repressing slams into me like a tornado, and my eyes glaze over. "Viv," I whisper. "You came." My mouth lifts in a small smile as I reach for her.

My heart plummets to my toes and the smile slips off my face when she shakes her head and steps out of reach. Pain splays across her features as she wraps her arms around her body. I see her cast is gone, which is good.

I slouch against the door and tuck my hands in my pockets so I don't move to touch her again. It's clear she doesn't want that. But I'm okay with baby steps. Whatever she needs, she's got it. "I miss you," I tell her.

"I miss you too, but it changes nothing."

What? "Why are you here then?"

"I came to tell you I'm leaving."

My brow puckers. "Leaving? Leaving for where?"

"I'm moving to Dublin, Ireland. My plane leaves at noon."

I blink repeatedly as I stare at her, sure I must have heard her wrong. This cannot be happening! This wasn't the way it was supposed to be. I thought if I gave her space, she'd process her emotions and come back to me so we could put it behind us. How can I fix things if she's leaving? And why? I don't understand this at all. It's entirely come out of left field. I run my fingers through my hair as panic wreaks havoc inside me. "How? Why? For how long?"

"UCLA has a transfer program with Trinity College Dublin. It's usually for junior year students, but Dad knows the president, and he made it happen for me. I'm going to complete my sophomore spring semester there."

I rub my hands over my face, still in complete shock. "You're going away for five months?"

"At least. If I like it, I'll probably stay during summer break too. As for why, I think that's obvious. I need to heal, and I can't do that in L.A. I need to go someplace the media won't find me. I need to leave all the noise behind."

"Leave me behind, you mean," I croak as a sharp pain lances my chest.

Her tongue peeks out, wetting her lips. "Yes. I can't put you and our relationship behind me when your face is everywhere and reminders of you are everywhere."

She cannot mean that! Why is she saying these things? It's just a setback! We're not breaking up. We can't. I need her. She needs me. We're meant to be together. What about everything we've planned for our future? She can't just turn her back on that. This can't be true. Taking her hand, I pin her with pleading eyes as I prepare to beg. "Viv. I love you. I don't want to lose you. I don't want her. I've never wanted her. I only want you."

She wrenches her hand from mine. "I don't want to leave on bad terms, Reeve. I will never forget what you did, but maybe one day I can find a way to forgive you. You're a free agent now. You can be with her with a clear conscience."

What is she talking about? I don't want anyone but her! She can't seriously think I want that bitch? "Viv, please, just *hear* me. I don't want her. She means nothing to me and you're everything." I yank on my hair as my heart thumps against my chest cavity, adrenaline courses through my veins, and I struggle to breathe. It feels like I'm on the verge of a full-blown panic attack. "You're fucking everything, Viv."

Tears roll down my face as the reality of the situation hits home. I haven't allowed myself to consider the very real possibility of us breaking up in the weeks since Christmas Day, preferring to cling to hope. I fully believed we would find our way back to one another because we share too much to just walk away. This is like someone has taken a chainsaw to my heart and sliced it to a bloody pulp.

"You made a lot of mistakes that hurt me, but I don't want to hold on to the hurt and the pain. I don't want our relationship to be defined by our final days. I hope someday to be able to look back and remember the good times, because there were a lot of those."

How is she so calm? How is she all right with this? Does none of it mean anything to her? "This isn't the end, Viv. Please, baby. I can't lose you."

She rubs at her brow and sighs. "Reeve, stop. Please stop. I can't do this again. You're making this harder. I didn't want to leave without telling you in person, and now I've told you."

She turns to leave, and I can't let her go. I reel her into my arms, fighting the incoming panic attack. "Please, Viv. Please don't say it's the end. It's not the end. It can't be. I'm not going to stop fighting for you."

I'm not.

She is *my girl*.

The only woman I will ever love.

I'm never, ever, letting her go.

Her composure cracks, and she sobs, shucking out of my arms and backing away from me. "If you love me, you won't fight, Reeve. You'll do this one thing for me." She cries out as tears pour down her face. "Look what you've done to me! I'm destroyed. I'm so lost and in so much pain. Please just let me go. Let me go, and don't come looking for me. Don't contact me, because clinging to what we had won't help either of us," she whispers.

This is killing me. I don't want to let her go, but I can't force her either. Maybe she just needs more time. I try to quell the raging storm rising inside me, drawing a deep breath as I rein my emotions in. "I hate what I've done to you. What I've done to *us*, and I will get you back because I love you too much to let you go forever." I hold her beautiful, beautiful face in my hands, using my thumbs to wipe her tears. "But I'll give you space. Take whatever time you need. I'll wait for you."

My heart is shattering and it's a miracle I managed to get those words out. I don't want to do any of that, but I have no choice. This isn't about me. This is about doing what she needs. Prioritizing her needs even if it means sacrificing my own. It's the least I can do for her now. Though it will kill me to not be with her, it's only temporary.

I'll win her back.

I can't imagine a world where I don't.

She steps out of my reach again, and it hurts. It's like she can't bear to be touched by me at all. "No. I don't want any loose ends. We are over, Reeve."

Resolve flows through my veins as I silently vow to do everything in my power to get her back. "Not for good, Viv. Never for good."

"I don't know what the future holds, but I can't go to Ireland with things hanging in the air. The past two years of my life have been spent in limbo waiting for you, and I can't do it anymore. For my sanity, I need a clean break. If you love me, you'll stop fighting my decision. You need to let me go. I can't heal otherwise."

My initial instinct is to refute her sentiment. I can't ever let her go. But I want her to heal and to be happy. I know I have robbed her of that, and I've never been more ashamed. Reminding myself this is about Vivien, I acquiesce. "Okay, if that's what you want, but this isn't goodbye, Viv. Only goodbye for now."

"I need to go, or I'll miss my flight."

"Take care of yourself. I'll be thinking of you." Every second of every minute of every hour of every day.

She looks me straight in the eye as she breaks my heart. "I'm not saying this to hurt you, but I'll be trying not to think about you at all."

That fucking hurts.

I swallow over the messy ball of emotion in my throat. "I deserve that." My eyes lower to her neck. "You're not wearing your locket." Since I gave it to her before I left the first time for Boston, she has only taken it off Christmas Day to wear the opal necklace I bought her.

"It hurts too much to look at it, and I meant what I said about a clean start."

I risk moving in closer, needing to look straight into her soul when I say this. "Someday, I'm going to correct my mistakes and win back your heart. I won't stop until I prove I'm worthy of your love again." As long as there is oxygen in my lungs, I will never stop fighting for her.

She cups my cheek, and I lean into her touch, greedy and desperate for it. "Be happy, Reeve. That's all I've ever wanted for you."

Letting her walk away is one of the hardest things I've ever done, but I have no choice.

I fucked up.

I caused this.

Which is why it'll be up to me to fix it.

Chapter Forty-Five
Now - Age 20

Hugging the framed photo to my chest, I sob uncontrollably as pain lays siege to every limb, every organ, every ligament, and every tissue. Resting my head back against the headboard, I hug the picture even tighter as tears leak from my eyes. Heartache bleeds from my pores as my mind replays the words written in the report.

Devin helped me to hire a security firm in Ireland to watch over Viv. I know she wouldn't approve, so she doesn't know. I couldn't bear the thought of anything happening to her while she was so far away, so I took matters into my own hands and hired bodyguards to watch over her twenty-four-seven. They send weekly reports to Devin, and he forwards them to me.

I knew she made new friends. Guys and girls. But I really didn't think anything of it.

Until today.

Sobs wrack my body as I curl into a ball on my side hugging the picture. I framed one for Viv too. It's the photo from the Harry Potter premiere we attended as kids. The one Rudy found online. I contacted the photographer and bought copies.

It's just one of the gifts I've been compiling for my love. A way to remind her of all we have shared, confirm how deep our connection runs and how intense our love is.

But it was all in vain. Pining away the past three months and not jumping on a plane because I am trying to give her space didn't work. Everything I've done to show her how much I love her has had no impact either. The sewing machine and supplies, the flowers, the tattoo, commissioning the architect drawings of our dream house, the album I worked on for months since she left me. Staying off drugs and trying to keep clean for her. Focusing all of my energies on finding ways to prove my love, making concrete plans for our future, and mapping out a strategy to take down our enemies.

All of it failed.

What was the point when she's already given up on us?

It's her birthday in ten days, and I have already organized the delivery of her gifts. Twenty bouquets of lavender roses—one for every year she's been born—and the package with the album and the architect's plans for our new house.

Wonder what her *new boyfriend* will think when they show up.

I already hate the guy, and I don't even know him.

My tears dry, and I sit back up against the headboard setting the picture down on the bedside table of my hotel room. I take it everywhere with me. I've found solace in it. In all the pictures I have of us together. But not today. Today, nothing can soothe my broken heart.

Vivien has *moved on*.

She's got a new Irish boyfriend.

She's forgotten all about me.

It hasn't even been four months since we broke up! Only three months since I last saw her, and she's already seeking comfort in some other guy's arms.

How could she do this?

I never see any other women. Not even when they proposition me, and it happens regularly. They don't even register, because Vivien is all I see, all I think about, dream about, and the only woman I want.

I am ruined.

I haven't stopped crying since I read the confirmation in the report. I know there are photos. The Irish security team is keeping some pictures on file. I'm tempted to look. To see who my competition is. But the stronger part of me does not want to know. The images my mind is conjuring are bad enough. I feel sick every time I think of her with another man. I can't look at any photos of them together or find out anything about that prick because I'm liable to jump on a plane and drag her back home.

I might still do it.

Go all caveman and lock her up in my apartment. I'll have the deeds and keys to the Pacific Palisades penthouse when we finish filming the final reshoots for *Sweet Retribution* in a few weeks. I have some time at home before I begin my next project. Then I'll be spending the summer in Toronto filming a new superhero movie.

Noise filters in from outside, and I climb off the bed and walk to the window. I look down at the pool where the cast members who traveled to Mexico are letting loose. Filming halted last week so we could attend a mini South American promo tour-slash-convention dedicated solely to the series. It was deemed a big enough deal to schedule the shoot around it.

Twenty-five of us have been staying at this boutique hotel for the last six days, and we return to Boston tomorrow evening. The studio rented the entire place so we have privacy, and I've been chilling out and avoiding my bitchy costar. The back of the five-star hotel, beyond the pool area, opens out onto a private stretch of beach, and I have gone surfing every morning.

Down below, the tequila is flowing, tacos are in plentiful supply, and loud music is playing while my costars frolic in the pool and the ocean or sunbathe on loungers while they get high and drunk. I hadn't planned on joining them despite Rudy's protests. I have kept to myself outside of official commitments, preferring to stay in my room than socialize. I haven't taken any drugs in months, and I don't want to be tempted.

Well, fuck that shit.

If ever there's a day for numbing my reality, it's today.

It's either get trashed or contemplate ending it all.

I splash water on my face and put eye drops in, but I doubt it'll help much. My eyes are bloodshot and red, and it's obvious I've been crying. It's nothing my shades won't conceal though. The last thing I want is for anyone to feel sorry for me. I can't stand the pitying looks I get from certain people these days.

I get changed into the board shorts Viv bought me in Greece with an ache in my throat.

I can't believe this has happened.

How can she bear to touch someone else? The thought of it alone brings me out in hives. I don't even look at other women, and she's already dating again?

How could she do this?

How could she do this to us?

I'm sick to my stomach as I make my way outside. I dismiss my bodyguards for the day, telling them to take off and let loose. No one is getting to me here, and I'd rather they not bear witness to my self-destruction. The throbbing ache in my heart is nothing new. It's been a constant companion since Christmas Day, but this is on a whole other level. I am destroyed. Saying I'm heartbroken doesn't come close to conveying how I feel.

"And the main man is in the house!!" Jacob yells when I

emerge poolside. Whoops and hollers surround me as someone presses a beer into my hand. "Dude, please tell me you've finally come to your senses?" Jacob slings his arm around my shoulders like there hasn't been complete animosity between us since I punched him for the part he played at the club. His eyes are rolling back in his head, and he's swaying on his feet, and that's my answer.

Right now, I don't give a shit about his insult or the fact I hate the guy. It's time I used him to serve my own needs. "You got any shit on you?" I ask.

"Hell yeah." He pulls a baggie out of the pocket of his shorts and hands me three pills. "Knock yourself out, man." He slaps me on the back, and it's no casual move, so I feel zero guilt when I push him hard and he lands in the pool.

"Reeve!" Rudy races toward me from the end of the pool, shaking his head as he watches me pop a pill and wash it down with beer. When he reaches me, he grabs my arm and pulls me over to the side where dense trees and thick shrubbery border the hotel from the road outside. "What the fuck are you doing?" He glares at me. "Don't throw away months of sobriety. You'll regret it."

"I really don't think I will," I say, knocking back more beer. "What's the point in staying clean? It's not like I've got anything or anyone to go home to."

His shoulders stiffen. "What's happened?"

"I've lost her." My voice cracks, and I feel like the biggest pussy. I clear my throat and pull myself together. The quicker I get out of my face, the better. "She's dating someone in Ireland."

"Ah, fuck." Rudy looks genuinely upset for me. He's the only person on set I trust now that Cora has finished her scenes and gone home.

"Try not to worry. It's not like he can compete with the

history you guys have, and remember her time there has an end date. You need to keep the faith. Vivien will come back to you." He drills me with a look. "Don't undo all your hard work, Reeve. Remember you're doing it for her as much as yourself."

"I can't do it today. I need to forget. I can't handle it without having a full-blown meltdown, and I refuse to do that in front of that bitch or any of her bitch boys."

I discovered Saffron has been fucking Wen and using him to mess with me too. And I spoke with Jeremy, the assistant director of *Cruel Intentions*. He's convinced Saffron distracted him with sex while Wen messed with the camera and the backup footage the night before my prom. I didn't realize Jeremy had dumped her after because he didn't make it public, and it was in her best interests to have me think she was still with him. Jeremy couldn't prove they sabotaged those scenes, which was why he lost his job and she got away scot-free.

At least until now. I'm determined to nail her scheming ass to the wall, and I've already got a PI on the case.

"Steer clear of her," Rudy says, "and stick to my side."

We claim a couple of empty loungers on the other side of the pool beside Ed, Darren, and Conrad. We pass a joint back and forth while drinking shots of tequila and local beer. Hours pass, and I pop the other pills while I continue to drink, and it doesn't take long to accomplish my mission. I'm blissfully happy in my own little bubble and no longer aware of my surroundings or the thoughts that led me to break my sobriety. I dance, sing, jump in the pool, and spend time on the beach talking to everyone. I'm buzzing and enjoying the vibe without a care in the world.

I laugh when someone pushes me, and I land on something cushioned. A weight settles on my thighs, and light caresses brush over the heart-shaped tattoo of Viv's name on my chest.

Heat floods my body, and it's like I've been injected with liquid electricity. My veins hum, and blood rushes to my cock.

Moans filter into the air, and my skin is on fire, my lips are tingling, and my erection is straining against my flimsy board shorts.

I'm swaying as I project forward and laughing as I rub my aching dick. Fuck, I'm horny. Everything spins as I walk. Voices are muted in the distance as I'm pulled away.

The rest is a blur until I wake in a room that most definitely isn't mine.

"Morning, lover," an unfortunately familiar female says when I stir in the bed.

My lungs stop functioning the second I hear her grating tone.

No! Please fucking God, no!

"How about a quickie before we have to leave for the airport?" Saffron says, draping her bare leg over mine and pressing into my side.

Gulping back bile, I turn my head on the pillow to face her. All the color leaches from my skin as I rake my gaze over her bright eyes, tangled hair, swollen lips, and the obvious smug expression on her face. My eyes narrow on the bite marks and raised skin on her neck and collarbone.

Lying flat on her back, she throws the cover aside exposing her naked body. "Go on, lover, admire your handiwork," she purrs before spreading her legs and running her tongue over her lips. Similar marks cover her tits, her stomach, and the inside of her thighs.

"No." I shake my head. I've never been that rough with Vivien in bed, and that's not my signature. This didn't happen. It wasn't me. This is another setup. I whip my head around the room looking for other male bodies. Someone else clearly did this, and I'm being framed because there's no fucking way I would ever screw this poisonous bitch. I don't care that I was completely wasted. I would still know better than this.

Right?

Right?

"I see the wheels churning, movie star, and I can guess what's going through that pretty little innocent mind of yours." She props up on one elbow, putting those monstrous things on her chest all up in my face as she runs her fingers over my brow.

"Don't fucking touch me." Shoving her hand away, I scoot to the edge of the bed to put physical distance between us.

She barks out a laugh. "That's not what you were saying last night, and it *was* you. You can try to convince yourself all you like, but you were the only man in my bed all night." Her lips kick up as her eyes glimmer maliciously. "I didn't think you had it in you, but you were like a fucking machine. A sexual beast." She reaches for my sore cock, and I stumble out of bed, falling on my butt. She laughs again. "We fucked all night long, movie star, and I'm reluctantly impressed. You've got stamina for sure though some of your technique could use work. But it didn't matter. It wasn't about pleasure."

I scramble to my feet, fighting terror and nausea as she crawls over the bed, coming toward me. "It was about *procreation*."

My eyes expand as her words launch a missile at my heart.

"That's right, lover," she purrs as I back up toward the bathroom, panicking and close to puking. "I'm ovulating, and you fucked me six times, coming inside me every single time, and I'm not on birth control." She cups her bare pussy. "What are the chances you knocked me up last night, movie star? I think they're pretty good."

I don't listen to any more of her hateful words, darting into the bathroom and bending over the toilet right before I start heaving. Saff follows me, gloating and laughing as I puke my guts up. "What did you give me?" I hiss in between vomiting. "I know you gave Jacob those pills for me."

But I was the fucking idiot who asked for them. She set me up, and I fell for it again.

"Speed." She flashes me a grin. "I knew it'd make you horny and give you the energy to go all night. I'm glad you didn't disappoint and grateful you made it so easy."

I slump against the side of the bath, nauseated and in complete shock, as I watch her snort a line of blow. "Don't worry, lover," she says. "You'll come around to the idea of us. I guarantee I'll be a much better wife than your pathetic ex."

"Vivien is worth a million of you, and you're fucking delusional if you think there'll ever be an *us*. I hate you. I loathe the very sight of you. You make me sick." I stagger to my feet, hating I'm naked. Staring at my reflection in the full-length mirror on the back of the door, I'm aghast at the scratch marks and bite marks covering my body. But it's the red rash on my cock that sends me reeling to the floor.

It's true.

I fucked her.

Oh my God.

I have just ruined any chance I had of ever winning Vivien back.

I dry retch into the toilet as Saffron cackles.

"Believe me now, lover?"

"I hate you, and I'm going to end you." I wipe the back of my mouth as I rise to my feet, towering over her.

"Now, now, movie star. Is that any way to speak to your baby mama?"

Chapter Forty-Six

I fall apart in the weeks following Mexico, and I'm not proud of it. But I can't stop my downward spiral. Especially after the photos appear in the media—on Vivien's birthday. Saffron timed the release to ruin another special day for my girl, and I flew into a violent rage. The bitch manipulated me into fucking her, gave me a rash on my dick because she had thrush, and is regularly taunting me about possibly being pregnant, and then she really had to stick the knife in by going to the press and ensuring my girl knew all about it. Pent-up emotion took control of my body, and I went for her. Nick had to call security when I lunged at the bitch, shouting obscenities and threats to kill her. I was promptly escorted off the set and told to go back to the hotel and calm down.

I'm popping more pills than ever in a desperate attempt to block reality out. I stopped receiving the security reports from Ireland after Vivien returned my birthday gifts and sent me a text that drilled her point home. Devin has promised to call if anything urgent crops up. He understands why I don't want the reports anymore. After the photo she sent to my phone, I can't stomach seeing more pictures of her with *him*.

Although I could only see the side of his face in the pic, because he was pressed into Viv's neck, he looks like a punk ass with his bleached hair, tattoos, and piercings. It's like Viv deliberately went out and found someone who looks nothing like me.

Every time I close my eyes, I see her in *his* arms, and I feel sick. I must enjoy torturing myself because it took me two days to delete the photo. I lost it at first and trashed the room in a vicious rage. Bobby and Leon had to restrain me and subsequently pay the hotel management for damages and compensation to stop them from booting me out.

After I calmed down, I probably looked at it a hundred times in those forty-eight hours. I'm clearly a masochist. It even haunts me in my dreams. It was Alex who convinced me to permanently delete it.

Audrey called me the day the photos hit the airwaves, wanting to know if I was with Saffron now. I was a complete mess. I'd left so many messages and texts for Vivien, and she wouldn't pick up, so I drowned my sorrows in a bottle of JD and some blow. I can't quite remember what I said to Audrey, but it was clearly enough for her to be concerned because she called Alex, and he showed up at the hotel the next day.

My buddy was shocked at the state he found me in, but I managed to downplay it as a reaction to the photo Viv sent. I'm not sure he believed me.

It's an all-out war on set with Saffron. She's acting like we're a couple, talking about moving in with me to other cast members, sneaking into my dressing room when my bodyguards are occupied, buying me gifts, offering me drugs, and trying to hang off me any chance she gets. I push her away, shout at her, and tell everyone I hate her and wouldn't touch her if she was the last woman on earth. I remind her repeatedly how much I hate her, but it's all some game to her.

I think she's legit batshit crazy.

Especially after she says she took a pregnancy test but refuses to tell me the results. I don't know what to think, whether she's pregnant or not, and it's driving me insane. I veer between thinking she made all this shit up to torment me, or she plans to trap me with a baby and she's enjoying dragging this out. Rudy thinks it's the latter. He's pressing me to call her bluff. To get Carson to send her a letter demanding a pregnancy test and subsequent paternity test if it turns out she's not lying. Because, let's be honest, even if she *is* pregnant, there is no guarantee it's mine. She fucks multiple guys, and she's high a lot, so it could be anyone's.

I don't reach out to my attorney or send her any letters. I don't trust her not to publish it, and I'm in enough hot water with Vivien as it is. Also, I suspect Saffron would enjoy receiving it, knowing she's torturing me by keeping me in suspense.

Thank fuck for Bobby and Leon. They are keeping her as far away from me as possible so I don't end up arrested for murder. My bodyguards feel partly responsible for Mexico, but it's not their fault. I told them to leave. What I did is on me. Maybe if I hadn't dismissed them, they might have been able to pull me away from Saffron, but I doubt it. I was too far gone to make any wise decisions. I most likely would have told them to butt out and fuck off.

"I'm glad you came," Alex says, handing me a beer as we sit outside in the garden of his friend's house, on deck chairs, in front of the bonfire dancing within a gray stone pit. Light spills out from the house behind us through open double doors, providing ample illumination in the dark. College parties aren't my typical scene, but I'm trying to put as much distance between me and that bitch, so hanging out with my buddy on my last Saturday night in Boston seemed like a good idea.

"Me too." I guzzle my beer as my knee bounces on the uneven terrain underfoot.

"I'm worried about you."

"Don't be. I'm fine." It's a knee-jerk reaction. We both know it's a lie.

"You're not, but you will be."

"I've lost her, Alex." I turn to eyeball my friend. "I've lost Vivien and my will to live." I knock back the rest of my beer and toss the empty on the ground at my feet.

"You'll get her back, and I'll win Audrey back, and then it will be like old times." He threads a hand through his hair before lifting his beer. "Want another?" he asks with some reluctance.

I nod, and he reaches back to grab a cold beer from the bucket.

"You've changed your tune," I supply before popping the cap and raising the bottle to my lips. In Australia, Alex was adamant he was never getting back with Audrey, and he made the most of his time while on vacation, hooking up with a different girl every night while I went home to an empty bed.

"I was full of shit, man." He leans back in his chair. "Trying to deny it to myself. I love Rey. I never stopped. None of the other girls I've been with have meant anything, and I wasn't happy."

"Hey, Alex."

We both look up, finding a blonde and a brunette looming over us, ogling us like we're their next meal.

"Who's your friend?" Blondie asks as the brunette bats her eyelashes at me.

Alex snorts out a laugh. "Yeah right, Jackie. You know who he is, and he's not interested."

"I find that hard to believe," the brunette says, landing on my lap without invitation. "All the gossip sites say you're done with Saffron for good now." She circles her arms around my neck, pushes her tits into my face, and grinds on my lap. "I'll let you fuck me in the ass, Reeve. You can do whatever you want to me."

I shove her off my lap, and she cries out as she lands unceremoniously on the bumpy, grassy floor. "One. I'm not interested now or ever. Two. Saffron and I were never together. I hate that fucking bitch with the intensity of a thousand suns. Three. Don't ever grope a guy without an invitation because we don't all want it. If a guy did what you just did, you'd call the cops on his sleazy ass. And four, have some goddamned self-respect."

"There's no need to be such a prick," the blonde, Jackie, says, helping her friend to her feet.

"There is every need. Just fuck off and leave us alone."

"Asshole." The brunette shoves her middle finger up at me before storming off, but the blonde is still standing here.

"Jackie, you heard Reeve. We're having a private conversation."

She crawls into Alex's lap. "I can wait until you're done." She plays with the hair at the back of his neck. "I thought we could hook up for old time's sake."

"I'm not interested." Alex is much more polite than me, lifting her up by the hips and setting her feet on the ground. "I'm back with my ex and strictly a one-woman man from now on."

"You can't be serious?"

"I'm deadly serious. Don't bother wasting your time because I'm off the market."

I'm guessing he's lying to get the women off his back. He's garnered more than his fair share of interest from the opposite sex tonight. Same as me. But none of them hold any appeal. I'm a one-woman man too, and I'm determined to get Vivien back. I have no clue how, but I'm not giving up.

We drink a few more beers, and I go to the bathroom to snort a few lines. Later, when we're hanging out with Alex's football teammates, I pop a pill when Alex is distracted, and by the end of the night I barely know my own name.

"We need to talk," Alex says, hovering above me when I finally blink my eyes open. My back aches as I pull myself upright on the couch, stifling a yawn as I glance around the large open-plan space.

"This your place?" I ask because I haven't been to the apartment he shares with one of his football buddies before.

He nods before handing me a mug of coffee and sinking onto the couch beside me.

My plan had been to go back to the hotel, not crash on Alex's couch. "How'd I end up here?" I cup my hands around the mug, inhaling the bitter aroma.

"You were completely trashed, and I didn't want to let you return to a hotel room alone." He points at the recliner chair across from the couch. "I spent most of the night there."

"You didn't need to do that." I sip the coffee, ignoring how my stomach churns unsteadily.

"What is going on with you? I want the truth, Reeve." His jaw pulls tight as he eyeballs me. I return his stare while contemplating if I'm brave enough to come clean. Alex has no idea how low I've sunk. "I'm still your best friend, and I want to help. I won't judge. Just tell me." His gaze latches on to mine. "Please."

I gulp over the lump in my throat, but the decision to fess up is an easy one. "I'm in a bad way," I truthfully admit before I launch into my story, holding nothing back as I explain how I got hooked on drugs, the attempts I've made to stay clean, and how what happened in Mexico a month ago has completely derailed me. My buddy listens without interrupting as I purge my soul, sobbing and shaking as I reveal the hideous truth.

"Some days, I don't want to live, and I'm not tossing that out flippantly. I mean it." I quietly admit my darkest secret, and pain flares in his eyes. "I miss her, Alex. I miss her so fucking much. It's like I'm lacking all the vital parts of me, and I feel empty inside. I don't know how to navigate life without her. She's in my blood. Every part of my life has always been inter-twined with Viv's, and I'm so lost without her. This isn't living. It's barely surviving. I don't want to live if she's not in my life, so numbing the pain with drugs and booze is the only way I can cope. It's either that or end it all."

"Fuck, Reeve." Alex pulls me into a hug, and I welcome his embrace. "I had no idea you felt like that. Why didn't you come to me? Or seek help from a professional because I really think you need that."

"I've been in denial. Facing up to it means having to deal with it, and I couldn't stomach it. We have hardly seen one another, and I didn't want to burden you with my shit."

"That's what friends are for Reeve." He hugs me tight before letting me go. "You're not alone. You've got me, and you've got Audrey. We're going to help you through this, I promise. Rey's really worried about you since your call, and she plans to talk to you in June when you're home for a week."

I was planning on going to Ireland that week, but I obviously blabbed that idea to Audrey, and she must've told Viv because Viv's message made it very clear I wasn't to show up. That I would not be welcome.

I promised myself I'd give her space, so even though it kills me thinking of her over there with another guy—knowing the longer she dates him the more likely she is to fall in love with *him* and fall out of love with *me*—I'm respecting her wishes. I will stay away and pray like hell that she comes back to me in August.

"I'm pulling out of the superhero movie," I say, startling myself. It's been at the back of my mind, another thing I couldn't confront. Unburdening myself to Alex has freed something inside me. "I need to go to rehab, and it's more important than my career. I need to get clean before I can tackle those bitches who set out to destroy me and Viv. I'm going to get my head on straight, take them down, and then I'm going to win my girl back and set everything to rights." Steely determination flows through my veins as a tentative plan starts writing itself in my mind.

Lauren said I needed to take care of myself before reuniting with her daughter, and that's exactly what I'm going to do.

I don't care about that Irish prick. Even if she falls for him, he can't hold a candle to what we share. I know she still loves me. I know she always will. Because that is who we are to one another.

I'm going to pull myself together and prove to Vivien I'm the same man she loves and that the future we always dreamed of is still ours for the taking.

Chapter Forty-Seven

My newfound resolve is tested just five days later when we wrap up the last of the reshoots for *Sweet Retribution*. It's bittersweet to be at the end, and it seems like a long time coming. Although the studio is talking about making more movies in the franchise, I'm done.

"You're making a huge mistake, Reeve," Bianca says, failing to hide her irritation.

"I'm not." This is where my involvement with the Rydeville Elite series ends. It doesn't hold good memories for me even if I have won a lot of accolades and support for my performances. It has set me on the path to the career I always dreamed of, and I will forever be grateful to the franchise and the studio for that. But everything else is tarnished, and I need to leave it behind. Vivien is my priority, and signing up for more of these movies would be the final nail in the coffin of our relationship. I won't do it. I don't care how much money they throw at me.

I remove the envelope from my bag and remind myself of everything I've put in place the past few days. I can do this. For

Viv. But mostly for me. I owe it to myself to clean up my act and start being the man I know I can be.

"We can make it a condition of your contract that Saffron has to be replaced," Bianca says, clearly clutching at straws. She reeks of desperation, and it's pathetic. "You won't have to deal with her anymore. You already have a studio agreement to promote *Sweet Retribution* separately, and you don't have to go near her on the red carpet. You won't be the leading actor in the later films, and it's not a huge filming commitment, but the money is fantastic. You'd be a fool to turn it down."

I slap the envelope on the table in front of her and place my hands on either side of it as I put my face all up in hers. "I'd be a fool to agree to anything you've negotiated or anything that ties me to you for any longer."

"What's this?" She eyeballs the envelope like it's a bomb.

"Official notification of termination of our agreement. You can stick your renewal where the sun doesn't shine. Saffron isn't the only one I won't be dealing with anymore."

"You can't do this after everything I've done!" She stands as I straighten up, waving her finger in my face.

"All you have done is fucked up the best things in my life."

I've lost a lot of my enjoyment for acting through this experience, and I lost the woman I love. I'm determined to reclaim both, and I'm taking active steps to fix things. I signed a new contract with Margaret Andre, and she's already proving her worth, willingly agreeing to extract me from the superhero movie after we discussed my reasons. It's not a smart career move, but she understands why I'm doing it and supports my plans. She said if the studio wants me badly enough they might wait for me. I'm not holding my breath, but it's good to know she can free me from the commitment—hopefully with minimal damage to my reputation.

Margaret flew to Boston a few days ago, and I was

brutally honest with her, explaining everything I have been through, my upcoming stint in rehab, and my need to get clean and get back on track. She was shocked when I told her some of the shit Bianca has pulled and reassured me that's not how she conducts business. I believe it because Lauren wouldn't have stuck with Margaret all these years if she wasn't the best at what she does. It feels good to have someone on my side who cares about me as a person, not just as an actor.

"I'm not letting you do this!" Bianca's shrill tone stabs me in the ears.

"You don't have a choice. Our contract has come to an end, and I'm not renewing it. I have signed with Margaret Andre, and she's managing me from now on." I fix her with a smug grin, wishing I could confront her with all the truths I've learned to date.

I am going to hang her out to dry. But I'm waiting to have that conversation. There are still a few gaps to fill in, and I want to get clean before I pull the rug out from under Bianca, Cassidy, and Saffron. D-day is fast approaching, and I can't wait to run them out of Hollywood.

"I'll ruin you," she hisses as I walk toward the door.

I glance over my shoulder, pinning her with a sharp look. "Not if I ruin you first."

I'm packing the last of my things the following morning as I prepare to bid adieu to the hotel that has been home on and off for the past two-plus years when there's a knock on my door. I open it, revealing a grim-faced Leon. Behind him, Bobby is holding a grinning Saffron back. "Can we talk inside?" Leon asks, and I nod, stepping aside to let him in while I eye the evil bitch outside. Nerves fire at me from all angles, and I don't have a good feeling about this.

"What does she want?" I ask Leon when the door is shut.

"She's saying she has something important to tell you in private, and if you don't speak with her, she'll go to the media and announce the news there."

All the blood drains from my face. There can only be one thing she's talking about. "Send her in."

Leon peers deep into my face. "Are you sure?"

I nod.

"If you're in trouble, Reeve, we—"

"I can handle her," I lie, clamping a hand on his beefy shoulder. "But thank you for always having my back."

"It's what you pay me for, sir." True, but I get a sense most bodyguards are not as committed or loyal as Bobby and Leon. Or maybe it's just how Devin Morgan trains his guys. Either way, I'm grateful for both of them.

Leon and Bobby are not happy to leave me alone with Saffron in my hotel room, but I do not want them to hear this. While it's not a requirement that they like or respect me to do their job, I like that they do, and I'd rather they didn't realize how far I've fallen.

"Why are you here?" I ask, folding my arms and glaring at her as we stand across from one another beside the closed door.

"You know why." Her eyes glimmer with self-righteousness, and I want to gouge them out with pliers.

"Spit it out, Saffron. I don't have all day."

"I'm pregnant."

My heart jackhammers against my rib cage, but I channel Simon Lancaster and fix a cold expression on my face. "I'm expected to just take your word for it?"

She removes a pregnancy test from her purse and thrusts it at me.

I blink repeatedly as I stare at the line which clearly indicates she's pregnant. But I still don't trust her. "This could be anybody's."

She rolls her eyes as she removes a paper bag from her purse. "You're nothing if not predictable, lover."

"Do not call me that," I snap as she takes a brand-new pregnancy test from the bag.

"You can't erase history, *lover*." She purrs the word, and I want to strangle her with my bare hands.

"You can pretend all you like, but we both know what happened was more like rape."

She laughs as her grip tightens on the box in her palm. "You truly are pathetic. It's not rape if you beg for it. You never once said stop or no. It was all fuck, yes, baby, just like that. Ride me ha—"

I slam my hand over her mouth to shut her up, quickly retracting it when she licks my palm.

"I loathe you," I remind her.

"Doesn't change the facts." Her grin is borderline manic. "You knocked me up, movie star, and now it's time to pay the price."

"Give me that." I yank the box from her hand, inspecting it for tampering, but it seems intact.

"I haven't messed with it." She hands me the receipt, showing she bought it from the drugstore on the corner fifteen minutes ago.

"I'm coming in with you." I don't trust her not to have brought someone else's pee.

"I'm not complaining." She waggles her brows as we move to the bathroom, making a show of removing her skirt and her panties before she pees on the stick.

"Don't try anything," I warn when she moves toward me semi-naked after finishing her business and flushing the toilet.

"I won't be responsible for my actions if you put one finger on me."

"Would you really hurt me when I'm growing your baby inside me?" Her hands land on my chest. "I don't think you would."

The words slam into me like a ten-foot pole in the gut, cranking my rage to new levels. If she is pregnant, and it's mine, this is only the start of her planned manipulations. Well, she can go fuck herself! She has manipulated me for the last time, and I am going to beat her at this game.

I'm suddenly aware her hands are roaming my chest, and she's grinding her bare crotch into my pelvis. I push her away and step back, putting distance between us. "Don't fucking touch me, and don't think that baby will save you because it won't."

Her eyes narrow viciously, and she opens her mouth to retaliate.

"Get dressed," I snarl, denying her the opportunity as I snatch the test and head back into the bedroom.

I look at it repeatedly as I silently pray. Saffron emerges from the bathroom fully dressed, wearing a gigantic smile I'm dying to wipe off her ugly face. Sensing I'm close to breaking point, she doesn't push it, sitting up on the desk and swinging her legs while I wait for fate to be revealed.

Nausea swims up my throat when the test confirms a clear positive result. She *is* pregnant. Fuck.

"Told ya!" She flings her arms around my neck. "You're going to be a daddy."

It takes effort to gently remove her arms from my body. "This could be Jacob's or whoever else you were fucking last month."

"I haven't fucked anyone but you these past two months. I wanted to eliminate the risk of it being anyone else's baby. I fully expect you won't believe it without proof, which is why I have a paternity test booked for next week." She pulls a card from her purse and hands it to me.

I can barely read the details of the appointment because I have gone into complete shock. If this truly is my baby, I am completely fucked. Vivien will never, ever, take me back if I have a baby with a woman she despises.

"Why are you doing this? What do you want?"

She giggles, and I want to knock her the fuck out. "I'd have thought it's obvious by now. *I want you*, Reeve. I want to be your wife, and I want to get married soon before I'm showing." Her eyes are out on stalks, and she's waving her hands animatedly as she talks. "Imagine how powerful we'll be?! Everyone will want a piece of us. You can command record fees. Of course, I'll have to give up acting to raise our family, but I don't mind being a trophy wife." She giggles again, and I swear that laugh will forevermore feature in my nightmares. "We're going to be Hollywood's next golden couple and really stick it to the Mills."

"Are you fucking insane?" I roar as anger bursts through my veins. "Like, are you clinically crazy? Because what part of I hate you and I fucking loathe you did you not understand?" I pin her with a menacing glare. "I cannot stand to even look at you knowing what you've done! Hell will fucking freeze over before I ever put a ring on your finger, you junkie whore!"

"I'll tell the world. I'll tell Vivien, and you'll never get her back," she hisses.

"Try it. I dare you." I step right up to her, and it takes enormous effort not to throttle her. That innocent child is the only thing stopping me. "I know you've done shit to mess up my relationship with Vivien. I have a fair idea of what it extends to. Trust me when I say you don't want to make an enemy of me any more than you already have done. Push me, and I will push back a million times harder. I have the contacts and resources to fucking end you, Saffron. I will ensure you never work in this town again, and if that child is mine, I'll take it from you. You'll have nothing, so consider your next words very carefully."

I'm trembling with rage and fear and a host of other emotions, and she looks genuinely shaken, but one can never really tell with Saffron. For someone who is wooden on screen, she sure can fake it well in real life.

"I know I've upset you with my behavior, but we could be so good together. It won't be like before. I'll be a good wife, Reeve."

Oh look, there's a flying pig.

"Not happening," I yell. "There is no scenario where I would ever marry you. Vivien is going to be my wife, and if you try to fuck that up for me, I will kill you." I clench my fists and grind my teeth, putting every ounce of hatred and venom into the look I stab her with so she's left in no doubt of her only option.

"Ten million," she says, hurriedly composing herself.

I arch a brow.

"Give me ten million dollars, and I'll have an abortion and sign an NDA."

If this child is mine, there is no way I'm letting her abort an innocent baby. As shell-shocked and devastated as I am, I already know that much. But it won't serve me to admit that now. My mind churns as I try to figure out how to handle this. "You'll sign an NDA today, and after the paternity test results are back, if this baby is mine, we will discuss terms."

"I want one million to sign the NDA, or I'm not doing it."

"No deal." She can fuck off if she thinks I'm giving her a penny now.

"Fine. I'll take my chances with the media."

She moves for the door, and I grab her arm. "Did you not hear what I just said?"

"Do your worst, movie star. I'll already have the money banked before you can stop me."

She's calling my bluff, and it's pointless. We both know the money these kinds of stories command, and it wouldn't be enough to sustain her drug habit for long. She won't go to the press. Her best leverage is me, so she'll play ball. Saffron might think she holds all the power, but I'm going to show her she holds very little.

There is no way this bitch is leaving my sight until I have secured her silence. Yanking the door open, I call my bodyguards into the room while Saffron protests and tries to get out of my hold. "Take Saffron to her room to collect her things, and then take her to the car. Use the staff elevator and avoid people."

"I'll scream."

"No, you won't." Time to add some extra fuel to the fire. I show her the text from Jeremy confirming he has proof of Saffron and Wen's sabotage. It's clear they deleted the footage and the backup on purpose to stop me from attending prom with Viv. Jeremy asked a tech friend to investigate, and he found a login trail that led back to an account owned by Wen and a laptop owned by Saffron.

I have asked Jeremy to hold off on revealing it until I'm ready to confront the three women. While he is keen to clear his reputation, he agreed because he knows I have more clout and contacts, and I will ensure none of them ever works in the business again. I also promised I'd put in a good word for him with my dad.

"One call is all it will take, and Jeremy will leak the proof," I threaten. "Your name will be mud, and you'll never work in Hollywood again. The studio will ensure you're arrested for tampering and breach of contract, and your word will no longer mean shit."

Fear flares in her eyes, and I know I've just bought her silence. If I have learned anything about her, it's that appearances matter. What people think of her matters. She loves being the center of attention, but only for the right reasons. This would ruin not only her career but also destroy her reputation. I don't expect this to hold her off for long, but it should work at least until I get her to sign an NDA. "Cooperate with me and I'll make this go away," I lie.

"You better not be lying to me, Reeve, because I swear I'll make your life miserable if you double-cross me."

"Do what I say, and that won't happen."

After she leaves, I call Carson, explaining the situation, and he hooks me up with an attorney friend of his in Boston. A few hours later, Saffron signs the NDA with her shady-as-fuck lawyer in the room.

I call my PI, and he sends some guys to shadow her in the following days. I don't trust her, and I want to ensure she doesn't blab to the press. I also told him to document everything as I might need it to build a case against her.

I have no choice but to remain in Boston while I wait for the paternity test appointment. Carson's lawyer friend puts me in touch with a reputable ob-gyn. She verifies the lab where the test is being conducted is legit and confirms she has a contact there so we can ensure the results are not falsified.

I'm attempting to wean myself off the pills, so the timing of all of this is extra shit. I'm booked into an outpatient program in L.A. for the next two months, and I've had a couple of sessions with a therapist and a medical team via Zoom to begin the detox process under their strict guidance. I had to attend a local clinic for some regular tests before starting. Alex has been calling every day to see how I'm doing, but he's still finishing exams, so he can't physically be here. I wouldn't want him to see me like this anyway. Bobby and Leon grab whatever supplies I need, and they've been really supportive since I fessed up to them about the drugs.

I am hibernating in a luxury Manhattan apartment I have rented for the short-term, battling fatigue, nausea, the shakes, nightmares, and a slew of other side effects, and it's a miracle I'm not drowning my sorrows in a bottle because I'm terrified Saffron is telling the truth, and this baby is mine. I need a clear head to beat Saffron at this new game, and that's plenty of motivation to stick to the program and get clean.

What the fuck am I going to do?

I really don't have a clue.

All I know is I need to protect the baby somehow while containing the news and ensuring Vivien never finds out, but I have precisely zero ideas on how to achieve it.

I wish I could talk to Alex or Rudy, but the fewer who know, the better. While Rudy has been a good friend on set, I don't think we'll be keeping in touch, so I can't trust him with this secret. When he asked again, I told him Saffron lied and isn't pregnant. To burden Alex with it would be asking too much. If he succeeds in getting back with Audrey, I'd have to request he conceal it from her, and that's not fair or right.

If I'm being one hundred percent honest with myself, it's mostly because I'm not sure I can deal with their likely reactions if I tell them my priority is Vivien and not my unborn child. That getting the woman I love back takes precedence over everything else in my life. Because it makes me sound too much like my father, and I've always been adamant I'm nothing like Simon.

I have a feeling that sentiment is about to be challenged in the worst way.

Chapter Forty-Eight

The baby is mine. The bitch did it. She tricked me into knocking her up, and now she's trying to blackmail me so things go her way. But I'm not playing ball and we're in a limbo state.

Carson advised I get her to sign legal paperwork to confirm she would not travel out of the US, abuse drugs or alcohol, or abort the baby until we have reached an amicable agreement. Her sleazy lawyer demanded a "goodwill payment" of one million dollars in exchange for her signature. Carson negotiated it down to 250K, and now I have two months to find something I can use to force her hand so we can do things my way. By that time, she'll be four months pregnant and will most likely be showing. I need to reach an agreement with her by then and ensure it's a term of the contract that she goes into hiding because the press can't know she is pregnant.

As part of the interim agreement, she conceded to the supervision of a medical team I have hired so I can ensure my baby is okay. I don't trust that bitch to do the right thing for my unborn child, so I'm also paying for permanent surveillance during her pregnancy. If she breaks the terms of our agreement or does anything to jeopardize my baby, I will ruin her.

I'm still in shock, and my emotions are all over the place. I'm going through the motions, trying to find a solution that doesn't completely detonate my life, and I'm focusing on that rather than thinking about the fact I'm having a baby with someone I hate and someone who isn't Vivien. It tears me up inside every time the thought lands in my mind. As does imagining Viv's reaction. I can't lose her for good. It's not something I could live with, and I need to fix this so I don't lose the love of my life forever.

I have to push those thoughts aside for now. If I let my mind go there, I'll crack up, and I need my wits about me to deal with Saffron. I can't abandon an innocent baby, and I need to prioritize him or her because Saffron has already proven this baby is only a pawn in her game to extract as much money from me as possible.

Saffron might think she has me by the balls because my actions prove I care about the child, and I don't want her to have an abortion, but she's also shown her hand.

She's desperate for cash, and she'll take whatever I offer.

She doesn't have much choice.

My PI discovered she's up to her eyes in debt. It seems her agent screwed her over on the contracts, and she got a pittance compared to me. No studios are beating her door down to offer her other parts. Her performance as Abby has been widely criticized by fans and movie critics, and I wouldn't be surprised if this is the end of her acting career.

"I need you to find those girls who assaulted Vivien," I tell my PI over the phone a couple of days after I'm back in Cali. "Now that we have evidence proving it was Cassidy who paid off the guy to wipe the street cam footage and a copy of Bianca's text to Saffron with Vivien's location, I am more convinced than ever it was Saffron who paid those girls to attack my love. Those girls are the key to everything."

"If you want more manpower on the case, I'll need a bigger retainer."

"That won't be a problem. Do what you must, but I need results fast." I have approximately ten weeks before Vivien comes home in mid-August, and I need to have this all wrapped up by then.

"How are you feeling today?" Craig—Dr. Buchman—asks after I'm settled in his office at the behavioral health center where I'm attending my outpatient rehab program.

"Better." I wipe my clammy hands down the front of my pants.

"And how are your symptoms?"

"Mostly gone. The insomnia is still there, but that was an issue before all this started."

"And what is *this?*" He poses the question with his pen poised over his notepad.

"You know." I squirm on the leather couch and rub the back of my neck.

"You need to say it, Reeve. We have already discussed this."

I wet my dry lips. It's still so hard for me to admit this. Drawing a brave breath, I force the words from my mouth. "Before my drug addiction started."

He nods. "Good. You need to accept you have an addiction if you are to have any success of permanently overcoming it."

He jots something down before lifting his head to me. "Are you ashamed?"

"Yes." I don't hesitate to reply.

"Why?"

I stare at him like he's grown two heads. He knows why. We've already had several video sessions where we have discussed it, but this is the first time we are meeting face to face. "Because it's not who I am. Because I let everyone down. Because it blinded me to the things staring me in the face. Because I lost my way and lost the woman I love. Because I couldn't fucking cope without using uppers and downers, and it was weak."

"And?" he prompts me to continue.

"And I hate the person I've become, which says a lot because I've hated a lot of things about myself for a long time before I started taking drugs."

"That is something we definitely need to address, but I want to stick with this for now. Are you ashamed you've had to seek help?" he asks, casually crossing one ankle over his knee.

I think about it for a few seconds before answering. "I thought I would be because I have always prided myself on doing things independently, but I know when I'm beat. I can't do this alone, and I need to understand how I got myself into that place so I can avoid it again. Addiction is an illness, and I wouldn't be ashamed or resist seeking help if I had a physical illness. So, no, I'm not ashamed I have sought help."

He smiles. "This is progress. That's good."

It is? It feels strange to accept his praise for something like this.

"Have you spoken to Alex and Audrey? Lauren and Jon?"

I shake my head. "I only returned home a few days ago, but I asked them to drop by my new apartment tonight. I intend to sit down and fully explain everything." I spoke to Jon by phone yesterday. They probably want nothing to do with me after everything I did to Vivien, but I was totally honest and told him I'm in an outpatient rehab program and I'm trying to get healthy and fix my mistakes. I explained I needed to talk to him and Lauren about some things and it was necessary for my recovery. Thankfully, he agreed they would speak with me. I'm not sure how I would have reacted if they'd completely washed their hands of me.

"Will your father be there?" he inquires.

I shake my head again. "My views have not changed since our last conversation about Simon. He will not support me in this. He never supports me in anything. If I told him I was attending this program, he'd call me a pussy, tell me to man up, and it's only a problem if I let it become one."

I'm glad my new penthouse was ready so I didn't have to go back to Simon's house. I don't want him witnessing any of this, and I'm going to great lengths to keep this private so the media doesn't get a hold of it. I'm willing to pick my brain apart and stretch myself out of my comfort zone on the road to recovery, but the one thing I refuse to do is involve my father.

Simon has the potential to derail everything I hope to achieve, and I won't let him mess with my head any more than he has.

We have mostly talked about my childhood during these sessions, so Craig is aware of the fractured nature of our relationship. While he isn't pushing me into anything with Simon, he said it's important I talk about it to help identify the underlying cause behind my addiction—the reasons and behaviors that drove me to turn to drugs instead of my loved ones.

"And what of the situation with Saffron? Have you given any more thought to what will happen when the baby is born?"

I exhale heavily. "She has made it clear she doesn't want

the baby. Not unless I come as part of the deal, and that will never happen."

"Will she sign her rights over to you?"

A growl slips unbidden from my lips. "For the right price, she would." I grip the arm of the couch hard.

"She provokes strong anger in you."

Yeah, no shit Sherlock. "She is trying to ruin my life! She trapped me with this baby thinking I would marry her, and now I'm screwed."

"Is it all her fault?"

I sit up straighter. "What? Why would you even ask me that?" Hasn't he been listening to everything I've told him?

"Is Saffron being pregnant *all* her fault?" he repeats.

Bile creeps up my throat. "Yes. She set out to do it on purpose."

"Did she force you to leave your hotel room that day in Mexico?"

I look everywhere but at him. I'm not complicit in this. He can't make me acknowledge something I don't believe.

"Did she force drugs down your throat?" When I don't answer again, he adds, "Did she force herself on you and make you fuck her repeatedly without protection?"

"No!" I shout, dragging my hands through my hair. "No, she didn't, all right? But that doesn't make this my fault."

"Work with me here. There is a point to this." His placid, nonjudgmental demeanor makes me want to punch him in the face, but it equally calms me. "I will ask again. Is it all her fault she is pregnant?"

"She set out to do it."

"And is that the reason she is pregnant?"

"Yes."

He says nothing, just stares at me, and I'm squirming on the seat again.

"This only works if you are honest with yourself, Reeve. You are wasting your time and mine if you can't be truthful. I am under an oath of confidentiality. Nothing you say to me leaves this room. This is a safe, judgment-free zone where you can admit your darkest secrets and fears, and I will not cast sentence on you. I am here to help, but you must help yourself too."

I swallow thickly. "I can't help going into defensive mode. It's what comes naturally to me."

"Don't be too hard on yourself. It's a protective mechanism you've had to rely on since an early age. But if you want to make real progress, we must change some of those self-destructive habits."

"I know." I truly do, but saying it is far easier than doing it.

"Is Saffron being pregnant all her fault?" he asks again in a softer tone, and I understand what he is getting at now.

Pain splinters in my chest. Admitting this feels like the ultimate betrayal of Vivien. Although I didn't set out to bed Saffron and I sure as fuck never planned on having a baby with her, I cannot deny all responsibility, and the thought guts me. It seriously slays me inside to admit this, but I want to get better. I want to be a better man. And that means I can't lie to myself any longer. "No," I whisper before clearing my throat and saying it more loudly. "No. It is not all her fault. No one forced me to join the party. I sought out Jacob because I wanted to get high. I had impaired judgment because of the decisions I made. I let myself be manipulated, but I was a willing partner. I am also partly responsible."

He sets his pen and pad down and leans forward on his elbows. "Accepting responsibility for your actions is a huge step forward, Reeve. You need to own your decisions, the bad ones as well as the good ones." He smiles at me. "I think we'll leave it there for today." He rises to his feet at the same time I do.

"Thanks, Craig."

He shakes my hand. "You're doing good, Reeve. This will be a long process, but you're on the right path. Good luck with your talk later. From what you have told me about your loved ones, I think it will be fine."

Chapter Forty-Nine

"Oh, Reeve," Lauren whispers, before covering her mouth with her hand. I have just finished telling them everything about my addiction, the things that were going on during the filming of the Rydeville Elite movies, and how I had reached rock bottom. The only truth I haven't revealed is the news about the baby. Tears fill her eyes. "I can't believe you went through all of that and didn't reach out for help!"

"How much does Vivien know?" Jon asks from his position beside Lauren on one side of my L-shaped couch. Audrey and Alex are seated side by side at the other end while I'm standing in front of the floor-to-ceiling window.

"Not much," I truthfully admit. "I didn't tell her because I didn't want her to worry."

"That was your first mistake," Audrey says, swiping at the silent tears rolling down her face.

"My first mistake was not listening to her about that bitch. My second was not being completely open and honest. If I'd told her everything, she wouldn't be in Ireland, and I wouldn't be this broken mess you see in front of you."

"You're not a broken mess, son," Jon says, and his words crack open the emotional tsunami swirling in my chest.

"You lost your way," Alex says, "but you're taking steps to redress it now. That takes strength." I notice he has his arm around the back of the couch behind Audrey, and they are sitting thigh to thigh.

"You've made a lot of mistakes, Reeve," Lauren says, climbing to her feet. "Mistakes that hurt yourself, our daughter, and us." She rubs at her chest as she walks toward me. "It helps to understand the background, and thank you for sharing it with us, but it doesn't exonerate you. You have a lot to do to make amends."

"I know, and I'm prepared to do whatever it takes. My biggest regret is hurting Vivien. I never meant for that to happen. My life feels so empty without her in it. Without all of you," I tack on the end, and it's no lie.

"We have missed you too." Lauren stops in front of me, studying my face. "And we've been worried."

"Extremely," Jon concurs.

"But you forced us to pick sides, Reeve." Lauren takes my hand and squeezes it. "It hurt so much to cut you out of our lives, but we had no choice. We will always prioritize our daughter and what we believe are her best interests."

"I understand, and I would've been angry if you hadn't supported Viv. It was the right thing to do. It proved you are the people I know you to be. I'm the one who messed up. This is all on me."

Lauren clasps my face. "We love you and are proud of you for doing the right thing now. It can't be easy."

"It's not, but losing Viv was the wake-up call I needed to

stop taking drugs, to admit I had a problem...an addiction, and to deal with things I probably should've dealt with years ago."

Lauren's head bobs slowly before she leans in and kisses me on both cheeks. "Your father has a lot to answer for, Reeve. I have told him time and time again. But you're a grown man now, and you need to acknowledge your mistakes and accept full responsibility. You have a choice now." She lowers her arms, clasping my hands in hers again. "Choose to be clean. Choose to be thoughtful. Choose to be the best version of yourself, the man we know you can be. There is so much goodness in you, Reeve. You are not your father, and the cruel things he has said and done do not define you. Rise above it. Fuck him if he doesn't see the things we see."

"Lauren."

"No, Jon." She glances over her shoulder at her husband. "We are done making excuses for that man, and honestly, I don't understand how you can still call him a friend."

"We go back a long way, and I have always believed maintaining a friendship with Simon was one of the best ways I could look out for Reeve."

"What do you mean?" I have often wondered how Jon could be friends with my father. They are polar opposites, and Jon is a million times more the man and the father Simon is.

"At first, it was because he needed our help. Losing Felicia broke him. Later, I tried to get through to him. Tried to get him help, but he refused to help himself. I stuck around for you, Reeve. I know he wasn't kind, and I tried to influence him to do the right thing or to take him out of the house if he needed to blow off steam so he didn't vent his anger on you."

"I didn't know that," I quietly admit, but it makes complete sense.

"From the time you were born, we have done our best to

protect and love you," Lauren says. "There wasn't much either of us wouldn't do for you."

"Thank you both for everything you did for me. I've been ashamed of how I repaid your trust and love. You mean the world to me. Vivien too. I hope you know that."

"We do, son." Jon rises and walks to where Lauren and I are standing.

"I don't know about you, but I'm starving," Alex says, palming his stomach. "How about I order food?"

"Sounds good," Lauren says, and I arch a brow in surprise. "We're not leaving yet," she explains, stepping aside as Jon pulls me into a bear hug.

"We'll support you every step of the way, Reeve." Jon pats me on the back before letting me go. "And I know I speak for Lauren too when I say we will attend the group therapy session with you."

"Just let us know when it is, and we're there," Lauren says.

"Us too," Audrey pipes up as Alex walks off to order takeout.

Lauren and Jon move into the kitchen to grab plates, glasses, and silverware. I'm so glad I hired an interior designer and had her fit out the entire apartment so it was ready to walk into.

Audrey pats the seat beside her on the couch. "Come sit."

I drop into the space beside her, and she immediately wraps her arms around me. "I had no idea you were going through all of that." Tears prick her eyes. "I thought you were having the time of your life and you'd forgotten all about Viv, but it wasn't like that at all."

"No, it wasn't."

She thumps me in the arm. "That's for being so stupid. You should have told her everything."

"I was a dumbass." My eyes drill into hers. "Answer me

honestly. Do you think I have a chance at winning her back? And how much competition is the Irish guy?"

"He is...very different from you. I think that's probably the appeal."

I wince and rub at my heart as pain spreads across my chest.

"Sorry." She squeezes me tight. "I don't mean to upset you. I'm just trying to explain it. She was in a bad way when she first arrived, but the scenery and space change has done her good. She didn't plan to date. It just happened, and she sounds happy. But here's the thing." She tosses long red hair over her shoulder. "He's not you. No one can replace your role in her life. I'm not betraying her confidence when I say she will always love you, Reeve. You don't just immediately stop loving someone even if they have broken your heart."

Audrey looks over her shoulder as Alex returns. "I know from personal experience you can't dig that person out of your heart no matter how much you might want to."

Alex settles on the couch behind her, circling his arms around her waist and kissing her cheek. "True love doesn't die, and Vivien and you are soul mates. You're going to get her back. I'd stake my life on it."

"I guess you two worked things out?"

"We did. My love is back in my arms where she belongs."

Audrey beams up at him as she clings to Alex's arms.

"I'm really happy for your guys." It's the truth.

"Thanks, Reeve." Audrey refocuses on me as Jon and Lauren finish setting the table out on the balcony and start filling drinks. "And thanks for telling us everything. It means a lot, and we want you to know we are here for you. Whatever support you need, just ask."

I nod over the messy ball of emotion in my throat. Craig

will be happy when I relay how tonight has gone. I couldn't have asked for more. "I appreciate it."

"As for your other question," Rey continues, "I can't tell you Vivien will definitely come back to you or even if she should. There is a lot to forgive, and the trust has been broken, but she still holds a lot of love in her heart for you, and I really don't think her new relationship will last beyond the end of the summer."

"How can you be so sure?" I ask as Lauren and Jon return with a tray of glasses, a couple of large bottles of soda, and some water.

"He's not into relationships." Audrey isn't mentioning his name, so I'm guessing Alex told her I don't want to know anything about him. Knowing nothing makes it easier to pretend like he doesn't exist.

I'm sure my therapist would have a field day with that thought.

"And while I think he genuinely likes Viv and seems to care for her, he's definitely not the long-distance type."

"Do you think there's a chance she might stay longer in Ireland?" My gaze bounces between Audrey, Lauren, and Jon as I ask the question.

"We don't believe so," Lauren says before asking everyone what they would like to drink. Jon pours and distributes sodas as we talk.

"We're already making plans for next semester, and I'm actively apartment hunting," Audrey confirms. "Viv has also signed up for an evening costume design course, so all indications are she's definitely returning to L.A."

A layer of stress lifts from my shoulders at her words.

"But anything is possible," Jon cautions, handing me a glass of soda. "You should prepare yourself for any eventuality."

"Is she happy?" I ask.

"She is." Lauren pats my hand before she settles back on the other side of the couch with her husband. "Ireland has been good for her."

"I'm glad. I want her to be happy even if it's not with me." I suck air in and out of my mouth. That was hard to admit. I hate some other guy is putting a smile back on her face, but I'm genuinely relieved to hear she is doing better. And the guy is temporary, I remind myself for the umpteenth time.

"I put her through hell, and while I want the chance to make it up to her, I won't do anything that will upset her again." Everyone sips their drinks, listening attentively as I speak. "It's been hard not hopping on a plane to go see her, but she asked for space. You told me to focus on myself before even attempting a reconciliation," I say, looking over at Lauren, "and that is what I am doing. I can't be a loving boyfriend if I don't love myself first."

"She's not your girlfriend anymore, Reeve," Lauren quietly says, compassion etched upon her face.

"Believe me, I know, and it's devastating for me, but I have hope. We have shared our entire lives together, and I love Vivien more than I can describe. I won't pressure her or make demands, but I'm hoping she'll let me make it up to her when she returns. I hope to gradually earn back her trust and her heart because she still owns mine. She is the only woman I love and the only woman I want to marry. That hasn't changed for me. It never did. It never will."

Lauren snuggles into Jon's side while a myriad of differing emotions flickers across her face.

"I am going to turn my life around, and I'm going to ensure those who deliberately hurt us will pay, and then I will dedicate the rest of my life to making Viv happy. Nothing matters more to me than her."

"We believe you mean that, son, but your actions need to

prove it this time. I won't stand by and watch her being hurt again."

"They will, Jon. I swear on my life I will never hurt Viv again. It will be my life's mission to make her happy. To give her everything her heart desires." I speak confidently because I fully believe I can rectify my mistakes and be the man Vivien deserves.

As long as I get the opportunity to prove it, and that's a big if.

"I know you're visiting her in Ireland next month, and it's probably asking a lot, but I'd like it if you didn't say anything to her about this. Vivien is happy, and it should stay that way. I plan to tell her everything when she gets home, and I really want her to hear it from me." Jon, Lauren, and Audrey have had the July trip planned for months according to Alex.

"I won't lie to my daughter, Reeve. If she asks me a direct question, I will be truthful," Lauren warns.

"I don't think she'll ask," Audrey says in a soft tone, sending me a pitying look I hate.

My heart thuds painfully, a constant reminder of everything we have lost. "She left to heal, and I don't want to make this about me. I also don't want her to be influenced at all. If she comes back to me, I want it to be for the right reasons and because she's made that decision herself."

"I respect that," Jon says. "And we would never interfere."

"As long as she doesn't ask directly, I have no issue maintaining your confidence," Lauren replies. "You have the right to explain it to her yourself, but make sure you do, Reeve. There can be no more secrets or lies."

Chapter Fifty

I am busy in the coming weeks with therapy and trying to get back to a healthy place. I go running early each morning on Santa Monica Beach, practice meditation and yoga, and I'm consulting a nutritionist and altering my diet so it's optimal. She put me on a variety of different supplements to boost my immune system, and I'm taking an herbal remedy to help me sleep at night. It is still a work in progress, but gradually things are improving, and I'm feeling much healthier and better all round. In between self-help, I focus on my plans to take Bianca and Cassidy down and deal with Saffron.

Gordon—my PI—tracked Viv's ex-college friend down, and Danny confirmed Cassidy and Bianca approached him to spy on Vivien. He was paid a lot of money to record her at the frat party that night. Enough to cover his dad's medical bills and pay for him to disappear. Gordon said the guy was hugely remorseful, but he's lucky I wasn't there because I would have gone to town on the bastard.

It was the last piece of evidence we needed to hang Cassidy

and Bianca out to dry, and we didn't hesitate to organize a meeting with Ken and the other studio execs to share our findings. Cassidy was fired on the spot, and she'll never work in the industry again.

I spent a huge amount of time this summer organizing meetings with several of Bianca's other clients, and it became obvious straightaway that her dirty tactics were not limited to me. She has routinely abused her position and invaded her clients' privacy. Five other actors sided with me, and we filed a joint class action lawsuit.

When news of the lawsuit hit the media, she lost the rest of her clients, and her business and reputation are in the toilet. Confronting her was most satisfying, especially seeing the sheer look of terror on her face when she was served. In a last-minute effort to save herself, she tried shoving most of the blame on Cassidy and Saffron. When I asked her why they did it, she said Cassidy had plans for setting up her own PR company and Bianca was going to sign her clients up. Saffron was going to sign with Bianca when her current agent contract expired, and Bianca planned for Saffron and I to be Hollywood's new golden couple.

All of it was self-serving, and none of them gave two shits about what I wanted or how badly they hurt my girlfriend. It was all about using us to further their own agenda.

All of this has helped to distract me from thoughts of what might be happening in Ireland. Any time I think about Vivien over there with some other guy, I feel ill. The thoughts of that punk ass touching her, kissing her, *fucking* her is almost enough to send me hurling down that dark hole again. But I stop myself from regressing by remembering his time with her is limited, and she'll be coming back to me soon.

He can't replace me in her affections, so he can enjoy his time with her now.

When she returns to L.A., she will be mine forever. I won't stop until I win back her heart and reset our future.

My cell rings, breaking me out of my head, and I stare anxiously at the incoming call before I pluck up the nerve to answer it. A lot rides on this, and I'm praying it's the news I'm waiting for.

"We're back," Gordon says. "How quickly can you come downtown to meet us?"

"Give me an hour."

Nerves fire at me the entire drive to my PI's office as I contemplate what I'm about to hear and whether it will give me the leverage I need to handle Saffron once and for all. I'm seething over my call yesterday with the ob-gyn I hired to take care of her during pregnancy. That bitch is drinking alcohol and taking drugs while carrying my child, and time is of the essence.

I need leverage to force her into rehab overseas before she causes permanent damage to my kid. I found the perfect place in Switzerland that has a maternity wing where her and the baby can be monitored and where she can give birth. We had a blazing argument over the phone last night, which ended with me hanging up after she point-blank refused to go overseas for the remainder of her pregnancy and the birth.

It's going to take more than money to keep her in line, and I'm hoping Devin and Gordon have news for me.

"Reeve, how are you?" Devin asks when I enter the room, moving forward to shake my hand.

"I'm doing good. Anxious to finish this now," I tell the owner of Morgan Security. This is the last loose thread, and it's a big one.

"Have a seat, Reeve," Gordon says, also shaking my hand before he ushers me toward the table.

"How did it go?"

Devin and Gordon exchange grim smiles. "We got what we needed," Gordon says, and I wait with bated breath for the intel.

"We spoke with two of the girls who were part of the assault on Vivien," Devin supplies. "They wouldn't tell us anything until we threatened to call the cops and go to the media unless they spoke with us. That loosened their tongues pretty quick, and they confirmed Saffron set it all up."

"One of them was real mouthy," Gordon says, "but she was a smart bitch. She recorded Saffron without her knowledge, and we have a copy of the video."

"What's on it?" I ask, not sure I have the stomach to watch it.

"It shows Saffron asking them to attack Viv and her handing over a quantity of drugs," he replies.

That fucking bitch. Bianca had been adamant Saffron was behind the attack and Cassidy and her only helped by providing Viv's location and covering her tracks, but I wasn't entirely sure until now. As much as I'd been hoping for this news, I'm still shell-shocked, upset, angry, and conflicted.

"Supplying to minors is a felony under California law," Devin says. "It's enough to get her put away for up to five years before we even consider the charge for organizing the assault on Viv. This evidence means she is going to prison."

I slowly nod as my mind processes this new information. Images of Viv lying in that hospital bed return to the forefront of my mind. Remembering how broken and battered she was makes me want to throw the book at Saffron. I wish I could do it. I want that bitch to spend time in jail for the physical pain and emotional torment she's inflicted on my love, but it's not an option. It makes me sick to have to let this pass, but if I hand this evidence to the cops, everything will come out, including the pregnancy, and I will lose Vivien forever. I just can't do it.

"I have contacts at LAPD. Just say the word, and we'll get things moving." Devin used to be a cop before he left to set up his own security firm years ago.

"I need to think about it." I'm cringing as I look between both men. I can only imagine what they must be thinking of me.

"She shouldn't get away with this." Devin stares pointedly at me. "I know you need something to negotiate with, but if you don't report this, there is no justice for Vivien."

"You think I don't know that?" I grind my teeth and sigh. "It's all that's been keeping me up at night lately."

"Is there really no other way?" Gordon asks.

Both men are aware of Saffron's pregnancy. I had no choice but to tell them. Gordon has a team watching her movements, so it's not like I could hide the pregnancy indefinitely. When Devin volunteered to travel with my PI to Utah to interview the girls, I decided to fess up to him too. Both men have signed NDAs, and they are reputable and reliable. I'm not the slightest bit concerned they will leak the intel.

After Gordon found those little cunts, I wanted to tag along on the interview trip. I wanted to give them a piece of my mind. To show them what they did to an innocent woman and have them look me in the eye and tell me they weren't sorry. I wanted them to see the disgust in my eyes and to feel shame. But it was deemed too risky for me to be there, for a variety of reasons, so Devin went in my place.

Saffron filmed a miniseries for Netflix in Utah last year, and the schoolgirls were all big fans. Apparently, they became friendly, and she clearly kept in touch with them if she could call them up and ask them to do this for her. She organized getting them in and out of L.A. undetected. She really thought of everything except one of the little bitches was smarter than Saff and recorded her.

There is a certain poetic justice in Saff being taken down like this.

"I have nothing else I can use to make Saffron toe the line. I hate I have to sacrifice justice for Vivien, but if I report Saffron, I will lose the love of my life and my baby will be born in prison. If I use this as leverage, I'm protecting my unborn child and protecting my future with Viv. I don't see how I have any other choice."

"Are you sure you want to do this?" Craig asks me later that day after I have told him about my meeting this morning with Devin and Gordon.

"I have to. I am all out of options."

"But are you really?" He quirks a brow while looking casually relaxed.

"Yes. I have to get Saffron out of the US and ensure she's cared for during the pregnancy. I want my baby safe. And I need to fight for Vivien when she returns home in two weeks. I need something to threaten Saffron with, to force her into signing that contract tomorrow, and this is it."

"What about telling Vivien the truth? Why is that not an option?"

My eyes almost pop out of my head. "Of course, I can't tell her! Vivien despises Saffron! I have never seen Viv hate anyone so much. She'll be heartbroken if she discovers I knocked that bitch up, and she will never forgive me."

"I'm sure she would be at first, but she could come around. You said it yourself, the child is innocent in all of this, and he or she will carry your DNA. The baby is not just Saffron's; it's yours too."

"I can't ask Viv to take on another woman's child. Especially when that woman took pleasure in inflicting pain on Vivien. How could she ever look at the child and not see his mother?"

"You'd be surprised, and you won't know unless you give Vivien that chance. She loves you. Isn't it possible she could learn to love your child?"

It's not as if I haven't thought about this. Of course, I have. Despite how much I have tried to stop thinking about the baby, I can't. I wish I could talk to Alex about it because he knows Vivien and would be best qualified to contemplate the answer to that question with me. But he's back with Audrey now. Confiding in him is out of the question. This decision is all on me, and it's painful in the extreme.

"I don't see how. Everything is still so raw, and I know my girl. Viv has a big heart, and she loves kids, but this is too much to ask of anyone. She would not be able to forgive me. The baby will be a constant reminder of my betrayal, and I can't ask that of her. Nor can I take the risk. If I ask her and she says no, then I'll have lost her. And I—" I can't verbalize these thoughts. I'm aware of how brutally selfish they sound. I ball my hands into fists and stare out the window.

"No judgment, Reeve," Craig reminds me.

I wet my dry lips before swinging my gaze to his. "If I tell Viv and I subsequently lose her, I'm afraid I'll turn into my father. That I'll direct my resentment and pain at my child, and I refuse to do that to an innocent."

"Do you really think you could do that?"

"I'd like to say no, but his DNA flows in my veins. My father has only ever loved my mother, and he never got over losing her. I hate to admit I'm anything like Simon, but we have that in common. If I lose Viv, I will never get over it. I won't ever marry or commit to any other woman. She is all I want, and if I can't have her, I won't be pleasant to be around. I'm the best version of myself with my love. Without her, I'll be my worst self. I'll succumb to my addiction, and my child will suffer. I couldn't tolerate treating any innocent so cruelly, and I refuse to inflict the childhood I had on him or her. The best way I can protect that baby is to ensure he or she grows up in a loving environment."

"In an ideal world, where there are no obstacles, what does that look like to you?"

A ghost of a smile curves the corners of my mouth. "Viv and I married, raising this baby along with our other kids. Living in our dream house. A house full of laughter and love."

"It sounds wonderful," Craig says before jotting notes on his pad.

"It does, but it's also out of reach right now. I can't deal in what-ifs. Saffron does not want this baby. She doesn't care what happens to it, but I do. I am all this child has right now, and I'm making the best decisions for me and for him or her. I couldn't raise it if I lost Viv. I would take it out on the child especially if there is a resemblance to that bitch. Having to look at my child and see *her* face in him or her knowing it cost me the love of my life? I would resent my own kid. I can't do that to either one of us. Letting my baby go is the right thing even if it hurts."

"It sounds like you have definitely decided on adoption."

"I have. It's the only option."

"I'm concerned you will be carrying so much extra guilt. How will you handle knowing your child is out there being raised by someone else and you'll have to keep this a secret from Vivien forever? How will you live with the knowledge you tracked down the girls who assaulted her, but they will never be punished for their crime and neither will Saffron?"

"I don't know." Air expels from my mouth. "I don't know how I'll handle the guilt, but I've got to try because the alternative is losing Vivien, and I would never survive that."

Chapter Fifty-One

"Are you okay?" Alex asks as we hang out at his place a week before Vivien comes home. "You seem troubled."

I bark out a laugh. That's the fucking understatement of the century. I got Saffron to sign the legal agreement. It didn't take any persuasion after I showed her the video. She got five million, and in exchange, she signed away her parental rights, agreed to stay away from me and Viv, and agreed to attend rehab in Switzerland and remain under the care of an experienced medical team who will assist her with the pregnancy and labor. She agreed not to return to US soil until after the baby has been born and all signs of the pregnancy are no longer evident.

I should be relieved I solved the problem, but I'm not.

I'm giving up my own flesh and blood because I selfishly can't let Vivien go. I feel like the worst human on the planet. Yet it doesn't change my mind. Carson is discreetly looking for a couple to adopt the child, and I gave him strict instructions that I want him or her to go to a loving home.

It doesn't erase the guilt or hurt though. I wish I could raise this child. I wish more than anything it was mine and Viv's, and then there would be no dilemma.

I have been thinking about my own upbringing a lot. I wonder, would my life have been better if Simon had given me up for adoption? If I had gone to a loving home, would I be the person I am today or a better version of myself? Then I remind myself if that had happened I would never have grown up next to Vivien, never have known Jon and Lauren, or fallen in love with the woman of my dreams. So, I guess things worked out the way they were meant to, and I must have faith it'll work out that way for my child.

"Reeve." Alex's concerned tone drags me from my inner monologue.

"I'm just anxious about Viv coming home and whether I'll be able to get her back." It's no lie. Audrey didn't say much after her trip to Ireland except that it's more serious with the Irish guy than she thought, but it seems one-sided because he didn't even make an effort to meet with Lauren and Jon while they were visiting. If she has fallen in love with him, is there any chance for me? The closer it gets to her return, the less confident I feel and the more on edge I am.

"Keep the faith. I didn't think Rey would give me another chance, but she did, and we're happier than ever."

"You aren't worried about the long distance?" I ask because they're both starting their junior year in a couple of weeks on different sides of the country.

"It won't be a picnic, but I'm not worried. We're rock-solid. I'll miss her like crazy, which will be the challenge, but we'll make it work, and it's only for another couple of years."

The following morning, I receive an urgent call from Carson asking me to come to his office ASAP. He wouldn't discuss the matter over the phone, just saying I needed to get my ass there stat.

So here I am, listening to what he has to say with my mouth trailing the floor. "You can't be serious, Carson? On what planet would this ever be a good idea?"

"Lori is nothing like Saffron, Reeve, and I'm only asking that you listen to what she and Travis have to say."

"How does she even know? That bitch is not supposed to have talked to anyone!"

"It seems Saffron turned up on her sister's doorstep one night before she left for Switzerland. They hadn't spoken in years, but she was drunk, and she blurted some things. Don't worry," he says when I open my mouth to speak, "I will send a reminder of the NDA along with a warning to her attorney and a note we'll be deducting 250K from the next payment."

We split the five mil in three equal payments. One has already been paid. The second will be paid after the baby is handed over for adoption, and the third payment will be issued two years after the child's birth, provided she upholds her end of the bargain. As an additional incentive, I'll give her another million after five years have passed, provided she is still playing ball. Any minor breaches of the terms mean a financial deduction from the next payout. The NDA is in place indefinitely, and I'll sue her ass for every penny if she ever talks publicly about this. We may also be able to pursue her for the assault or drug charges at a later stage, subject to the statute of limitations. It should be enough for her to hold her tongue, at least for the first few years. After that, I may have to resort to other measures to keep her quiet as I don't trust her not to try to cause more trouble in my life.

But I'll be ready for her this time, and forewarned is forearmed.

"I also lodged those restraining orders for you and Vivien too," he adds.

"Okay, good." I prop my elbows on the table. "But how did Lori know to come to you?"

"She spoke with Saffron's lawyer. She told him she and Travis wanted to adopt the child, and he told her to come and talk to me."

"I don't think it's a good idea. I don't want Saffron anywhere near my child, and this would make it too easy."

"You said yourself Saffron has no interest in the baby, and Lori and Saffron are estranged. From what she has said, keeping her sister away from the child would be her primary concern."

"Saffron would know where the child lives. If he or she is adopted anonymously, she won't have any access. That is what I want."

Carson gets up from his desk to sit down at the meeting table across from me. "I understand your concern, Reeve, but wouldn't it be better for the child to be raised by his own flesh and blood if there is that possibility? Lori is his aunt, and she's a good person. Just meet her. She's been waiting hours to see you. At least hear her out. They both readily signed an NDA so you can speak openly."

He raises a valid point, but I'm still not sure. But the least I can do is talk to the couple. "Okay. I'll talk with them."

I try not to stare at Saffron's older sister as she enters the room with a tall, dark-haired man, but it's challenging because she looks absolutely nothing like her sibling. Where Saffron has long dark hair, Lori's golden-blonde hair is cut into a sleek bob. She has big blue eyes, and she's wearing a modest black dress that ends below the knee under a fitted red jacket. Although they are both around five feet tall, Lori is much thinner and more petite.

She offers me a tentative smile as her husband pulls a chair out for her to sit on.

"Reeve, this is Lori and her husband, Travis." Carson makes the introductions.

"It's nice to meet you," I say, shaking their hands one at a time. Lori's soft grip is firm but not aggressive. "Carson says you are Saffron's older sister?"

"Half-sister," Lori replies. "We lived with our mom, but we had different dads."

Ah, that explains it.

"I helped to take care of Saffron after our mother passed, but she's always been wild."

"Lori sacrificed a lot for her sister over the years, but Saffron always took it for granted," Travis supplies, clasping his hands together on the table.

"I tried so hard with her, but eventually I had to cut ties for my own sanity. We don't have a relationship. We hadn't even spoken for years when she just showed up on my door."

"Is that the truth, or are you saying it for my benefit?" I don't hide my skepticism.

"It's the truth, but you're welcome to check it out. We have nothing to hide."

"Why would you want to adopt this child? What's in it for you?"

"Travis and I can't have children. We tried for years, and after going for treatment, I discovered I'm infertile. We have been exploring adoption, and then Saffron showed up, and it seemed like a sign."

Leaning forward in her chair, Lori pins me with earnest

eyes. "This baby is my flesh and blood too, and I would hate to see him or her go to anyone else when he could come live with us. I would love to raise my niece or nephew. Nothing would give me greater joy. We can't wait to start a family, and we have a lot of love to give. I promise the child will not want for anything. We both have good jobs and our own home, and we can provide for him or her. They will be well cared for."

"We really want to do this," Travis reaffirms. "And think about the medical implications. If anything were to happen in the future, we have access to you and Saffron for medical history. If the baby goes to strangers, that information would not be available."

That is an additional benefit for sure. "Saffron has been abusing alcohol and drugs while pregnant," I supply. She swears she only fell off the wagon one time, but I don't believe a word out of her mouth. She's a pathological liar, and she doesn't care about the baby. "I don't know how bad it is or whether the child could be born with health issues. She's in rehab now under strict supervision, so she'll get clean, but she might have already caused harm to the baby." I asked this question of the medical team, and all they could say was everything looked okay on the scans, but that doesn't mean there could not be complications at birth.

Lori shakes her head. "I'd like to say I'm disappointed and shocked, but I'm not. Saffron is selfish in the extreme. I truly hope she hasn't caused any harm to the baby, but no matter what happens, we still want to do this." She eyeballs her husband.

"That won't change our minds or our commitment," Travis confirms.

These are good people. How did Saffron turn out so poisonous when her sister seems compassionate and kind?

"I am sure you have concerns," Lori continues. "All we are

asking is if you can give us a chance. Do the usual background checks. Get to know us. We can meet and talk, or you can come out to the house if you want to see it. Do whatever you need to do to reassure yourself, but please don't rule this out without serious consideration."

Emotion shimmers in her eyes, and I can tell she's sincere. She means it, and even though I've only been in her presence a few minutes, she is warm and open, and I think she's a good person. "I don't want Saffron around the child. What if you reconcile with her in the future? What if she tries to take him from you? I'm not going to mince words. Your sister is not a nice person. She helped to sabotage my relationship, and she tried to trap me into marriage. She has been vocal about not wanting this baby, and I want to ensure she is nowhere near that child growing up. As much as I like the idea of him or her being brought up by family, strangers hold greater appeal because Saffron won't have any access."

"This will sound harsh, but I don't want my sister anywhere near this child either."

"There is no reconciliation in the cards," Travis says. "Saffron has burned her bridges with us. She has hurt Lori far too many times. She's not welcome in our home and wouldn't be welcome around our son or daughter. You can add that into the adoption paperwork, and we'll sign it."

Lori reaches across the table to hold her husband's hand, and tears glisten in her eyes when she turns to look at me. "Additionally, we were talking before you arrived, and while it's not legal, we would be prepared to put our names on the birth certificate if you wanted an extra safeguard. She couldn't take the child from us then, and there would be no paper trail linking him or her to you."

That holds appeal, but I'm not sure we could do it or should do it.

"I need time to think about it," I say.

"Of course." She smiles as she stands. Her husband wraps his arms around her waist and holds her close. "Mr. Park has our contact details. Reach out if you have any questions or if there is anything you need to know."

Chapter Fifty-Two

My knee bounces on the floor of the black Mercedes as I stare out the window from the back seat while waiting for Viv to appear. Bobby is behind the wheel, and I sent Leon inside the airport to collect her because I can't show my face even at this early hour. LAX is a regular paparazzi hangout, and I don't want to be papped.

My heart stutters, and butterflies swoop into my stomach when I spot her coming toward the car with Leon carrying her cases. Tears prick the backs of my eyes as emotion swirls in my chest. Fuck, I have missed her pretty face. The urge to run to her and scoop her into my arms rides me hard, but I manage to restrain myself. My heart rejoices, bouncing around behind my rib cage as she advances.

It's been seven long months since I last saw her in the flesh, but it feels like an eternity. She's only wearing jeans and sneakers with a fitted shirt under a hoodie, but she has never looked more gorgeous. Her long hair tumbles around her shoulders as she approaches the car, and I swallow over the ball-sized lump in my throat and wipe my clammy hands down the front of my shorts. Butterflies skate around my chest and my stomach is doing cartwheels.

Calm down, I remind myself. She is still Viv. Still the girl I have grown up loving even if we haven't seen each other for so long.

She climbs into the back seat and freezes on the spot when she sees me.

Today is important for a bunch of reasons, but it's my best shot at winning her back, and I need to bring my A game. I have gone over what I would say hundreds of times, so I just need to keep my cool and not blow it.

Here goes nothing.

"Hey, beautiful." I turn around fully to face her and smile, hoping she can see the love radiating from my every pore. "You are a sight for sore eyes."

Relief whittles through me when she flings her arms around my neck. I band my arms around her back and hold her close, struggling to hold back tears as her familiar scent wafts around me. Everything always feels so right when Vivien is in my arms, and this is no exception.

"I'm happy to see you." She eases back, her gaze skimming over me through her ginormous shades. "You look good."

"So do you." This is better than I hoped for, and I can't suppress the excited grin that spreads over my mouth or the way my gaze automatically lowers to her lips. I want to kiss her more than I need to breathe.

"What are you doing here? Where are Mom and Dad?"

"I've spoken with your parents a lot this summer, and we're building bridges. I asked them if I could pick you up, explaining my reasons, and they agreed." I move in closer until our knees touch. "I missed you so fucking much."

I'm not sure what I said that upsets her, but her brow puckers and confusion swims in her eyes. Then she hangs her head. Pain bubbles in my chest, never far from the surface. "Viv, look at me. I need to see your eyes, baby." I lift her chin with one finger and carefully remove her sunglasses, smothering my fear when I spot her swollen eyes and tearstained skin. She's been crying, and they weren't happy tears. I swallow heavily, guessing why she's been crying, and I'm terrified she won't ever be mine again.

"Am I too late?" I whisper, reaching out to touch her face because I can't *not* touch her when we're this close. She leans into my hand, but it only brings a modicum of relief. I'm strung tight and trying not to panic. "Viv?" I peer deep into her eyes, summoning strength as I ask a difficult question. I made a promise to myself during therapy that I would always speak my mind and communicate openly, and I intend to start now. "Have I lost you for good?"

Tears pool in her eyes. "I don't have the mental or emotional capacity for this conversation right now, Reeve. I feel lost all over again." A single tear rolls down her face, and I can't hold back any longer. Wrapping my arms around her, I pull her in close, providing what little comfort I can. Warmth settles in my chest when she rests her head on it, and it's a good thing she's letting me hold her and not pushing me away. It means all isn't lost, and I cling to that hope.

I don't mind how long it will take me to win her back as long as she gives me the chance to fight for her.

So far, all indications are that she will. I put a leash around my fear, attempting to keep a cool head. "It's okay, baby." I hold her tight as I run my hand up and down her hair. "I'm here now, and I'm going to make everything better." I ask Bobby to head for my apartment as Leon pushes the button to engage the privacy screen. I didn't even have to ask. They just know what I need. I swear both guys are worth their weight in gold. If Devin ever attempts to try and remove them from my detail, we'll be having words.

"I understand you're not in the mood for talking, but can you just listen?" I ask, and she nods against my chest. "I need you to know I still love you. I've never stopped loving you. I wanted to hop on a plane to Ireland at least once a week, but I promised I'd give you space to work through things, and I wanted to keep my word."

A weird sound rips from her throat as she shucks out of my embrace. "This is all sounding far too familiar and not in a good way."

"You are right, but things are different now. I'm me again, Viv." I link our fingers, silently fist pumping the air when shivers cascade over my skin as usual with her touch. Not that I was worried I wouldn't feel the same, but it's nice to have the affirmation. Her fingers twitch, which means she felt it as well, and it bolsters my confidence. We still share the same connection. It's buzzing in the air and in our touch, and I'm going to reclaim her heart like I promised. There is no other outcome that is acceptable to me.

"What does that mean?"

I sweep some of her hair behind her ear. "You were right about everything, and I should have believed you. You have always had my back, and instead of letting you in, I shut you out. I'm disgusted with myself. I made a lot of bad decisions. I chose to believe the wrong people, and it cost me the most precious thing in the world—*you*. I'm not excusing my behavior. Not at all. I'm just trying to explain how I ended up in such a bad place. At the start, being away from you unsettled me more than I could have imagined. I was overwhelmed with everything expected of me on set and really feeling my age. The other actors were all older and more experienced in movies and life. I felt lost and young, and I was definitely out of my comfort zone. Bianca and Cassidy were pushing me to break up with you, and the stress of that, combined with the movie responsibility and the long hours, took its toll. Saffron—"

Her face contorts, her eyes narrow, and a growl slips from her lips at the mention of her archnemesis. "I know you hate her with good reason. I hate her too, but I need to tell you everything. You need to know it all, and I can't not mention her name."

"Fine," she clips out.

"She suggested I pop a few uppers. She said it was how everyone coped with long shifts on set. She said everyone was doing it. I'd seen the guys snorting coke, so I stupidly believed her." I wet my dry lips. "I hid the true extent of my drug use from you because I was embarrassed. I had always been anti-drugs, as you know. It was a slippery slope, and I was plunging headfirst down it. I know now that I should have confided everything to you, but I didn't want to see the disappointment in your eyes. I wanted you to be proud of me. I wanted Dad to be proud of me."

It is still so hard to admit this because I was such a fool, and I let stupid pride get in the way of common sense. "I should have gone to your mom and sought her advice before signing that new contract, but I was already fucked up from pills and coke and Saffron was mouthing in my ear, saying fake relationships were the norm and if you loved me you wouldn't have a problem with it."

Viv leans back, looking ready to commit murder.

"I'm doing all the things I should have done from the start," I continue. "I will explain everything I've discovered back at my place. For now, I need you to know I'm done with letting assholes manipulate me. I've cut ties with Bianca. I have a new supportive team around me who genuinely cares about me and my best interests. I've signed with Margaret, and Edwin Chambers is my publicist. I pulled out of the movie I was due to film this summer so I could get to the bottom of things and make amends."

"What about her? I need to know what happened, and I don't want you holding anything back. This is your only chance to fess up, Reeve. You're lucky I'm even giving you a chance to explain."

"I know that, Viv, and I'm grateful."

"Have you fucked her?"

Internally, I'm screaming. Wishing I didn't have to admit this truth, but I can't deny it. Slowly, I nod, hating the pain that races across her face before she briefly closes her eyes.

"Have you fucked other women since we broke up?" she asks as her eyes reopen.

I shake my head. "Nope. I haven't so much as looked at another woman. The only woman I want is you. With Saffron, it was only one time," I explain. "In Mexico, when those pictures were taken. I was high and drunk, and I have no recollection of it. All I know is I woke up beside her, and it was obvious what we'd done."

Anger stabs the backs of my eyes. I hate remembering this. It was one of the worst days of my life. "I threw up the second I realized the truth and what it meant for us. That fucking bitch laughed. She stood over me while I puked my guts up in the toilet, laughing and smiling while snorting a line." My anger cranks up a few notches. "She had the audacity to assume we would be together after that, but I made it abundantly clear I would never have fucked her if I'd been sober and I wanted her nowhere near me. I went to the studio and told them I would walk if they didn't keep her away from me when we weren't filming. I told them the only way I'd promote *Sweet Retribution* was if she was nowhere near me."

I stop for a few seconds to draw a breath and attempt to

contain my anger. "They agreed, and that pissed her off. I found out afterwards she had staged the whole thing. Had a photographer hiding close by to take the money shot. She timed it perfectly to ruin your birthday. I'm so sorry."

"What a pity you hadn't done that the first time it was obvious she was interfering."

She isn't snarling the words like she would have in the past, which is progress.

I don't think I'm the only one who has changed.

Maybe separation was good for us.

"I should have. Everything would've been different if I hadn't been so weak. So stupid. I failed myself as much as I failed you." I twirl a piece of her hair around my finger. "I won't ever fail you again, Viv. If you give me one more chance, I will prove to you I'm worthy of it."

Chapter Fifty-Three

"Where are we?" she asks as Bobby pulls up to the underground parking lot underneath my apartment building.

"My apartment in Pacific Palisades."

"You own an apartment?"

I bob my head. "It's only a stopgap. I found a couple of perfect sites to build our home, but I wouldn't dream of buying anything without your involvement." That's what I was up to this past week to help distract me in the run-up to her return.

She chews on the corner of her lip while moving around in her seat. "Reeve..."

I flash her an excited grin as I let my hope shine through. "I know I'm probably coming on too strong. I promised myself I wouldn't do that, but I'm going to win you back, Viv. I'm not giving up." The smile slides off my lips. "Not even if you tell me that Irish guy has a fighting chance."

Tears instantly flood her eyes, and her lower lip wobbles as the most anguished expression crawls over her face. Air filters from her lips in exaggerated spurts. "Fuck." I gently grasp her upper arms. "I've got you, Viv. Breathe in and out. Nice and slow." I inhale and exhale with her until her breathing returns to normal.

All the blood drains from my face when my gaze snags on her fingers stroking the necklace resting on her collarbone. It's not one I've bought her, which can only mean... "Did he buy you that?" I briefly shut my eyes to disguise the visible pain.

Audrey said it was serious for Viv, but I didn't fully believe it. However, it's impossible to ignore the potential truth when faced with it. I don't want to ask this, but I need to know where I stand, or how big of an uphill struggle I'm facing. "Do you love him?"

Strained silence rings out for a few beats, as Bobby parks the car, before she says, "Yes."

I drop my head in my hands as my heart pounds painfully against my rib cage and screaming fills my ears. Now I'm the one who can scarcely breathe. *She loves him. She loves him.* How has this happened? It's my worst nightmare, and this pain is every bit as bad as the pain I felt the day we broke up and the day she told me she was leaving for Ireland. I'm crushed, but I pull myself together and remember I'm in this for the long haul. I need to know another truth, so I steel my emotions and lift my head, staring deep into her eyes as I ask, "Do you still love me?"

"Yes. I do. I love you," she answers without hesitation, and my body instantly calms like I've just ingested a truckload of Valium. All isn't lost. There is still hope. "I can work with that."

"Reeve..."

"I know, Viv. You don't need to say it. I know you, remember?"

I help her out of the car, into the elevator, and guide her along the hallway toward the place I now call home. "I got the penthouse, but it's not huge. At least, not compared to where we both grew up." I open the door and step aside to let her enter first.

"I lived in a penthouse in Dublin, and I actually loved that it was smaller. Much easier to clean."

"I can't wait to hear about your trip. What is Ireland like?" I ask, guiding her into the main living space.

"It was amazing. I'll tell you all about it, but wow. This view is to die for." She marches straight to the window, and I take a second to memorize this moment. I have imagined her being here so many times, and now she is. For so long, I didn't dare to dream. Afraid of setting myself up for a fall, but I'm going to indulge it now. She still loves me, and she's not pushing me away. She's here with me and we're talking and it's going to be okay. *We* are going to be okay. I feel that truth resounding deep in my bones.

"I bought this place for the view," I confirm as I stand beside her at the expanse of floor-to-ceiling windows that offer a magnificent view of the ocean in the near distance. "I probably should've bought a place in Beverly Hills or West Hollywood to be closer to the studios, but I wanted to be near the ocean. Now that I'm clean and sober, I've taken up running again, and I jog every morning at five a.m. down at Santa Monica Pier."

"Clean and sober?" She turns to look at me.

"I attended an outpatient rehab clinic for a couple months to wean myself off all the shit I was doing. I saw a therapist there too."

"It was that bad? Why didn't I see it?"

"It was hella bad after those photos surfaced. I reached a real low point, but ultimately, it was a turning point. It was at that juncture I decided to turn my life around. As for why you didn't see it—I didn't want you to see it, Viv. And, before you ask, I didn't do much shit when I was with you. I didn't need to." I caress her cheek, refamiliarizing myself with her silky-smooth skin. "You're the only drug I need."

"No drug is healthy, Reeve. They're all addictive and damaging to your health."

True. "Except you. You were always good for me. I was a fucking fool to have vented my frustration at you instead of confiding in you and letting you help me make the right decisions. I've grown up a lot these past few months. I missed you like crazy." I cup her stunning face. "You're so fucking beautiful, Vivien. I have missed your gorgeous face." I peer deep into her eyes. "Do you think you can ever forgive me?"

Her hands wrap around my wrists. "I already have."

Shock whistles through me. I thought it would take a long time to earn her forgiveness because I fucked up a lot and made a ton of mistakes. To hear her say she has already forgiven me is more than I dared to hope for. I have never been worthy of Vivien Grace Mills, but never more so than in this moment.

"I needed to forgive you to heal. I saw a therapist in Ireland, and she helped me to that realization. I know you didn't intentionally set out to hurt me, Reeve. I'm angry you made so many stupid decisions. I'm mad you turned to drugs and that bitch instead of me, but hearing your explanation helps me to understand it a little better."

I lean in on autopilot, needing to kiss her so badly. She pulls away before my lips make contact.

"That doesn't magically solve everything. You still betrayed me, and that's not something I can forget in a hurry. Earning my trust again will not be easy, and I can't promise you anything, Reeve. You don't own my full heart anymore, and I'm a bit of a hot mess now, in case you didn't notice."

That's not a no. Hope swirls in my chest, and I feel like doing a Leo DiCaprio from the corner of my balcony. "I know I have a lot to do to prove my intentions are true. I need to work hard to regain your trust, but I'm going to do it. I've already set things in motion, and I won't stop until I've got you back." I reel her into my arms, knowing touch will ground us. "I can't exist in this world without you, Vivien Grace Mills. I've tried, and it's not worth living if you aren't there by my side."

Her stomach rumbles, and I make her sit down on the couch while I fix us some food.

"California sun, oh, how I've missed you." Viv tips her face up to the sun as she leans back in her chair and pats her stomach after we have eaten our chicken wraps on the balcony.

"You *are* looking a little pasty," I tease, and she shoves her middle finger up at me.

It feels so normal. While we have a lot of shit to work through, we have fallen back into familiarity with ease. Our connection is still strong, as is our love. Resolve is the blood flowing through my veins as I drink her in, basking in a warm glow that only comes from her company.

I love her so much.

It resonates through every tissue in my bones.

She is my home. My everything. I never want to be apart from her again.

"I'm really glad you're home," I say softly, my eyes raking over every delectable inch of her. "You look good, Viv."

"I am good."

"I love seeing you here. I knew when I was buying this place you'd love it. And wait until you see the properties I've earmarked for our forever house. They will blow your mind. Did you even look at the architect plans before you returned your birthday gift?" The word vomit just spews from my mouth. Despite her earlier pleas, it's so hard to contain myself when I've spent months apart from her and months planning for our reunion. I'm all up in my feels, and it's hard to rein myself in.

"Reeve, enough with the heavy. Please. I've had the most horrendous forty-eight hours. Can't we just chat and catch up?"

The smile drops off my face as some of my euphoria dies. "I know I'm getting carried away, but I've been waiting for a chance to start making it up to you for months, and I'm a little anxious."

Her features soften. "I understand, and I like that you're trying to make amends. It reminds me you're still you, but I just got off a plane, Reeve, and I'm tired and emotional."

"Of course. I won't overburden you, but I do need to fill you in on the Bianca, Cassidy, Saffron situation, as well as what I've been doing this summer."

"So, fill me in." She takes a sip of her sparkling water and listens attentively as I explain everything.

"It will really piss me off if she gets off scot-free," she says about Saffron a few minutes later, and I inwardly cringe.

Omitting part of the truth is still a lie, and I hate having to do it, but there is no other way. I have made the decision, and I need to own it. Craig says it's part of accepting who I am. Guilt and self-loathing will only hold me back. Beating myself up every five seconds won't change the choice I have made, so I need to own the decision, accept the guilt, and focus on moving forward with the next phase of our lives.

"She hasn't escaped unscathed." I top off her water. "She's officially finished with the production. She won't be at the premiere, and she won't be doing any promotion."

"How come?"

I'm protecting her, protecting us, I remind myself as I lie. "She OD'd, and her sister has sent her to rehab." I stretch my arm across the table and hold her hand. "She's gone from our lives now, Viv. She can't hurt us anymore, and in case she gets any ideas when she emerges from rehab, I have already instructed Carson Park to apply for a restraining order in both our names."

"Thank you."

"One final thing." I stand and pull her into my arms.

"I did a thing."

"Oh God, Reeve. What now?"

"A good thing, I hope you'll agree. I did an exclusive interview with Oprah, and I told her everything. I needed to publicly clear your name and let everyone see how viciously you've been treated and how stupid I was not to believe you from the outset. I came clean about the drugs and the stress of carrying such a big movie and how I didn't respond well to the pressure. Obviously, I had to be careful what I said about Bianca with the impending court case, and I can't accuse Saffron of shit when I have no proof to back up my claims. Bianca's and Cassidy's words don't count because they're both nasty backstabbing bitches, and their reputations are in the toilet."

"How the hell did you get the studio to agree to that?"

"When it airs next month, it will generate a huge amount of publicity for the franchise, ahead of the release of the last movie. All publicity is good publicity, so they're on board."

"Thank you, Reeve." She hugs me, and my heart soars. "Thank you so much for doing that. It helps. It really does."

"Yeah?" I wasn't sure if she would like me discussing our personal lives, so it was a bit of a gamble. I'm glad it paid off.

"Yeah."

"Come and watch the interview. If there is anything you don't like, I can have it edited out. Margaret helped me get a clause added to the contract that gives us editorial rights."

We watch the interview together, gradually moving closer on the couch until we're holding one another tight. Viv is sobbing by the end, and I'm starting to grow concerned. "Hey."

I wipe the moisture from her cheeks with my fingers. "Happy or sad tears?"

"More happy than sad." She circles her arms around my neck. She's trembling, clearly overcome with emotion, and I'm not exactly immune either.

"I love you, Viv. I love you so much. I'm sorry you ever felt like that wasn't true. I am going to spend the rest of my life making it up to you, whether you'll let me or not."

She barks out a laugh. "Always the charmer."

I see the adoration in her eyes, and I'm struggling to contain the myriad of emotions charging through me.

I need her.

I want her.

I love her so fucking much.

It's time to remind her she's mine.

Chapter Fifty-Four

"Every word is true, Viv." I can't hold back any longer. I need to kiss her, so I move in for the kill, bringing my mouth closer to hers. "I lost my way for a while, and I hurt us both in the process. I will not make that mistake again." Then I slam my lips down on hers and kiss the ever-loving daylights out of her.

Warmth fills every lonely inch of me, and I'm greedy as I ravish her mouth, kissing her with a primal longing that emanates straight from my soul. Every sweep of my lips and every glide of my tongue papers over the cracks in my heart, and I'm silently rejoicing that she's in this with me, meeting me kiss for passionate kiss, clawing at me as desperately as I'm clawing at her.

I didn't plan on this happening today even though I longed for it and dreamed of it. I'm not going to stop it unless she asks me to because she's moaning into my mouth, pushing her body against mine, and clinging to me with the same need driving me to demand more.

We shed our clothes, and I lay her out on the couch, my

gaze roaming over every gorgeous curve of her body, reminding me of everything I have been missing.

I'm insatiable for her, exploring the expanse of her creamy skin with my lips, my tongue, and my fingers. I can't stop kissing her and touching her, and I'm afraid if I pause she'll disappear like it was all a mirage.

Her soft fingers on my flesh are heavenly, and to know she desires me as much as I desire her makes all the pain of the past few years worth it. Nothing or no one can rip us apart because our connection is too strong. Vivien and I are meant to be together, and I have never once stopped believing in that.

I stroke my fingers inside her, finding her ready and willing. My cock is almost bursting at the seams as I give it a few quick tugs. Pulling her hands up over her head, I carefully press my body against hers before claiming her lips in a searing-hot kiss. "I love you, Viv. Over everything and everyone. The only thing that matters to me is you. You have my heart for now and eternity." She spreads her legs, and we stare at one another as I move inside her slowly, filling her inch by inch, and it's fucking everything. "God, Viv." Emotion wells in my eyes as she peppers my face with kisses.

"Let me feel your love, Reeve. Show me you mean everything you've said today."

Gladly, my love. I kiss her deeply as I make love to her, pouring everything I'm feeling into every sweep of my lips and every thrust of my cock. We're both greedy, clinging to one another with a feverish need, and it's everything. I try to prolong it because it's sheer ecstasy being intimate with her like this. I don't know when it'll happen again. I know we can't just pick up where we left off, no matter how incredible the sex is or how potent our connection is. It doesn't excuse my sins. There is a lot I need to do to prove myself to her again, but knowing she still wants me and loves me means we will get there. All is not lost, and the future we have planned is ours for the taking once again.

After we're done, I hold her against me on the couch, smelling her hair, inhaling her scent, and reveling in the feel of her bare skin pressed to mine. Her fingers dance over the tattoo of her name on my chest, and then she starts crying. It cracks a new fissure in my heart.

Please let her not regret something so special.

Please let her not have second thoughts.

I hold her as she sobs, whispering reassurances as I dust her face with kisses, willing my love to seep into her pores and remedy all her broken pieces. I comfort her when she makes herself physically ill from inner turmoil, holding her hair and rubbing her back as she pukes into the toilet.

Maybe I should have stopped it from going so far, but I can't find it within myself to regret it.

I take care of her, helping her to brush her teeth and clean her face before carrying her out to the living room where I ply her with water. Then I just hold her. Cradling her in my arms as she releases more pent-up emotion. I glance at my phone, wishing there was time to reschedule with the photographer. I don't want to do this when Viv is clearly fragile, but it's obvious how much she loves this Irish guy, and he's no idle threat.

When I said I would fight for Vivien, I meant it.

I will fight dirty if I have to.

He's not stealing her from me.

She's *mine*. She always has been, and she always will be.

I just need to ensure that Irish punk ass understands it.

He had his time with her, and now it's over.

She's back in my arms where she belongs.

Where she's staying.

Edwin was the one who planted the idea in my head, but I'm sure he didn't mean it like this. My new publicist said getting ahead of the media is the key to managing them. Putting out stories before they break means we control the narrative, not the other way around. He has a few firms he uses when he wants to push a story or an angle, and it gave me some ideas of my own.

There are a couple of photographers who follow me religiously. Most of them are scum of the earth, and I wouldn't piss on them if they were on fire, but I like Federico. He acts like he's human. He's always friendly and polite, and he has backed down at times when I've asked him to. He has earned my respect, so it seemed natural to agree when he proposed an exclusive working arrangement. I'll give him the heads-up on stories or my whereabouts so he can get the scoop and I'm in control of the narrative.

This is our first time working together, so I can't bail at the last minute. I'm sure he's already in situ. Vivien is vulnerable right now, and if I could postpone it, I would, but I can't. I'm doing this for us anyway. I'm helping her to clear the fog in her head. After this, there will be no third parties standing in the way of our future.

That's how I reconcile it within myself as I help her into her underwear and then pull on my boxers. I scoop her into my arms and carry her out to the balcony, ensuring her chest is hidden from view. I made it very clear to Federico that no bare tit shots were to be taken or the deal is off, and I expect him to comply.

We stand on the balcony facing the ocean, and I wrap my arms around Viv's naked chest from behind, ensuring her tits won't be visible in the photo. I'm choosing this position on purpose because it's similar to the pose in the photo she sent me when she was with him.

I want him to get the message loud and clear.

She is *mine*, and he can fuck off.

Reeve

Holding Viv with her back to my chest, I worship her with a slew of drugging kisses, dragging my lips back and forth across her face, her jaw, and the elegant column of her neck. Heat from her body embeds deep inside me, thawing all the previously frozen parts. This feels so right because we were meant for one another. I have never doubted that conviction, and I'm not going to start now. Viv needs that spelled out so my intentions are crystal clear.

"I know you're upset, and I can guess why," I say. "I'm not going to lie and say I'm happy you love this Irish guy, but it's my fault you were even there in the first place, so I've got to man up and accept the situation." I spin her around and brush a soft kiss to her lips. "He's not here, Viv. I am. And I'm all yours in every sense of the word. I won't be making any decisions about my career without your involvement. Everything I do from here on out will be done placing your needs above mine. I know you need time, and I'll give you that, but please say you'll give us another chance. If we try and you say it's not working for you, it will kill me, but I'll walk away. I will do whatever it takes to make you happy, because that is the only thing that matters to me anymore. You are my entire world, Viv, and I won't stop until I have proven that to you."

A couple of hours later, I leave her fast asleep in my bed after staring at her like a creeper for an indeterminate amount of time. Long wavy hair fans out across my pillow, and little puffs of air trickle from her full lips. Her skin is lightly flushed as she sleeps deeply, and I capture the image in my mental gallery. She's so beautiful. And she looks perfect curled up under my comforter, looking peaceful and content.

She is back home where she belongs, and I am never losing her again.

Viv stayed awake as long as she could, but jet lag kicked her in the ass. I'll have to wake her later to drive her home because

Lauren and Jon want to see her, but for now she can grab a long nap.

When I see it's dead, I plug in her phone to charge in the living room, and it pings with some new notifications. I shouldn't look. But I need to know what I'm up against if the just-published photos and impending TV coverage don't drill the point home. I tap in her pin, glad she's still using the same code, and retrieve the text and call log. There are a bunch of missed calls and new texts from *My Toxic God*.

What the fuck does that even mean?

I glance at one of the messages to ensure it's *him* before I wipe his calls and texts and block his number. Then I take a shower and get changed while I wait for enough paps to arrive outside the apartment building before I wake Viv up.

Chapter Fifty-Five

I frown at my cell as my call drops. I know Viv has a break now in between classes, and I only have a short window to talk to her before I'm due back in the TV studio. I hated having to leave her less than two weeks after she returned home, but the release of *Sweet Retribution* was moved up to October, so we're on the first leg of the promo tour. Sans Saffron, thank fuck. I'm sure it kills her knowing she will miss the promo and premiere, but the media has been fed the rehab story, and they know she's overseas trying to heal herself. I snort out a laugh. What a joke. I bet it won't take her much time to snort most of my money up her nose once she gets back to the US.

I call Viv again, and this time, she picks up. "Hey."

"Hey, beautiful. Have I caught you at a bad time?"

"I have a few minutes to talk."

"I miss you." I tell her every day because it's the truth.

"I miss you too," she agrees. "What are you up to?"

"I'm over at Universal Studios with some of the cast. We're being interviewed by Kelly Clarkson today."

"Oh, get me an autograph. You know how much I love her music."

Vivien is rarely starstruck, a consequence of growing up how we did. But there are a couple of notable exceptions, and Kelly is one. It's cute she thinks she has to ask. As if I don't know her inside and out. I chuckle. "I already have it in my pocket along with a few goodies she gave me for you."

"Thank you."

"Anything for you, babe. You know that." I would literally bend over backward to please my woman. Anything she wants, it's hers.

"You can stop sending flowers now. If you send more, there won't be any room for Audrey and me." I've been sending daily deliveries of lavender flowers, chocolates, and other gifts.

"I need to show you how much I love you, Viv. I need to remind you of who I am and who we are. I need you to remember all the good times because there were way more of them than bad. I know we can be amazing together again if you'd just give me a chance to prove it."

The day after our reunion, I dropped by her house to return the album I made for her birthday and to just spend time with her. Viv explained her head was a mess and I needed to give her some space. Granting her more space is the very last thing I want, especially with my forthcoming work commitments. We've been separated enough in the past few years. But I didn't protest. I haven't crowded her, but I make sure I contact her every day so she knows she is my priority.

"I'm not disputing any of that, Reeve, but you can't pressure me. You need to give me space to sort through my feelings."

"I'm scared of losing you, Viv," I admit. "I can't live without you."

A few tense beats of silence ensue before I clear my throat

and ask the question that's been toying on my mind these past few weeks. "Are you talking to *him*?"

"No. I haven't heard from him since I left Ireland."

Relief flows through me like water bursting the banks of a dam. The prick got the message, or maybe it was never as serious for him, as Audrey thought. Which is ludicrous.

I understand what it's like to be with this woman and what it's like to lose her. I can't imagine any man willingly walking away from her.

"I love you, Viv, and I want you by my side. I want our dream to come true. The one we talked about endlessly as kids. We have the resources to make it happen now, and I want that with you. I want our forever. I'm ready for it." I want to make appointments to view those sites I found with a private real estate agent a few weeks ago. They won't remain on the market for long. I'm itching to buy a plot and hire a contractor so we can begin building our dream home. But I haven't mentioned it to Viv yet because I'm trying not to move too fast.

"I wish it was as easy for me, but we can't just pick up where we left off, Reeve."

"Why not?"

"Because too much has happened, and we still have stuff to work through."

"Let's work through it then because I'm not letting you go, Viv. Never again."

"We'll talk when you get home in a month. This isn't the kind of conversation we can have over the phone."

"Just remember I love you, Viv. I have loved you since I was a little boy, and I never stopped. I never will."

"I love you too, Reeve, but you need to give me some time."

What does she think I'm doing? This is not easy for me, but I'm holding back for her. "I'm trying, my love. I am trying to be patient, but it's hard when I've been without you for so long."

"I know it's coming from a good place."

Her soft, sultry tones do something to my insides, and I wish I could project myself through the phone so I could hold her and kiss her. "If you just give me a chance, I will make it up to you."

"You agreed we'd rebuild our friendship first. It's all I can offer you right now."

"And I'm grateful for it and for your forgiveness. But you can't blame a guy for trying for more with the only woman he has ever loved."

"I don't, but it's making it harder for me."

It hurts to hear that because I promised her, and me, I wouldn't do anything to make life difficult, and I'm trying to stick to that vow. "That's not what I want, but I can't stay away, Viv. Please don't ask for that because it'll kill me."

"Just back off a little, Reeve. That's all I'm asking."

I exhale heavily, reminding myself of the endgame. I can be patient. I can wait longer for her. "Okay. I will try."

"Thank you."

"You're my entire world, Vivien. Don't forget it."

"I won't, but I've got to go. Have fun at the interview, and give Kelly my love."

"I will. Have a great rest of the day. Love you, baby."

"Love you too."

"How was the tour?" Carson asks as soon as I'm settled at the table in his office with a steaming mug of coffee in my hand, thanks to his efficient assistant.

"Tiring, but it's almost over now. We have three weeks of promotion after the premiere next week, and then I can finally put this experience to bed."

I can't wait. As much as I'm proud of this movie, promoting it has been a chore. I want to punch something every time I see myself with that bitch on screen. I asked Viv to walk the red carpet with me at the premiere, but she said no, which I was expecting. While part of me was saddened, the other part agreed with her and was relieved. I don't want her seeing me with that bitch on screen. It might drag everything to the surface again. She has tentatively agreed to attend the premiere of the movie I filmed in Sydney two summers ago in January, and I'm hoping she won't back out.

"I'm glad. I've seen how much stress you've been under." Carson walks to the table with a folder in one hand.

"It's an experience I'm glad to relegate to the far corners of my mind." I take a sip of my coffee before adding, "Thanks for all you've done to help me these past couple years. I'm not sure I ever said that, but I appreciate the support."

"I'm happy to help, Reeve." He claims the seat across from me. "And I'm here for you with anything you need." He opens the folder and pulls out two stapled documents. "It's good to see you looking so well," he adds, pushing the documents and a pen across the table to me.

"It's good to be well."

"How is Vivien?"

The smile is instantaneous on my face. "She is great. I'm dropping by her place after I leave here." I came straight from the airport to Carson's office, wanting to get this handled so I have a free schedule the next couple days to spend with the love of my life.

"That's wonderful. She's a lovely girl, and I'm glad it all worked out for you."

I don't bother telling him I'm stuck in the friend zone for now because I'm confident it's only a temporary situation.

"For what it's worth," Carson says, jerking his eyes at the

documents in front of me. "I think you're doing the right thing. You are too young to be saddled with a child, and Lori and Travis will make excellent parents. They will take care of your son, and you can rest easy knowing he is well loved and provided for."

I rub at a pain in my chest. I found out last week that we're having a little boy. It was a bittersweet phone call. Even though the decision has been made, I still have moments of doubt. Moments where I wish I didn't have to give my son up. But I have made the decision and I need to own it which is why I'm here to sign the adoption agreement. The formal adoption paperwork has been signed and submitted. These are the terms of our personal agreement.

I had a meeting with Lori and Travis before I left L.A., and we talked extensively for hours. The background checks all panned out, and the only reason for not letting them adopt my son was Saffron. But they have reassured me she will not have contact with the boy, and they'll reach out to Carson if she tries anything. It's a small risk to take to ensure my child has a good life and he is brought up with family. I can't deny him, so I told them I agreed before I left that day. The look of sheer joy on their faces told me I'd made the right call, and I haven't regretted it since. "I don't want to read it. Give me the Cliffs-Notes version."

"Lori and Travis will be listed as the bio parents on the birth certificate, offering you more protection against Saffron. Even if she was to blab to the press at a later date, the official paperwork will refute her claims and label her a liar and trou-blemaker."

"I don't want any hint of this coming out in the future. Viv would ask questions, and I don't want to lie to her face. What we're doing isn't legal. Are you sure it'll hold up to scrutiny if examined?"

"It's rock-solid, trust me. The only way it could be challenged is if a court ordered a DNA test at a future time. That scenario is highly unlikely, and I would put it out of your mind."

I suppose no plan is fail-safe, and this is the best we can do. It doesn't just protect me; it protects my son. This way, he can grow up without a media spotlight on his head, and I like that for him.

"Okay, what else?"

"It confirms your commitment to buy the property Lori and Travis have selected as their new family home, states the generous monthly allowance will be paid up until the child turns eighteen, and confirms thereafter his trust fund will kick in."

"Where do I sign?"

"Page four and page six. It's marked with tabs."

I scrawl my signature in both places on both copies and hand them back to him.

"Your commitment to finding the right family for your son and ensuring he's well cared for is commendable, Reeve. This isn't the ideal scenario, but I truly believe you have done the best you can."

"I hope so," I say, draining my coffee and pulling my jacket on. "I just want him to be happy, and I truly believe he'll be happiest with Lori and Travis."

Chapter Fifty-Six

I stand outside Vivien's door wearing a ball cap and keeping my head low as I shield a bouquet of lavender roses and lilies in my arms. I got back in the early hours of the morning, and I'd been dying to see my girl, but she had classes all day, so I had to summon patience from somewhere.

The door swings open, and my automatic smile fades a little when it's Audrey, not Viv, who greets me.

"Wow. Could you be more fucking obvious?" Rey arches a brow as she steps aside to let me enter. "You could at least pretend like you're happy to see me too."

"Sorry, Rey." I lean in and kiss her cheek before I hand her a box of those French chocolates she loves. "Hopefully this makes up for it."

"It so does." She gives me a quick hug before shutting the door. "Thank you. This is sweet and thoughtful."

"Alex mentioned you were a little stressed with your upcoming exams, so I thought some chocolate might help."

"It wasn't necessary but much appreciated." Audrey

deposits the box on the counter. "And exam stress is the norm for both of us at this time of year."

Maybe that's why Viv has been acting weird these past couple months. I haven't been home a lot, but she's been avoiding me despite telling me she wants me in her life. I look around their open-plan living area, but there's no sign of Viv. "You still have a few weeks, and I'm sure you'll nail it. Where's Viv?" I ask just as the distinct sounds of someone vomiting echo from the bathroom. "She's sick?" My feet are already moving in her direction.

Audrey grabs her jacket, purse, and keys. "I'm meeting Alex for dinner and a movie, so you guys have the place to yourselves," she says, avoiding answering my question.

I swing around just outside the hallway that leads to the bedrooms and main bathroom. "Okay, have fun."

"Reeve," she calls out before I walk off. Rey worries her lower lip between her teeth. "Go easy on her. It's been a tough time."

Now I'm officially worried.

I race to the bathroom, spying Viv hunched over the toilet bowl through the half-opened door. I put the flowers down on the counter and walk over, crouching beside her. "Hey, baby."

"Reeve," she whispers, lifting red-rimmed eyes to mine. Sweat beads dot her skin, plastering hair to her forehead and cheeks, and she's so freaking pale. Her lips are chapped, and her movements are lethargic as she leans back against the tub.

"Shit, Viv. You don't look so hot. Have you seen a doctor?"

Her tongue darts out, wetting her dry lips as she slowly nods. Then she heaves, dry retching over the bowl because there's clearly nothing left in her stomach to expel. I hold her hair back and smooth a hand up and down her back until she's done.

"Fuck, this is horrendous," she moans, and I prop her up as she stands.

"What did the doctor say?" I ask after she's cleaned her face and brushed her teeth. "And how long has this been going on?" I scoop her up into my arms when she sways, happy she doesn't protest.

"A while." She leans her head against my chest, and I kick the door to her bedroom open. I've only been in her room one time. When she showed me the framed Kelly Clarkson auto-graphed poster she mounted on her wall. "Ugh, I'm so sick of this, and I'm so drained," she says as I lay her down gently on her king bed.

"Let me get a cool cloth and some water." I press a kiss to her brow as she curls on her side on top of the comforter.

When I return a few minutes later, I have a thermometer, a cold cloth, a glass of water, and some crackers. I called Bobby and Leon and asked them to pick up meds and some chicken noodle soup. I'll be having a stern talk with Leon when I see him. He's assigned to protecting Viv now, and he should have told me she was sick.

After my Oprah interview, interest in Viv and me hit record highs. I'm deflecting questions on a daily basis, and I didn't want Viv to be harassed, so I spoke with her and suggested Leon leave my detail to look after her. Thankfully, she agreed immediately, and it meant I could sleep easier at night knowing she was safeguarded. It's just Bobby and me now, and so far, it's fine. If it gets nuts, I can hire a couple more bodyguards for additional protection for both of us.

"Let me help." I set the supplies down on the bedside table and help her to sit up against the backrest. I dab the cool cloth against her clammy skin and take her temp. It's within normal range, which is a huge relief. She's probably caught a tummy bug, but it doesn't seem serious. Releasing her hair from the hair tie, I brush it before securing it again so it's out of her way if she vomits some more. "Do you want to get changed?" I ask, guessing she's probably uncomfortable.

"I don't have the energy."

"I can help."

She peers deep into my eyes, and I hate seeing her so pale and so fragile. Her stare is intense, and I wonder what is going through her mind. "I won't look," I say in case she's worried about me stripping her down. "Though it's nothing I haven't seen before," I quip to lighten the tense atmosphere.

Her lips kick up at the corners before she lifts her arms. It looks like it takes enormous effort to move her exhausted body as I help her undress down to her panties. Then I grab a clean silk nightie from her dresser and help her into it. Viv crawls under the covers, and I perch on the edge of the bed as I pull the comforter up to her chest before handing her the water. "Drink that. You're probably dehydrated. I asked Leon to grab some Liquid I.V. from the pharmacy and Gatorade. We need to get electrolytes back into you. Then maybe you can try some peppermint tea or ginger ale to help settle your tummy."

Tears fill her eyes, and her lower lip wobbles.

"Hey," I softly say, gently cupping one cheek. "What is it?"

She gulps a couple of times as tears roll silently down her face, and I'm starting to panic.

"Reeve." Her voice croaks.

"Yes, baby." I softly sweep my fingers over her cheek.

"I'm pregnant," she whispers, and my fingers stall as my entire body turns rigid.

I blink repeatedly, staring at her in a daze as blood rushes to my head and knots form in my stomach. I can't be sure I didn't just imagine it. "Did you just say you're pregnant?" I choke out.

Slowly, she nods.

My brain struggles to comprehend this as all kinds of thoughts flutter through my mind. Fear creeps up my throat as one potent thought lands like a punch to the head, and I have to know. "Is it mine?"

"Yes," she whispers, clutching my arm.

"We're having a baby?" I splutter as my thoughts continue racing. What are the fucking odds of knocking up two women within such a short space of time and both being pregnant together?

She nods as she swipes at the tears pouring down her face.

Oh my God. I can't wrap my head around this. Vivien is pregnant with my kid? Swirling happiness builds momentum inside me as a hundred different thoughts fire at me from all angles. This is incredible news! The absolute best thing that could happen. My baby is growing inside the love of my life, and I want to shout it from the rooftops because I am so deliriously happy. This is everything I have ever wanted, and my heart is filled to bursting point.

"Are you mad?" she asks, and I realize I've just been staring into space and probably freaking her out.

"No, baby." I clasp her gorgeous face in my hands and smile the biggest smile. "Not even a little bit. You have made me the happiest man on the planet." Tears stab my eyes as I stare at her equally emotional gaze. "This is the most fantastic news. I'm so excited!" I lean in and press a tender kiss to her lips. "I love you, and I can't wait to see your stomach swollen with my baby." The grin on my face is so wide it threatens to split it in two. "This is the best news ever. I'm over the moon, babe. I have always wanted kids with you." This feels like a sign. I had to give away one child, but I'll get to keep this one. Viv and I will get the family we've always wanted.

"You're really happy?" Creases line her brow as she stares at me.

"So fucking happy I want to tell the world!" Not literally, of course. I climb up beside her and carefully lift her into my lap, setting her head down on my chest as my arms encircle her. My heart is beating to a new rhythm, and everything feels right in my world again. We are exactly where we're supposed to be, and I'm getting everything my heart has ever desired. I offer up silent thanks to whomever made this happen. This is officially one of the best days of my life. "This is what I've always wanted, Viv. You know this."

"We're so young, and we're not even together."

Twenty-one is not that young, and we have the resources to give this baby the best of everything. He or she will want for nothing. As for us, that's just semantics. "Say the word, and I'll rectify that now." *Marry me* is on the tip of my tongue, but I'm not about to blurt it out. I still remember the last time I proposed. It was a rash decision and the completely wrong call. I'm not making the same mistake again. Vivien knows I will always take care of her. She knows deep down I want to marry her. I'm only asking when the timing is right and she'll say yes.

"I won't rush this, *us*, just because I'm pregnant." Her eyes pierce mine. "I can't change how I feel. I can't cut him out of my heart like he never existed. I still need time to process all my emotions, and my hormones are going crazy, and it's only adding to my confusion."

"Are you happy? Do you want this baby?"

"One hundred percent. The timing isn't ideal, but it's a baby. One created out of love. How could I be anything but happy?" Tears cloud her vision again.

I was pretty sure that would be her answer, but I'm glad to confirm it and ecstatic we're on the same page. "Do you still love me?"

"Yes, absolutely. That won't ever change."

Another smile graces my lips because it seems I just can't keep smiling. "Then we'll work things out. We'll take it one day at a time. One step at a time, and I will be by your side throughout." I brush my lips against hers again, happy she's letting me. There has been no kissing or anything intimate beyond hugs since the day she arrived home. The day we made love and created new life.

"I should move in. So I can take care of you."

She shakes her head. "That is not giving me space or taking it slow."

"You're pregnant, and if this is the norm, you need me to help."

"I have Audrey, and I'm not sick every day. Today has been the worst. The doctor said the nausea usually goes after the first trimester."

"How far along are you? When is the baby due, and how long have you known?"

She chews on the corner of her lip. "I'm thirteen weeks pregnant. Our baby is due in early May, and don't get mad, but I've known for two months."

Not going to lie, but it hurts she's sat on this news for that long. "Why didn't you tell me?" I have a suspicion I might know why.

"I was trying to come to terms with it myself, and you've been gone most of that time. I didn't want to tell you over the phone."

I'm not sure I fully believe that, but I'm not going to do or say anything to upset her now. "It's okay. I understand, and I'm not mad."

More tears fill her eyes. "Gawd." She giggles over a sob. "It feels like my tear ducts are broken today. I can't stop crying. My hormones are going haywire."

I bundle her in my arms, pressing her head to my chest. "It's okay. It's par for the course, I'm sure. And I meant what I said. I can move in here, or you could move in with me. It's only a twenty-minute ride to UCLA from my place." I stroke her arm. "I want to take care of you, and I don't want you doing this alone. I want to be there for every milestone, and I want to attend every appointment."

"I want you involved too, but I'm not rushing back into a relationship. I still have trust issues, and there are other things we need to resolve."

I don't agree, but it's not about what I want. Slow and steady wins the race. "So, I guess that means I'm still in the friend zone?" I try not to let my hurt shine through my words.

"For now, but I won't exclude you from this. I promise."

"Do you have an ob-gyn?"

She nods.

"Is it possible to get a list of appointment dates so I can block them on my calendar?"

"I can schedule all my appointments in advance. I'm sure that's no problem."

"Okay, cool. Also, I was planning to talk to you about my next career moves, so we might as well discuss it now." I shift her back onto the bed beside me so we can have a serious conversation. "I've been offered a starring guest role on *Euphoria*. It'll be four episodes in total. Filming will take place mostly at Sony Culver City and a few locations around L.A. and Cali. Filming starts just after the *In a Different Life* premiere next month, but one *Euphoria* episode takes a month to film, so it will take me up until the end of March. It would mean I'm around more for you, although sometimes the shoots can be long. But I'd be close if there was an emergency or anything."

"It sounds perfect." She runs her fingers back and forth

across my chest, through my shirt, and I'm not even sure she's aware she's doing it. "Audrey and I love the show. I'd get a kick out of seeing you on it."

"Okay, that's agreed then. I'll tell Margaret to give it the green light." I clear my throat. "I was going to ask what you thought about me filming a movie in Italy over the summer. It's being directed by Anthony Minghella, and he's already secured a lot of A-listers. He personally asked for me, and the role is incredible. I was hoping you might agree to come with me, but the baby obviously changes things."

"I want to support you, Reeve. Truly I do, but I won't be moving overseas with a newborn."

"And I won't be without you or our baby, so I'll pass on that one."

She sits bolt upright. "Are you sure? If it's that good of a role and Minghella is a big deal, then maybe you shouldn't pass." She stares off into space, looking lost in thought. "We could come out for a few weeks, maybe half the time? Mom and Dad could come to help me with the baby."

"You'd do that for me?"

A genuine smile ghosts over her mouth. "Yes. I realize now it must have been so lonely for you in Sydney that summer. If things hadn't been so fractured between us, I would have altered my plans so I could spend time with you there. I'm trying to make better choices now, and we need to learn to compromise more. If you really want to do this movie, you should agree to it, and we'll make it work."

I slam my lips to hers and drive my fingers into her hair. Viv kisses me back with the same passion, and my heart is so full it feels like it might burst. We're both panting and red in the face when we break apart.

"You'll be the death of me," she says, but there's no heat behind her words. Only love.

"I fucking love you, Viv, and this is officially one of the best days of my life. We're having a baby, and we're talking things through like adults." I pull her into my arms and press a kiss into her hair. "I respect your need to take things slow, so I'll be patient, but we're going to make it. I just feel it in my bones."

Chapter Fifty-Seven

"Reeve! Vivien! Look here!" Flashbulbs go off in our faces, and I tuck Viv in closer to my side, angling our bodies and trying to shelter her from the worst of the glare. "Is it true you're moving in together?" some reporter shouts while we smile for the cameras and wave at the crowds beyond them. So many fans have turned out for tonight's premiere, and I'm walking on air. It has more to do with the vision in gold at my side than my pride, which there is a lot.

"Are you getting married?" another reporter calls out, but we ignore them. "Is it true you turned down Anthony Minghella?"

Yep, I answer in my head. Viv was willing to find a way to make things work, but I didn't want her to feel forced into traveling with our baby when he or she is only a few weeks old. I'm prioritizing my family, and it was easier than I thought to turn the high-profile role down. What the media doesn't know is the director has postponed the movie to the following summer, all so I can be there.

It blew my mind when Margaret told me.

I can't believe any director, let alone one of his status, would delay a movie just so I could take the leading role. I spoke to Vivien before accepting it, and she's on board with moving to Italy the following summer with our baby. To know she's looking that far into the future is proof of her intended commitment, and it has eased those tiny niggling doubts that have been in the back of my mind in the three weeks since she told me she is pregnant. As did the conversation we had last night.

So, today is a great day. I'm on top of the world, celebrating another movie, getting more glowing reviews, and having a baby with the love of my life. Now she's on the red carpet with me, sharing in the moment and supporting me. This is how it was supposed to be during the Rydeville Elite movie premieres.

I make a silent promise to myself that I'm never walking the red carpet without Vivien ever again.

The photographers and reporters heckle us some more, but we tune them out. As if we've mentally communicated, we turn toward one another at the same time. My hands rest on her back as her palms land on my jacket. Our gazes connect and hold for a few minutes, and the intensity of our connection crackles in the space between us. I reach out and touch her skin, staring at her with all the love swelling my heart. Flashes surround us, but nothing or no one else exists in this moment but her.

"You look beautiful," I tell her again. Pressing my lips to her ear, I whisper, "Pregnancy looks so good on you." Vivien is radiant now her sickness has passed, but her glow is the only visible sign she is pregnant. She is sixteen weeks along now, and her stomach is still flat. It bodes well for Viv's desire to attend school as long as possible, and then she plans to switch to online classes from home.

Reeve

We told Viv's parents two weeks ago, and while they were shocked, they were overjoyed at the prospect of becoming grandparents. Lauren wants Viv to move back to the house, but Vivien is insisting on staying at the apartment she shares with Audrey. She won't let me move in either, and even though I spend most nights at their place, I'm never invited to stay over.

We're firmly in the friend zone, but I'm sneaking the odd kiss here and there. It reminds me of being thirteen when we were doing the same thing while I was trying to work up the courage to ask her to be my girlfriend. Man, they were such simple, easygoing times, and we didn't have a clue. I remember how I tied myself into knots that year, all because I wanted to ask her to be mine. It seems so silly now, but at that time, it was everything to me and all I obsessed over for months on end.

Anyway, I'm looking forward to our scan on Monday. I want to ensure everything is okay even though Viv tells me the doctor said it's perfectly normal not to be showing at this stage. Is it wrong that I can't wait for her stomach to grow? That I want everyone to know she's carrying my baby? "I love you," I say, dropping a kiss on her cheek. The crowd goes nuts, and Vivien steals all the breath from my lungs with a showstopping, glorious smile. I wouldn't be surprised if this image of us is broadcast around the world or shown on the front pages of newspapers tomorrow.

One of the PR people gestures toward me, indicating it's time to start moving inside.

"I love you too, Reeve." Her fingers thread in mine as we shuck out of our embrace. "And I'm so happy to be here and proud to walk the red carpet with you."

"Fuck, Viv. You can't say things like that to me in public. It makes me want to drag you into the bathroom and bury my cock deep inside you."

She squirms a little, and a faint blush crawls over her

cheeks. She jabs her finger playfully in my chest as we turn and walk off, hand in hand. "And you can't say stuff like that to a perpetually horny pregnant woman," she whispers in my ear.

"You are?" First I'm hearing of it.

"Forget I said anything."

"Not likely." I bend down and speak directly into her ear. "I told you I'd take care of you. If you need me to get you off, I'll get you off. You only have to ask."

"Not helping," she mumbles, drilling me with a warning look I'm well accustomed to.

"Just making sure you know I'm down with that. It would hardly be a chore." I waggle my brows, and she rolls her eyes.

The movie was well received, and we're at the after-party in a five-star hotel in the city. A table was reserved in my name, and I'm here with Vivien, Alex and Audrey, and Lauren and Jon. Simon was a no-show. To the premiere and the party, and I'm trying not to let it get to me.

"Where is everyone?" Alex asks, returning to the table with two whiskeys. I only drink in moderation now, and this is my first drink even though we've been here for hours. While alcohol isn't the issue, it might be easier to get tempted to abuse drugs if I'm drunk. So I limit my alcohol intake these days to be safe. "The girls went to freshen up in the bathroom. I think we exhausted them on the dance floor, and Jon and Lauren are talking to some industry heads."

"Did you ask her last night?" Alex asks as he slips back into his seat.

I nod, glancing around to ensure there are no prying ears in proximity. "She says it's not his, that it's mine." Although I asked Vivien the day she told me she is pregnant, it's been playing on my mind, so I worked up the courage to ask Viv last night if there was any chance the baby could be *his*.

My best bud studies my face. Audrey already knew Viv was pregnant, and I told him when they came back to the apartment that night. He was a bit pissed Audrey had known the entire time and said nothing, but he understands they are best friends and she couldn't tell him before I knew. Just because we're all trying to be more truthful in our relationships doesn't mean there can be no secrets. We talk and keep some stuff to ourselves, and I'm sure the girls do the same.

Craig says it's normal and only a problem if one of us hides something important. I'm continuing with therapy, and it'll be an ongoing thing at least for now. It's good to have someone neutral to talk to, and it's helping to keep me straight. I haven't been tempted to turn to drugs, but all it might take is one incident, one trigger, to send me back to that dark place. I want to avoid that at all costs.

"This is a good thing, right?"

I take a sip of the amber liquid. "I want to believe her, but I'm not sure she's telling me the truth. He was her boyfriend right up until she came home. I thought she might not have told me for two months because she was doing one of those DNA tests. I'm hoping that was it. But there's still a small part of me that's worried. That thinks this is why she's keeping distance between us."

"You could ask her to do a test."

I shake my head. "Then she'll think I don't believe her, and it will set us back." I loosen my bow tie. "I trust Vivien, Alex. Her heart is pure. She wouldn't string me along if she truly believed the baby wasn't mine. Perhaps she's just being cautious with her heart. I'm choosing to trust her and believe her."

"I agree she wouldn't deliberately mislead you. Definitely not about something this serious."

I smile at my friend. "I'm giving her the benefit of the doubt, and I'm fully on board."

I have to trust Viv and shove those nasty voices whispering in my ear into a lockbox in my head.

On nights where I'm struggling to sleep, I contemplate the irony of giving up one child only to be told the other is not mine and losing Vivien to my competition. It's a very real fear, and it threatens to unravel all my progress. So, I have no choice but to toss that suggestion into the lockbox and pretend it doesn't exist. Vivien would not lead me to believe this is my baby if she genuinely didn't think it was. That's the only truth I need to believe in, and it's the one I am choosing to accept.

He looks around before lowering his voice. "You're going to be a dad. Wow. I still can't believe it."

I flash him a megawatt grin. "I know. I can't wait."

I end the call and slump to the floor in my kitchen, curling my fingers around my cell as tears stream down my face. Today was always going to be difficult because last Christmas Day was when I broke Viv's heart and ripped us apart, so this news only adds to my pain.

I have a son.

Bodhi was born an hour ago in Switzerland. Three weeks early. Possibly because that fucking whore bribed an orderly to give her drugs, and who knows what kind of damage she has done to him.

The doctor said he's slightly underweight, but he seems healthy. They are going to run some tests to ensure there are no issues, and provided he is given the all-clear, he will fly to the US with Lori and Travis in a week. Carson organized a private jet to fly them there and back. I'm paying for it on the down-low. I didn't want to use the Studio 27 jet or have Dad involved for obvious reasons.

I sit there in a daze, my mind churning, my heart heavy, until my cell rings. I pick up when I see it's Lori calling. She's crying happy tears, and we talk for a few minutes. She wants me to come to the house when they get home. She wants me to meet him. I'm not sure it's a good idea. I don't want to get attached, but we have spoken at length about when he's older and telling him the truth. It doesn't seem right to deny him that knowledge.

Every person should know where they came from, even if it's not a pleasant story.

She thinks it might be a good idea if I've played some role in his life even if it's only silent interest. I'm still not sure what to do.

Lori and I have grown somewhat close. We talk at least every couple of weeks. Even though the paperwork is all signed and the adoption is confirmed, she seems determined to include me, to let me know the preparations they have made for his arrival and the things she has planned to do with him.

She is going to make an amazing mother.

Just like Vivien.

"I've got to go," I say. "I'm expected at Vivien's house for Christmas lunch. I don't want to be late and worry her."

"How is Vivien doing?"

"She's doing great." Picturing her glowing face helps to bring a smile to my face.

"And your son?"

I told Lori we're expecting a boy. "All is good with the baby." My heart soars like usual, but today it's a little bittersweet.

"I wonder if they will look alike?" she muses, and I really can't do this today.

"Merry Christmas, Lori. Pass my regards to Travis."

"Same to you, Reeve. I hope today isn't too difficult for you. I'm here if you need me, and I'll keep you updated by text."

I hang up and move into autopilot mode, showering and dressing before I grab the bags filled with gifts and set out for the thirty-five-minute drive to North Beverly Park.

***

Everyone is in good spirits at the Millses, and it mostly helps to distract me. I sit beside Viv at the dinner table, leaning in to kiss her or squeeze her hand or rest my palm on her thigh. I need to be touching her to be reminded of why I sacrificed my child. Why I let him enter this world alone. The doctor said Saffron refused to hold Bodhi and barely even looked at him. It should please me she has no interest in him, but it only makes me sad for my son. He's thousands of miles away with only a team of doctors and nurses caring for him.

It feels wrong.

I should be there.

There should be someone who loves him holding him in the first few minutes of his life. It had been decided Lori and Travis would travel to Switzerland a few days before the birth to avoid this very scenario, but his premature birth ruined that plan.

My heart hurts, but I try to snap out of it. Lori and Travis will be on a plane tomorrow and in the meantime, there is an excellent team of caring doctors and nurses taking care of Bodhi. He will be fine. I made this decision, and I stand over it, but I suppose it's only natural to feel like this when things have happened unexpectedly and thrown me for a loop.

"Come take a walk with me." Viv palms my face, and I realize I've zoned out and everyone is finished eating.

"Wear your jacket. Rain is forecast," Lauren says, drilling me with a look I can't decipher.

I help Vivien into her rain jacket and borrow one of Jon's before we slip outside to the garden. Lauren built a walking trail around the perimeter of their property at the rear, with the start commencing at her infamous rose garden.

Viv loops her arm through mine as we walk, heading in the direction of the rose garden. "Are we going to talk about the elephant in the room?" she asks.

"I can't imagine you want to." The grass is damp underfoot thanks to an earlier shower.

"Pretending it never happened won't erase it, and I don't want Christmas to be forever ruined for us."

A lump lodges in my throat. Will it ever be anything but for me? It's not just the anniversary of one of the worst days of my life—the day I lost the woman I love—it's now the day my first-born son entered the world, and I suspect it will forever be a day where I'm nostalgic and sad.

"I forgive you, Reeve." She pulls me to a halt a few feet from the entrance to the rose garden. "*I forgive you.*" Tears stab her eyes as she cups my face. "Please forgive yourself."

"I don't know how," I croak. My emotions are balanced precariously on a tightrope today, and I'm not sure I can hide it from her.

"Oh, baby, please don't cry," she says, and I didn't even realize I was.

Anguish pours from me as I sob, falling against her, accepting her comfort as I concede to my emotions. I'm the worst human to seek comfort from her when another woman has just given birth to my child across the ocean.

"I love you." She hugs me tight and peppers kisses on my face.

"I don't see how," I sob into her neck.

"This time last year was the worst day of my life, but look how much difference a year makes?" Taking my hand, she pulls me over to the bench just inside the rose garden. "Reeve." She turns to the side, and our knees brush. She holds my hands in her softer, smaller ones and kisses me. It's tender and loving and I don't deserve it.

"I don't know how you can bear to even look at me." I lower my eyes to my lap.

"Reeve," she snaps, gripping my face and forcing my gaze to hers. "She tried to break us, and she didn't succeed because our love is so strong. Our connection too intense to deny. We still love one another." She pulls my hand and places it on her still-flat stomach. "We're having a baby. We're going to be a family, and she can't take it from us." She sniffles, and emotion glimmers in her eyes. "We both made mistakes, but we have learned from them. We are stronger than we were before. Strong enough not to let her ruin Christmas Day again this year."

She plants her hand over mine on her stomach. "This time next year, our son will be celebrating his first Christmas." Her entire face lights up as if she's been touched by an angel. "We'll be making new happy memories, and every Christmas will be a time for joy, not sadness."

She can't know how much those words mean to me or how they lift my spirits. There is so much to look forward to, and Bodhi will be well loved and cared for. This is a time to celebrate, not to wallow in a pity party for one. Only Vivien can ground me and help me to see the light. She has always been that for me. "I'm not worthy of you." I rest my brow against hers. "I'm so not worthy of you."

"Don't start this crap again," she teases. She weaves her

fingers through my hair. "Have I ever told you how much I love your hair?"

"Maybe a time or two." Some of my stress eases, and I drop my head to her shoulder, letting her play with my hair because it feels so good.

"You're my best friend, Reeve, and in time, you're going to be more again."

My head whips up. "Do you mean it?"

She brushes longish strands of hair out of my eyes. "Yeah, I do." Tears shine in her eyes. "But I still want to keep things lowkey until after the birth."

The lockbox in my head rattles, but I reinforce the bolts. I can't deal with those thoughts today, and I made a promise to myself to give her the benefit of the doubt, and that still stands.

"Can we at least be friends with benefits?" I suggest with a cocky grin because I really need her today. I'm not talking about sex per se. It's intimacy I crave. And feeling connected to her in every way because I need to know we're in this together, and I'm vulnerable today.

She rolls her eyes. "You love pushing boundaries, babe."

I shrug. "Can't help it if I want you every second of every minute of every day."

"I love Romantic Reeve."

My heart blooms like always when she refers to me as Romantic Reeve. "Enough to let me make love to you?" I'm not expecting her to say yes, but you can't blame a guy for trying.

Her arms wind around my neck before her lips descend in a passionate kiss I feel all the way to my toes. "Yes." Her eyes bore into mine. "Stay tonight? I need you, and I think you need me, and I'm done denying both of us or questioning whether it's a good idea."

"I'd like that."

"Good."

Her smile bathes me in warmth, helping to heal some of my fractured parts. I should probably be questioning the right or wrong of this, but I'm too selfish today to deny myself either.

Later that night, I make love to Viv in her bed for hours, and not that I needed the affirmation, but it cements the decision I made and helps bring me to a place of acceptance and peace.

Chapter Fifty-Eight
Now - Age 21

My heart is battering against my rib cage, and my stomach is tied into a million knots as I cradle my son in my arms and stare at his sleepy little face, his tiny little hands, and perfectly formed feet. "He's so small," I whisper as I stare at him in awe. I can't describe the things I'm feeling or regret taking Lori up on her offer to meet Bodhi even though this is going to tear my heart into shreds.

"He is underweight but not worryingly so, and all the other tests came back fine," Lori says, smiling as she leans against Travis and they watch me with my son.

"He's beautiful." I thought I would look at him and only see that bitch, but I see none of her in him. He is the spitting image of me as a baby. Lauren has a ton of baby pictures of me, and I asked her for the album this week. Of course, she thinks I'm getting emotional because of the impending birth of my other son, and it only adds to my guilt.

So much for acceptance. I have struggled to handle my emotions in the two weeks since Bodhi was born, and I've had to schedule extra therapy sessions with Craig to work through all my feelings.

"He truly is. Inside and out. He's the best little baby, and we couldn't be more in love with him."

I glance around the inviting living room of their new house. Baby stuff, blankets, and cuddly toys are littered around the room, and it gives off cozy family vibes. It warms my heart to know my son will grow up here with these people.

"Thank you," I whisper, lifting my head as I hold my son closer. "Thank you for doing this for him."

"Thank you, Reeve." Lori comes forward with tears in her eyes. "You cared when my sister didn't give a shit. You made the ultimate sacrifice to give him a good home, and I understand your motivations. I know what Viv means to you, but I see how hard this has been. You're a good man. Don't let anyone tell you differently because you made this choice."

I raise him to my chest and lower my head, inhaling the lavender smell emanating from his skin and feeling the warmth of his little body. I press a kiss to his soft brow. "Goodbye, my son. I love you very much, and I hope you have a lifetime of happiness with Lori and Travis. If you want to come find me when you're older, I promise I'll be there for you." I have already decided to tell Vivien about him at some point in the future. I cannot fathom carrying this secret in my heart until the day I die.

Tears leak from my eyes as I hand him to Lori. "Do you want to get a picture?" she asks, concern radiating from her gaze.

I shake my head. "Thank you for letting me see him, but it's best if I don't see him again. It will only make it harder." I can't tear my eyes from him as I pull the sealed envelope from my pocket. "If it would be okay with both of you, I'd like to write to him once a year. I wrote this the day after Christmas. When he is older, if he wants to know about me, maybe you can give them to him?" I wipe my damp eyes before extracting the other letter.

Lori's brow puckers when she sees the name Vivien written on the envelope. "Every year, when I send a letter for Bodhi, I'll send an updated one for Vivien. If anything should happen to me, I want to ensure she is there for you if you need any help. You can't just show up at her door without some proof. That letter will do it."

"Are you sure about this, Reeve? I can always go to Carson."

"You can, and that is your choice, but none of us knows what lies in store, and I want to prepare for all eventualities."

"You are mature beyond your years, Reeve."

Some days I feel ancient, like I've lived many lifetimes already. I have matured since everything went down, because I had to, but I don't fully agree with her sentiment. Some days, I still feel like a little kid who hasn't a clue what he's doing.

She takes both letters. "I will safekeep all your letters, and if you like, I could send you a letter in December too with an update of how he is doing."

I don't have to think about it for long. Even though it might hurt, I want to know how he's doing. "I would like that, thank you." I rummage through my bag, sitting on the coffee table, remove the soft toy, and hand it to her. "I hope it's okay I bought this for him."

"Of course. You can send gifts, Reeve. We meant what we said. We won't stand in your way if you want to be involved in his life."

"I appreciate it, but I think minimal involvement and contact is best."

"If you change your mind, you know where I am." She pats

me on the arm as the baby stirs, and that's my cue to leave. "If you ever need us, we're here."

"Thank you for everything and take care."

The months fly by in a whirlwind of activity. I'm filming *Euphoria*, and on days when I'm not working, I'm hanging out at Viv and Rey's place. Alex flies in once a month when the season finishes, and Audrey flies out to Boston to see him once a month, and they are making it work in a way Viv and I didn't.

Viv is showing now, and I think her days on campus are coming to an end, at least for this semester. She wants to finish her degree, and I have agreed not to book more than one or two projects next year so I can care for the baby while she attends classes. Lauren is dying to help out, and we can always hire a nanny if we need to, so we'll manage.

"Oh my God, quick, Reeve, come and feel this," Viv hollers from the bedroom the instant I return to the apartment laden down with the goodies she sent me to buy. Driving back took me twice as long since I picked up some paparazzi attention at the store. I needed to shake the guys so I didn't lead them directly to Viv. Interest in us is still crazy, and Viv has to wear layers of baggy clothes to disguise her bump. We want to protect our unborn child and keep the news out of the press until we are ready to reveal it.

I dump the bag on the counter and race to her room. "What's up?"

"Look." She wears the biggest smirk as she lies propped up on the bed with her back against the headboard and her swollen, bare tummy on full display. My eyes are out on stalks as I watch her stomach visibly move before a limb pushes upward, almost like it's trying to protrude.

"What the fuck?" I ask as her stomach deflates.

She grabs my hand. "He's trying to kick out of my stomach. He's been doing this for the past ten minutes. Wait." I watch her stomach moving in complete awe. It blows my mind to see this shit. It makes it all so real. To think that's our little boy in there, being nurtured by Viv, and he's growing big and strong. He'll be with us in nine short weeks, and I cannot wait. I physically tick the days off on a calendar every day and I'm growing more excited the closer we get to his birth. "There." She moves my hand over the raised part of her bump, and I feel his little limb pressing into my palm.

"Is it his foot?"

She shrugs. "Could be, or maybe it's his hand or his elbow?" Excitement is etched all over her face.

I dot kisses all over her stomach. "Hello, Easton. What are you up to in there, hmm?"

Viv and I chose his name together from a list we compiled over several weeks. We had it narrowed down to five, and we both like Easton the best. Easton Jonathon Lancaster is a solid name, and I cannot wait to meet him. "Are you that excited to meet us you're trying to come early?" I ponder as my hands roam Viv's warm stomach. "As much as we're excited to meet you, you've got to stay in there, buddy, and continue growing."

Vivien stares at me with tears in her eyes.

"What?" I ask as our little thrill seeker quiets down.

"I love how you talk to him and sing and read all the classics. If I wasn't already in love with you, that would do it."

I move up the bed so my head is on the pillow beside her. "I love him so much already. Like my heart feels fit to burst every time I think about him."

"Me too. I loved him from the moment I found out." Her fingers toy with my hair and I wish I could freeze-frame this perfect moment forever. "I think he's gone to sleep. At least it means a reprieve from the kicking for a while!"

"Maybe he's going to be a football player."

"Or a troublemaker." Viv winks.

My eyes lift to hers as my fingers glide over her taut skin. "I wonder where he gets that from, hmm?"

She giggles, and my heart soars into space. I sit up beside her and peck her lips. She's still holding me at arm's length, but kissing is generally okay. We've had sex since Christmas, but she hasn't let me stay the night, always careful to keep that boundary in place. "Love you," I say before nuzzling into her neck.

"Love you too." She turns slowly onto her side, resting her belly on the bed. "I spoke with the administration team today, and I'm switching to online classes starting next week." She drags her fingers through the stubble on my cheeks. "I'm going to move back home. Mom wants me close in the final stages."

I want her close, but I don't get to dictate this. However, I obviously give something away.

"I know you want me to move in with you. I know you're keen to make things official and I want that too, Reeve."

"Marry me," I blurt, and it's no surprise the words finally break free. I've only felt like asking her at least once a day.

Her face contorts, and I can read her like an open book.

She doesn't need to say *no* for me to understand that's her answer.

Chapter Fifty-Nine

Swinging my legs off the bed, I prop my elbows on my knees and rest my head in my hands. "I'm sorry, Reeve." The bed dips as she moves closer, circling her arms around me from behind. "It's too soon. We're not there yet, but I do love you, and I still want that one day."

I pull myself together and turn to face her. "I'm sorry I blurted it out. I'm just so freaking happy, Viv. This is everything I've ever wanted, and I want to make it official. It feels like I've been waiting forever."

"It will happen, babe." Her lips press to mine softly and sweetly. "I love you so much, Reeve. I have loved you my entire life, and these past few months have reminded me of all the reasons why. I'm hurting you, and I hate that, but can you be patient for just a little while longer?"

I take her hand and press a kiss to her palm. "Absolutely." I stand and smile. "Now, how about some chocolate ice cream and gherkins?"

She pats her chest. "You know the way to satisfy a woman."

"Not just any woman; only *you.*"

"Thank you for taking such good care of me. For coming to all the appointments and being so excited. I can't express how much it means to be doing this with you."

"You never have to thank me for that. It's what I want to be doing."

I shove the pain of her rejection aside as I head out to the kitchen to fix her gross snack, and then we watch TV in bed together. After, I rub her sore feet and massage oil into her stomach while spouting Shakespeare to our kid. Viv giggles like a lunatic, but she secretly loves it, like when I sing to our little boy. I walk to the kitchen to grab her a glass of water and her antacid medication before I prepare to leave.

"Would you stay?" she asks.

This is unexpected and probably a pity gesture, but I'm too greedy and pathetic to decline. "Of course."

She bites down on her lip. "Only if you want to."

I quirk a brow. "I always want that."

"Okay then." Her eyes light up.

I brush my teeth using her toothbrush and take a piss before washing my hands and staring at my reflection in the mirror.

Please let this baby be mine.

The thought slips out of the lockbox unbidden before I shove it back inside.

When did my life get so fucked up? With Saffron, I prayed for the baby to be any other guy's, and now I want it to be mine, and there's a slim chance it might not be. I said months ago I would give Viv the benefit of the doubt, and I have done that. It hasn't been hard. I haven't been this happy for years. We're both floating on a cloud and giddy for our new arrival. I truly don't think she would do this to me if she thought Easton wasn't mine. She is not cruel.

It's only sometimes at night, when I'm struggling to sleep, that some lingering niggles resurface. Mostly because she's still keeping distance between us, and it's honestly the only reason I can find as to why Viv keeps knocking me back, being that things are amazing. We laugh, smile, and hang out a lot, just like old times. I know she loves me because she tells me often. I know she wants me because I see the desire she tries to keep hidden on her face. We're having a baby, something we are both thrilled about. Something we have talked about growing up.

It's all coming together, so why is she holding back?

While I understand her need to get over that douche in her own time, and she needed time to learn to trust me again, I don't see how we still aren't there.

Unless she's holding back out of fear the baby could be his.

Nope. I splash water on my face and steady my resolve.

Easton is mine, and Viv is just being cautious with her heart.

I'm just feeling mopey because I stupidly blurted a proposal when neither of us was ready, but I won't read into it.

Viv loves me, and she wants to be with me.

I just need to channel more patience, and everything I crave will be mine.

I'm feeling more content as I leave the bathroom and return to my love. The only light in the room is a soft glow from the small bedside lamps. Viv is tucked up in bed, rubbing lotion into her arms as I shuck out of my clothes and climb into bed in my boxers. "I made you some chamomile tea unless you have your herbal remedy on you?"

"I don't carry it with me, but I'll be fine."

We drink our drinks in amicable silence until she breaks it. "How about a back massage? That might help you to relax."

"You don't have to do that." It might take me a while to fall asleep, but I already know it will be the best night's sleep I've had in ages because sleeping with Vivien is always the perfect remedy.

"I want to."

"Can you?" I ask, eyeing her considerable bump.

She swats me playfully. "I'm not incapacitated, dufus!" She threads her fingers through my hair as she peers deep into my eyes. "It might not be the greatest massage in the world, but I'm game to try." Bending down, she presses her lips over the heart-shaped tattoo on my chest. "Have I ever told you how much I love this?"

I fold my arms behind my head. "You know, I don't believe you have."

"Well, that was seriously remiss of me." She kisses the ink again, and I caution my dick to quiet down. I don't think he'll be getting any action tonight, and I'm A-okay with that. Getting to sleep beside her and hold her is more than enough. "I love it and you. Now turn over."

"Yes, bossy boots."

"You love when I boss you around."

"Everywhere but the bedroom," I remind her as I get into position.

"There's a first time for everything."

I chuckle as I lie down while she warms the oil in her hands, but I'm not laughing when she starts working it into my tense muscles. It's a little awkward for her with the bump, but she manages to knead the knots from my back and summon the snake in my pants. "Ugh, that feels so good."

"How good?"

"Very good. Extremely good."

"Hmm." There is movement on the bed, and a grunt rips from my lips when she reaches between my legs to cup my crotch. "Turn around," she commands. The bed dips up and down as she changes position, and when I flip around, she's sinking to her knees at the foot of the bed. "Take off your boxers and come here."

"You don't have to do that."

Her brows climb to her hairline. "This again?"

I chuckle but stay where I am. "You don't have to blow me, Viv. I'm okay."

"No, you're not, and I'm not doing it because of that. I'm doing it because you need the release and because *I love you*, Reeve, and I want to show you how much. Now quit arguing with me, and get your sexy, *naked* butt down here stat."

I do as I'm told and lean back as she works my cock with her mouth and her hand. Watching my very pregnant love pleasure me shoots my arousal to new levels, and it's not long before I'm coming in her mouth. "Damn, babe. I needed that."

"I could tell." I climb off the bed and help her to her feet, before guiding her back to bed.

"My turn?" I ask as I round the bed to get in on the other side.

"That was for you, and I'm too tired. This little trouble-maker kept me awake all last night."

I prop up on one elbow. "Are you sure?"

She tilts her head back to look up at me. "Yes, maybe in the morning."

"You got it." I kiss her passionately before moving to her tummy and kissing my baby. "Night, Easton. Don't keep your mom awake tonight." There's no movement, and I hope that means he's sleeping too.

We turn off our lights, and I spoon her from behind. Viv takes my hand and places it firmly on her stomach. "Reeve?" she whispers after a few minutes.

"I'm awake."

"Could we visit those sites you found? The ones for our dream home?"

A jolt pumps through my heart. "Why?"

"Because we need a home for our family, and I think we should start making plans now."

"You're kind of giving me mixed signals, babe."

"I don't mean to." She angles her head back to look at me, and I can just make out her features in the dark room. "I want to show you I'm committed to our future. I want you to know I choose you. No matter what, I want to be with you."

"Do you mean it?"

"With every beat of my heart."

Chapter Sixty

"I love it here," Viv says, standing in front of the large window of the cabin I rented for the weekend in Big Bear. While there is still snow on elevated ground, I didn't reserve a cabin near the slopes this time, choosing one with a stunning lakeside view. We didn't drive this weekend as I wanted to have a private jet on standby just in case Viv's water breaks early. Should anything happen, we can be at Cedars-Sinai in a little over an hour.

I finish unpacking the takeout we bought at the village and walk over to her, wrapping my arms around her from behind. To look at Vivien from behind, you would not know she is eight months pregnant because she's still slim. It's only when she turns around that you see her large, neat bump and realize she's got one in the oven. "Do you still want to buy a place here?" We talked about it in the past.

"Yes, but let's concentrate on our dream house first." She tilts her head back to look at me. "I presume there's been no news yet from the realtor?"

"Nope." I tweak her nose and hold her close. "I promise I'll tell you the instant I receive his call."

"I really hope we get it." Her eyes sparkle with an expectation that mirrors my own. "Imagine waking up to that view every morning?"

"It would be a dream come true."

We viewed ten different sites in the past few weeks, but we both fell in love with the plot on Mulholland Drive. It's only a ten-minute drive from North Beverly Park and less than thirty minutes from downtown L.A. and the studios, so the location is perfect.

Set off the iconic road, it has stunning views which encompasses the ocean, the city, and the Santa Monica mountain skyline. There is ample land to build our French château-style two-story dream home. I already have the architect plans. But we're requesting modifications, as Viv has a few changes she'd like to make.

It will be 9,300 square feet inside with formal and informal living rooms and dining rooms, a massive open-plan kitchen, a laundry room, a study, a library, a game room, a playroom, an indoor pool, a gymnasium, a theater room, five bedrooms, seven bathrooms, and a sunroom, along with copious balconies to enjoy the expansive views and glorious California weather.

Outside, we have a pool and terrace area, an outdoor kitchen, grill and dining area, and plenty of room to build a playground, treehouse, and obstacle course for Easton and his future siblings. Viv wants a garden with trees and shrubs and a rose garden, and I'm going to give it to her.

"I have a good feeling about it," she says, turning in my arms.

"Me too." I claim her lips in a tender kiss before taking her hand and leading her over to the table. "Take a seat, my love, and I'll serve dinner." I load her plate with a little bit of everything and pour her a glass of water before piling pasta, gnocchi, and pizza on another plate for me and grabbing a soda. We sit side by side at the table, eating in comfortable silence as we look through the window at the lake as nighttime slowly descends.

After, I run her a bath and leave her to soak while I clean up and set a fire. It's not super cold, but I want her toasty warm and comfortable.

We watch movies in front of the fire on the couch with Viv snuggled under my arm and a blanket tossed over our legs. We munch on snacks and talk about the nursery that is almost completed at Lauren and Jon's place.

I haven't shown Viv the nursery I've designed at my apartment yet because it's a surprise. It's been done in pastel colors with white furniture, and one wall has a large mural with owls, scarves, letters, scrolls, wands, books, and feathers dotted across the painting. It's a restful, calming space while indulging my inner child.

"You need to have a word with E," Viv says over a yawn as she smooths a hand over her bump. "He seems to have his routine all messed up. He's kicking like crazy right now when he should be sleeping."

I slide to the floor and cradle her bump in my hands. "Time for sleep, buddy. You're wearing your mom out." Viv is having difficulty sleeping, and she's been a little grouchy this past week. It's why I whisked her away here, hoping the change of scenery might help her to relax.

Movement glides across her stomach, and we both smile. "I think you might be right. We could have a troublemaker on our hands."

"I don't mind." Viv covers my hands with hers. "As long as he's healthy and happy."

I lean in and kiss her. "Love you."

"Love you too." A loud yawn rips from her lips, and I help

her up and tuck her into my side as I walk her to the mezzanine-level master bedroom.

Viv is fast asleep when I emerge from the bathroom a few minutes later. Despite her protests downstairs, I'm not surprised she's out for the count. I tired her out on purpose today. We went shopping and had lunch in the village before a game of mini golf, and we finished with a boat tour on the lake. Shucking out of my clothes, I crawl under the covers. Propping up on one elbow, I stare at her for a few moments, just drinking her in.

My entire world is in this bed, and I never want to lose sight of it again.

"Come with me." Viv extends her arm and waggles her brows as I sit on the couch, absently reading a book on parenting.

"You should be resting." She's three days overdue, and I'm on edge. The doctor has said everything is fine, and it's not unusual to go over with your first child, but I can't help worrying. I've been living at Viv's house since we returned from our weekend at Big Bear. Mostly sleeping in my old bedroom, but she lets me stay with her some nights. I don't mind as long as I am here. I have completely cleared my schedule so I can be hands-on when Easton makes his grand entrance.

"Resting is the last thing I want to do. I want to move around, to encourage our stubborn son to come out!"

I climb off the couch and rub her tense shoulders. "I think he's stubborn like his mother," I tease, and Lauren grins, looking over at us from the desk where she's working.

"I don't hold the monopoly on stubbornness, Reeve." Viv fixes me with a sharp look before whispering in my ear, "I read something online, and I want to try it."

"Color me intrigued," I whisper before kissing her.

She takes my hand and leads me out of the study and into the hallway. Jonathon approaches as we move toward the stairs.

"Hello, princess." He kisses Viv on both cheeks. "Any movement?"

"None, but we're working on it." She waggles her brows, and I almost choke on my tongue with the blatant insinuation. I'm even more intrigued now.

Jon closes his eyes briefly, and I'm guessing he's counting to ten in his head so he doesn't punch me. "I hear congratulations are in order."

"Yes." Vivien circles her arms around my neck. "We are now officially homeowners."

"Well, plot owners," I correct, snaking my arm around her back and keeping her close. "We've hired the same firm I commissioned to complete the architect drawings last year, to manage the build, and we're paying extra for a rush job."

"They're pulling a team together now and hiring a main contractor," Viv explains.

"They are hoping to break ground in August, and we're aiming to get the keys before Christmas."

"That's a lot of house to build in five months."

"We're hiring a lot of manpower, so it's built as quickly as possible."

"While not compromising on the quality," Vivien adds. "We've hired a project manager to oversee the build so it goes smoothly and safely."

"Well, good luck with it, and if you need anything, let us know."

"We will." Viv grabs my hand and pulls me upstairs.

"What are you up to, baby?" I purr as we walk hand in hand up the stairs.

"Apparently sex and spicy food work to bring on labor so I

want you to fuck me good and hard, Reeve. Pound this baby out of me."

"Fucking hell, Viv. I can't decide if I'm turned on or turned off."

She yanks me into her bedroom and strips as fast as a heavily pregnant woman can. We slide naked into bed with Vivien lying on her side. It's the only angle that is comfortable for her at this stage.

"It's going to work," she says, arching her head back to look at me. "I can feel it."

"Let's hope so. I'm so ready to meet him."

"Me too."

I kiss her slowly and passionately as my hands roam her body, and my dick hardens behind her back. I'm gentle with her nipples because her tits are extra sensitive, and I lay her flat on her back as I part her folds and lick her pussy. Viv would prefer me to be rougher, but I just can't do it. It goes against every protective instinct, so I take my time, gently coaxing an orgasm from her, and then I reposition her on her side and push inside her.

"You okay?" I ask as I thrust gently in and out.

"Peachy." She grabs my hand and kisses it. "You can go harder. I won't break."

"I don't want to hurt you, and I can't be rough with you right now." We had sex a few days ago, and it was a little painful for her, so I need to be gentle.

"It's not hurting. It feels good," she says as a hint of pain glides across her face and her stomach seems to tighten.

"That doesn't look like it feels good," I say, easing out of her.

"I'm fine," she pants, reaching her arm around to hook the back of my neck. "Please don't stop, Reeve. I want you to make love to me."

It's impossible to resist Viv when she pins me with those big Bambi eyes, so I inch back in and watch her carefully for any signs of distress, but she seems fine now. We kiss as I drive in and out of her, and when I feel she's close, I rub her clit and speed up my thrusts until she's coming over my dick and I'm shooting my cum inside her. After we take a bath together, she sits on the side of the bed while I comb her hair and suddenly her water breaks.

"Oh my God!" Viv stares between her legs at the liquid soaking the floor. "It worked!" Her eyes are glassy when she lifts them to meet my gaze. "It actually worked!"

"But did it?" I'm trying to remain calm as I quickly get dressed. "You were having contractions, weren't you?"

"No, I... shit, yes." She winces and clutches her stomach.

"You need to time them." I hand her my cell. "I'll grab some clothes and your bag." Viv has had it packed for weeks, and I'm grateful she is organized as it helps to keep my anxiety at bay. I pick a soft, pink maternity dress, a white cardigan, and silver pumps from Viv's closet and grab her bag.

"I haven't had another one," she says when I reemerge.

"Okay, that's good." I'm glad we did those classes now, and I'm not in a complete panic.

"Keep the timer on, and I'll help you to get dressed." Viv props the cell on her bedside table and drops the towel as I help her into her underwear and her clothes.

"Umph." She grabs onto my shoulder and leans forward, clearly in pain.

"Is that another one?"

She nods, and I check the timer on my cell. "Five minutes apart. I'll call Dr. Freeman, and then we'll go downstairs and tell your parents. They'll want to come with."

Chapter Sixty-One

"Congratulations, Daddy," the nurse says, lifting my newborn son into my arms. "He's beautiful, and although a little small for a full-term baby, he's absolutely perfect." I can hardly see through the tears blurring my vision as I cradle Easton to my chest. I burst into tears when his first cries rang out around the room, and Vivien and I were hugging one another, both crying tears of joy when the doctor laid him down on Viv's chest for a couple minutes before the medical team whisked him away to do the usual checks and tests. They are stitching Vivien up now, so I'm on dad duty.

"Hello, buddy." I rock him gently as I admire his perfectly formed features. "Welcome to the world." He's swaddled in a blanket, wearing a soft, blue hat on his head, hiding most of his dark hair. Pale blue eyes stare intently into mine, and my heart is swollen with so much love. I press a kiss to his warm cheek, marveling at how smooth and soft his skin is. "You're so tiny," I say, touching his delicate fingers. Breath stutters in my lungs when he grips my finger. My chest heaves as powerful emotion charges through me. Easton is staring up at me, blinking and studying my face, and his look is one of trust and innocence, and it blows me away.

The enormity of the responsibility smacks into me, and I take the seat beside Viv's bed in case my legs go out from under me.

She smiles at us with fresh tears in her eyes. "My boys. I love you so much." She blows us a kiss.

"Look at your beautiful mommy," I whisper to my son, angling him in my arms so Viv can see him. "She took care of you for nine months, and you owe her everything."

He stares at Vivien with the same intensity as the nurse finishes and fixes the covers over Viv before elevating the back of the bed.

I walk to the love of my life and carefully lay our son in her arms.

Viv sniffles. "Reeve, look at what we made. He's so perfect." A sob rips from her lips.

"You're perfect." I lean down and kiss her lips and then my son's brow. "You're a superstar, Viv. I don't know how you did that." It was a long ten-hour labor, and Viv was a fucking trooper. She didn't whine or scream or do any of those things you see on those horrific real-life birthing shows. My love is dignified even when in labor. "I'm so proud of you," I say as she coos at Easton, swaying him in her arms.

"I couldn't have done it without you." Her face shows signs of exhaustion, not surprising with the late hour, but she's bursting with happiness too. "I love you so much, Reeve, and I want to make lots more babies with you."

I perch on the edge of the bed, wrapping my arms around the love of my life and our son. "I'm down for that." I caress his soft cheek again. "It just hit me now how we are responsible for this tiny human. He can't do anything for himself, Viv. He's entirely reliant on us for his needs and—"

"It's scary," she finishes for me.

"I'm fucking terrified. What if we fuck up?"

She rests her head on my chest as we both stare adoringly at our son. "I'm sure we'll mess up a lot, Reeve, but we won't mess *him* up. We're going to be great parents." Confidence threads through her tone. "We'll learn as we go, and Mom will help."

"I should go get your parents and Audrey. If they're still awake." It's after four a.m. now, and they've been here all night.

"Wake them up if they are sleeping. They won't want to miss meeting their grandson." She worries her lip between her teeth. "Did your dad contact you?"

"Nope." I grind my teeth to the molars. I messaged him when we were en route to Cedars-Sinai and then again after Easton was born, and I have heard nothing. "He's an as—A-S-S-H-O-L-E."

Vivien attempts to smother her smile. "We've known that since we were kids, and you don't need to spell it out. Pretty sure E doesn't know what it means."

"I don't want to corrupt his innocent ears."

"Oh, Reeve." She beams up at me. "I do love you so."

"We made a baby, Viv. Look at him. Look at how incredible he is."

We both stare at him in awe. "He looks just like you in your baby pictures, and I'm not even one bit unhappy about it." Tears wrack her body, and I take Easton from her. "It's okay, Viv." Her hormones are obviously still going crazy. "Don't cry, babe."

"I'm just so freaking happy right now."

"Me too. Not even my dad can ruin this moment."

"Screw Simon. You don't need him. You have your own family now."

I circle my arm around Viv just as an anguished wail

escapes Easton's mouth, followed by more cries. The nurse approaches with a wide smile. "I think someone is hungry."

I hand Easton back to Vivien as the nurse helps her to breastfeed for the first time and I go out to get Lauren and Jon.

Lauren is fast asleep with her head on Jon's lap and her legs up on the couch when I enter the private waiting room. Audrey is dozing in the armchair by the window. Jon's drowsy eyelids perk up when he sees me.

"You have a grandson," I tell him. "And he's perfect."

"Where is he?" Lauren says in a sleep-drenched tone, swinging her legs to the floor before her eyes have even opened. "Take me to my grandbaby."

"Me too." Audrey gets to her feet and rushes me. "Congrats, Reeve. How is Viv?"

"She's doing great, and she's asking for you."

Vivien is feeding Easton a bottle when we return, and I wonder what happened to the breastfeeding. Maybe she didn't want to do it in front of her parents and best friend, or she could just be too tired. "Hey, Mom, Dad, Audrey." She grins at her parents. "Come say hi to your new grandson."

"Oh, Vivien." Lauren clasps a hand to her chest. "Look how beautiful he is." She leans back on her husband as they smile at our son while he greedily sucks the formula milk. "Look, Jon, isn't he beautiful?"

Audrey peeks over Lauren's shoulder, swiping at the tears leaking from her eyes. "He's the most beautiful baby I've ever seen."

"I totally agree." Jon leans down. "Hello there, little guy. Welcome to the family."

Lauren sniffles as she gives Viv an awkward one-armed hug. "I'm so happy for both of you." She pulls me into a hug. "Congratulations, Reeve."

Emotion consumes me, and I can only nod. Audrey leans into my side, squeezing my arm.

"He looks so much like you too. Doesn't he, Jon? It's like seeing Reeve for the first time all over again."

When I saw Easton for the first time, I instantly knew he was mine, and the stress I didn't realize I'd subconsciously carried lifted from my shoulders. There was never anything to worry about, and I was right to trust Viv.

"That's what I said." Vivien's grin is out of control, but her eyes are welling up again. She and Audrey exchange a look.

"Can I feed him?" Lauren asks, unable to wait any longer to get her hands on her grandson.

"Any time, Mom."

"Why don't you sit down, and I'll hand him over to you," I suggest, chuckling as Lauren races around the bed to claim the chair before anyone else does. Viv holds the bottle to his tiny mouth as I lift him into my arms before passing him to his grandma. Then I whip out my cell to take a few pics of a besotted Lauren Mills and circle my arm around my girl.

Life doesn't get better than this.

I live at Lauren and Jon's for the next couple of weeks as Viv and I get used to this parenting lark, and it's honestly two of the best weeks of my life. I am obsessed with my son. I can't stop looking at him. Holding him. Touching him. At night, when he's asleep in his crib, Viv and I stare at him for ages, both of us reluctant to leave him for any length of time.

I get up to do the night feedings so Viv can rest. She's doing online exams, and I'm trying to do as much of the heavy lifting as possible. Viv wanted to breastfeed, but it would have put too much additional stress on her with the exams, so our son is being formula-fed. He's thriving and already putting on weight.

In the middle of the night, after I've fed him, he falls asleep on my chest, and I enjoy those special moments when it's just me and my boy bonding. I force myself to put him back in his crib, because I could stay all night in the recliner chair with him snuggled against my chest.

"Our little prince is asleep," I say, entering the living room and flopping down on the couch beside Viv. Lauren and Jon tend to use the other living room at night so we have privacy, and I appreciate it. Everything is centered around Easton right now, and I don't want to neglect our relationship.

"You're amazing." Viv turns to me on the couch, handing me a glass of champagne.

I arch a brow. "What are we celebrating? Besides the obvious."

"I finished my exams, and I have the entire summer off." She bites on the corner of her lip in an obvious tell.

"And?" I cajole, taking a sip of the champagne.

"And." She gulps, tucking herself into my side. Her eyes probe my face, and her expression is full of love, and it's like a balm to my soul. I never gave up on her, on us, and I'm glad I fought back because what we have is worth fighting for and then some. "And I'm ready." The words rush from her mouth as she levels me with a look, urging me to get the meaning behind them.

"Are you sure?"

"I have never been surer. I'm yours, Reeve." She takes the flute from my hand and places it on the end table. "I'm sorry I made you wait, but I wanted to ensure we weren't rushing things. That we were taking the necessary steps to repair our relationship the right way. I didn't want to make this about Easton because it had to be about you and me. I needed to trust you again, and I do. You have more than proven yourself to me these past ten months." She crawls into my lap. "You're my Reeve again. The boy I have adored since the dawn of time."

My hands land on her hips as her hands suction to my chest. "I love you for now and forever, Reeve Elon Lancaster, and I want to officially be yours and you to be officially mine. I want us to be a true family. I want everything with you."

I grab her face and kiss her gorgeous mouth, and my heart is beating wildly in my chest. I hold her face as I worship her lips before forcing myself to break away. "Do you mean what I think you mean?"

She vigorously nods. "Ask me, babe. Ask me again."

"Now?" I have plans for a big elaborate proposal in front of the Eiffel Tower.

"Now. I don't want to wait any longer for our forever."

I lift her off my lap and set her down on the couch. "Hold that thought. I'll be right back."

I race up the stairs to our bedroom, tiptoeing into the room carefully so I don't wake our precious bundle of joy. I grab the box from my duffel bag, grateful I had the foresight to bring it with me. Maybe I had a sixth sense despite my plans.

My heart is doing somersaults as I run back downstairs and race into the living room, almost skidding on the hardwood floor in my socks. I'm a little breathless as I round the couch and sink to one knee before Viv. Her eyes swim with joy as I take her hand and gaze into her gorgeous hazel eyes.

"I wanted to do this differently, and I planned to take you to Paris to propose, but I'm not wasting the opportunity because it feels like I've waited a century to do this. I love you, Vivien Grace Mills. I have loved you from the moment you opened your pretty eyes in this world, but I just didn't know it yet."

I pause for a second, swallowing thickly over the lump in

my throat. "My entire life, you are all I have seen. You have been my best friend, my lover, my closest confidante, my cheerleader, my shoulder to cry on, and the mother of my son. The very best part of me comes from loving you, and now the very best parts of us exist in Easton. You have given me many things, my love, but the gift of our son is the greatest gift of all."

I lift the lid on the ring box, and her eyes pop wide. She was probably expecting it to be the same ring as the one I first proposed with, but I couldn't keep that one after everything that happened. I returned it and exchanged it for this three-carat pear-shaped diamond engagement ring with tapered baguette side stones and a platinum band. It's a different design and style ring but every bit as classic and elegant as the first one. I hope she likes it, but if she doesn't, we can return it and she can pick a ring herself.

I clear my throat and try to steady my nerves. "You have always been my family, Vivien, but now I want to make it official. Please do me the honor of marrying me. Will you be my wife?"

Happy tears stream down her face. "Yes, Reeve." Her voice projects confidence, and I'm silently fist pumping the air. "Yes, I will marry you. Nothing would make me happier or prouder, and I can't wait to be your wife."

Chapter Sixty-Two

Our wedding day is the second most perfect day of my life after Easton's birth. Neither of us wants to wait, so here we are, about to enter the grand ballroom of the best five-star hotel in L.A. as Mr. and Mrs. Lancaster only two months after she finally said yes when I proposed.

Vivien is resplendent in a custom Dior lace wedding dress with a low back and a small train. She considered making her own gown, but it was too much pressure when we have a newborn, we're building a house, and we wanted to get married quick. Looking at her sleek silhouette, you would never guess she only gave birth eleven weeks ago. "I love you, Mrs. Lancaster," I say, leaning in to kiss her lips. "I'm the luckiest man alive because you're the most gorgeous woman in the world."

I can't stop looking at her today, and I can't stop touching her. Our private wedding ceremony at the chapel was small, just for immediate family and friends. Audrey was Viv's bridesmaid, and Alex was my best man. Lauren and Jon were there, as was Simon. It was fifty-fifty if he would show, and I wouldn't be surprised if he's not in the large crowd waiting behind these ballroom doors for the wedding dinner and party.

Easton gurgles in my arms, and Viv's expression melts. "He's definitely saying ah-ah." She dots a kiss on his brow. "Aren't you, cutie?"

He smiles at his mom and we're both mesmerized, like always. I swear, every time he does something new, we both act like he's the only kid in the world to ever do it. We already have tons of photos, and Viv started a book where she's recording all the key moments. Last week, she noted he made the "ah-ah" sound for the first time.

I've been in love with Vivien my entire life, and it's always been this big, intense love, the kind you read about in books and think isn't real. But it pales in comparison to how I feel about her now she's a mom. Watching her with our son intensifies my love to an unprecedented level. She's incredible and such a natural, and I can't wait to have more kids with her.

"I'm so lucky you're mine, and I'm so incredibly in love with you," I tell her while the hotel manager waits patiently for us to give him the nod to open the doors.

"Romantic Reeve was always my favorite, but Daddy Reeve trumps him every time."

The manager fights a smile, and I press my lips to her ear. "Not sure you should be admitting your kink in public, wifey. Unless you want it splashed all over social media tomorrow." Viv read some steamy romance novel last week that introduced both of us to Daddy kink. I'm not opposed to role-playing in the bedroom, and I'm encouraging her to read all the romance books for inspiration.

"Oh my God." Her cheeks stain pink. "You know I didn't mean it like that."

"Babe, it's fine." I wrap my arm around her and waggle my

brows. "You can call me Daddy in the bedroom any time you like."

The manager is fighting a losing battle with his mouth, and Viv notices. "I didn't mean it like that! I swear!" she says, looking directly at him.

"Relax. He signed an NDA. All the staff did, and the hotel is empty of guests who aren't wedding guests, and all of those signed NDAs too." I slide my hand down and squeeze her lush ass. "I'm just teasing." My lips twitch. "But I'm totally cool with the Daddy part."

"Reeve."

I chuckle as Easton wriggles in my arms. "I think we should get this show on the road before my little milk monster decides he's hungry again." Easton is insatiable and hungry all the time. He's put on enough weight to bring him up to his peers, and the pediatrician is pleased with his progress.

Vivien nods at the manager, and I hold her close to one side as I cradle our son.

The doors open, and the crowd cheers as we are announced into the room. The space is packed with friends and extended family members, as well as some industry heads and friends of Lauren and Jon, and my dad. Margaret is here as is Edwin.

He negotiated and coordinated an exclusive wedding feature with *Vogue* magazine and our photographer has already sent the editor a select number of shots to be included in the feature, which is being published the day after tomorrow. The interview was conducted a few weeks ago, and we've already approved the editorial.

To keep Federico happy, I tipped him off about the location of my bachelor party, and he got the scoop. So far, my relationship with the photographer is reaping benefits. It's satisfactory denying the predatory paps the money shots they're craving.

The party lasts until the early hours of the morning.

Lauren and Jon relieved the babysitter at midnight. The woman was thoroughly vetted, and Bobby and Leon were in the hotel room the entire time. You can never be too safe when it comes to children. Kidnapping threats are a genuine concern in celebrity circles. Devin provided the security today, and everything went off without a hitch.

"Husband, come dance with me," Viv says, throwing her arms around me from behind as I sit at a table with a few of the guys. "I've missed you."

Alex and Nate chuckle. Nate and I buried the hatchet a few months ago, and he's here with his fiancée and a bunch of our old schoolmates.

"I see you two are as sickening as ever," Nate drawls, and Viv flips him the middle finger.

"I've got two words for you," Audrey says, slurring her words a little as she jabs her finger in Nate's direction. "Pot. Kettle. Black."

Viv sinks into my lap and circles her arms around my shoulders, giggling at her best friend.

"Babe, that's three words." Alex grins.

"Oh shit, yeah." Rey giggles. "Oops."

"No more champagne for you." Alex stands and wraps his arms around her.

"I'm just so freaking happy!" Rey flings her arms in the air and shimmies her hips. "Our best friends are married; our godson is the cutest fucking baby ever; we're back together; Nate's stopped being a douche, and everything is right with the world!"

We're all laughing as we make our way onto the dance floor to catch the last few songs before the DJ calls it a night.

"Happy, babe?" I ask as I twirl Vivien around the dance floor.

"Ecstatically happy." She rubs her nose against mine.

"You're my husband." A wide grin spreads over her gorgeous mouth. "I just love saying that."

"I know." I hold her tighter, my hands moving lower on the bare skin of her back. "I've been calling you my wife all night, any time I get the opportunity." I lean in and nip her earlobe with my teeth. "But what I'm really looking forward to is making love to my wife for the first time. What do you say, baby? Ready to ditch this party and start a private one upstairs?"

"I'm ready. I thought you'd never ask." She grinds her hips against mine, and I curse under my breath as all the blood in my body instantly rushes south. I swear Vivien just has to breathe on me and I get hard.

"Say your goodbyes and be quick." I tap her ass and smother a chuckle. "Daddy Reeve is dying to play with Mommy."

Chapter Sixty-Three

The next year flies by in a whirlwind of activity. Christmas comes and goes, although we're not in our dream house yet. The building work is finally finished in April, and we move in in time to celebrate Easton's birthday. He turned one on May fifth, and we throw him a big birthday party. Vivien completes her senior year and graduates with an honors degree, and then we leave for Italy. We rent a gorgeous house on the Amalfi Coast for the duration of filming, and Easton is a bona fide water baby by the time we return to L.A. in late August. We love Italy so much we return the next year and buy a stunning cliffside house with an infinity pool. Audrey and Alex come out for two weeks, and Lauren and Jon spend the entire month of July with us.

When we return home, Viv decides she wants to find some part-time work. She loves being home with Easton, but she doesn't want to let her degree go to waste. I'm happy for her to do whatever she wants, and I'll always support her.

Together, we interview for a nanny and hire Angela after passing on at least twenty others. Viv gets offered a part-time permanent role with a leading production company, but after much discussion, she turns it down in favor of going freelance. It's not long before she's hired to work on an adaptation for Netflix, and after that, they send her regular work along with a few other clients.

Working freelance suits Viv because she can choose her own hours and work from home most of the time. As long as she meets her deadlines and attends the odd few meetings in person, her clients are happy. It means she's at the house when Angela is taking care of Easton, and that's important to my wife.

Another couple years pass by, and I'm home more regularly since I'm at the stage in my career where I can pick and choose projects. I won't book more than three projects per year, and I always ensure to slot them around family time. Viv and I plan our work commitments together around family life, and we never take each other for granted.

In a way, losing one another as we did was good for our relationship. We know what it's like to live without one another, and we're more protective of our relationship and our family time. We're also more respectful of one another, and we have the kind of setup a lot of other couples only dream about.

Mostly, I try to pick roles that won't take me too far from home so I'm not absent for long periods like I was when I was filming the Rydeville movies. Long separations aren't good for any of us, and I refuse to put my family through that again. Exceptions are made on occasion for a passion project, and then we work it so Viv and Easton come and visit me. The beauty of Vivien's work is she can do it from anywhere, which is handy.

Easton turns four in May, just before I head to Portland to film a movie with Jim Cameron. I negotiated time off for four weekends during the nine-week shoot, and I fly home to be with Viv and Easton. When the movie wraps in early August, I return home just in time for Easton to start pre-kindergarten. Vivien and I take him together on his first day, and it's a little bittersweet because it's Bodhi's first day at school too.

"Daddy," Easton says, from the back seat as I drive out through our gates and onto Mulholland Drive. Bobby and Leon are in the SUV behind us. One addition we made to our architect plans was the installation of a house for the security team. We now employ a team of eight bodyguards, and they rotate shifts and alternate between days and nights. We also installed a high-level security system with cameras all over the exterior of the property and panic buttons inside the house. On top of the tall walls bordering our property are high-tech sensors that send a text alert to security if anyone tries to climb over it. A fully stocked panic room is housed in our basement.

After the shit Vivien endured at the hands of trolls and so-called fans of mine years ago, I want only the best protection for her. There are still some idiots that hate I married her and not that bitch.

"Yes, buddy." I eye my son through the mirror.

"What was the name of your teacher when you started school?" Easton asks.

"Ugh." I scramble to remember. I was only four or five, and even if I could remember that far back, I purposely blanked a lot of stuff from my mind.

"Mrs. Pitson," Vivien says without hesitation.

"How do you remember that?"

"How do you not?! She had purple hair and blue-framed glasses, and she called everyone sweetie pie, and her breath always smelled like sickly sweet air freshener."

I stare at my wife with my mouth open. "You're not human," I tease.

She shrugs, smiling as I round the next bend and head

toward the junction. "You have a photographic memory for learning lines, and I'm good at remembering teachers."

"I hope my teacher has purples hair and she smells like freshener."

"It's purple, E," Vivien corrects, "and I doubt Mrs. Pitson still teaches at Blackrock Kindergarten, but if she does, and she's your teacher you can tell her your mommy and daddy say hi."

"I hope I meet my wife at school," Easton adds a few beats later, and Viv and I share a goofy grin.

"You do, huh?"

"Like father, like son," Viv whispers while grinning.

"Yep, and she's gonna be buuutiful like Mom."

"Hate to break it to you, buddy, but there is no one else in this world as beautiful as your mom. She's one of a kind."

Vivien looks at me like she wants to strip me naked and bounce on my cock. I'd be more than happy with that plan if we didn't have an inquisitive kid in the back and it wouldn't be wholly inappropriate.

"And there she goes again." Easton sighs, shaking his head as he looks out the window.

My lips kick up at the corner. This boy slays me in all the best ways. He's got so much personality already. I get a lump in my throat whenever I'm with him or thinking about him because he makes me so goddamn proud to be his dad.

"Want to explain that one, E?" Viv turns around to look at our son with amusement in her eyes.

"You made that kissy face at Daddy again. It's gross."

I bark out a laugh as I take the exit and turn down the road toward the school. "I hate to break it to you, buddy, but if you want a wife, you've got to kiss her."

"And it's not gross, it's nice," Vivien says. "But you should save your kisses until you're older and keep them for the right girl."

"I'm not kissing anyone except Mommy 'cause I love her."

Vivien practically melts into the seat, and I get it. Easton has a way of plucking our heartstrings without even trying. "Ditto, buddy." I squeeze Viv's hand.

I live for these moments.

This is what's important in life.

Easton's face pulls into a grimace. "I've changed my mind. I don't want to meet my wife today."

I pull through the school gates and park in the rear parking lot. It's busy, and almost every space is full.

Vivien climbs out her side, taking Easton's bag while I unstrap our son from his highbacked booster seat. The security car pulls into the spot beside us. "It's okay to be nervous," I tell him as I watch him looking left, right, and all around. "I was really nervous my first day of school, but it was cool. I had fun, and I bet you will too." Only because Vivien was there. I was really shy when I was a young kid, and Vivien was my lifeline. I remember how she made the teacher—Mrs. Pitson as I've just been reliably informed—seat us together, and she held my hand under the table until it stopped shaking.

"Don't be silly, Daddy." Easton climbs down and takes my hand. "I'm not nervous, and I'm going to have fun. Oh, look! There's Lewis. From summer camp. He's gonna be my best friend. Lewis!" Easton hollers, and I grip his hand tight as he tries to run off across the parking lot to his friend.

Bobby chuckles and Leon smiles. They adore Easton, and they're really good with him.

"Easton!" Lewis shouts back, and it looks like his friend's mom is having difficulty keeping a hold of her son too.

"E, you can meet Lewis at the entrance. You can't go

running off across the parking lot. It's dangerous with so many cars around."

"Okay, Mom." He lifts his free hand to take Vivien's as I swipe my son's bag from my wife. "Let's go." He lifts his head. "Hey, Bobby. Hey, Leon. Today's my first day at school." He puffs out his chest, and he looks so fucking adorable in his little uniform. My chest hums with pride.

"Awesome, little dude." Bobby lifts his fist for a knuckle touch, and Easton eagerly obliges.

"Have the best day, Easton." Leon high-fives my son, and then Easton practically drags us to the front door. The instant he sees Lewis, he takes off, and we let him go this time because it's safe.

Oh, to be that enthusiastic and confident at four years of age. He might be my mini-me in physical looks, but he definitely takes more after Vivien in personality.

"Easton!" Vivien calls after him, running to catch up before he disappears inside the school. "Hold up, buster. We need to take you inside."

"And you forgot this," I add, holding up his bag.

"Okay, come on, come on. We want to see if we're in the same class." The boys loop arms and charge through the doors with us hot on their heels. I take Vivien's hand, ignoring the odd cursory looks coming from a few of the parents. This is a private school, and you need to be well-connected to get in. Most of these people are wealthy and successful, and they aren't all that concerned with celebrity, but there are always a few nosy fuckers.

"Hi, Amy," Vivien says, smiling at Lewis's mother.

"Vivien, it's good to see you." Her eyes dart briefly to mine.

"This is my husband, Reeve."

"Nice to meet you," I say while keeping one eye on the boys in front of us.

"It's nice to meet you too. I believe you know my ex-husband and Lewis's father, Ken Cooper?"

"I know Ken, though we haven't spoken in years. He's a good man."

"We'll agree to disagree." Her mouth pulls into a grimace, and I'm not touching that.

"Easton was asking if Lewis would like to come over for a playdate this week," Viv says, riding to the rescue. "Is there a day that would suit you?"

I zone them out while they make arrangements. Mention of Ken brings back memories of Rydeville Elite and that bitch, and my mind automatically wanders to Bodhi. He's starting pre-kindergarten at a private school in San Jose today because Lori mentioned it in her December letter. She has kept to her word just as I have, and I send her letters and gifts every December. It's the one time of the year when I allow myself to think about my other son for more than fleeting minutes.

Lori said Bodhi didn't speak until he was three, and then he had a slight speech impediment. Doctors said it might be attributable to the shit that bitch put into her body while carrying him. He attended speech therapy for a year, and he speaks fine now. Though she said he's a quiet boy, and he doesn't naturally talk a lot. He sounds a lot like me at that age, and he looks a lot like me too.

Lori encloses a photo with her letter every year, and it's hard sometimes to look at Bodhi and not feel bad for denying Easton and him the opportunity to be brothers. They look so much alike they could pass for twins.

Thankfully, Saffron has no interest in him, and she has never seen him. She's a full-blown addict now, and her Hollywood career is long over. Her new porn career doesn't count. It's good to see karma catching up to her, but I hope Bodhi never wants to know who his bio Mom is because that shit would hurt.

"Reeve." Vivien calls me from the door to the classroom, and I snap out of it, realizing I had just stopped in the hallway.

I stride toward her and smile, ignoring Amy's curious stare. "Are the boys in the same class?"

"They are," Amy says, smiling. "I'm glad. Lewis struggles to make friends, and he likes Easton a lot. I was hoping they would be put together."

I chuckle as I watch Easton offer his hand to his new teacher—not Mrs. Pitson—and I can tell he's made an instant fan by the way she smiles warmly at him. It's hard not to like our kid because he's amazing, and I'm not saying it 'cause I'm biased. It's the truth. We couldn't have asked for a better son. Easton is a bright, inquisitive, confident child, but he's very mannerly, and he hasn't given us any trouble. It's a joy to be his father, and I love him more than I can say.

We put his bag in his cubby, place some supplies on his desk, and then make our goodbyes. Lots of the kids are crying and clinging to their parents, but Easton waves us off without a shred of concern, and it's Vivien who's wiping at her eyes as we leave.

We say goodbye to Amy at the front door, and then I take Vivien's hand, and we stroll leisurely toward our car. Bobby and Leon fall into step behind us. "We're raising an amazing kid," I say, lifting our joined hands and kissing her knuckles.

"I'm not sure we can take much credit." Vivien leans into my side. "He's just naturally outgoing, confident, and kind. He makes me so proud."

Her voice cracks, and I circle my arm around her shoulders and keep her tucked into my side, ignoring the few side-eyes we're picking up. You'd swear they'd never seen a celebrity before, which is bullshit in L.A. "I am so incredibly proud of him. Being his dad is an honor, and you're an awesome mother. We're totally taking some of the credit."

Viv smiles.

"That kid is gonna rule the world someday," I say.

"I wouldn't be surprised in the least if he did," my wife agrees.

Chapter Sixty-Four
Now - Age 25

"What are you up to?" Vivien asks, looking over her shoulder at me as she finishes drying her hair.

"Who says I'm up to anything?" I tease, arching a brow as I fit my cufflinks into the cuffs of my dress shirt.

"You haven't stopped staring at me, and I see that twinkle in your eye, Reeve, but we don't have time. Our guests will be here shortly, and E is probably hyped up on sugar and driving poor Charlotte insane." Except for a skeleton security staff, we send everyone else home at Christmas. This year, our house-keeper-slash-lifesaver asked if she could stick around, so Charlotte is joining us for dinner.

"What if I want to give you an extra Christmas gift." I walk toward her as she gets up from her dressing table, tying the belt on her silk robe tighter. As if that would stop me.

"You have already spoiled me too much." We were up at the crack of dawn with Easton, and after he opened all his gifts, we exchanged ours. I did go overboard this year with jewelry, rare collector's edition books, La Perla lingerie, salon vouchers, a private table with a personalized menu at her favorite restaurant, a box full of various dressmaking materials for her to create to her heart's desire, and a surprise trip to the Seychelles in the new year.

I also bought her a Lamborghini Spyder, but I haven't shown her it yet. It's possible she'll kill me because we already have seven cars in the garage between us, but what good is earning all this money if I'm not spoiling the people I love? Besides, her other two vehicles are SUVs, and I want her to have something nonpractical. Something that will indulge her love of cars.

I love spoiling my wife, and nothing will stop me from giving her this last gift. I need it, and I need to feel close to her. These past few weeks have been trying, and I've been attacking Viv like a horny teenager who's just discovered his dick. I've been fucking her twice daily for weeks, and it reminds me of those early years as teenagers exploring sex when we were greedy for one another and obsessed with that pleasurable high.

"Reeve?" Concern is etched upon her face as she grips my arms. "You spaced out." She runs her hand up and down my arm. "You've been doing that a lot lately. Is everything okay? Do you have something on your mind?"

Yes. But we're not going there today.

"I'm fine, babe. I just zoned out. It's known to happen when I've had about three hours of sleep."

"God, I relate. Every year, it's like E wakes up earlier. It'll be a miracle if I don't fall into my dinner by the time we're all seated."

"We should have organized caterers," I say, reeling her into my arms.

"Never." She shakes her head as my hand glides down her back toward her shapely ass. "Mom always cooked on Christmas Day, and I'm continuing the tradition." Her fingers wind around the nape of my neck. "Is it Simon? Is he fucking with your head again?"

"No more than usual," I admit, squeezing her ass in both hands.

"Fuck him if he's a no-show. He makes no effort with his grandson, and E barely knows him. If it was up to me, I'd cut him out of our lives completely, but he's not my father."

This isn't the first time she's made the suggestion. Viv hates how he toys with my emotions, and she wishes what he thinks didn't matter to me so much. I do too. I want to cut him out because the way he virtually ignores my son irritates me to no end, but E doesn't care. He adores his grandpa Jon, and he doesn't need Simon.

When I was in therapy years ago, I spoke to Craig at length about my relationship with my father, and it's complicated. He is a shit dad, a shit father-in-law, and a shit grandparent, but he's the only parent I've got. It might seem silly, but I think my mom would be upset if I gave up on him. Which is ridiculous because I never knew her to know whether she'd be upset or not, and she's not here to criticize.

But I can't help how I feel.

No matter how often he disappoints me, I still can't cut him out completely. There have been times he has come through for me, and I like to believe that, deep down, he does care but just can't show it.

"I don't give a fuck whether Simon shows up or not, and we're not talking about him today." I grab her ass and pull her in flush. "There is time for one more gift, and don't deny me what I need."

Her face shines with unadulterated love. "I love you so much, Reeve. You make me so happy. I hope you know that."

"I do, and you make me insanely happy as well. The only thing that would make me happier is another bun in your oven." I place my hand over her flat stomach. "But I'm sure it'll happen in the new year." She's been off birth control for four months, and I was hoping we'd be pregnant by Christmas.

She averts her eyes and links her fingers in mine. "About this extra gift?" She pins me with a flirty smile that does twisty things to my stomach even after all these years.

"Lose the robe, get on the bed, and spread those pretty legs for me, baby. I'm about to rock your world."

Ensuring the door is locked, I eat her out in record time, and then I fuck her against the wall like a man possessed.

"Wait for it, E!" Alex calls, preparing to throw the ball to my son as the three of us play in the rear garden after dinner. The girls have gone for a walk, and Jon is helping Charlotte finish the cleanup. Alex and I had to take Mr. Impatient outside to let him run off some of his sugar high.

"Yay!" Easton whoops. "Look, Daddy! I caught it this time."

"Great job, buddy."

"Must be your coach." Alex puffs out his chest, and I chuckle. Alex teaches at a high school in Boston, and he seems happy, but I'm gutted he didn't get to fulfil his NFL dream.

I can't wait until our friends move home to L.A. next year. They've been in Boston for years, and I've missed having them close by. They got married last year, and Alex is itching to try for kids as soon as Rey finishes her medical studies. It's been a long road, but she'll be a fully qualified doctor next year.

She doesn't know this—neither of them does—but I bought her a modern office building downtown. I thought maybe she could use it as a base for her medical practice when they return home. Of course, if she doesn't want it, she can just sell it or do whatever the hell she wants with it. It's a gift for her to use however she sees fit.

"When you move here, will you be my coach?" Easton asks, throwing the ball back to my best buddy and his godfather.

"Absolutely, little dude."

"Yay!" Easton jumps up and down, and I smile at his enthusiasm.

Most Christmases, it's enough to yank me from my head, but not this year. This year, things are different. They have been since I went to the toy store to buy identical superhero gifts for both of my sons and had an epiphany.

I'm denying Bodhi and Easton the opportunity to be brothers, and I can't live with it any longer.

Lori's annual letter cemented the sentiment. That prick Travis had an affair, and he divorced Lori and left her and Bodhi behind to move to the UK, where he's already married to this other woman, and she's expecting a child.

"Dad, catch!" Easton yells, pulling me from my inner monologue, and I move in time to catch the ball. We throw it back and forth for a while, until the women return. After placing Easton on my shoulders, we head back inside to play board games. Then Alex, Jon, and I play Nerf wars with Easton, racing up and down the hallways, ducking and diving into rooms, as we fire at one another.

"Gotcha, Daddy." Easton points his gun at me when I enter the game room where I knew he was hiding.

I hold up my hands. "Don't shoot. I surrender."

Three foam bullets pop at my chest, and I dive at my son, scooping him up and throwing him over my shoulders. "You're going to pay for that, buddy." I fling him on the couch and tickle him all over as he shouts and giggles and tries to worm away.

"Enough. I render!" he says, and I take pity on him.

"Let's call it quits." I bundle him into my arms, pressing kisses to his hair and holding him tight. Feeling close to him usually helps to assuage my grief, but today it's an extra reminder of all I'm missing.

"Daddy?"

"What's up?" I brush his messy hair back off his brow.

He looks up at me with his big trusting eyes, and my heart melts. "Was I really naughty this year?"

My brow puckers, wondering where this is coming from. "Not at all. Why'd you ask?"

"'Cause Santa didn't bring me the one thing I really, really want."

I mentally flip through his Santa list, and I can't think of anything we forgot to buy.

"Is it because I asked him in my head instead of putting it on my list? 'Cause I forgot to add it, and Mom says I can talk to Holy God in my head and he'll hear me, so I thought Santa would too."

"What did you ask for?"

"A brother."

My heart stutters behind my chest.

"Or a sister. I don't mind." He shrugs his little shoulders. "I just want a brother or a sister. Do you think if I give him back all my toys he'll give me one instead?"

Fuck me. How the hell can I answer that? Vivien is normally the one to have these conversations with him because I never know the right thing to say.

"It's not about being naughty, and Santa can't bring you a brother or sister. It's down to God and me and your mom, and I promise you will have a sibling. You just need to be patient. Can you do that?"

His cute little brow creases. "If I have to." He pouts. "But how is it up to you and Mommy? I don't ur-stand."

Where is Vivien when I need her? "Go ask Mommy. She'll explain."

"Okay." He jumps up off my lap and runs out of the room, almost knocking over the table in his haste to get to Vivien.

A sad smile crests over my face. The irony is I could give him a brother tomorrow. I lean back on the couch and sigh, dragging my hands down my tired face. My insomnia has been raging as badly as ever this month, and it's all because I haven't been able to stop thinking about Bodhi. I'm worried. Although Lori is capable and a fantastic Mom, I didn't picture my first-born growing up without a father. I believed I'd made the best choice for him, and now I'm floundering.

I can't reverse the adoption. It would be complicated legally, but it could probably be done; however, I can't take it that far. Bodhi is Lori's son, and trying to take him from her would not be right.

But I want to be involved in his life.

Preferably as his father so Easton can get to know his brother.

Maybe we could come to an arrangement where he'd come to stay with us every second weekend or something, and Lori and Bodhi could come to us for the holidays, and we could integrate them into our family. It's not unheard of. Family means lots of different things these days, and there are all kinds of arrangements in place.

It's about the kids.

It's about doing what's best for them, and keeping them apart doesn't feel like it's best.

I abandoned Bodhi, and I want a chance to rectify that.

Of course, I can't say anything to Lori until I've told Vivien and we've worked through it. It's not going to be easy news to hear, and she'll be devastated. Not just that I had a baby with that bitch but the fact I concealed it from her even if I still believe it was my only choice back then.

I stand over the decision I made five and a half years ago. Vivien would never have accepted Bodhi then, but I...I think she would now. I have thought about it extensively, and I firmly believe Vivien is in a place where she can accept the situation and make room for my other son. I can't keep this a secret from her any longer nor deprive Easton of his brother.

It's killing me.

I want to have a relationship with my other son, and I want him to know I love him as much as I love Easton.

This has the potential to rock my marriage to its core. However, Vivien will fight to keep her family together, and she won't deny an innocent child. She might hate me for a while, but she won't end our marriage, and she won't deny Bodhi a place in our lives.

I would stake my life on it.

If I didn't believe it, I wouldn't even consider this, because losing her is not an option.

My wife is good and kind, and she will come around once she gets over the initial shock. Especially when she sees how much Bodhi looks like Easton. It would be impossible to refuse him when they are so close in age and look like they are twins.

Regardless of how happy I am with my life, Bodhi is always at the back of my mind.

I need to do right by him and do it in a way that will support Lori, now she's a single mom, and not usurp her role as his mother because that won't change. Bodhi will gain a stepmom in Viv and he'll be a lucky boy with two strong women guiding him as he grows.

My mind is made up.

I'm going to talk to Vivien after the holidays and fess up.

"There you are."

I jump on the couch, startled by her arrival. Viv's heels click on the hardwood floor as she walks toward me. "I just had an interesting chat with our son." She eyeballs me with one of her infamous looks as she drops onto the couch beside me. My arm goes around her on autopilot. "Thanks for that, by the way." She jabs me in the chest.

"I froze, and we both know you're better at this stuff. What did you tell him anyway?"

She cringes a little. "That mommies and daddies kiss and hug, and they make the baby grow in mommy's tummy."

I crack up laughing. "Oh my God. That's too funny."

"He caught me off guard, and it was the best I could come up with on such short notice. I would tell him a simple version of the truth, but he's not even five yet, and it just seems way too young."

"I agree, and I was right to send him to you. You always know the perfect thing to say."

Her fingers sweep through my hair. "I wish you gave yourself more credit. You're amazing with Easton, Reeve." Tears prick her eyes. "You're the best father and husband. We're so lucky to have you."

"Hey, hey." I lift her onto my lap and cup her face. "What's brought these tears on?"

"I just love you and hate seeing you so melancholy every Christmas."

I gulp painfully.

"It's in the past. I never think about it anymore. We're in the best place and happy, right?" she adds.

"Absolutely." I wipe her tears with my thumbs.

"Then please forgive yourself. I want you to enjoy Christmas in the here and now, not dwell on the past."

This is another reason why I need to tell her about Bodhi. She thinks I'm remembering that awful Christmas we broke up when that's not it. I try never to think about that because it was one of the worst days of my life, and she's right. We have moved on from there. We're together and in love, and we have a dream life I cherish. I barely think about that time now.

"I enjoy Christmas, and I am happy. I promise that is all in the past."

"Do you mean that?" Her skepticism bleeds into her tone.

"Yes." I rub my nose against hers. "Stop worrying. I'm happy. I get to love you for the rest of my life. We have an amazing son, and hopefully, we'll give him a sibling next year, especially since he wants one so bad."

"About that." Tears shine in Vivien's eyes, and butterflies swoop into my chest.

"Babe?" I croak, already on tenterhooks.

"I only found out ten days ago, and I didn't want to tell you on the phone." She plucks a pregnancy stick from someplace behind her and hands it to me. "Merry Christmas, Reeve. We're giving Easton that sibling he's dying for."

I stare at the clear PREGNANT written on the stick through blurry eyes.

"How far along are you?"

"Six weeks. The baby is due early in August."

"I fucking love you. You've just made me so incredibly happy." I wrap her in my arms and kiss her over and over. I dot kisses all over her face while telling her I love her repeatedly.

My heart is so full, and while it doesn't change the decision I've made about Bodhi, it does change the timing. I'm not dropping a bombshell on Vivien while she's pregnant. It would stress her out, and that could put the baby at risk.

I will wait until after our baby is born to tell her about Bodhi.

Chapter Sixty-Five
Now - Age 26

Simon Lancaster dies the night I win my first Best Actor Oscar. Figures that asshole would find a way to ruin one of the best nights of my life. I struggle in the aftermath of his death as I'm forced to confront my emotions head-on. I didn't win his love or his pride before he died, and now I never will. Until his last breath, I was still craving his approval, and it makes me sick. Why am I so weak when it comes to my father? Why did his approval matter so much? Why can't I move past it?

My family is my lifeline during this time. I cling to Vivien with a desperation that sends me tumbling into the past. At first, I don't cry, and then I can't stop. I'm having major trouble sleeping again, and I'm all over the place. When my wife suggests therapy, I return to Craig because I refuse to let Simon's death derail me or force me back down the path to addiction. It helps to talk it through, as does concentrating on my family. I cancel a planned project to stay home with Vivien and Easton.

I take Easton to and from school each day, to Little League

practice, and to drama classes. We spend tons of quality time together. It brings us even closer, and my son really helps me through this difficult time.

Focusing on Viv's pregnancy and our new baby helps enormously too. We're having a girl, and we've chosen Lainey as her name. Easton and I sing to her every night, and getting to share this experience with our son this time only adds to the joy.

The day after Vivien's twenty-sixth birthday, Carson calls me and asks me to come to his office the following day. I have no clue what it's about, and he refuses to say anything until we meet.

"Your mother died during childbirth, but it wasn't giving birth to you," my attorney says.

"What do you mean?" I splutter, totally confused.

"You have a twin, Reeve. An identical twin brother."

I stare at him in shock for a few beats, and I feel all the blood leaching from my skin. I imagined I heard that, right? Carson did not say what I think he just did. "What? No? I don't…" I grip Viv's hand tighter. She's seated beside me in front of Carson's desk. "How is that possible? My father said nothing to me about a brother." I glance sideways at my wife. "And your parents never said anything about my mother expecting twins."

"Your parents didn't know they were expecting twins, Reeve. One twin was hiding behind the other. It can happen with identical twins where the babies share the same amniotic sac. It's extremely rare, and usually, later scans detect the second fetus, but this was almost twenty-seven years ago, and ultrasounds were not as advanced as they are now. There are examples all over the world where the parents didn't find out it was twins until the delivery. That is what happened in this case."

"What happened to my...twin? Did he die?" I ask, bracing myself for his reply.

Carson links his hands together on the table, wearing a sympathetic look. "You were born first, and everything was fine. Your mother held you in her arms and smiled for a picture."

"I know. I have it in a frame on the wall in our living room. It's the only photo I have of me with my mother." For years, I kept it safeguarded in my bedroom at Viv's house, getting it framed when I bought the penthouse in Pacific Palisades.

Vivien reaches around my back to comfort me, and I lean into her arm, needing her support. I still haven't processed this. It doesn't seem real.

"Then they realized there was another baby, and that's when the complications arose. Your mother died on the table, and they had to deliver your twin brother by cesarean section."

"Oh God." Vivien gasps, covering her mouth with her free hand.

"What happened to my brother?" I ask through gritted teeth. He still hasn't answered me and I need to know.

Carson clears his throat. "I have known your father my whole life, and I have never seen a man love a woman as much your father loved your mother. You two remind me of them."

"Carson," I snap, not in the mood to be reminded of the ways in which I resemble that asshole.

Viv crawls into my lap, wrapping her arms around me, and I'm grateful for her warmth because an icy chill is snaking its way through my bones, and I'm shivering.

"Your father was holding you in his arms, crying over your mother's lifeless body, when his other son's cries rang out in the room."

"He blamed him," I surmise. "He blamed my brother for my mother's death."

Carson nods.

"He was only an innocent baby! It wasn't his fault," Vivien cries, wearing a look of utter horror.

I imagine it's how I would feel if I was capable of feeling anything other than shock. "He couldn't bear to look at his son knowing it had cost him his wife, so he wanted to get rid of the baby," I say, and my voice sounds hollow to my ears. It's another reminder of how similar we are. While the circumstances are different, I did the same thing Simon did, and it's not sitting well with me. I stare at Vivien as I purge another thought. "He might as well have gotten rid of me too. This explains so much. Deep down, he must have blamed me too." All the puzzle pieces are slotting into place now.

"My understanding is the medical staff tried to make him see that," Carson continues explaining, "but he was inconsolable and absolutely determined he wanted nothing to do with your twin. He told me all this many years later, and I don't mind admitting I was in complete shock. It's not my place to judge anyone, and I never said it, but your father went downhill in my estimation when he confided that in me. I had thought things were different between you and your father, and it pains me to hear they were not."

"He didn't want me either," I deadpan.

"What happened to Reeve's twin?" Vivien asks as she holds me close before peppering kisses into my hair.

"Your father arranged for a quick hush-hush adoption."

If anyone could organize something like that in record time, it would be Simon.

"Does he know?" I rub at my stinging eyes.

"That's something you'll have to ask him. If you would like, I can set up a meeting."

"You know where he is? You know who he is?" I grab Vivien as my heart jackhammers in my chest.

I have a brother? A twin? He's out there somewhere alive?

"I do. I can get a message to him."

"What's his name? Does he look like me?" My brain is firing all kinds of thoughts and questions at me now and my head is a jumbled mess.

"I have never met him in person, so I can't say. However, it's a common misconception that identical twins look identical. Even though they share the same DNA, they aren't necessarily exactly alike. They can be different in appearance, temperament, or personality, and environmental as well as chemical factors play a part. As for his name, I can't reveal that until I have spoken to him and gained his permission. Let me reach out to him and see if he would be agreeable to a meeting."

"Reeve might need a little time," Viv supplies.

"I understand, and I won't arrange anything until we have spoken. I will just test the waters."

***

"I feel sick," I whisper to Viv, dragging my hand through my hair and messing up the careful styling. "What if he doesn't like me or he doesn't want to form a relationship with me?"

It's been two weeks since Carson revealed I have a twin brother, and I have veered all over the place in the intervening time.

It's been the biggest shock of my life, and I have run the full gamut of emotions. Craig has been helping me to decipher my feelings, and I have spoken exhaustively with Lauren and Jon too. They had no idea I had a twin or that Simon had given him away.

The parallels with Bodhi haven't helped. I'm drowning in

guilt again, and floundering a little because I did the same thing my dad did. It sickens me and strengthens my resolve to tell Vivien about Bodhi after Lainey's birth. Craig agrees with my plan, and he's trying to help me to let go of my guilt, but it's hard.

But I can't think about Bodhi today because my twin is here. Downstairs, waiting to meet us. I know nothing about him except he's my flesh and blood, and I desperately crave him in my life.

I always wanted a brother growing up, and now I have one.

I'm trying not to dwell on the fact we have missed out on twenty-six years because I fly into a rage every time I think about that bastard Simon, and it's best for my sanity that I don't focus on it. Instead, I'm concentrating on all the years we have yet to come—if he wants me in his life. I don't know if he grew up with siblings or his circumstances. He might be here purely to sate his curiosity and then walk out of my life.

Those fears, and others, have kept me awake for the past few nights, and I'm running on adrenaline today.

Vivien palms my face, forcing my attention on her. "He's your *twin*. It's probably been as big of a shock for him as it's been for you, but how could he not love you? You're an amazing person, Reeve. A wonderful husband, son-in-law, and father, and I know you'll be an excellent brother too. If he doesn't want to get to know you, that's all on him." She grips my hips. "It's a good sign he's here. That must mean he's open to it. Just don't expect miracles. It might take both of you some time to come to terms with everything, but I'm sure it'll work out. You're not just brothers. You're *twins*. That's an extra special connection."

"True." I have been reading up on twins, and I think the emptiness I've always felt inside comes from having him ripped from my life. I kiss my wife, holding her close as I let her melt some of my stress. "I've been a basket case these past few months. Thank you for putting up with me."

She runs her hands up my chest. "Reeve. I love you. I love you so much." Her arms encircle my neck as she brushes her lips briefly against mine. "Supporting you is never a chore. I've just been worried, but I think you're about to turn a corner." She smiles. "We should go. We don't want to leave the poor man waiting too long."

I wonder if he looks like me, I ponder as we walk hand in hand downstairs. What Carson said about identical twins is true, so we may not be exactly alike. I wonder if it's like Bodhi and Easton. They share a striking resemblance, but I'm guessing they won't be identical. I can't fully tell as I've never met my eldest son in the flesh since he was a baby, and I only have photographs to go on.

Drawing a brave breath, I open the door and enter our formal living room. My brother is facing the window with his back to us. He looks a little taller and a little broader than me. His hair is similar to mine. He's dressed casually, all in black, and I'm suddenly self-conscious in my dress shirt and pants. Should I have worn jeans too?

Why isn't he turning around? Surely, he heard us walking in? I clear my throat as I glance at Viv. She looks a little weirded out too. "Hello," I call out, and he slowly turns around.

Knots twist in my gut, and I hold myself still as he walks toward me. I study his features, and the similarity is uncanny. Except we're not exactly alike. We have the same blue eyes and the same shape face, but he has a bump on his nose and a small scar over one eyebrow. He doesn't have a beauty mark over his lips like I do. I'm tan, and he looks a little pale. He definitely banks more time in the gym, and he's probably got a couple of inches in height on me. Ink covers his arms, and he's got a nose and eyebrow piercings.

A strange sensation crawls over me as he comes to a stop in front of us. I can't explain it. It's almost like déjà vu, yet I've never met him before.

I snap out of it and smile as I make introductions. "I'm Reeve Lancaster, and this is my wife, Vivien."

"It's nice to meet you both," he says in an accented tone that is definitely not American. "I'm Dillon O'Donoghue."

Chapter Sixty-Six

Vivien sways, and my arm goes around her back as I hold her up. "Darling, what's wrong?"

She clings to me as her gaze bounces between me and my twin. The shell-shocked expression on her face confirms she's struggling to wrap her head around this, and I get it. It's all pretty surreal.

"Viv. Baby. Talk to me," I ask, starting to get a little concerned. She is almost seven months pregnant, and stress isn't good for her or the baby.

"I'm okay," she rasps. "I just got a little dizzy."

"Come and sit down." I steer her over to the couch, and I feel her trembling against me. Now I'm worried. I help her to sit and then push her head down between her legs. "Deep breaths, babe, and keep your head down. It will get rid of the dizzy spells. I'll grab you some water." I move to grab a bottle of water and look up at my twin. He's standing with his arms folded, staring at Viv. "It's been a particularly stressful time for both of us recently," I explain. "Stress isn't good for the baby, and I've been trying to get Viv to take it easy, but she's been worrying too much about me."

"Congratulations. This is your second child, right?" Dillon says, and a strangled sound rips from Viv's mouth as if she can't breathe.

Is she sick? What's going on? I don't like this at all. "Shit." I rush back to her, putting the bottle of water and a glass down on the coffee table. "Maybe you should lie down upstairs." She's been under enormous strain lately having to support me, and it's clearly taken more of a toll than I realized. I need to do better. I've got to get my shit together and be there for my wife.

"No!" she says, her tone elevating a notch. "I'll be okay in a minute."

I realize I'm being rude. "Take a seat," I say, smiling at Dillon as I fill a glass of water for Viv.

He sits on the couch across from us.

"Drink this, babe." I hand Viv the glass and rub her back. My brows knit together as I watch her hand trembling around the glass. Something is very wrong, and prickles of apprehension lift the hairs on the back of my neck. "Perhaps we should call the doctor." I help her to hold the glass while she drinks and lift my free hand to her brow. "You don't feel too hot, but you're a little clammy."

"I'm feeling better now. Stop worrying." She pushes my hand away and takes a drink by herself.

"Are you sure?"

"Yes." She puts my arm around her shoulders and cuddles into me. "I'm sorry I derailed your meeting. Talk to your brother."

Charlotte enters the room with a tray, leaving it on the coffee table. She shoots Dillon and me an inquisitive look before smiling and exiting the room.

"Would you like something to drink?" I ask my twin. It's so

weird to say that and even weirder to be sitting across from him. I'm definitely in a bit of a daze, and that weird sensation is still there. "I can get something stronger, if you like?"

"Coffee is fine."

"Why do I get the feeling I know you from somewhere?" I ask as I fix his coffee.

"I'm the lead singer for Collateral Damage," he says, accepting the mug I hand him.

Ah, that explains it. "Yes! That's it. We saw you perform at the Oscars in February, didn't we, Viv?" I was vaguely aware of them before the ceremony. Music is more Viv's thing. But I know they're very successful and they're from Ireland, and now I can place his accent.

"We did." A fake smile is plastered on her face, and she's acting very odd.

"Congrats on your win, by the way," he adds. "I loved your acceptance speech."

"Thanks. I'm sorry things didn't go the band's way that night." I remember they were nominated for best song, I think, but they didn't win.

Dillon shrugs, but a muscle pops in his jaw, and I guess it's a sore point. I would be the same if I hadn't won that night even though it's still a massive honor to be nominated.

Tension thickens in the air, and to say things are awkward would be an understatement.

I tap my fingers on my knee. "So, you grew up in Ireland? Viv spent some time there, and she loved it." I smile at my love, trying to leash my anxiety. When I turn my head, I see Dillon looking at Viv in a very intense manner. I frown, picking up some strange vibes between them.

"I did. Ireland is great." Viv clings almost possessively to my side.

"Did you like growing up in Ireland?" I ask, trying to shake the stress free from my shoulders.

"It was good. I grew up on a farm with my adopted parents, three brothers, and my sister."

"Wow, so you have brothers and a sister. That must've been nice." Jealousy coils in my stomach. What would it be like to grow up in a big family like that? And on a farm too. It all sounds so normal, and I'm envious. It doesn't sound like he needs another sibling, and I'm wondering if there'll be any place in his life for me.

Dillon appears to relax, and a genuine smile crosses his face. "Yeah, it was cool. Things were fairly wild growing up as teenagers in Ireland."

"Are you close to them?" I blurt.

"We're a close family." Dillon is still smiling, but his gaze is fixed on Viv in a way I'm starting to resent.

Why the fuck is he looking at her when responding to my questions?

"I'm especially close to my sister, Ash. She manages the band. And my younger brother Ro is our drummer."

Vivien closes her eyes like she's in pain. "Are you okay?" I tighten my arm around her shoulders.

"I'm fine." The fake smile on her face says that's a lie, and I watch as it slowly slips from her mouth. "Did you know?" she asks Dillon. "Did you know you were adopted? Did you know who your bio parents were?"

I'm grateful she asked the questions I wanted to.

"My parents told me I was adopted when I was six, so I've always known. I toyed with the idea of finding my birth parents as a teenager, but I didn't pursue it." He arches a brow, and a hint of a smirk appears on his lips. "Why would I? I have the most amazing family. I didn't need to find the parents who abandoned me."

"Our mother didn't abandon you," I rush to correct him. Our mother is innocent in all this. Simon is the villain of the piece, not Felicia Lancaster. "She died giving birth to us."

"So I've just discovered." He rubs his face, and I spot confusion and frustration only because I've felt the same since I discovered the truth.

"You just found out too?"

"It's been such a shock."

"I know. Simon was wrong to do what he did to you. To us." My voice cracks as a tsunami of emotions sits heavily on my chest. Viv links our hands, and I welcome her grounding touch. "It's just another reason in a long list of reasons why he was a shit dad."

Dillon leans forward on his elbows. "You didn't get along?"

I shake my head. "No. He might have kept me, but it was in name only. He could hardly bear to look at me sometimes."

My brother looks at the floor as his knee bounces. When he lifts his head a few seconds later, no sign of emotion is evident on his face. It's like he wiped it all clean. An icy chill tiptoes up my spine. The way Dillon just did that is eerily reminiscent of Simon. Scarily so. "Well, he's not here now, and there's nothing to stop us from getting to know one another. Brother to brother." His eyes drift momentarily to Viv again. "Twin to twin."

"I would really like that," I say as his gaze returns to mine. Despite the strange tension in the air and the weird way Vivien is acting, I still want the chance to get to know my brother. First meetings are bound to be awkward, right? We're virtual strangers, and we've only recently discovered the truth. We're both still in shock and this is a big upheaval.

A good one, I hope.

At least he seems willing to try, and that is all I had hoped for today.

"I would also really like it if you'd accept half of my inheritance. It rightfully belongs to you." I have discussed this with Viv, and I wasn't sure if I would mention it today, but it seems appropriate. Dad left everything to me, including his shares in Studio 27, the house, his bank accounts, and his other property portfolio. It's more than I know what to do with, and an equal share of it is rightfully Dillon's.

"I don't want anything from that man," Dillon barks, digging his nails into his thighs. "And I don't need his money anymore."

What does *anymore* mean? It's an odd thing to say. I don't blame him for his vitriol though. Simon gave him away without more than fleeting consideration. Although it sounds like it all worked out for Dillon, it's still got to hurt.

"It's not just money. There's some property and shares in Studio 27. You don't have to decide now. We can talk about it again."

"I need to go." He climbs to his feet, looking seriously pissed, and I regret bringing up the inheritance. I should have waited before talking to him about it.

"You can't stay a little longer?" We have barely had time to talk, and I didn't think he'd be leaving so soon. We scheduled Angela today to take care of Easton so we have plenty of time to talk with my brother. Hurt blooms in my chest, but I try not to read too much into it.

"We have time booked in the studio, and the guys are already waiting on me. But let's meet up at the weekend, yeah?" He steps up to me, and all trace of his anger is gone now.

I wonder what he'd say if he knew he'd inherited some of Simon's traits? Not that I can talk. I inherited plenty of them too.

"It was good meeting you," he says.

"I wish we hadn't lost so many years." I rise to my feet, surprised when he pulls me into a hug.

"We have plenty of time to catch up," he says.

"Daddy!" Easton bursts into the room, and I shuck out of my brother's arms as my son comes barreling toward me. "I made extra cookies for my sister. Look!" He holds out a napkin with two cookies as I lift him into my arms.

"Yum." I chuckle as cookie crumbs land on my shirt.

"Who are you?" Easton fixes his wide-eyed blue gaze on Dillon.

Dillon stares at Easton in that same intense way he stared at Vivien, and it unnerves me.

"This is your Uncle Dillon," I explain.

"Cool! Is he coming to my birthday party tomorrow?"

"Tomorrow?" Dillon says, and there's a strange edge to his tone. "I thought your birthday was in June?"

Ice replaces the blood flowing through my veins. How the fuck would he know that? We didn't exchange any personal details in advance of this meeting. All Carson told him is that I would prefer to meet privately, at my house or his. He asked to meet here, and Bobby picked him up from somewhere downtown. There is no way he should know Easton's birthday is reported in the media as being in June. It's not inconceivable to think he knows who I am and that I have a wife and son, but knowing something this specific is not usual.

An ominous sense of dread washes over me, and I want him out of my house now. Something is not adding up, and I'm on high alert. I don't like how he was looking at Vivien, and I don't like how he's currently looking at my son. I tighten my hold on Easton and step back as I mask my concern. I force out a chuckle. "The media thinks it's June because we manipulated them into believing that, but he was actually born five weeks earlier."

I observe his reaction, and he loses the shield he's been wearing, showcasing his shock.

Unease crawls up my spine.

"Why would you do that?" Dillon asks.

"We've had issues with the paparazzi in the past. The last thing we want is them hounding us every year on Easton's birthday. This way, we get to celebrate without them breathing down our necks. Win-win." It takes effort to sound so blasé.

Dillon stares at Vivien in a familiar way, and all the hairs lift on my arms. What the fuck is going on here?

"I don't feel so hot," Viv tells me. "I need the bathroom." She races out of the room before I can say a word.

"Daddy." Easton's pale face locks on mine. "I don't feel so hot either."

Then he throws up all over me. He starts crying, and I rub his back as I murmur assurances. I set his feet on the ground and grab the trash, telling him to puke into it if he thinks he's going to vomit again as I strip him out of his soiled clothes. I rip off my ruined shirt before lifting Easton into my arms.

"Sorry to rush out like this, but I need to get him into the tub. He must have the same stomach bug Vivien has," I lie. I'm pretty sure Easton ate one too many cookies, and I don't think Vivien is sick either.

"It's no problem. Do what you need to do. I can see myself out, and I'll be in touch."

Chapter Sixty-Seven

"Are you sure you want to see these, Reeve?" Devin asks, keeping his palm on top of the large white envelope on his desk containing the photographs from Vivien's time in Ireland.

I came straight here after Carson's office. I signed the paperwork to change my will and put some of my other affairs in order. I knew I would probably not go through with it tomorrow if these pics prove what I think they will, and I wanted to do the right thing by my twin. Giving him his share of Simon's inheritance is only fair, and even if I end up hating Dillon, I'm not sorry I put that in place.

"You can't unsee them, and some of them are intimate," Devin adds.

"What?" I clip out, whipping my gaze to meet his as horror stabs into me.

"I had no idea the Irish firm was capturing such private moments. It's an absolute breach of privacy and completely unprofessional. I have already given them a piece of my mind. I sent a couple guys to Dublin to ensure all paperwork and photographic evidence was deleted from their hardcopy files and digital systems."

I thought Devin had the pics on file at his offices, but he explained he never asked for them after I requested not to receive them. He received written reports summarizing activity only.

Devin asked me if I wanted the photographs after Vivien returned home from Ireland and I told him I didn't. I thought the Irish company would have just destroyed them, but they've been sitting in their offices gathering dust for years.

I am livid but also grateful they exist because they hold the key to ending the torment I've been in for the past nineteen days ever since that disastrous meeting with my twin.

He slides the envelope across the desk to me. "These are the only copies. We deleted them from our server after printing."

"Thanks."

He sits forward and scrutinizes my face. "Are you doing okay?"

I shake my head and rub at my tired eyes. I've barely slept in weeks, and things are shit at home. Vivien is hiding something from me, and I think I've figured it out.

I hope I am wrong.

I really do, because if I'm not, my entire world is falling down around me.

"I have a lot going on, and things are strained at home, but it'll work itself out." I'm not sure if I'm trying to convince him or me.

I thank him, take the envelope, and head out to the car. Bobby opens the back door, and I instruct him to take me to my penthouse. I'm not sure why I held on to the place when we rarely use it anymore, but I'm grateful I have somewhere private to do this.

We stop on the way so I can buy a bottle of scotch and a few beers. I cannot do this sober, if I can do it at all. I wish Alex was here. I've mentioned my concerns and made him swear not to say anything to Rey. He promised he wouldn't, and he's kept his word because World War Three hasn't occurred yet.

Bobby watches me with concern through the mirror, but I ignore him.

The chunky envelope sits on my lap like a ticking time bomb. I rest my head back and close my tired eyes, praying that I'm wrong about this. That I've slotted the wrong puzzle pieces into place.

That Dillon making excuses to cancel our planned meetup is just because he's busy.

That Vivien giving Leon the slip last week was innocent and not because she was meeting my twin.

That Dillon isn't Vivien's Irish boyfriend.

That my wife hasn't been concealing it from me when she should have told me the second I laid eyes on my brother.

Because if it's true, it means... I can't continue the thought. It's too painful to consider. I shove it in a lockbox for now. Instead, I remember how beautiful my wife looked earlier tonight as I made love to her from behind while we were lying on our sides on our giant bed. My hands roaming her firm stomach where my daughter is currently cocooned. Viv's tight walls gripped my dick as I shot my load inside her. Her sleepy expression as I kissed her goodnight was like tiny pinpricks to my heart because I knew once I left our bedroom that everything might never be the same again.

I really hope I've got it wrong.

I hope the guy in these pictures is someone other than Dillon.

I kick off my shoes and swing my legs up onto the couch, knocking back a healthy mouthful of Laphroaig before I pluck up the courage to open the white envelope. My hands are trembling as I remove the photos and set them upside down on the couch beside me. There are hundreds of them. My heart beats overtime as I drain my drink and pour another two fingers of scotch. I definitely need the liquid courage. I'm sweating bullets as I reach for the photos.

This is it.

There can be no going back now.

I try to brace myself, but nothing could have prepared me for this.

Pain rips through me as I look at the first photo, and my worst fears are confirmed. The man Vivien was in love with in Ireland was my twin. After she returned to L.A., she told me he'd always own a part of her heart, but I held most of it.

Does that part still love him?

And does he love her?

From the way he was looking at her that day in the living room, I would say *yes*.

They have both been lying to me, and I fall apart in a nanosecond.

What if I lose her to him?

What if I lose both of them to him?

Tears flow freely down my face as I flip from one photo to the next, each damning one flaying another layer off my heart until the organ rests in tatters inside my chest.

"Alex. It's true. It's him," I say the instant my buddy picks up my call. I'm in my car on the way to the charity event where

I'm the guest speaker. Talk about the shittiest timing in the world.

"Are you sure?"

"I have the photographs. It's him. It's my twin. I fucking knew it! Dillon is Vivien's Irish boyfriend. She lied to me. She has been fucking lying to me for weeks!"

I don't blame her for not telling me who he was back when she first returned home. I didn't want to know his name or any intimate details. I just asked her to tell me what had happened so I could try to understand exactly how heartbroken she was. She never even told me he was in a band.

I can't criticize her for not telling me everything when I didn't want to know. But I *can* hold it against her for not telling me the fucking second that prick walked into our house. That's when she should have fessed up.

I feel like a fool.

Like they've both been laughing behind my back.

"Fuck, Reeve. I don't know what to say except I really don't think Vivien would cheat on you or risk your marriage. Whatever her reasons were for ditching Leon last week, there must be a logical explanation."

"I think I'd prefer if they were fucking over the alternative." Bile churns in my gut, and nausea swims up my throat.

"You don't mean that."

"No, I don't." I grip the wheel harder as I take the exit off the highway. "Either scenario will kill me stone dead. What if..." I can't say it. I can't even bear to think it without wanting to hurl myself off a cliff.

"Don't go there. You need to talk to Vivien, Reeve. You need to tell her you know about Dillon and ask her directly what's going on. Don't jump to conclusions until you understand everything. It might not be as bad as you think."

"I have a real bad feeling about it."

"Did you say anything to her today?"

"I haven't seen her since last night. I crashed in the guest room when I got home. I was trashed, and I couldn't bear to look at her knowing she was lying. How could she do this to me, Alex? After everything we've been through? How hard we fought to get back together? Why wouldn't she just tell me when Dillon showed up?"

A pregnant pause ensues. We can both guess why she said nothing, but it doesn't excuse her behavior.

I take the turn for the hotel. "I've got to go do this charity thing. I'm meeting Vivien here, and I'm going to talk to her when we get home. I'll call you tomorrow."

"Call me tonight. I don't care if I'm asleep and you have to wake me. Just call me later."

"I love you, man." I'm feeling hyper-emotional tonight, and my friend has been a rock for me recently.

"I love you, too. Keep the faith, Reeve. Vivien loves you, and you two were always meant to be together. This is just a speed bump, albeit a big one. You'll get through it."

I hope he's right, but I'm scared he's not.

I deliver an emotional speech, grateful I wrote it last week and thankful for my stellar acting skills that hide the emotional turmoil rampaging through me like a hurricane. I avoid Vivien as much as I can.

Looking at her tonight hurts.

It hurts so fucking much.

She has betrayed me, and she might as well have stabbed me repeatedly in the chest because that's how this feels. I am clinging to my sanity by my fingernails. I stand to lose everything, and I won't survive it. I just won't.

I feel Vivien's eyes on me at the dinner table, but I ignore her and talk to the other guests. She knows something's wrong. She has probably figured out I know by now.

We pose side by side for photos with the charity directors, looking like the picture-perfect couple even though it's all turning to shit. "Can we make our excuses and leave?" Viv whispers when we are finally alone.

"Eager to get home, or eager to get away from me?" I snarl. I'm trying to contain my anger, conscious she's heavily pregnant with my daughter, but it's hard when the rug has been pulled out from under me.

"We need to talk, and this can't wait."

"You're right," I snap. "It can't." My anger fades a little when she rubs her belly and her eyes well up. Pain slices through me at the thought of all I could lose. I'm crippled. Shattered into pieces on the inside.

It takes a while to say our goodbyes, but we finally get through the well-wishers and exit the ballroom. I stride toward the entrance, and we stand under the awning as we wait for our car. Torrential rain plummets to the ground, covering the roads in a fine layer of water. Tension bleeds into the air between me and my wife, and I'm struggling to control my anger again. My emotions are ping-ponging all over the place, and I'm terrified of what's about to come.

I hold on to my wife as the umbrella-carrying porter walks with us to our car when it pulls up in front. It's slippery, and I don't want her to fall. I open the passenger door of my Maserati for Vivien. She looks around at me. "You've been drinking. I'll drive."

A muscle locks in my jaw. "I only had a few, and I'm not drunk."

"But it's raining and—"

"You really don't want to push me right now, Vivien." I

glare at her because what the hell? She knows I wouldn't get behind the wheel if I was impaired. "Do you honestly think I would drive if I wasn't fit to drive? Do you think I'd put your life and our unborn child's life at risk by driving if I wasn't in full control of my faculties?"

Reluctantly, she shakes her head.

"Then get in the damn car, Viv."

I tip the porter and the valet and slide behind the wheel. I start the engine and drive away, heading for the back roads rather than the highway. Pileups on the 405 are the norm in bad weather, and I'd rather avoid a collision.

Vivien stares out the window with her arms folded around herself. The silence is painful in the extreme. My head and my heart are at war right now. My brain is screaming for the truth while my heart wants to delay the inevitable for as long as possible. I'm quietly seething, like a pressure cooker about to pop its lid. The more I think about her and Dillon sneaking around behind my back, the less control I maintain and the more I feed the rage festering inside me like poison.

When we reach a quieter portion of open road, I can't hold back any longer.

I need to know, and it can't wait.

"Is there nothing you want to say to me?"

Vivien is slow to look at me. "I think we should wait until we get home to talk."

My fingers dig into the wheel, and my nostrils flare. She's not going to deflect. We're having this conversation, whether she likes it or not. "Are you fucking him?" I glance at her quickly, not wanting to take my eyes off the road for long when it's still raining cats and dogs. "Are you fucking my *twin*?" I snap.

Panic splays across her beautiful face. "What? No! Of course, I'm not! Why would you say that?"

"Where did you disappear to when you gave Leon the slip last week?"

She bites her lip. "I can explain, but not like this, and you should slow down. The rain isn't showing any signs of stopping."

"Just answer the goddamn question, Vivien!" I slam my hands down on the wheel.

"I was with Dillon, but it's not what you're thinking. I haven't been with him. I would never cheat on you, Reeve. Never. You've got to believe me!"

"I waited for you to tell me. It's been over two weeks, and you said nothing!" I roar.

"You've known all along? Why the hell didn't *you* say something?"

"Because I needed to hear it from my wife! I needed to know the trust I've placed in you all these years wasn't for nothing. I needed to know we are a solid team." Pain ricochets around my chest, spreading to other body parts.

"We are, Reeve." She reaches for me, but I shove her hand away. "How did you find out?" She brushes the tears rolling silently down her face.

Why is she crying?

What has she to cry about?

I'm the one who's been wronged.

I'm the one who stands to lose everything. If anyone should be crying, it's *me*.

"Your reaction the day he showed up at our house tipped me off, and I saw the way he was looking at you. His reaction to Easton's birthday was a major trigger." She looks perplexed, so I elaborate. "He said he thought E's birthday was in June." She still looks confused, so I go further. "We hadn't exchanged names in advance. Our identities were supposed to be hidden. I can understand how he might have recognized me, but knowing our son's birthday was reported as being in June, not May, was a major flag. I knew for sure something was amiss. Then I remembered that photo you sent me when you were in Ireland, and I recalled seeing a guy with the same kind of hair behind you in the hallway at the Oscars. Things started slotting into place. I was praying I was wrong. That it was just a coincidence your ex had bright blond hair and my twin used to."

I slow down a little as we drive over the slick road. "Until last night when I met with the owner of the private security firm I'd hired to watch you in Ireland."

"What the what? What do you mean?" she shrieks.

I level her with a pointed look. "Did you really think I'd let the love of my life wander around Ireland without someone protecting her from harm? In case you've forgotten, you'd been viciously assaulted a couple of months previously, and I wasn't taking any chances."

"You had someone spying on me the entire time?" Incredulity splays across her face.

"Not spying. *Protecting.* I hired a guy in L.A., and he found a reputable local firm in Dublin. They had guys watching you twenty-four-seven to ensure you were safe."

"That is... I can't believe you did that." Shock lingers behind her words and on her face. "What did they tell you? Have you known who Dillon is all along?"

"If I knew who he was, I would've thrown the motherfucking asshole out of my house the second I laid eyes on him!" I yell, and my voice breaks at the end as a fresh wave of emotional torture slams into me. "Back then, I knew there was a guy before you told me because the security firm sent me weekly reports."

"That is such a massive invasion of my privacy. I can't believe you did that, Reeve. I asked you for space!"

"And I fucking gave it to you!" I shout. "Every week when I

got the reports, I wanted to hop on a plane and bring you back home. It took colossal willpower to stay away, but I did it because you asked me to. It almost killed me, Viv. I legit felt like my heart was breaking on a daily basis. I knew you were with him, and I risked losing you permanently. The only thing I could do was try to make amends and hope to fuck you were still mine when you came back. *If* you came back."

"You need to slow down," she cautions. "Please, Reeve." She touches me lightly on the arm. "Why don't you pull over and I'll drive?"

"That day in Mexico was the day I found out about him. There were photos, but I refused to look at them. I knew my heart couldn't bear to see that, so I never saw any photographic proof." A solitary tear glides from one eye as I cast a quick glance at her. "They were left out of my reports because I couldn't tolerate seeing you with him. I got trashed that day to numb my pain." I laugh bitterly as the irony crashes into me. "My twin was fucking shit up for me even then. This is all his fault. I found out about him, got drunk and high, and ended up screwing that psycho bitch."

Chapter Sixty-Eight

Anger is like a second skin covering me from head to toe. I'm burning up from the inside, consumed with toxic flames that won't be extinguished. The pain is so raw, as if I've sustained deep cuts over every inch of my skin. "I saw the photos last night. They confirmed my suspicions about everything." Images I would rather scorch from my brain flit across my subconscious, and Dillon is lucky he's not in this car because I'd pummel his face until it's unrecognizable. "You let him fuck you against a cross at the top of a hill in the middle of the night? And in the sea when others were around?"

Viv pins angry eyes on me while jabbing her finger in the air. "You don't get to judge me, Reeve. I was with my boyfriend, and everything was consensual. At least my photos didn't end up splashed all over the tabloids and social media. You were spared that humiliation."

Wow, she really went there, and it feels like we've regressed in time. She's trying to turn this around on me when all I was trying to do was protect her. And you can't compare a few photos in a magazine to the hundreds of pics I endured, many of them highly intimate. It makes me sick thinking about it. "Do I even know you? Do you have any idea what it did to me seeing that?"

"Well, maybe you shouldn't have invaded my privacy in such a revolting manner! Do *you* have any idea how it feels to know someone was watching me with *my boyfriend*? Capturing our most intimate moments on film?" she yells, gesticulating frantically. "Those photos should never have been taken! And they sure as fuck shouldn't be sitting in some pervy PI's office like a ticking time bomb."

"I didn't know they'd done that because I didn't ask for it, and I never looked at the photos. After I got you back, I didn't give them a second thought." Taking the envelope from the glove compartment, I throw it into her lap. "There you go. That's all of them. Carson already got signed declarations from the US and Irish security firms confirming no other copies are in existence in physical or digital format."

The leather of her seat squelches as she moves position. "Did you arrange that photo of us on the balcony the day I came home?"

I grind my teeth repeatedly. What the fuck has that got to do with this?

"Answer me, Reeve. We might as well bring all the skeletons out of the closet."

I really don't want to have this conversation now, but she's right. We might as well air all the dirty laundry. My anger dissipates a little as I beseech her with my eyes for understanding I know she won't feel like giving. "I was so scared I'd lost you. You were really upset. I knew you were in love with him. Possibly more than with me, and I wasn't risking losing you forever. I'd gotten friendly with a photographer. He'd suggested we could have a mutually beneficial arrangement. I called him that day and set it up."

Her head falls against the headrest, and she closes her eyes. Tears roll down her cheeks as rain continues to pour from the heavens. "You seduced me on purpose so the photographer would get the money shot and you'd use it to drive Dillon away."

What. The. Actual. Fuck??

"Don't rewrite history, Viv." Gripping the wheel tight, I work hard to not lose my temper again. "I seduced you because I fucking love you and I missed you. I wanted to feel close to you again. Staking my claim, and warning that prick off, was secondary." I look at her briefly as we round the next bend. "You're mine, Viv, and that's never going to change."

I'm hoping if I repeat that mantra enough it'll be true.

Viv stares at me like I'm a stranger, and I hate it. She knows me. She's the only person on the planet who knows me so well. "I always thought you stopped to talk to the reporters that day to send a message to Saffron. To let her know we were back together and to not try anything. I never stopped to consider you were sending Dillon a message too. I was so fucking naïve."

"Two birds. One stone."

"Don't act so freaking flippant! You lied to me! Manipulated me! How often have you done that in our marriage, Reeve? What else don't I know?"

And my anger returns tenfold. "Oh no, Viv. You don't get to throw that shit at me. You've done exactly the same! You should've confessed the second we stepped foot in our living room that day. You should've told me immediately who Dillon was. Instead, you sat there and let him try to make a fool out of me."

How fucking dare she try to turn this all on me! I'll accept I've made mistakes, and she doesn't know about the biggest one yet, but she's messed up too.

"I wanted to tell you. I was planning to, but he blackmailed me into keeping quiet."

"He what?" I roar. That fucking prick. I am going to rip that Irish asshole a new one and ensure he stays the hell away from my family. I don't care what his agenda is. I don't care if Vivien thinks she loves him. He isn't worthy of my family or me. I'll take out restraining orders to keep him away.

He is not stealing what is *mine*!

"He took photos of me when we were together without my permission. He threatened to post them online along with the truth that he was your twin and that E..." She sobs in earnest, and the urge to pull over to the shoulder and comfort her rides me hard..

I have always hated seeing Vivien crying. "He has no intention of developing a relationship with me. He's here for you. You and...my son." I have suspected this all along, but this proves it.

"We are yours, Reeve. He can't take us from you."

I wish those words brought total relief, but they don't. They can't. "If you didn't meet with him to fuck him, there is only one other reason you would." Something vital ruptures in my chest, and I start crying. "You did a paternity test. Didn't you?"

She nods. "He insisted on it. I wanted to tell you, but he blackmailed me into keeping silent. Then I thought maybe it was for the best to wait until we had the test results, but..." She breaks down again, and we're both being torn apart by this.

How could everything that was so perfect be ruined so quickly? "No, Viv. Please, God, no. Don't say what I think you're going to say." I won't survive if she tells me my son isn't mine. He can't be his. He can't be.

"I'm sorry, Reeve. I'm so sorry," she pants, and I hear the panic in her tone.

Pain eviscerates me from every angle, and I'm a giant mass of heartbreak.

"I didn't know you were twins! I kept my distance when I first returned from Ireland because I wasn't sure you were the father. I'm sorry I lied about that, but I was trying to protect you. I was so happy when Easton was born and the test confirmed he was yours." She sobs again.

"I knew you lied," I quietly admit.

"What?"

"You told me you'd been sleeping with him. I'm not an idiot. Of course, I knew there was a chance the baby wasn't mine. I knew you were refusing to commit to me, to accept my proposal, because you wanted to make sure. I don't hold that against you, Viv. I respect you for trying to do the right thing by me and your baby. It's why I never said anything, and if you're beating yourself up over that, don't."

"Oh, Reeve," she puts her hand on mine as she quietly cries.

I'm terrified I know the answer before I ask this question, but I have to know. Denial won't change the facts, and it's killing me. It's time to rip the Band-Aid off. "Please tell me Easton is my flesh and blood? Please tell me he's *my son*. I love that little boy with everything I am. Please don't say he's his. I can't lose him."

"Pull over, please," she begs.

"No, Viv. Just say it. I can't bear it a minute longer!"

Tears are dripping off her chin and rolling underneath the top of her dress. "You are still Easton's dad, Reeve. In all the ways that matter, he is still your son."

"Vivien," I croak, barely able to breathe. "Is he my biological child or Dillon's?"

Strained tension bleeds in the air, and the only sound is the whoosh-whoosh of the wipers and the pitter-patter of rain as it continues tumbling from the dark night sky. "He's Dillon's," she whispers, and intense pain races through me obliterating everything in sight.

"No!" I cry. It feels like my heart is being yanked from my chest. "No. He can't be. He's *my* son! He's mine. *You're* mine. He can't have you!" I plead with my eyes, silently begging her not to leave me. I need her. I need Easton. They are mine. Mine, not his.

"I'm sorry, Reeve. I'm so sorry." She rubs at her chest. "But he's still your son. You're still his father, and I'm still your wife. That won't change."

I want to believe that so badly, but how... "You can't tell me this doesn't change things, Viv, because it does."

The car jerks forward, and I lose it.

Easton isn't my flesh and blood.

He's Dillon's.

Dillon's and Viv's.

They created the most perfect little boy. I didn't.

I bash the horn repeatedly as my rage and hopelessness mushrooms until it feels like a suffocating force swirling like dark clouds through the car.

All I know is pain.

It's everywhere.

Consuming me.

Choking me.

Snuffing the air from my lungs.

Squeezing a hand around my heart.

"Calm down, Reeve. Please. You're going too fast."

"Don't fucking tell me to calm down!"

Pain, pain, pain.

It reaches out, hugging my bones, tightening and tightening until it feels like I'm going mad. "I have sacrificed so much for you! For our family. And he's going to try and take it all from me!" I pound my fist into the dashboard over and over.

I hate Dillon O'Donoghue.

I am going to fucking end him.

He doesn't get to take my world from me.

"What the hell does that mean?"

"My heart is breaking, Viv." I stare at her, and I feel equally destroyed and hollow inside. "I don't want him near my son. I don't want to have to explain this to Easton. I can't lose him. I can't lose you. I won't. I—"

"Watch out!" she screams, and I glance at the mirror, spotting the car emerging onto the road at the last second.

I press down on the accelerator and swerve to avoid them, but they clip the rear end of our car and we spin out on the wet road. Vivien screams as I fight to reclaim control of the car. We're spinning and bouncing, and panic jumps up and bites me as I struggle to gain traction. I yank the wheel hard, trying to right it, but we bank sharply to the left, crashing through the fence at speed.

Wooden debris litters the exterior of the car as we barrel forward. I press my foot to the brake as I wrestle with the wheel. Adrenaline is coursing through my veins as Vivien continues screaming. A giant tree looms right in front of us, and we're going to hit it.

Acting on sheer instinct, I unbuckle my seat belt and throw myself across Vivien and Lainey. I grip her body tight as I cover her as much as possible. A piercing, screeching sound reverberates in my ears, and we're thrown around with the force of the impact as we plow into the tree.

I love you. I love you.

Please be okay.

Keep Lainey safe.

Tell Easton I love him so much.

I don't know if I say the words or think them, but I pray she hears it anyway.

As I peer into Vivien's panicked eyes, I take one last lingering look at my love because I know this is it. The last time I will ever see her.

There isn't enough time to panic because a crushing weight presses down on me, and I instantly lose consciousness.

Then, I float away.

Epilogue

"You should do something, Daddy. Bodhi needs you," Lainey says as we both stare into the rippling purple waters of the observation pool. The scene unfolding in the garden of Vivien and Dillon's home is grim.

"My heart is broken, Reeve," Vivien says, looking distressed. "Help me. Help us!"

She looks up at the sky as she calls for me, like she has done so many times.

"We love him. We love him as much as we love Fleur, Easton, and Melody. He's our son. He owns an equal part of our hearts. He's an integral part of our family. He's the only part of you still with me, but it's way more than that. I love him for the person he is. I love the quiet introspection he gives to every decision. I love the intensity on his handsome face when he's scribbling songs in his journal or playing his guitar. I love the adoration in his gaze when he watches his sisters and the joyful laugh he emits when he chases them around the play-ground. I love the respect shining in his eyes when he speaks with Dillon and the fierce way he protects his brother when

Easton doesn't even notice it. I love his intelligence and his fight and his focus. I love how he hugs me. I love when he calls me Mom."

Vivien is an amazing mother, and both my sons are with her, exactly how I wanted it.

She sobs, and if I still retained normal human emotions, my heart would ache for her.

But there is only peace, light, love, and happiness now.

"He's the sweetest boy, Reeve. You would have been so proud of him, and you'd be so worried now if you knew how messed up he is. A lot of that is your fault, and I'm pissed at you, but I can't get mad at you without turning that lens around on myself. I have tried to be the best mother to him and Easton, to my daughters too, but I'm failing. I'm failing my boys. They are both floundering, and I don't know how to help them!"

Vivien's beautiful face is soaked in tears. "Easton will be okay. I know he will. It doesn't stop me worrying about him, but I know he'll get through this. With Bodhi, I am genuinely terrified, Reeve. I know he is still the same sweet boy deep down inside. I know he is hurting and lashing out, but I'm so scared."

Vivien walks to the tree, tracing her finger over the spot where my name is etched in the wood before doing the same with Lainey's name.

"Love you, Momma," Lainey says.

I curl my arm around my daughter and surround her with my love. Lainey looks so much like Vivien, and if she had taken human form, I think she would have shared her pure heart too. As my daughter's soul hadn't taken physical form on Earth when we ascended, she was given a choice when we arrived. To return to Earth in another body and get to live or take ethereal form and remain here with me.

Lainey chose to stay, and the form she took was a reflection of what she would have looked like had she lived on Earth.

Because Lainey never lived down below, she can't connect to our loved ones in the same way I can.

She can observe, but she cannot visit.

There are rules, and I abide by them. You cannot intervene with fate. If Bodhi is meant to die in that alley tonight, I cannot save him. But we will be here to greet and guide him.

The early days are a tough transition as you let go of your human form and emotions. There is no time limit and an abundance of acceptance as the transformation takes place. Lainey and I had one another, and Felicia and Simon were here too.

I continue to watch my love through the waters. "I can't lose him too, and I'm fearful he's following a path he won't return from," Vivien says. "It's a path I can't follow, and that hurts so bad. I'm supposed to hold my kids' hands and be with them for everything. But I can't follow Bodhi down this particular path, and I am terrified. If anything happens to him, I will die!" Vivien falls to her knees and presses her brow to the tree. "Help him, Reeve. I know you're still out there. Please help our son. Help me and Dillon to do the right thing. Just...help."

"Go, Daddy." Lainey floats to her feet. "Give Mom a kiss from me."

I wander to the pools of destiny and ask my question. It isn't Bodhi's time, so permission is given. Once granted, I visualize myself in the rose garden and I am there.

Vivien's pain surrounds her in a deep purple aura, confirming she suffers. Reaching out, I sweep my fingers across her face. She's still so beautiful, even shrouded in sadness.

"Reeve," she whispers, lifting her hand, and it touches mine. "You're here."

I am always here, my love. Watching over you and your family. Protecting and supporting wherever I can.

Vivien is happy and surrounded by love. It's everything I wished for her. I hold nothing but love in my heart for my brother. Dillon cares for her the way I did. He loves Easton and Bodhi with his full heart. Their beautiful daughters too.

I wrap my essence around Vivien, cradling her in my heavenly warmth, and the strain leaves her face as serenity replaces it.

I will protect our son now.

I kiss her cheek. *Lainey sends her love. Be happy.*

I picture the alleyway beside the bar, and then I am there. I go to my son. He's lying injured on the ground, bleeding from a knife wound in his side.

Move, Bodhi. I send my will to his subconscious. He tries to get up, but he doesn't move.

I press my mouth to his ear. *Get up, son. This isn't your time. You need to live.*

He still doesn't move, so I project into his mind and wrap my essence around him, urging him to stand. *Fight, Bodhi. Fight to survive.*

This time, he does it, and I watch him stumble out of the alley and onto the sidewalk, collapsing in front of a couple who will take him to a hospital.

I close my eyes and picture home.

"Thanks, Daddy." Lainey pulls me into a hug, and we take a seat at the side of Mount Blessed, admiring the stunning view spread out before us.

"Everything is as it should be," I say.

Lainey nods, smiling lovingly at me.

When Vivien ascends, after leading a long and happy life, Lainey and I will be waiting to shower her with love and support.

Time moves differently here, and it won't be long until I'm holding my love in my arms again.

Exactly where she belongs.

Growing up in Ireland, I always felt like something was missing.

I had an idyllic childhood, yet I was never happy.

After Mum explained about the adoption, I constantly questioned my existence.

Despite being surrounded by love, I struggle to accept it or reciprocate.

Then my bio-dad shows up, trying to buy my silence, and a switch flips inside me.

I let my demons run free.

Nothing matters except revenge.

Then *she* lands in my lap—the love of my twin's life—and it feels like fate.

Except nothing goes according to plan.

I was supposed to steal her heart—she wasn't supposed to steal mine.

After she runs back to him, I'm left heartbroken and shattered.

The hits just keep on coming and my pain turns to anger.

Revenge takes center stage again and the perfect opportunity presents itself when Simon dies.

Meeting my twin sets a devastating chain reaction in motion, and I'm drowning under the weight of my sins.

Vivien is struggling to cope in the aftermath of her crushing loss. Repairing the damage is my number one goal, because I won't leave her to handle this alone. She can hurl hateful words at me and do her best to push me away.

But I am going nowhere.

Protecting my family is my sole priority.

Vivien and Easton need me, and this time I won't let them down.

A Final Word from the Author

I didn't intend to write Reeve's book, but in December 2022 he popped into my head, and he refused to leave. I had a vision of him on a bed, clutching Viv's photo, as he broke down in tears. It haunted me FOR WEEKS, and it was at that point where I committed to writing his book. I knew he had a lot to say, and I felt it would be an injustice not to share his story because there was so much we didn't see in the original novels.

Starting this project, I wanted to ensure we had tons of new content so it would read like a new book. But I also knew it was important to show some of the key scenes from the duet in Reeve's point of view. I asked the readers in the All of Me spoiler group on Facebook to tell me what scenes and what things they would like to see in this book, and I tried to incorporate all their feedback. Thank you so much to everyone who contributed. I cannot tell you how much I appreciate it, and your love for these characters and this world!

Readers seem divided on Reeve. Some love him, some loathe him. I knew when I committed to writing this book that a lot of readers might not pick it up, but I still felt compelled to write it and I'm so glad I did. For me, it has enhanced the experience of reading this series. I didn't set out to change readers from Team Dillon to Team Reeve, but I wanted to show how this troubled, complicated man had so many layers and he truly wasn't a bad person. He was a good person who made bad choices. I hope I have shown how things were not as black and white as they may have seemed. Yes, he made mistakes, and he was downright manipulative, at times, but it was always coming from a place of love. It doesn't excuse his behavior, but I hope it has helped to explain it. They were all so young and dealing with some pretty big stuff. Simon Lancaster's influence on both his sons was considerable, and he has a lot to answer for!

I didn't want to leave this book at the point of the accident and have everyone come away feeling sad or mad or down. Before I started writing this book, I envisioned an epilogue in heaven for Reeve and Lainey. When I wrote the last word, I felt a sense of peace knowing Reeve is with his daughter, watching over his family, and waiting for his love to come join him. While I'm still sad that was his fate, I'm happier knowing he is content. I hope it might have given you some closure, too.

I was partway through writing this book when I realized I had to write a Dillon companion novel too, as there is so much we didn't see from his POV during the series either. I have a lot of content to work with and I'm excited to write his book in 2024.

If you want to discuss the book with other readers, I suggest you join the spoiler group on Facebook: https://www.facebook.com/groups/allofmeduet

Thank you so much for reading my series and for taking these characters into your heart. This book exists because of readers like you.

more pain. Until Jared rocks up to the art gallery where I work, with his fiancée in tow, and I'm drowning again.

Seeing him brings everything to the surface, so I flee. Placing distance between us again, I'm determined to put him behind me once and for all.

Then he reappears at my door, begging me for another chance.

I know I should turn him away.

Try telling that to my heart.

This angsty, new adult romance is a FREE full-length ebook, exclusively available to newsletter subscribers.

Type this link into your browser to claim your free copy:
https://bit.ly/TITMHFBB

OR

Scan this code to claim your free copy:

About the Author

Siobhan Davis™ is a *USA Today, Wall Street Journal,* and Amazon Top 5 bestselling romance author. **Siobhan** writes emotionally intense stories with swoon-worthy romance, complex characters, and tons of unexpected plot twists and turns that will have you flipping the pages beyond bedtime! She has sold over 2 million books, and her titles are translated into several languages.

Prior to becoming a full-time writer, Siobhan forged a successful corporate career in human resource management.

She lives in the Garden County of Ireland with her husband and two sons.

You can connect with Siobhan in the following ways:

Website: www.siobhandavis.com
Facebook: AuthorSiobhanDavis
Instagram: @siobhandavisauthor
Tiktok: @siobhandavisauthor
Email: siobhan@siobhandavis.com

Books By Siobhan Davis

NEW ADULT ROMANCE
The One I Want Duet
Kennedy Boys Series
Rydeville Elite Series
All of Me Series
Forever Love Duet

NEW ADULT ROMANCE STAND-ALONES
Inseparable
Incognito
Still Falling for You
Holding on to Forever
Always Meant to Be
Tell It to My Heart

REVERSE HAREM
Sainthood Series
Dirty Crazy Bad Duet
Surviving Amber Springs (stand-alone)
Alinthia Series ^

DARK MAFIA ROMANCE

Mazzone Mafia Series
Vengeance of a Mafia Queen (stand-alone)
*The Accardi Twins**
*Taking What's Mine**

YA SCI-FI & PARANORMAL ROMANCE

Saven Series
True Calling Series ^

---

*Coming 2024
^Currently unpublished but will be republished in due course.

www.siobhandavis.com